CRYPTOZOOLOGY ANTHOLOGY

CRYPTO ZOOLO GY

ANTHOLOGY

strange and mysterious creatures in men's adventure magazines

EDITED BY ROBERT DEIS, DAVID COLEMAN & WYATT DOYLE

MENSPULPMAGS.com   # new texture

CONTENTS

DAVID COLEMAN

"That Fondness for the Marvelous So Common to Mankind..."

How did the lore and research of cryptozoology—the search
for unknown but purported creatures—enter the consciousness
of the American reading public? While newspaper accounts
contributed to the groundswell of early interest in sightings of
cryptids such as Bigfoot, Sea Serpents, Thunderbirds and beyond,
reports were often isolated to the local newspapers in which
they were published. Given that sightings typically occurred in
rural areas (for obvious reasons), many published encounters
by witnesses were often regional news items in small town
newspapers. It is true the Associated Press and other national
newspapers such as *The New York Times* frequently ran stories
about cryptids. However, many of these posts were published
without follow-up or left unexamined, without thorough analysis
prior or after publication. Take for example a November 28, 1959
Chicago Times editorial that originally appeared earlier that year
in the *Kansas City Star*. The editor, without sarcasm, congratulates
the residents of Kamloops, British Columbia, for their "acquisition
of a fine full-grown monster" secured using unspecified native
rituals. He concludes the specimen's exhibition "certainly won't
hurt the tourist business in Kamloops." In the absence of a

subsequent story denying the claim, uncritical readers of both
the *Chicago Times* and *Kansas City Star* could be understandably
forgiven if they assumed that Bigfoot had indeed been proven to
exist.

This kind of sensationalized story—"selling the sizzle" of
the possibility, but lacking a balance of critical information in
the coverage—helped establish the legend of such monsters as
Sasquatch and the Loch Ness Monster. As a result, it was difficult
for early cryptozoologists to later fact-check these reports,
as they often lacked accurate or complete contextual details.
The disbelieving, if not mocking, tone taken by some skeptical
journalists could hinder later verification. Skeptical writers
ridiculed what scant evidence was offered as unreliable, in effect
prejudicing future researchers as to its veracity. Adding to the
confusion, these were mostly one-off items, and unless one kept
a subscription to all major newspapers in America during most
of the 20th century (and maintained a proper index to them), key
data and witness reports were difficult to find by even the most
dedicated cryptozoologists. There was, in essence, an information
gap. And in an age prior to the internet, that simply meant *that*, so
to speak.

Enter the men's adventure magazines (MAMs). Their
historical and creative importance is highlighted by Messrs.
Deis and Doyle in their introductory essay as genre publications
that offered professional outlets for a diverse, exciting array
of talented writers and commercial illustrators. But for now,
consider they also worked as the earliest source of reliable
cryptozoological reporting and cryptid community building, as
well. Loren Coleman (no relation), a renowned cryptozoologist,
author, lecturer and curator of the International Cryptozoology
Museum, explained to me when I queried him in regard to the
influence of men's adventure magazines on cryptozoology:

*When I first became intrigued in March of 1960, by what was
mostly then called "romantic zoology," I searched far and wide
for reading resources on the search for Bigfoot, Sasquatch, Loch
Monsters, Yetis, Sea Serpents, and other creatures (that would*

"The Indian, a comparative newcomer to this continent, has known of the existence of the Sasquatch or Bigfoot for centuries; he lives in peace with this hairy, primitive 'cousin' of man, and respects his claim to the high passes and the deep ranges. But the white man, quick to teach, is slow to learn." Sasquatch portrait by John Duillo. ("On the Trail of the Sasquatch, America's Abominable Snowman," Man's Action, April 1970)

be called "cryptids" after the word was coined in 1981).

As the years of the 1960s unfolded, and the words "Abominable Snowmen," "Bigfoot," and "cryptozoology" occupied more and more of my time, I still found few books on the subject. Any I did discover were due to librarians at the Decatur Public Library or a mail order used book dealer, Atlantic Book Service in Boston, who helped me find some gems.

But soon I stumbled across a grand resource for nonfiction, usually firsthand accounts and field-investigator written articles on this new science of cryptozoology. I had noticed in Ivan T. Sanderson's 1961 book, Abominable Snowmen: Legend Come to Life, that he had written some articles in True magazine. Not knowing what this was, and not finding it at my local library, I finally hunted down the current issues at a local newsstand on the main thoroughfare in Decatur, Illinois.

A brand new world opened up and was revealed before me: True, Argosy, Saga, Adventure, For Men Only, Stag, Man's Magazine, Male, True Men, and Man's Life. Field & Stream, Boy's Life, and Outdoor Life were there too, but it was the "men's" magazines that most often carried the fearsome, factual, and sometimes borderline cryptid articles, with no shame.

Soon I found I could go from barbershop to barbershop in Decatur, looking for old, and some very old, issues of men's magazines that contained articles cited in Sanderson's and others' books. I would buy the out-of-date magazines from the barbers, as they were mostly interested in keeping the current issues for their customers.

I would go home with my cache of treasures, and search the magazines for the stories of bipedal bears attacking campers, Alaskan Indian tales of their Bigfoot, or Sea Monster accounts from war zones. The good and great authors, like Ivan T. Sanderson, John A. Keel, plus others using numerous pseudonyms, as well illustrators like the historical artist Mort

Künstler, filled the pages full of resource materials for long hours of speculation on cryptozoological species.

The content varied in believability, but I was a skeptical reader, always conscious that the article could be fabricated from whole cloth. I checked and double-checked sources, locations, eyewitness names, and incidents. I built an enormous library of articles from these sources.

I was a big fan of the genre, and considered even the fictionalized stories a form of influence on the public. They increased interest in Bigfoot and Lake Monsters, kept them in front of casual readers at newsstands and barbershops, and directly affected an entire generation of mostly male readers. The cryptids became a part of popular culture, more and more, and certainly I was positively impacted by the availability of these resources for my research. I learned critical thinking skills, thanks to these magazines, but I also found good, solid articles by nonfiction authors who were willing to share their material with a wider audience through men's magazines.

Here the nexus between men's adventure magazines and real world cryptozoology is made clear by one of its most influential practitioners, and the link is profound, if largely culturally unacknowledged. For without the wide readership of those articles, eagerly devoured by untold millions of bored American males awaiting their latest butch cut or flattop, cryptozoology as a growing concern would have likely been seriously impaired, delayed by perhaps decades in popular appeal. It is even possible some of the most respected researchers in the field, such as Coleman and others, might have lost interest and/or abandoned further research if not for the continual coverage in MAMs. Let us be thankful we do not live in that quantum reality!

The connection between published monster accounts and cryptozoology as endeavor is so intertwined, it is difficult to separate them in terms of mutual dependency and combined cultural impact. Take one persistent, paradoxical example: Bigfoot, aka Sasquatch. The idea of Bigfoot arrived conjoined

with speculative zoology from their earliest printed appearances
together. The *Oregon Historical Quarterly* #15 from 1814
published what could later be considered an early Sasquatch
encounter. In a journal entry, surveyor David Thompson (a
renowned stargazer, mapmaker, and explorer of the Canadian
wilderness) records while on an expedition in the Rocky
Mountain area near Alberta, Canada: *"I saw the track of a large
Animal—has 4 large Toes abt 3 or 4 In long & a small nail at the
end of each."* Thompson admits he and his fellow hunters were
reluctant to pursue whatever left the tracks, owing to a setting
sun and their silent fear at imagining what left them. He likewise
introduces his own rationalist explanation as to the tracks'
origins. For Thompson, writing forty years later, the cryptid
tracks were perhaps made by a gargantuan "Monster Bear," as he
speculatively concludes. He references the legendary aspects with
which the mountains have been imbued via the native population
and their accounting for all that is unexplained as monster-
caused. As Thompson writes in a style common to his era:
*"These reports appeared to arise from that fondness for the marvelous
so common to mankind."* But in offering his own sober assessment
with decades' worth of hindsight (and, some might reasonably
argue, embellishment and/or fading of memory), Thompson still
concludes on a cautious note of chilling uncertainty as to his own
deduction. He ends by confessing: *"But the sight of the track of that
large a beast staggered me, and I often thought of it."*

   And I often thought of it...

   It is this lingering air of vague unease, of speculative
possibility, that drove so much of the earliest accounts of
cryptozoology.

These stories did not exist in a cultural vacuum, outside the
influence of other forms in their era. Consider that most
perennial of popular influences, the movies. There were
occasional movies dedicated to the cryptid phenomena, often
influenced by men's adventure magazines. The early Yeti film
The Snow Creature (1954)—directed by Billy Wilder's brother, W.
Lee—featured lurid posters with large ballyhoo insets reading:

"It is hard to think of any horror filmmaker who made movies that were as cheap or as ridiculed as Jerry Warren's."
—Tom Weaver, IMDb

"Man Beast was somewhat ambitious for a low-budget independent '50s monster film. While a number of rungs below a Universal '50s monster film, or even an American International one, it was an entertaining film by Jerry Warren's standards. It aspires to the heights (or depths) of a film like Monster From the Ocean Floor *(1954)."*
—Bill Shute, Kendra Steiner Editions

"Himalayan Monster Captured 20,000 Feet Above the Earth! Millions Gasped When They Read About It in *Life*, *Time*, and *Argosy* Magazines!" Similarly, the poster for Jerry Warren's *Man Beast* (1956) promised: "Hair-raising excitement in the icy lair of the man-like creatures roaming the roof of the world! ... You read about them in *Time*, *True*, *Argosy*, *Newsweek*, *Pageant*, *Popular Science* Magazines!" While *Time*, *Life*, and *Newsweek* were included in the roster to add luster, high-end MAM titles *True*, *Argosy*, and others were the real populist proponents of the cryptozoological phenomena. Where mainstream publications reserved judgment and offered less variety, MAMs were all over the proverbial cryptid map. And where the early Yeti movies were typically constrained by inferior budgets, the men's adventure magazines set no such limitation on the authors' imaginations. Setting their stories in the most exotic, remote regions of the world, the narrator inevitably encountered a threatening monster lurking in the local shadows. With a few notable exceptions (such as 1957's *The Abominable Snowman of the Himalayas* from Hammer, and 1958's *Half Human* from Toho), cryptid movies of the Cold War era were but pale reflections of their MAM inspirations. No Hollywood special effects could compete with a reader's imagination.

The influence ran both ways, but a likely greater inspiration than movies on MAM cryptid coverage was the press-sensationalized Himalayan explorations of the early 20th century. These exotic affairs were headed by Westerners with such regal names as Major C.H. Shockley, George Leigh Mallory and Lt. Col. Charles Howard-Bury, and funded by such prestigious groups as the Royal Geographic Society. Though these early excursions were not Yeti searches per se, they nonetheless had a profound impact on cryptozoology. Press accounts of the Everest Reconnaissance Expedition of 1921 (headed by Howard-Bury) introduced the term "abominable snow men" into the lexicon, and by mid-century, explorers of the Himalayas such as Eric Shipton, Edmund Hillary and others could not avoid the inevitable Yeti questions when they returned to face a cryptid-obsessed press that often seemed more interested in the creature than any summit conquest. These newspaper accounts were not only instrumental in popularizing the Yeti, but they also helped kickstart subsequent well-financed expeditions—again underscoring the symbiotic nature of printed accounts and cryptozoology. On December 20, 1959, the esteemed *World Book Encyclopedia* announced $20,000 in financing for a four-month Mount Everest Yeti quest. The Ringling Brothers and Barnum & Bailey Circus hyped that it had hired game hunter McCormick Steele to trap a Yeti and bring it back for exhibition. Texas millionaire Tom Slick, a Yale grad with a trust fund to burn, financed well-publicized cryptozoological expeditions in search of not just the Yeti, but Bigfoot and the Loch Ness Monster, too.

Nor were merely Brits and Yanks interested in the Sherpa

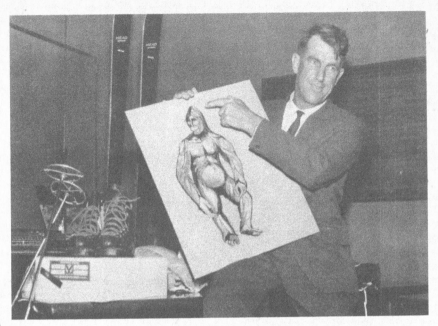

"Sir Edmund Hillary beat Mount Everest but though he followed up every clue, couldn't solve mystery of Himalayan yeti—the original Abominable Snowman. His conclusion: it's a 'myth.'" ("*Russia Claims 300 Sightings of the Abominable Snowman,*" Stag, *November 1968*)

monster of lore. The Chinese and Russian governments also financed expeditionary forces in search of the elusive snow beast in this Golden Age of Yeti exploration. MAMs were not only right in the middle of the growing cryptozoological phenomena, but likewise contributory to its very continued existence—and vice versa in terms of magazine sales, too. The plethora over decades of such marauding monster tales included in this book alone reveals how commercially dependent publishers of MAMs were in keeping cryptid interest alive and growing. Once the beast—*whatever* the beast—was out of the bag, MAM editors knew a good thing when they saw it selling magazines. And so a long-standing dependency between media and monster continued, in perhaps one of its most potently viral waves of popular influence: tales of the Yeti.

Another clear influence on these stories was the Professor

Challenger adventures by Arthur Conan Doyle. The Challenger archetype echoes through this collection's manly explorers and gun-toting cryptozoologists, well-equipped but small-banded in their dangerous trips. Far from the pushover later filmic adaptations may have implied, the Challenger of the stories is a Hemingwayesque man of aggressive attitude. At the start of *The Lost World*, Doyle offers that Challenger has assaulted numerous reporters who have dared to ridicule his cryptid claims. (Indeed, the "challenge" of overcoming public disbelief in the adventurer's unorthodox endeavors is another potent theme that would run throughout the real world of cryptozoology.)

In the novel, Challenger not only discovers a "lost world" plateau of living dinosaurs, he also encounters a tribe of man-ape creatures known as the Doda, an early literary invocation of Bigfoot (albeit without the usual solitary aspect attributed to most Sasquatch sightings). *The Lost World* was first serialized in 1912 in *The Strand Magazine*, a popular British predecessor of sorts to the American MAMs of a later era. Such fictional explorations of mythic locales (and encounters with legendary creatures found there) were a clear influence on the stories gathered in these pages.

EVERYTHING good comes to an end, and everything great, too soon (it can feel) rather than too late. The popular influence of the MAMs and their codependent dance with cryptozoology stories would fade by the end of the 1970s, the mutual admiration society finally dissolving with the demise of the MAMs. Cryptozoology would become more influenced by books, films, and popular shows such as *In Search of...* by the late 1970s, and far less, if any, from lurid newsstand periodicals. As Lyle Blackburn, author of *The Beast of Boggy Creek: The True Story of the Fouke Monster* and an avid cryptozoologist from a later generation, told me when I asked him about the possible influence of MAMs on his interest: "I didn't read or collect any of those mags. I think they were a bit ahead of my time or I just wasn't aware of them when I was a kid. I have since bought a few collector's copies of *Argosy* for the nostalgic cryptozoology articles, but they didn't

"Abominable Snowmen Behind the Iron Curtain" by yeti scholar Odette Tchernine. *Author of the books* The Snowman and Company *and* In Pursuit of the Abominable Snowman. *Her three decades of global cryptid research from the 1950s through the 1970s coincided with the lifespan of the men's adventure magazine genre.*

(Argosy, *February 1971*)

FEBRUARY ARGOSY

A scientific reconstruction of a primitive manlike creature, without the usual coarse hair covering, was prepared by a Polish anthropologist, Wsenczyslaw Pisarzak.

ABOMINABLE SNOWMEN BEHIND THE IRON CURTAIN

HERE IS THE FIRST REPORT ON THE FANTASTIC RESEARCH LAUNCHED BY SOVIET SCIENTISTS INTO THE LIVES OF YETIS OR ABOMINABLE SNOWMEN ARTICLE BY ODETTE TCHERNINE

have any affect on my knowledge of the subject like books and television did."

Indeed, the coming deluge of cable TV shows, fictionalized and documentary movies, bestselling paperback books, and the dawn of the internet all but ensured the need for exposure to a MAM for cryptozoologic updates would become as extinct as *Gigantopithecus.* But oh, what tantalizing literary remains, and hardly fossilized! Likewise, Blackburn's fellow cryptozoologist, author Nick Redfern (whose works include *Monster Diary, There's Something in the Woods* and *Monster Files*) reported to me the MAMs were negligible on his own interest and early research, as they were not readily available for import in the UK, where he grew up before moving to the United States. But like others before him, Redfern appreciates the historical importance they had on many others. "Looking back at the old scene from today's perspective, I don't think there's any doubt—at all—that all

Russian Yeti coverage paired two men's adventure perennials: Bigfoot and the Red Menace. Art by Gil Cohen. ("Russia Claims 300 Sightings of the Abominable Snowman," Stag, November 1968)

of those magazines massively contributed to the visibility of the subject of cryptozoology and the people and players in the subject," said Redfern. "They helped to highlight significant cases, helped writers in the field to get established, and definitely contributed to the growing awareness."

As for myself, I was fortunate enough as an impressionable child to have felt the full, if fading, effect of such publications in the 1970s. Not unlike a younger Generation X version of Loren Coleman, I haunted the local newsstands that featured the "good stuff" such as *Argosy* and other tantalizing titles, always in hopeful search of my next cryptid kick. If after standing on my tiptoes (for the titles were always placed top shelf to make it more difficult for tyke browsers like myself to glance them over) and discovering the latest issue didn't feature a story dedicated to a Giant Squid, Sasquatch or at least a modest Lake Monster rehash of some type, I would place said issue back in the rack, disappointed. It would be a long series of weeks, if not months, before perhaps I would be lucky enough to find a new run of stories about Bigfoot or Nessie. The best I could hope for would be a quick glimpse of some rare cryptid photos on this week's episode of *In Search of…* during its hypnotic title montage during the interim, as well as zealously re-reading each treasured MAM featuring a cryptozoologic entry in my collection. And it is through this perspective, from the viewpoint of a time prior to "everything, all the time," that you will best experience reading the many wonderful stories to follow.

No one can entirely place aside the present for a pure experience of the past, of course. Our own histories color our present realities, which are largely subjectively based, at any rate. But imagine yourself back in an era when such stories had major impact on their devoted readers and a growing field of research. Place yourself in that barbershop, timidly asking the barber if you might purchase those old back issues. Feel the vicarious tingle of hiding a particularly sensationalized issue of a men's magazine in a stack of comic books, with nary a discerning glimpse from the bored clerk at the check-out point. As you explore story after story, consider the long waits so many passionate, dedicated cryptid lovers endured between the publication of new creature tales, while you need only turn the page to satiate your next monster thrill.

Be transported to a time and place where discovery and adventure go bloody hand in bruised fist, where the heights of imagination share a precarious, precipitous peak with that oldest of human fascinations: the mysteries that arise from "that fondness for the marvelous so common to mankind." For these stories remain marvelous in the fondest ways imaginable.

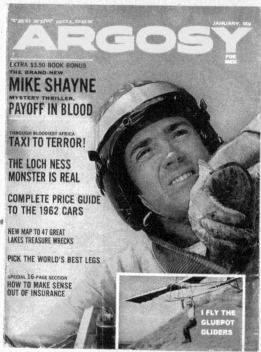

Right: Detail from a truly spectacular Nessie portrait by artist Paul Lehr. The piece accompanied Tim Dinsdale's exhaustive account, "The Loch Ness Monster Is Real," in the January 1962 issue of Argosy. Below: The complete 2-page spread.

Clenched Fists, Big Feet, and Loch Ness Monsters

Night. The kind of pitch-black night you only find deep in the woods, far from civilization. As the campfire is extinguished, the flickering glow emanating from the heart of the ring of tents dims and darkens. A few charred, skinny branches, their whittled ends still sticky with the baked residue of melted marshmallow and chocolate, lay abandoned in the now-smoldering fire ring. The whoosh of zippers punctuates murmurs of conversation as tent flaps and sleeping bags are opened and resealed for lights out. And as the sounds of campers are overtaken by cricket song and the occasional hoot of an owl, sleepy thoughts of the next day's plans are edged out by chilly memories of the evening's ghost stories.

And then...

A rustle of dead leaves, crunching as they're pushed across the forest floor... Something's moving in the woods! The sharp crack of a dry branch snapping underfoot is followed by the sound of heavy, wet panting... *Something* is sniffing and snorting as it lumbers its way through the campsite...

What's out there? A bear? A hungry wolf? A mountain lion? Or is it... Bigfoot?

One of many men's adventure magazine pieces by author/researcher Ivan T. Sanderson, a leading light in early cryptozoological investigation, with Sasquatch art by Mort Künstler. ("A New Look at America's Mystery Giant," True, March 1960)

It seems like he's been out there forever. Those who came of age in the 1970s will recall an era when fascination with Bigfoot, the Loch Ness Monster and related creatures reached a cultural high point, along with other mysterious subjects like UFOlogy, spiritualism, and the occult. It was a time when books by Erich von Däniken topped the lists of paperback bestsellers, and producer Alan Landsburg (who'd adapted Däniken's books into a trio of successful documentary features) *really* blew the lid off things with his fondly remembered television program, *In Search Of...* In addition to Däniken's ancient astronauts, that show brought man-monsters, sea monsters, and other weird phenomena to prime time, beaming them into America's living rooms weekly, and sparking the interest of a new generation in the process. The '70s also saw an explosion of movies and memorable TV episodes that featured such creatures, especially Bigfoot.

Nowadays, Bigfoot, Abominable Snowmen and other legendary "monsters" are the focus of a revived and steadily

I LAY THERE, FEELING THE MONSTER SHAKING ME LIKE A RAG DOLL, ITS GREAT JAWS CLAMPED ON MY ARM, CHEWING IT INTO A BLOODY PULP...

The monster out there in the moonlight was balancing its half ton of fighting fury on silent pads.

by Vincent Dolce

I FED MY ARM TO A KODIAK

In addition to cryptid conflict, violent encounters with all kinds of savage creatures were a hallmark of men's adventure magazines. Here. a "true" story of survival is presented with MAMs' typical subtlety.

("I Fed My Arm to a Kodiak," Rage, March 1961)

growing subgenre, powered by TV shows, movies, books, 'zines, websites, podcasts, and videos—all eagerly devoured and debated by millions of people hungry for more information about fantastic creatures from a realm that some people call myth, but that true fans call *cryptozoology.*

Some sources credit Belgian zoologist Bernard Heuvelmans with coining that term in his seminal book, *On the Track of Unknown Animals,* first published in 1955. Heuvelmans himself attributed it to his friend and fellow expert on arcane zoology, Ivan T. Sanderson—about whom more later. *Cryptozoology* is a fusion of three Greek words: *crypto,* meaning "hidden" or "unknown," *zo* meaning "animal," and *ology,* "the study of." In short, it's the study of hidden or unknown animals. *Cryptid* is the general term used for such creatures. If you look into the growth of interest in cryptozoology and cryptids, you'll find that a key role was played by stories featured in the pulpy men's adventure magazines that emerged after World War II and were read by millions of men in the 1950s, 1960s, and 1970s.

For the three decades they existed, men's adventure magazines provided a unique form of entertainment for the large subset of American men who enjoyed the genre's mix of gritty war stories, action and adventure yarns, exposés and "sexposés," true and fictional crime and detective stories, gonzo animal attack tales (*à la* "Weasels Ripped My Flesh!") and stories about strange and unusual topics that were generally ignored by the mainstream media—and that included creatures like Bigfoot, Yetis, the Loch Ness monster and UFOs.

Since their demise in the '70s, men's adventure magazines (which we sometimes shorten to MAMs, to prevent repetitive typing injuries) have been recognized as a fertile early training ground for writers who would go on to greater fame. The Men's Adventure Library featured stories by some of those writers in our inaugural collection, *Weasels Ripped My Flesh!*, including Lawrence Block, Jane Dolinger, Robert F. Dorr, Harlan Ellison, Bruce Jay Friedman, Mario Puzo, Robert Silverberg, and Walter Wager.

If you're already a fan of vintage men's adventure magazines, you know that they also featured cover paintings and interior illustrations by some of the greatest illustration artists of the 20th century. The stories in the anthology you are now reading are accompanied by artwork by Stan Borack, Gil Cohen, Clarence Doore, Rafael DeSoto, John Duillo, Jack Dumas, Norm Eastman, Robert Engel, Denver Gillon, George Gross, Warren Knight, Mort Kunstler, Tom Lovell, John McDermott, John Pike, and other talented illustrators.

In putting together this collection, several new realizations struck us. One is that the role MAMs played in the modern growth of interest in cryptozoology and cryptid creatures was huge—and not widely known. Another is that very few of the

many stories about cryptids we discovered in men's adventure
magazines had ever been reprinted. We also recognized some
clear and interesting cultural parallels between the readers
of the men's adventure magazine genre and modern fans of
cryptozoology.

In the world of 1950s magazine publishing, the battle lines in
the fight for male readers were drawn early. *Playboy*, other slick
"bachelor magazines" of the time, and most MAMs featured
"cheesecake" photos of scantily clad women, though the photos in
MAMs tended to be less explicit until the late 1960s.

However, as Hugh Hefner wrote in his editor's introduction
to the first anniversary issue of *Playboy* in 1954, there was a
bigger difference in the overall content and readership of the
two genres: Hefner noted that most popular men's magazines
at the time—hunting and fishing periodicals and MAMs—were
"concerned almost exclusively with action, adventure, and the
great out-of-doors." In contrast, Hefner said, *Playboy* was a
magazine for "urbane fellows who were less concerned with
hunting, fishing, and climbing mountains than good food, drink,
proper dress."

Those "urbane fellows" tended to dismiss, scoff at, and look
down on men's adventure magazines and their readers—as did
any literary critics or social commentators who were even aware
of them. Similarly, the realm of cryptozoology and its modern
fans are often dismissed, scoffed at and looked down on by
"urbane" social commenters and mainstream scientists.

But we doubt the original blue-collar working guys reading
men's adventure magazines in their heyday or modern fans of
cryptozoology would give a damn about that. They'd surely agree
that there's a lot social and scientific authorities, eggheads, and
bosses of the world don't know—and that there's plenty they've
been wrong about in the past.

Many cryptozoology buffs are aware of Ivan T. Sanderson's
pioneering book *Abominable Snowmen: Legend Come to Life*. First

"Is There a Lost Race of 'Dawn Men'?" Frame 352 of the famed Patterson–Gimlin film from 1967 makes one of its many appearances in men's adventure magazines. The controversial footage was still a hot news item when Stag *ran this image in its November 1968 issue. MAMs afforded many readers (and budding researchers) their first real opportunity for an unhurried look at the creature in the footage.*

("Russia Claims 300 Sightings of the Abominable Snowman" Stag, *November 1968)*

published in 1961, it is still in print and now available in ebook format. It may be the best-selling book ever written about the manlike cryptids.

But something only the more serious cryptozoology fans know is that Sanderson's most significant contributions to the lore about legendary "hidden creatures" were the articles he wrote for mid-20th century men's adventure magazines. From the late 1940s to the early 1970s, he wrote dozens of heavily researched articles about mysterious creatures for *Argosy* and *True*, two of the top tier, high-circulation men's adventure magazines.

For years, Sanderson held the title of Science Editor at *Argosy*. In that role, he contributed many widely read and influential articles about the Loch Ness Monster, various other lake and sea monsters, and man-like "Hominid cryptids" such as Bigfoot, Sasquatch, and the Abominable Snowman, or Yeti. One of his blockbuster scoops was an article about the film of Bigfoot taken by Roger Patterson and Bob Gimlin. Titled "First Photos of 'Bigfoot,' California's Legendary 'Abominable

Snowman,'" it appeared in *Argosy*'s February 1968 issue. That story made Sanderson, Patterson, and Gimlin superstars in the burgeoning field of cryptozoology. Still frames from the film stamped the now iconic visual image of a female Bigfoot walking with swinging arms into the consciousness of people around the world. It played an instrumental role in making Bigfoot famous and led to a slew of other Bigfoot-focused magazine and newspaper stories, books, and movies in the 1970s.

What's less well known is that men's adventure magazines made a contribution to the history and lore of cryptozoology that goes beyond the articles written by Sanderson. Throughout the 1950s and 1960s, men's adventure magazines were publishing scores of stories about cryptid creatures by various authors. Some, like Sanderson's, were historically significant to the development of cryptozoological lore.

For example, in 1948, *Sir!* magazine, one of the pioneering periodicals that helped shape the men's pulp adventure genre, scooped the mainstream magazines and other media by printing one of the first stories about Sasquatch published in the US. We've included this rare treat here as our opening story, "Wild Giants of British Columbia" (pg. 27).

Cryptid encounters of every stripe enjoyed frequent coverage and could arguably be considered nearly as much a hallmark of the mags as sadistic Nazi villains or animal attack stories. In the early 1950s, *Sir!* and other early MAMs that emerged in that decade published some of the first stories written about the Abominable Snowman, or Yeti. In 1962, *Argosy* published a high-profile article about the Loch Ness Monster by Tim Dinsdale, showing stills of his grainy footage of "Nessie" that became world famous. In 1963, the popular men's adventure magazine *Saga* published a seminal cryptid story by Jack Pearl (pen name of writer Jacques Bain Pearl) titled "Monster Bird That Carries Off Human Beings!" That story has been credited with generating modern awareness of legends about a huge flying cryptid called the Thunderbird—and for inspiring a wave of other stories and books about giant birds.

"Only those who had seen him believed he existed, for the tales the witnesses brought back were incredible." "Kill the Mad Giant of Idaho," a cryptid yarn set in the pioneer era. (Real Men, *February 1965*)

Many of the most influential cryptozoology-related stories were written and published as non-fiction. Other cryptid creature stories were the type of pulpy, often bloody action yarns that were common to the genre. Both types of stories appeared in many of the most popular men's adventure periodicals published in the 1950s, 1960s, and 1970s, such as *Man's Magazine* (pg. 59), *Male* (pg. 73), *Adventure* (pg. 91), *Saga* (pg. 173), *Argosy* (pg. 249), *For Men Only, Man's World* (pg. 267), *Men, Stag,* and *True.* Fiction stories and purportedly true articles about cryptid creatures also appeared in many of the more obscure men's adventure magazines, like *Courage* (pg. 172), *Showdown* (pg. 118), *Rage* (pg. 220), and *True Weird* (pg. 44).

Some were penned by notable writers of speculative fiction, like the great Arthur C. Clarke ("The Reckless Ones," pg. 91). Others were by authors known for their articles and books about strange and paranormal subjects, including Ivan T. Sanderson and John Keel ("Incredible Monster-Man Sightings in the US," pg. 73), the world-famous author of a series of popular books about UFOs and strange creatures. (Keel is best known for his 1975 book, *The Mothman Prophecies*, which inspired the spooky 2002 film starring Richard Gere.)

Movies, television, books, comics, and now the internet have all contributed significantly to a renewed fascination with creatures that blur the line between fact and fantasy. But the relative obscurity of vintage men's adventure magazines since the 1970s has meant few newcomers are aware of the myriad ways these unique, frequently outrageous magazines helped lay the foundation for today's cryptozoological lore and media.

We hope this anthology will help increase awareness of that fact, and point the way to a wider appreciation of men's adventure magazine stories in general.

Notes on the Text and Terminology

Since this is an anthology of stories about "hidden creatures," we've also included a special hidden story that doesn't show in the table of contents. It's a long lost article by one of the (human) giants in the realm of cryptozoology mentioned above. You'll know it when you see it.

In the interest of historic preservation of both men's adventure magazine stories and cryptozoology lore, we've kept the spelling of the various names given to creatures and places as they originally appeared in each of the stories reprinted here.

Editors of *Sir!* claimed the creature depicted opposite is "*an artist's conception of the Abominable Snowman sketched from specifications detailed in the report by Shipton expedition.*" In fact, it's the work of Czech painter František Kupka, based on the La Chapelle-aux-Saints Neanderthal skeleton and the work of French paleontologist Marcellin Boule. The skeleton was

---

(cont'd)

discovered in France in 1908; Kupka's drawing was published in *L'Illustration* in 1909 and soon after reprinted in the *Illustrated London News*—predating the controversial 1951 Everest expedition of mountaineer Eric Shipton by four decades. ("The Abominable Snowman Seen Again," *Sir!* September 1953)

Discovery of the Piltdown Man, by artist Frank Soltesz. Once touted as proof of an evolutionary missing link, Piltdown Man is now ranked among the most notorious cryptozoology scams ever perpetrated on the public. ("The Monster Ape That Hoaxed the World," *Man's World*, April 1964)

"WILD GIANTS OF BRITISH COLUMBIA"

"WILD Giants of British Columbia" was an attempt by Chehalis Indian Reserve agent and teacher John W. Burns to record and popularize much of the native folklore he encountered in his government-sanctioned tenure. This was not Burns' only or even first attempt to do so. He published an earlier version of "Wild Giants of British Columbia" in *MacLean's Magazine* dated April 1929, then later, a slightly different telling of the same concepts in a January 1940 issue of *The Wide World, A Magazine for Men* called "The Hairy Giants of British Columbia."

More germane, Burns coined the term "Sasquatch" for his hirsute tribe of relic hominids. And though the term was an amalgamation of Indian terminology, the Anglicized moniker stuck, and the media soon adapted its continual usage. Burns was not only a writer, but also a firm believer in the truth of the accounts he recorded. As proof of his advocacy's lasting impact, Sasquatch is still commonly misunderstood to be a Native American name for Bigfoot—further demonstration of how published accounts affect perception and lingo associated with cryptozoology.

In this regard, "Wild Giants of British Columbia" echoes many memes now firmly associated with Sasquatch, and these go beyond Burns' popularization of the namesake cryptid itself. For example, Sasquatch in Burns' stories remains elusive in mountainous terrain, uses boulders as weapons, attacks cabin-sheltered humans, and leaves footprints which are often the only evidence of its terrifying visitations. (Note the latter similarity to surveyor David Thompson's 1814 account in this regard, which also occurred in the Canadian wilderness.) Sasquatch is herein revered by native tradition but also believed as factually existent, favors night prowling, traverses rivers as easily as dense undergrowth, survives as a cave dweller and is mistaken at first for a bear on its hind legs. All of these ideas, and many more, appear in Burns' seminal series of articles. Many of these tropes are still prevalent within the cryptozoological community, and likewise appear in subsequent Bigfoot movies and TV shows.

This is not to say Burns is *originating* the idea of an ape-man species living in the wilds, nor even most of the concepts delineated above, as other Bigfoot stories predate his published accounts. Teddy Roosevelt, in his 1892 memoir *The Wilderness Hunter*, recounts a savage Sasquatch encounter that results in a fur trapper's death by cryptid. *The Wilderness Hunter* tale features many of the same descriptive elements of Sasquatch as in the accounts by Burns, including its human-like tracks, bipedal gait, ability to dart across darkened terrain, powerful odor, and a sinister, low-moaning howl. But the cultural impact the men's adventure magazines had on the burgeoning field of cryptozoology—as well as the reading public's fascination—was more profound than any singular book entry. Rather than rare, sporadic accounts such as appeared in Thompson's and Roosevelt's books, the MAMs transformed cryptid stories into a fully fledged, continuously reported upon phenomena.

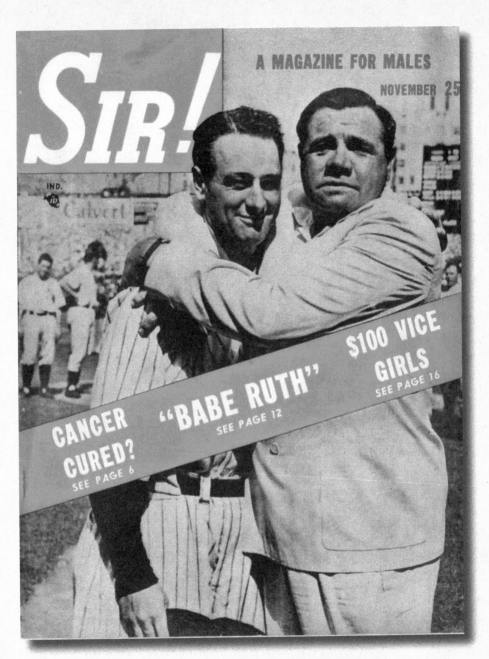

SIR!

A MAGAZINE FOR MALES

NOVEMBER 25¢

IND.

CANCER CURED?
SEE PAGE 6

"BABE RUTH"
SEE PAGE 12

$100 VICE GIRLS
SEE PAGE 16

"WILD GIANTS OF BRITISH COLUMBIA"
J.W. BURNS / C.V. TENCH
SIR! **NOVEMBER 1948**

WILD GIANTS OF BRITISH COLUMBIA

AS TOLD BY J. W. BURNS

Indian Agent, Chehalis Indian Reserve, B.C.

AND SET DOWN
BY C. V. TENCH

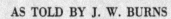

THE Indian was running. With stark fear showing upon his face he was racing madly toward the Chehalis River where his dug-out canoe was moored. In pursuit lunged a giant of a man all of eight feet in height and broad in proportion. A "Sasquatch" or wild giant of British Columbia, stark naked and covered from head to foot by a thick growth of black, woolly hair.

In his fright the Chehalis Indian, Peter Williams, completely forgot the rifle he clutched in one hand; made no attempt to stop and fight it out. At sudden sight of the monster standing atop a huge boulder all reason had fled, to be instantly supplanted by sheer panic as the giant sprang in growling attack.

Heedless of trees and tangled undergrowth, the Indian plunged wildly on, careening from side to side, panting in great gasping breaths and jerking his head to gaze behind him in the ultimate of terror.

The giant was fast overtaking him when at last he reached the river. A frantic heave and the dug-out canoe shot out into the turbulent stream. But the swift river did not in the least daunt the giant; he at once plunged into the water in continued pursuit.

The moment the prow of the dug-out scraped on the opposite bank, Peter Williams leaped ashore. A hasty glance showed the giant now almost in mid-stream, swimming strongly and forging slowly toward him. Once more the Indian took to his heels.

Panting and dazed from exhaustion he at last reached the poorly-built frame shack that was his home.

Hurriedly he herded his wife and children into the building. Bolting the door, he barricaded it with everything he could. Then, with rifle ready, he shiveringly waited the giant's arrival.

Presently there came the sound of a heavy body forcing its way through the brush. It was the wild man. Darkness had not yet set in and peering through a crack, Peter Williams had a good look at the monster. It was a Sasquatch, and a Sasquatch is a man, therefore the Indian could not bring himself to shoot.

Growling deep-chestedly the giant prowled all about the flimsy dwelling. Then, putting one huge shoulder against a wall he pushed with such tremendous force the frail building shook. Timbers creaked and groaned so much under the strain that Peter Williams was afraid that the roof would cave in, so he whispered to his squaw to crawl under the bed with the children. At once the badly frightened woman and youngsters obeyed, leaving the equally scared Peter Williams to face the monster alone if the wild giant did force entry.

But the Sasquatch did nothing so drastic. After prowling gruntingly around the house a few times the monster stalked away into the bush. Next morning, Peter Williams found the giant's tracks in the mud outside the shack. The footprints measured twenty-two inches in length! (The average man's are from ten to twelve inches).

THE foregoing is a graphic account of what actually took place in the "Saskahaua" or "The Place of the Wild Men" district of British Columbia, Canada. I have merely written what Peter Williams told me took place.

I have known Peter for a good many years. He is intelligent, honest and trustworthy. Personally, I do not question the truth of his story; it is but one of many such tales regarding the Sasquatch or Wild Giants I have heard first hand from Indians under my direct care.

But before I attempt to relate any additional stories about the Sasquatch, I should like to state that for fifteen years I have held my present position as Indian Agent, stationed at the Chehalis Indian Reserve, some sixty miles from the city of Vancouver, B.C. My Indian charges are also my friends, and because I have always reciprocated by trying to be their good friend, the Chehalis Indians took me into their confidence and have revealed to me the mystery of the Sasquatch, a thing they have *never confided to any white man before!* One reason is that they are naturally of a proud, somewhat aloof nature, extremely sensitive to ridicule. If a white man unknown to them asked about the Sasquatch he would be met with the reply: "No. White man won't believe. He make joke of Indian."

Although I have never personally encountered a Sasquatch, there is ample proof that the hairy giants once inhabited the Chehalis district of British Columbia in considerable numbers.

Legends tell of two tribes of Sasquatch who were deadly enemies and fought until they almost exterminated one another, fighting hand-to-hand with stone clubs on the wild, steep slopes.

The Sasquatch may be reduced in numbers, but there is abundant evidence that they are not extinct and that they are not merely a superstition or an exaggeration. When an intelligent young Chehalis Indian woman such as Emma Paul declared that she saw one of them near her house one evening last summer, it would be an injustice to suspect her of romanticism.

"I saw the Sasquatch," said Emma, "a few yards from the house. I was standing by the door at the time. He was watching me closely and I had a good look at his face. He was big and powerful in appearance. Other members of the family were present who also saw him.

"We bolted the door and he prowled around outside the house for some time. We have often heard one of them at night since then and one used to rub his fingers over the window panes. It was only last night that a Sasquatch was outside tramping loudly about the house. We all heard it and so did the white carpenter who lives next door."

The Indians maintain that each summer the Sasquatch have a gathering of the remnants of their race near the rocky, shelving

(Continued on page 54)

Mr. J. W. Burns, a responsible government official, believes that deep in the unexplored mountain fastness of British Columbia, Canada, there still lurk a few scattered survivors of the mysterious Sasquatch, primitive creatures of huge stature, covered from head to foot with coarse hair, who have figured in Indian legends for centuries. Supposedly these giants are extinct.

31

ART BY JOSEPH SZOKOLI

The Indian was running. With stark fear showing upon his face he was racing madly toward the Chehalis River where his dugout canoe was moored. In pursuit lunged a giant of a man all of eight feet in height and broad in proportion. A "Sasquatch," or wild giant of British Columbia, stark naked and covered from head to foot by a thick growth of black, woolly hair.

In his fright, the Chehalis Indian, Peter Williams, completely forgot the rifle he clutched in one hand; made no attempt to stop and fight it out. At sudden sight of the monster standing atop a huge boulder, all reason had fled, to be instantly supplanted by sheer panic as the giant sprang in growling attack.

Heedless of trees and tangled undergrowth, the Indian plunged wildly on, careening from side to side, panting in great gasping breaths and jerking his head to gaze behind him in the ultimate of terror.

The giant was fast overtaking him when at last he reached the river. A frantic heave and the dugout canoe shot out into the turbulent stream. But the swift river did not in the least daunt the giant; he at once plunged into the water in continued pursuit.

The moment the prow of the dug-out scraped on the opposite bank, Peter Williams leaped ashore. A hasty glance showed the giant now almost in mid-stream, swimming strongly and forging slowly toward him. Once more the Indian took to his heels.

Panting and dazed from exhaustion he at last reached the poorly built frame shack that was his home.

Hurriedly he herded his wife and children into the building. Bolting the door, he barricaded it with everything he could. Then, with rifle ready, he shiveringly awaited the giant's arrival.

Presently there came the sound of a heavy body forcing its way through the brush. It was the wild man. Darkness had not yet set in and peering through a crack, Peter Williams had a good look at the monster. It was a Sasquatch, and a Sasquatch is a man, therefore the Indian could not bring himself to shoot.

Growling deep-chestedly, the giant prowled all about the flimsy dwelling. Then, putting one huge shoulder against a wall he pushed with such tremendous force the frail building shook. Timbers creaked and groaned so much under the strain that Peter Williams was afraid that the roof would cave in, so he whispered to his squaw to crawl under the bed with the children. At once the badly frightened woman and youngsters obeyed, leaving the equally scared Peter Williams to face the monster alone if the wild giant did force entry.

But the Sasquatch did nothing so drastic. After prowling gruntingly around the house a few times the monster stalked away into the bush. Next morning, Peter Williams found the giant's tracks in the mud outside the shack. The footprints measured 22 inches in length! (The average man's are from 10 to 12 inches).

THE foregoing is a graphic account of what actually took place in the "Saskahaua" (or "The Place of the Wild Men") district of British Columbia, Canada. I have merely written what Peter Williams told me took place. I have known Peter for a good many years. He is intelligent, honest and trustworthy. Personally. I do not question the truth of his story: it is but one of many such tales regarding the Sasquatch or Wild Giants I have heard first hand from Indians under my direct care.

But before I attempt to relate any additional stories about the Sasquatch, I should like to state that for fifteen years I have held my present position as Indian Agent, stationed at the Chehalis Indian Reserve, some sixty miles from the city of Vancouver, BC. My Indian charges are also my friends, and because I have always reciprocated by trying to be their good friend, the Chehalis Indians took me into their confidence and have revealed to me the mystery of the Sasquatch, a thing they have never confided to any white man before! One reason is that they are naturally of a proud, somewhat aloof nature, extremely sensitive to ridicule. If a white man unknown to them asked about the Sasquatch he would be met with the reply: "No. White man won't believe. He make joke of Indian."

Although I have never personally encountered a Sasquatch, there is ample proof that the hairy giants once inhabited the Chehalis district of British Columbia in considerable numbers.

Legends tell of two tribes of Sasquatch who were deadly enemies and fought until they almost exterminated one another, fighting hand-to-hand with stone clubs on the wild, steep slopes.

The Sasquatch may be reduced in numbers, but there is abundant evidence that they are not extinct and that they are not merely a superstition or an exaggeration. When an intelligent young Chehalis Indian woman such as Emma Paul declared that she saw one of them near her house one evening last summer, it would be an injustice to suspect her of romanticism.

"I saw the Sasquatch," said Emma, "a few yards from the house. I was standing by the door at the time. He was watching me closely and I had a good look at his face. He was big and powerful in appearance. Other members of the family were present who also saw him.

"We bolted the door and he prowled around outside the house for some time. We have often heard one of them at night since then and one used to rub his fingers over the window panes. It was only last night that a Sasquatch was outside tramping loudly about the house. We all heard it and so did the white carpenter who lives next door."

The Indians maintain that each summer the Sasquatch have a gathering of the remnants of their race near the rocky, shelving top of Morris Mountain, which commands a wide view of the vast mountain solitudes all around. Prior to the gathering, the wild giants send out scouts, and it is these scattered scouts that have been seen by the Indians.

Naturally, anthropologists the world over are keenly interested in the reported existence of these hairy giants, and two years ago a party of Americans with movie cameras, fully equipped for an expedition into the wilds, visited me and asked for my assistance in enlisting the aid of Indian guides, packers, and general helpers.

In spite of being offered ten dollars per day and all found, not one of my Indians would volunteer, declaring that such an expedition would be in vain, as the Sasquatch, hearing and seeing the approach of the party toward their meeting place, would at once go into hiding. So the American party set out without the aid of native helpers. In less than two weeks they returned, gaunt, weary and covered with fly bites. They told me that ordinary white men could never reach the top of Morris Mountain because of its impassable ledges and ravines.

A FEW weeks later, another of my Indians encountered a Sasquatch.

The Indian—an old man named Chehalis Phillip—claims that he saw Sasquatch several times in his younger days. On this recent occasion he was fishing for trout in Morris Creek, a tributary of the Chehalis River. His canoe was gliding quietly along the sluggish mountain stream close to the rocky, terraced bank when without warning a rock was thrown from the shelving slope above, falling with a splash within a yard of the canoe, almost swamping it and drenching the Indian.

Startled, Phillip hurriedly looked upwards and saw a hairy monster leaning over the cliff and holding a bulky object which proved to be another heavy rock. This the wild giant deliberately hurled with terrific force at the helpless and by now thoroughly scared Phillip. The rock splashed into the water bare inches from the canoe.

Believing that the Sasquatch was about to dive into the water and attack him, Phillip cast free his lines and paddled frantically away.

But not all Sasquatch are unfriendly; apparently they have as strongly developed individual characteristics as ordinary mortals. Witness what an old Indian named Henry Napoleon has to say:

"The first time that I found out for sure that the wild men do still live around here," Henry told me. "I did not see any of them. Some years ago when I was young, three other young men and

I were picking berries on a rocky mountain slope. In our search
We suddenly stumbled upon a large opening in the side of the
mountain. The discovery greatly surprised all of us, for we knew
every foot of the area, and never knew nor heard there was a cave
in the vicinity. Outside the mouth of the cave there was a very big
boulder. We peered into the cave but could not see anything.

"We gathered some pitchwood, lighted it and began to
explore. But before we got very far from the entrance of the cave,
we came upon a sort of stone house or enclosure. We couldn't
make a very thorough examination, for our pitchwood kept going
out. We left, intending to return in a couple of days and go on
exploring.

"Old Indians, to whom we told the story of our discovery,
warned us not to venture near the cave again, as it was surely
occupied by the Sasquatch. But we paid no attention to them and
went to explore the cave again. To our great disappointment and
surprise, we found the big boulder rolled back into its mouth
fitting as tightly as if it had been made for the purpose.

"Then, some years later I was out hunting deer in the same
vicinity. It was almost dusk when I saw something I at first took
to be a big bear standing on its hind legs, but as I stopped and
raised my rifle the creature spoke in a tongue much like the one I
now speak. He invited me to come closer and when I did so I saw
that he was a man over seven feet tall and his body was very hairy.

"At first I was very scared, but his eyes were kind and he
asked me to sit down and talk. He told me that during the winter
the Sasquatch sleep like bears, that their home is on the top of
Morris Mountain where no Indian or white men could ever find
them; that they live on roots, fish and meat just like the Indians.

"Then suddenly it was dark and he was gone."

ANOTHER of my Indians, a man named Charley Victor, has this to
say of personal encounters with Sasquatch:

"I was hunting in the mountains near here. I had my dog with
me. I came out on a plateau where there were several big cedar
trees. The dog rushed up to one of the trees and began to growl
and bark. On looking up to see what excited him I noticed a large
hole in the trunk of the tree about seven feet from the ground.
The dog kept jumping and scratching at the trunk and looking to

me to lift him up. I did so and he dropped down inside the hole.

"Then there was an awful noise, the dog growling and barking and something screaming. I thought it was a bear my dog was fighting with and, with my rifle ready, shouted to the dog to drive the animal out. And then something just shot out of that hole. I fired and the creature fell to the ground. I stared and then I felt sick. What I had shot looked like a white boy of about twelve years of age. He was naked.

"Bleeding from a bullet wound in his leg the poor boy lay there on the ground. When I stepped forward he twisted away and let out a wild scream. From deep in the trees came a reply. Nearer and nearer came the voice and every now and again the wounded boy would cry out as if calling directions. Then out of the forest came a Sasquatch woman.

"I then not only felt sick but also scared. I lifted my rifle, not to shoot the woman but just in case I had to defend myself.

"The wild woman ran toward the boy. Her skin was as dark as mine and her long straight hair fell to her knees. In height she would be about seven feet and big-built all over. She looked so strong that I am sure that if she had laid hands on me she could have broken every bone in my body. But I was by then too scared to even run.

"She bent over the boy then turned on me savagely, her big eyes like balls of fire. In Douglas dialect she said angrily:

"'You have hurt my friend.'

"I replied in the same language—for I am part Douglas myself—that I had mistaken the boy for a bear, that I was very sorry, and that, anyway, he was not badly hurt.

"She did not reply, but picking up the boy as easily as if he weighed nothing, lifted him to her shoulder and strode off into the woods.

"I do not think that the boy belonged to the Sasquatch people," Charley concluded, "because he was white and she called him her 'friend.' No, she must have stolen him or run across him in some other way."

ANOTHER incident that is well-authenticated happened last September, when Indian hop-pickers were having their annual picnic near Agassiz, British Columbia. A young Indian man and

maid, William Point and Adaline August, both graduates of a
Vancouver high school, had walked some distance from the picnic
grounds when they suddenly encountered a Sasquatch. Hearing
of this occurrence, and anxious to verify it, if possible, I wrote to
William Point. Here is his reply:

Dear Mr. Burns:

I have your letter asking is it true or not that I saw a wild
giant at Agassiz last September, while with the hop-pickers there.
It is true and the facts are as follows: Adaline August and myself
started for her parents' house which is about four miles from the
picnic grounds. We were walking on the railroad track, when
Adaline noticed someone walking along the track coming toward
us. I also saw this person and at first thought it was another man
walking the tracks as were we. But as he came closer we noticed
that his appearance was very odd, and on coming still closer
we halted in amazement and alarm as we saw the man wore no
clothing at all and was covered with hair like an animal. We were
both very frightened. I picked up two large stones with which I
intended to hit him if he attempted to molest us, but within fifty
feet or so he just stopped and looked at us.

He was twice as big as the average man, with arms so long his
hands almost touched the ground. His eyes were very large and
as fierce as a cougar's. The lower part of his nose was wide and
spread over the greater part of his face, which gave him a very
repulsive appearance. Then my nerve failed me and I turned and
ran. I looked back later and saw that he had resumed his journey.

Adaline August had fled at first, and she ran so fast that I
did not overtake her until we reached the picnic grounds, where
we told the story of our adventure. Older Indians who were
present said that the creature we encountered was undoubtedly a
Sasquatch, a tribe of wild, hairy giants, now almost extinct, who
live in the district in tunnels and caves. Assuring you of the truth
of this,

Yours truly,
William Point

I myself do not doubt William Point's story, as he is both
intelligent and well-educated.

And now to show how extremely sensitive to ridicule

regarding the Sasquatch the Indians are, and how quickly and indignantly they resent being doubted.

ON MAY the 23rd and 24th, 1938, a festival known as "Indian Sasquatch Days" was held at Harrison Hot Springs, BC. After obtaining special permission from the Department of Indian Affairs at Ottawa. I took several hundred of my Indians to the event. And then, in his opening speech over the radio, a very prominent member of the British Columbia government made a bad slip, thus offending all listening Indians who understood English. And the same government official was promptly put in his place by old Chief Flying Eagle.

After a few preliminary words the official went on: "Of course, the Sasquatch are merely Indian legendary monsters. No white man has ever seen one and they do not exist today. In fact—"

He was drowned out then by a great rustling of buckskin garments and tinkling of ornamental bells as, in response to an indignant sign from old Chief Flying Eagle, more than two thousand Indians rose to their feet in angry protest. Chief Flying Eagle then stalked across to the open space where stood the government speaker surrounded by other officials. Absolutely ignoring them Chief Flying Eagle turned and, in excellent English, thundered into the microphone:

"The speaker is wrong. To all who now hear I, Chief Flying Eagle, say: Some white men have seen Sasquatch. Many Indians have seen Sasquatch and spoken to them. Sasquatch still live all around here. Indians do not lie. I have spoken."

During the many years I have been delving into this fascinating subject of the wild giants of British Columbia, I have come into possession of information that is both definite and well authenticated. The oldest written record that I have come across to date is that of the late Alexander Caulfield Anderson, a pioneer of note after whom a suburb of West Vancouver (Caulfield) is named.

As long ago as 1846, when he was an inspector for the Hudson's Bay Company, he was sent out to establish a post in the vicinity of Harrison Lake. In his official reports he several times mentions the wild giants of the mountains" and wrote that on one

occasion he and his party were met by a bombardment of rocks
hurled by a number of Sasquatch.

But perhaps the strangest experience any Indian has had with
the Sasquatch is that of a woman named Serephine Long. Now a
woman getting on in years, Serephine claims that many years ago,
when she was a young girl, she was abducted by a Sasquatch and
lived in haunts of the wild people for about a year. She has told
me the story many times. As nearly as possible I retell it in her
own words.

"I was walking toward home one day many, many years ago,"
Serephine commenced, "carrying a big bundle of cedar roots
and thinking of the young brave Qualac (Thunder) I was soon
to marry, when suddenly, at a spot where the brush grows close
beside the trail, a long arm shot out of the bushes and a big hairy
hand was pressed over my mouth. Then I was swept up into the
arms of a young Sasquatch. I was terribly frightened and fought
and struggled with all my strength, but it was no good; the wild
man was as strong as a big bear. Then holding me with one hand,
he smeared tree-gum over my eyes sticking them shut so that I
could not see. He lifted me to his shoulder and started to run.

"He ran on and on for a long, long time, not once resting; up
and down hills through thick bushes, across many streams. Once
he had to swim a river and then perhaps I could have got away,
but I was so afraid of being drowned I held on tightly with my
arms about his neck. But although I was so scared, I admired him
for his great strength and speed of foot.

"After reaching the other side of that river he began to climb
and climb until presently the air got very cold. I could not see but
I guessed we were near the top of a mountain.

"Presently I felt the Sasquatch stop hurrying and then he
stooped down and moved slowly as if entering a tunnel. He then
laid me down and I heard people talking in a low, throaty tongue I
could not understand. The Sasquatch next wiped the sticky tree-
gum from my eyelids and I was able to open my eyes and look
around.

"I sat up and saw that I was in a great big cave. The floor was
covered with animal skins soft to the touch and well-preserved.

"I then saw that beside the young giant who had brought me
here, two other giants were in the cave; a man and a woman. They

looked very old to me, but they were active and cheerful and
later I learned they were the parents of the young giant who had
stolen me. I cried and, asked them to let me go, but all three just
smiled and shook their heads.

"And from then on I was kept a prisoner; not once did they let
me out of the cave; always one of them was with me if the other
two were away.

"They fed me well on roots, fish and meat. Never having
seen them with any weapons, one day—after I had learned a few
words of their tongue, which is much like our tongue—I asked
the young giant how he caught and killed the deer and mountain
goats and sheep he often brought into the cave. He just smiled
and opened and closed his big hairy hands, indicating that he laid
in ambush for them and then choked them to death.

"When I had lived in the cave for about a year I began to
feel awful sick and weak. I told this to the young Sasquatch and
pleaded with him to take me back to my people. At first he got
very angry as did his mother and father, but I kept on pleading
with them and told them I wished to see my own people before
I died.

"I really was a sick girl and I suppose they could see that,
because one day, after crying and pleading with the young giant,
he went outside and then returned with a leaf full of tree-gum.
With this he stuck down my eyelids as he had done before, then
lifted me to his big shoulder as easily as if I had weighed nothing.

"The return journey was like a bad dream, for I was in much
pain. When we recrossed the wide river I was almost swept away,
for I was too weak to cling to the giant very tightly. But he held
me with one hand and swam with the other.

"Close to my home he put me down and removed the tree-
gum from my eyelids. When he saw that I could see all right he
shook his head sadly, pointed to my house, then turned back into
the forest.

"My people were all wildly excited when I stumbled into the
house, but I was too sick and weak to talk just then. I crawled
into bed and that night gave birth to a child. The little one lived
but a few hours, for which I was glad.

"But I hope that never again shall I see a Sasquatch."

AND that is Serephine Long's story, the only one on record of a wild man ever abducting an Indian.

I could relate more instances relating to the wild giants of British Columbia from data I have painstakingly collected over a period of fifteen years, but in a short article of this kind the few I have recounted must suffice.

Do hairy giants inhabit the mountain solitudes of British Columbia? Many Indians, besides those quoted, are sincerely convinced that the Sasquatch—a few of them at least—still dwell in the unexplored interior of the province. And with my Indians, whom I trust, I also need no further proof.

Sir! reprinted "Wild Giants" in 1952, replacing Joseph Szokoli's art with a grab bag of photographs and adding a breathless new Editor's Note at the start: *"The recently publicized stories of the Abominable Snowman which has been terrorizing the natives of Tibet, was no news to readers of Sir! magazine. While Life magazine printed the story December 31, 1951, Sir! scooped the*

(cont'd)

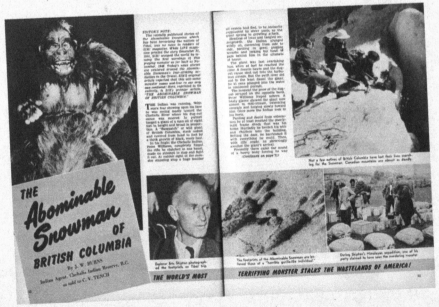

world by issuing the first warnings of this preying monster as far back as November 1948. Today's news stories are centered around the Abominable Snowman's fear-striking activities in the Orient. Sir!'s original article reported that this self-same monster **roams scot-free on our very own continent!**" (Emphasis theirs.) Rather less fear-striking is the unfortunate gorilla suit (above) in a photo that accompanies the article. ("The Abominable Snowman of British Columbia," *Sir!*, May 1952)

"'FISH' WITH HUMAN HANDS ATTACKED ME!"

BIGFOOT has become such a celebrated cultural phenomena, a reader unfamiliar with the field of cryptozoology could be understandably misled into believing the whole study is dedicated to relic hominids. But this is far from the case, as the long history of sightings of the Loch Ness Monster, Sea Serpents, Fish Men, giant squid and other water-based cryptids proves. And where there are recorded sightings and/or other evidence, cryptozoologists are bound to arrive, sooner than later, to collect and verify. Before the dawn of the internet, men's adventure magazines were a huge source of fact-based reporting by cryptid researchers and interested lay writers, as stories such as this one—"'Fish' With Human Hands Attacked Me!" from *True Weird*, November 1955—and "The Reckless Ones" from the October 1956 *Adventure* (included here on pg. 91) demonstrate.

"'Fish' With Human Hands Attacked Me!" by Arthur A. Dunn is a gonzo specimen of crypto mixology (that is, the blending of fact, superstition, and fiction). It purports to be a telling of encounters with a finned "fiend from hell," which resembles a horrific combination of human and fish origins, complete with arms and grasping webbed hands. True to men's adventure form, it plays fast and loose with known facts and assumed names.

Despite the pseudonyms employed throughout, the writer works in the *Coelacanth*, a rare order of fish that was once thought extinct for millions of years but is now known to exist in two extant species. In many respects, they are as close anatomically to reptiles and mammals (including the use of lobed fins as limbs) as they are classic fish species. More importantly, the discovery of remnant Coelacanths in the last century is often cited as proof that animals once thought extinct can actually, if rarely, turn out to be hidden in the ocean's depths. If such creatures exist despite the evolutionary forces that drove a majority of its contemporary species into extinction, then the argument can theoretically be extended, even if unlikely, to any and all cryptids. Likewise, the Coelacanth and other such discoveries can also be used to offer what might be called "plausible scientific denial." To wit: Cryptozoologists can argue that as long as their methods remain scientific and free of subjective bias, they are as legitimate as any other researcher exploring what is only posited, not proven, to be factual—no matter how outlandish the claimed species may appear to outsiders.

Fish Men may seem exotically improbable, but consider how they, too, find their place in cryptozoological history and lore. When I queried author/cryptozoologist Lyle Blackburn (*The Beast of Boggy Creek* and *Lizard Man: The True Story of the Bishopville Monster*), he mentioned precedents in prior crypto accounts that may have influenced this story. From his *Lizard Man* book, he cited a March 7, 1952, edition of the *Log Cabin Democrat* published in Arkansas, in which a similar cryptid was encountered by George Dillon, a local fisherman. The accounts are basically the same, with a fishing culture coming into contact with a human-like specimen heretofore never encountered, and both fleeing from each other in mutual, abject horror. Dillon's version even includes the salient detail that the frog-like creature he snared in the jaws with his trotlines reached up at the boat with a hand-like appendage, which it used to free itself from being hooked. According to Blackburn, another report from the 1950s is of a legendary half-man, half-fish creature said by witnesses to reside in the Chaco river region of Paraguay. An Amazon river variation of the latter, in fact, may be not only a possible basis for "'Fish' With Human Hands Attacked Me!" but the hugely popular movie *Creature From the Black Lagoon* (1955) as well.

In an interview from 1995, *Creature* producer William Alland told *Starlog*'s Tom Weaver that one night during the making of *Citizen Kane*, he'd enjoyed dinner with Orson Welles, Dolores Del Rio, and Gabriel Figueroa, a renowned Mexican cinematographer. Figueroa entertained the party with tales of

Creature From the Black Lagoon*'s Gill Man, in a life-sized interpretation by sculptor Mark Alfrey*

Photo courtesy Mark Alfrey / MarkAlfrey.com

a half-man, half-fish creature that annually snatched a young maiden from one of the human shoreline villages—after which, the villagers would not see the monster until its next yearly pilgrimage. Figueroa swore the legend was true, and it inspired Alland to launch *Creature From the Black Lagoon*. It is interesting to note that the fish men story included here uses the same basic "maiden meets an aquatic, bipedal monster" scenario. Again, the overlap among popular news accounts, MAMs, and the movies is such that settling which came first and what was more influential in cryptid reporting is difficult, if not impossible, to sort with complete clarity.

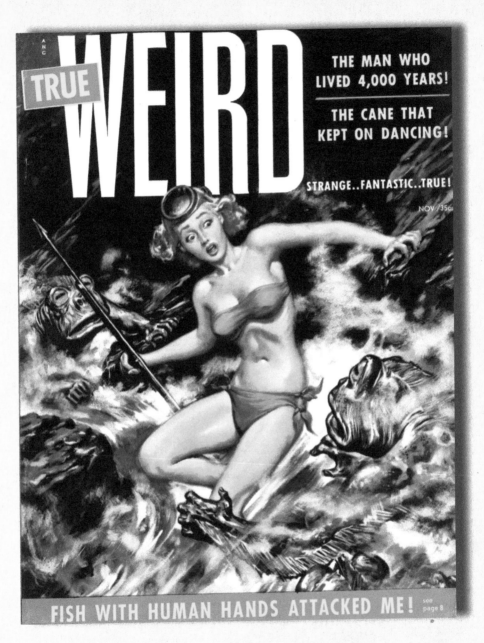

FISH WITH HUMAN HANDS ATTACKED ME! see page 8

"'FISH' WITH HUMAN HANDS ATTACKED ME!"
ARTHUR A. DUNN
TRUE WEIRD, **NOVEMBER 1955**
COVER BY CLARENCE DOORE

Terror stalked the lonely Nicaraguan beach when the Monster

appeared from the sea.

'FISH' WITH HUMAN HANDS ATTACKED ME!

Fish, believed extinct for 50 million years, have
been caught alive recently, and now this fantastic
monster of which the British Museum has a record,
appears in 1954

BY ARTHUR A. DUNN
ILLUSTRATED BY WARREN KNIGHT

IN THE spring of 1954 a paragraph item appeared in
a number of newspapers, to which most editors gave
facetious headings. The complete dispatch from Puerto
Cabezas, Nicaragua, read as follows:

"Senorita Madeline Fuercova, visiting friends at nearby
Bragman's Bluff, on the Atlantic side of this Central American republic, today claimed to have narrowly escaped an
attack by three strange fish. Each fish, she said, had the
head of a toad, the chest of a man and, instead of fins,
arms like a human being.

"The Senorita had wandered away from her friends and
was alone at the time. Unfortunately for science, there were
no witnesses to the extraordinary occurrence. Ichthyologists
who were asked to comment on the fish the Senorita said
she saw, were not very gallant. They asked if the beautiful

29

ART BY WARREN KNIGHT

In the spring of 1954 a paragraph item appeared in a number of newspapers, to which most editors gave facetious headings. The complete dispatch from Puerto Cabezas, Nicaragua, read as follows:

"Senorita Madeline Fuercova, visiting friends at nearby Bragman's Bluff, on the Atlantic side of this Central American republic, today claimed to have narrowly escaped an attack by three strange fish. Each fish, she said, had the head of a toad, the chest of a man and, instead of fins, arms like a human being.

"The Senorita had wandered away from her friends and was alone at the time. Unfortunately for science, there were no witnesses to the extraordinary occurrence. Ichthyologists who were asked to comment on the fish the Senorita said she saw, were not very gallant. They asked if the beautiful young woman had exposed herself too long to the tropical sun or had been celebrating before she went into the water.

"The Senorita herself said:

"'I had been skin diving for fish with a spear and was returning to shore when I noticed, coming toward me, what I thought were sharks. They were about the size of sharks and I was surprised to see them so close to shore. Naturally, I made for land as fast as I could with the monsters coming in my direction.

"'When I reached shore I noticed that one of the fish, which

She was spearing for fish when she was horrified by the appearance of the monstrous toad-like creature.

seemed more intent on reaching me than his companions, swam quite close. When about ten feet from me he reached out as if to grab me and I saw—instead of a fin, a human hand! I was terribly frightened. I jabbed him with my spear and he moved back. All three seemed to rise out of the water and, for the first time, I noticed that their heads, which were about the size of human heads, looked those of toads! As they rose half out of the water I could see they had chests like a man, and each fish had hands like a human being!

"'The leader, partly out of the water, approached me again and I jabbed him hard with my spear. This time he uttered what sounded like a grunt of pain, turned, and swam away. The other two followed him.

"'When they were gone I crept up the beach and I guess I fainted.'"

Those newspapers that did publish a paragraph or so of this dispatch did it with tongue in cheek, snide innuendoes, and heads like "Latest Fish Story." Creatures such as the young lady described were unknown, and to take it seriously would stamp the editor as a little gullible. But—

A year ago a fish was dredged up in Long Island Sound which was an entirely new species, hitherto unknown to science and, after study, considered a missing link in the long line of man's development. Almost two years ago a fish that scientists believed became extinct some fifty million years ago, was caught by fishermen off the coast of South Africa. Other strange fish believed to have died out millions of years ago, or never even to have existed except in fable, are now being sought by ichthyologists off the coasts of Africa and Madagascar, with large money prizes offered to fishermen who can bring them in alive.

What still lives in the depths of the great oceans is not known. Fish yet unseen by man's eye are known to live in the utter blackness of the deep, cold seas, and, the British Museum in London has a record of a fish similar to the ones described by the frightened Senorita—a fish that was caught alive and seen by hundreds of Englishmen!

The first weird record of the fish with hands of a man began between 4 and 5 A.M. on the morning of July 15, 1642, not far

A fish with pig eyes like a very fat man

A section of the British Museum which houses records of this weird occurrence.

from Wollage, near Dover on the Kent coast of England. As they had for hundreds of years, fishermen living in hamlets along the coast cast their nets that Friday morning hoping for a good catch.

One fisherman named Thomas West, who had worked these waters for years and knew the type of fish that came close to shore on the incoming tide, cast his net as he had innumerable times. As the tide receded he pulled in the net and felt an unusual weight and struggle as if he had a whole school of fighting fish or three or four very large ones.

With considerable satisfaction and happy visions of what so lucky a catch would bring at the market, he pulled hard and brought in his net. In the pale light of that early summer dawn he saw a creature thrashing about in the net in desperate efforts to escape the entanglement, a creature so strange and frightening that he screamed in fear.

His terrified screams brought the other fishermen along the shore running. When they saw what was entangled in the net they stood petrified with horror. As the ancient record in the British Museum tells it, Thomas West had caught "...Fiend, not a Fish; at the least a Monster."

No one, even in an age filled with beliefs in goblins, gnomes, witches and denizens of heaven, hell, and places in between, ever dreamed of a creature like this. These fishermen, who had lived their lives along the sea, had never, in their most drunken moments, envisioned such creatures. The animal struggled desperately to free itself, uttering noises that sounded like a mixture of angry growls and grunts. Its eyes seemed to pop and glare venomously at the people around it. Some fishermen, muttering prayers, rushed around and picked up stout pieces of driftwood to use as clubs.

The fishermen pleaded with Thomas West to throw the animal back into the sea. Some crossed themselves in terror, fearing they had captured "a fiend" in disguise. West, admittedly afraid to go too near his catch, also stood by with a stout piece of driftwood, ready to bash in the creature's head if it made a move toward him.

The old record describes this catch, subsequently seen by hundreds, as about five feet long, with the head of a toad and the chest of a man. Where two fins would normally be, two human arms protruded. The record states: "He is in breadth a yard over...his tail was a foot in length and was all made of whale bone"!

The wife of a fishermen who heard the shouts and screams also came running. She approached close for a better look. The monster's frantic thrashings had torn a small hole in the net through which one fin-arm protruded. Other villagers, seeing that the creature was safely entangled approached very close. One woman bent to see the shape of his head and the creature's arm shot out from the torn hole and seized her.

The woman screamed. The monster, clutching her close, dragged itself, the net, and the woman toward the sea. At this the other fishermen began pounding the fin-arms until the monster released its grip on the now unconscious woman.

While some were still beating the fish, others pulled the woman out of its reach.

With all these screams and shouts, more fishermen came running. One, upon seeing the catch cried:

"It is no fish but the Devil ye have!" and beat the beast over its head until it lay weak and trembling.

The fishermen called it a toad-fish with the hands of a man. Others called it "a Fiend from Hell." Every name the superstitious and frightened fishermen could think of was applied to the animal that was now breathing with difficulty due to the beatings.

Word of the catch spread almost as fast as a dry forest fire. By word of mouth, by news crier, by messenger on horseback, the news swept England and, eventually, the story was published in London.

The record in the British Museum, with its quaint spellings, tells of:

"...a terrible Monster taken by a Fisherman near Wollage, July the 15, 1642, and is now to be seen in King Street, Westminster."

The fishermen gave West a hand, and the monster from the deeps was carried in the net to Glove-Alley in King Street, where it was put on display. Other fishermen followed those carrying the monster, their clubs ready if the beast should try to escape.

Once it was on display, with an armed group of volunteers standing guard, those who came to view it increased in number. Several times the creature raised its head and made spasmodic

motions with its fin-hands, as if to appeal to the men surrounding
it. When that brought no response it turned over on its belly. As
the old record states, when it lay on its belly it resembled a toad,
but when it turned over, it had the perfect breast and chest of a
man. Upon close examination its ribs could be seen.

THE fish market was soon crowded with those who came from
all directions to view the incredible creature from the deeps. A
butcher's wife, rushing to see it, pushed her way through the
crowd and shrieked:

"This is the Devil in the shape of a Great Fish!" and passed
out cold.

Another woman, about to give birth, also came rushing to see
the monster and became so agitated that midwives had to attend
her on the spot.

With the passing hours the fish became weaker. It was
obviously dying. It opened its mouth as in one great surge of
hunger or supplication and revealed (what was verified after its
death) three sets of sharp teeth!

The superstitious villagers were certain it was some
harbinger of evil, for the ancient record states:

"...all unusual births either in men or bruit creatures, in sea or
upon land, especially out of their seasons, have ever been the fore-
runners and sad harbingers of great commotions and tumults
in States and Kingdomes, if not mournfull Heraulds of utter
desolation...."

Fish came out of the primeval waters to crawl on land

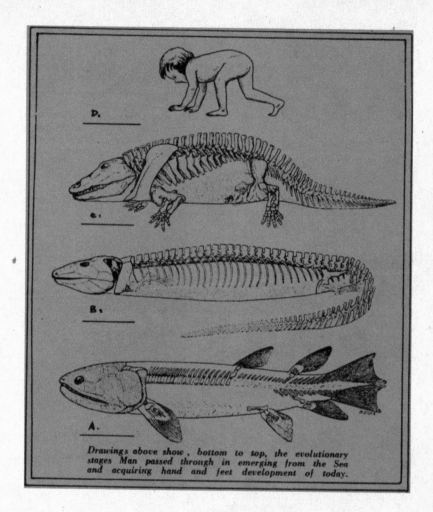

Drawings above show, bottom to top, the evolutionary stages Man passed through in emerging from the Sea and acquiring hand and feet development of today.

As evidence, the reader is reminded of the time a heifer calved a lamb on the altar in Jerusalem (mentioned by Josephus) and half a year later the beautiful city of Vespasian was sacked and destroyed!

Most fish cannot live long out of water but this monster apparently had air lungs, like a land animal or an animal that can live on both land and in water. It seemed to breathe without much trouble when it was on exhibition.

No one could advance a good reason why this monster appeared so close to shore. Nothing like it had ever been seen but, someone pointed out, for several days before, the summer being unusually hot, women had bathed at this spot. Whether this had anything to do with the appearance of the monster, cannot now be known. I mention it only to complete the record, which begins with the statement: "God sheweth his wonders in the deep."

There is no record of what eventually happened when the monster died—whether it was buried or cast back into the sea. The record simply ends the tale with a prayer: "God in his mercie grant that this ugly monster may not for our sins prove the like to us...." referring to the calamities that befell places where strange animals appeared.

Scientists have never reached more than a mile below the surface of the oceans and, in some places, the seas are seven miles deep. What still lives in the unplumbed depths, no man knows. But if fish though extinct for fifty million years have been caught alive, it is now believed there are many others, and perhaps even stranger fish in the sea.

The description of the monsters that appeared off the coast of Nicaragua is not too dissimilar to the catch by Thomas West. It opens possibilities that creatures as weird as this fish may be in the deeps or perhaps even more weird than anything yet seen by man.

Set in "the jungle between Yucatan and Guatemala," the ripping yarn "I Found a Lost World" (*Rage*, March 1961) posits the existence of an undiscovered "Neanderthal or Cro-Magnon" community with a yen for female *Homo sapiens*. Cover artist Clarence Doore's thrilling illustration delivers a monster more lycanthropic than the Stone Age creatures described in the tale.

"I STALKED
THE YETI"

"I STALKED the Yeti!" by Franz Kale appeared in the February 1953 issue of *Man's Magazine*. In many ways, it echoes the popular media coverage of the Abominable Snowman in those years, as the subheading *"You read about it in your newspaper"* indicates. Typical of fictionalized entries in MAMs, it is factually laced to provide a sense of verisimilitude. For example, Nuli Singh, the narrator's local travel companion, dismisses the weird tracks found in the mountain peaks as belonging to a bear. "A Himalayan black weighs no more than 200 pounds. Even in Nepal where I have hunted the biggest," Singh informs. While it is true the Himalayan Black Bear (*Selenarctos thibetanus laniger*) does not generally exceed a weight range of from 200 to 265 pounds most of the year, it actually can balloon upward of 400 pounds as it prepares for its annual hibernation.

Another confabulation of lore and imagination is provided in the detailing of Yeti reports by Sherpa natives in the story, which describe creatures approaching a staggering 14 feet (a height exceeding most accounts). The story's suggested indigenous name for the Yeti, the "Metehkangmi," is a variant of *Metoh-Kangmi*, or "man-bear snowman," first coined by Lt. Col. Howard-Bury in recounting his 1921 encounter with snow tracks left by the Yeti. And though some inaccuracies abound, "I Stalked the Yeti!" is remarkable for how much information about the actual history of the subject matter that it does present, and much of it is within the realm of reliable. For many readers (and avid cryptozoologists), such background detail was crucial to their first understanding of the exotic Tibetan culture.

There is a reason the Yeti is stalked, not studied, in this tale; as the author presents the snowbound cryptid, it is a suggested maneater. Indeed, blood is found spattered in the snow and it is presumed to be that of the fearful Bhotias, who have been devoured alive. Later still, the narrator will find a shred of human flesh in a tree's branches, with the conclusion the enraged beast first impaled, then ripped off, the hapless human's arm. This level of murderous intent on the part of the Yeti is not unknown to the local legends, but the sheer savagery of the way the narrator describes such incidents pushes the envelope in terms of how the Abominable Snowman was usually portrayed in more tame newspaper accounts. Here the cryptid is a full-fledged monster that shows no mercy whatsoever to any and all intruders into its majestic domain. This diabolical rendering of the Yeti, while atypical of documented reports, was embraced by men's adventure readers, who clearly preferred a menacing monster to a reclusive gentle giant in their two-fisted terror tales.

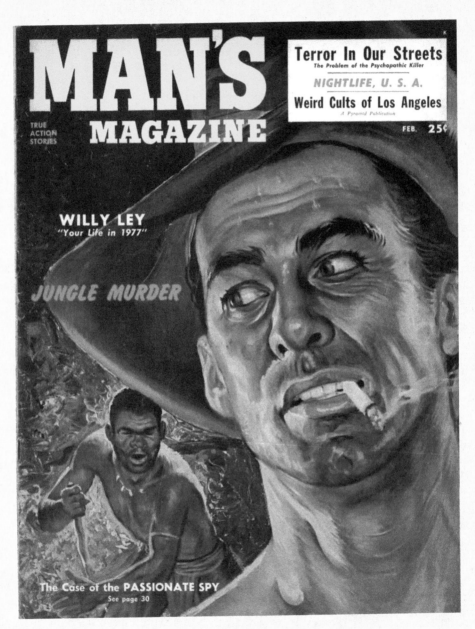

MAN'S MAGAZINE

TRUE ACTION STORIES

FEB. 25¢

WILLY LEY
"Your Life in 1977"

JUNGLE MURDER

The Case of the PASSIONATE SPY
See page 30

"I STALKED THE YETI!"
FRANZ KALE
MAN'S MAGAZINE, FEBRUARY 1953
COVER BY RAFAEL DESOTO

By FRANZ KALE

The beast must be at least eight feet tall according to this photo of Yeti's tracks brought back from Himalayas by a Mt. Everest expedition.

Mysterious Monster Sought Among Himalayas Icy Crags

NEW DELHI (AP).—The "Abominable Showman," that mysterious resident of the upper Himalayas most recently reported by a British climbing expedition.

I stalked the YETI!

You read about it in your newspaper. Now here is the amazing, true story of the Abominable Monster of the Himalayas by the man who dared to hunt it!

WE WERE skirting Rakoit Glacier in the Himalayan area of Northern India at an altitude of 14,500 feet in search of the rare snow leopard when we came upon the incredible footprints. It was Nuli Singh, my Gurkha assistant who first spotted them. I was a little distance behind him followed by our two Bhotia bearers.

The prints were big and bizarre and puzzling. In 17 years of collecting rare wild animals in Asia and Africa for Oosterweil Brothers of Amsterdam I had never seen anything like them. Deeply etched in the powdery snow, they had been left by an enormous and probably powerful creature with four broad toes and an even broader thumb. The foot measured more than twelve inches in length and six and a quarter inches in width.

With growing excitement and still-disbelieving eyes I stared up the snowy slope to where the tracks disappeared in the distance, lost in the blinding Himalayan sunlight. The space between each set of toed-in prints clearly indicated that the creature, when standing erect, was at least eight feet tall! Could there be such a bear?

Nuli Singh read my puzzled thoughts.

"No bear, sahib," he said gently. "A Himalayan black weighs no more than 200 pounds. Even in Nepal where I have hunted the biggest."

I nodded in quick agreement. These were not the tracks of any freak-sized bear. A bear print shows toes of equal size. Nor were they the cat-like tracks of the snow leopard with which I am quite familiar. There wasn't the slightest doubt in my mind that they had been made by a huge *two-legged* monster!

My puzzlement and excitement grew as I thought about this. The only two legged creature, other than man, I have known to inhabit the Himalayas at 14,000 feet and higher is the langur, a monkey which occasionally grows to a height of five feet. But langurs usually travel in troops. And the biggest langur track I ever saw spanned a scant eight inches.

THE TWO Bhotia bearers came up and dropped their loads. Then they caught sight of the tracks and their dark faces, framed in knitted Balaclava helmets, took on a greenish, seasick tint as Jumar, the older, pointed them out to the other, Utam.

"Metehkangmi! Metehkangmi!" they began to chant in fright. They cast anxious looks backward toward the friendly forest of pines and deodar cedars from which we had so recently emerged. They were about ready to bolt.

"They're afraid of the Yeti—the Abominable Snowman," Nuli Singh remarked. He looked scornfully at the terrified Bhotias, tapping the worn leather scabbard of his razor-sharp kukri significantly. At the same time I pretended to examine my rifle, making a confident show of being ready for any Yeti.

"Incestuous spawn of a Garhwali sheep herder!" Nuli Singh swore fiercely. "Ready to lose your bowels at the sight of the tracks of an aged, outcast langur. Pick up your packs."

Jumar and Utam looked at each other indecisively. Nuli Singh took a slow step in their direction, his hand on the hilt of his kukri.

An angry Gurkha, about to draw a knife that can lop off a head at a single blow, is a sight that inspires immediate obedience from any Indian between the Nepalese border and Cape Comorin. The Bhotias were no exception. To them the menace of Nuli Singh now seemed acute. That of the Yeti, for the moment, less formidable. They picked up their packs.

"Which direction, sahib?" Nuli Singh asked. I caught the challenge in his eyes. An ardent hunter, he was as determined to investigate the mysterious tracks as I was.

"We follow the langur," I said loudly. "It is a big one. I would add this monkey to my collection."

We started up the slope following the tracks and at the same time keeping a vigilant eye on the reluctant Jumar and Utam.

"These are no langur prints, sahib," Nuli Singh whispered to me. "Even were there one so big it would leave, here and there, a tail drag."

"I know," I agreed. "This is no tailed creature. The Bhotias are right. This is a track of the Metehkangmi, the Yeti, the Abominable Snowman, whatever it might be."

Even as I said it I realized that I was stalking the most fantastic, most elusive game of my life!

AS A SPECIALIST in the collection of rare wild animals I have bagged okapi in the Congo, the equally scarce saiga antelope in western Asia and once, on a visit to Tibet, a chiru, that weird member of the antelope family with swollen snout and abnormally long horns. But all these thrills rolled into one could not compare to that of finding the track of the Yeti.

Until I saw the prints with my own eyes I had refused to believe that any such creature existed, although I had often heard bizarre stories about it. The Yeti, according to Himalayan natives, was a ferocious, ape-like creature with a bare face and a powerful, gorilla-like body covered with thick, reddish hair. The female of the species, larger than the male, supposedly grew to a height of 14 feet. An insatiable meat-eater, the Yeti lived on yaks, and the occasional luckless native it caught in its habitat: the upper, snowy plateaus of the Himalayas.

Although no Yeti had ever been glimpsed by a credible authority, as early as 1921, while in the vicinity of Mt. Everest, Lt.-Col. C. K. Howard-Bury had come upon tracks very similar to those we were now following. From then on other white hunters and explorers occasionally had seen them too. One was Joseph Rock who encountered them on an anthropological expedition to the Amne Machin area. Another, the most recent, was Eric Shipton, noted British explorer who in (Continued on page 42)

From study of tracks, anthropologists have constructed a human-like beast which resembles Neanderthal man. Yeti may link apes and humans.

We were skirting Rakoit Glacier in the Himalayan area of
Northern India at an altitude of 14,500 feet in search of the rare
snow leopard when we came upon the incredible footprints. It was
Nuli Singh, my Gurkha assistant who first spotted them. I was a
little distance behind him followed by our two Bhotia bearers.

The prints were big and bizarre and puzzling. In 17 years
of collecting rare wild animals in Asia and Africa for Ousterweil
Brothers of Amsterdam, I had never seen anything like them.
Deeply etched in the powdery snow, they had been left by an
enormous and probably powerful creature with four broad toes
and an even broader thumb. The foot measured more than twelve
inches in length and six and a quarter inches in width.

With growing excitement and still-disbelieving eyes I
stared up the snowy slope to where the tracks disappeared in
the distance, lost in the blinding Himalayan sunlight. The space
between each set of toed-in prints clearly indicated that the
creature, when standing erect, was at least eight feet tall! Could
there be such a bear?

Nuli Singh read my puzzled thoughts.

"No bear, *sahib*," he said gently. "A Himalayan black weighs
no more than 200 pounds. Even in Nepal where I have hunted the
biggest."

I nodded in quick agreement. These were not the tracks of

any freak-sized bear. A bear print shows toes of equal size. Nor were they the cat-like tracks of the snow leopard with which I am quite familiar. There wasn't the slightest doubt in my mind that they had been made by a huge *two-legged* monster!

My puzzlement and excitement grew as I thought about this. The only two-legged creature, other than man, I have known to inhabit the Himalayas at 14,000 feet and higher is the langur, a monkey that occasionally grows to a height of five feet. But langurs usually travel in troops. And the biggest langur track I ever saw spanned a scant eight inches.

THE two Bhotia bearers came up and dropped their loads. Then they caught sight of the tracks and their dark faces, framed in knitted Balaclava helmets, took on a greenish, seasick tint as Jumar, the older, pointed them out to the other, Utam.

"Metehkangmi! Metehkangmi!" they began to chant in fright. They cast anxious looks backward toward the friendly forest of pines and deodar cedars from which we had so recently emerged. They were about ready to bolt.

"They're afraid of the Yeti—the Abominable Snowman," Nuli Singh remarked. He looked scornfully at the terrified Bhotias, tapping the worn leather scabbard of his razor-sharp kukri significantly. At the same time I pretended to examine my rifle, making a confident show of being ready for any Yeti.

"Incestuous spawn of a Garhwali sheep herder!" Nuli Singh swore fiercely. "Ready to lose your bowels at the sight of the tracks of an aged, outcast langur. Pick up your packs."

Jumar and Utam looked at each other indecisively. Nuli Singh took a slow step in their direction, his hand on the hilt of his kukri.

An angry Gurkha, about to draw a knife that can lop off a head at a single blow, is a sight that inspires immediate obedience from any Indian between the Nepalese border and Cape Comorin. The Bhotias were no exception. To them the menace of Nuli Singh now seemed acute. That of the Yeti, for the moment, less formidable. They picked up their packs.

"Which direction, *sahib*?" Nuli Singh asked. I caught the challenge in his eyes. An ardent hunter, he was as determined to investigate the mysterious tracks as I was.

"We follow the langur," I said loudly. "It is a big one. I would add this monkey to my collection."

We started up the slope following the tracks and at the same time keeping a vigilant eye on the reluctant Jumar and Utam.

"These are no langur prints, *sahib*," Nuli Singh whispered to me. "Even were there one so big it would leave, here and there, a tail drag."

"I know," I agreed. "This is no tailed creature. The Bhotias are right. This is a track of the Metehkangmi, the Yeti, the Abominable Snowman, whatever it might be."

Even as I said it I realized that I was stalking the most fantastic, most elusive game of *my* life!

As a specialist in the collection of rare wild animals, I have bagged okapi in the Congo, the equally scarce saiga antelope in western Asia and once, on a visit to Tibet, a chiru, that weird member of the antelope family with swollen snout and abnormally long horns. But all these thrills rolled into one could not compare to that of finding the track of the Yeti.

Until I saw the prints with my own eyes, I had refused to believe that any such creature existed, although I had often heard bizarre stories about it. The Yeti, according to Himalayan natives, was a ferocious, ape-like creature with a bare face and a powerful, gorilla-like body covered with thick, reddish hair. The female of the species, larger than the male, supposedly grew to a height of 14 feet. An insatiable meat-eater, the Yeti lived on yaks, and the occasional luckless native it caught in its habitat: the upper, snowy plateaus of the Himalayas.

Although no Yeti had ever been glimpsed by a credible authority, as early as 1921, while in the vicinity of Mt. Everest, Lt. Col. C.K. Howard-Bury had come upon tracks very similar to those we were now following. From then on other white hunters and explorers occasionally had seen them too. One was Joseph Rock who encountered them on an anthropological expedition to the Amne Machin area. Another, the most recent, was Eric Shipton, noted British explorer who in 1951, while on a plateau near Mt. Everest with Sen Tensing, his Sherpa guide, found Yeti tracks and photographed them.

In no instance, however, had any of these men been able to

follow the tracks to the source. Then and there I determined that was my objective. Langurs and snow leopards were forgotten. I wanted to be the first to bag a Yeti!

For some six miles by my pedometer, over the snowy rise and down the gentle slope beyond, leading to one of the many Himalayan high valleys, we followed the tracks, which took us to the pocket, a stand of deodar cedars and giant rhododendrons. Here the tracks disappeared into the woods. And here the Bhotias came to a halt. They put down their loads and stared fearsomely ahead into the woods.

Nuli Singh shot a questioning glance at me. I shook my head. It would do no good for him to threaten Jumar and Utam again. Stark fear of what might lie ahead had taken possession of them. I, myself, was a bit uneasy as well as curious as to what might be lurking in the woods. With my rifle held ready I strode forward, as nonchalantly as I could for the benefit of the Bhotias. Nuli Singh remained behind to keep an eye on them.

It was late afternoon and the woods, in the shadow of Buldar Peak, were already quite dark. I followed the enormous prints between the trees but soon lost them as the snow-line ceased at this point.

IT WAS, I decided, too late in the day to seek them further. So I rejoined Nuli Singh and the bearers.

"We will camp among the trees," I told them. "There is plenty of wood for a bright fire and a hot meal."

Jumar and Utam just stood there as I spoke. They gazed toward the forest with terror-riveted eyes, like the eyes of a Madrassi I had once seen just before he had been bitten by a deadly krait.

"If the *sahib* will permit," said Jumar slowly, "we will sleep on the snow near the trees with a bright fire. It is not good for us to sleep in these woods."

I shrugged my shoulders as though this was of no importance. That was the way the Bhotias wished it. No power on earth could compel them to enter the woods on this night.

"We will leave at dawn," I said sternly. "Then we shall follow the tracks to wherever they may lead."

This seemed to satisfy Jumar and Utam. They carried the

packs to the edge of the forest and busied themselves gathering wood. Then they built a big fire on the snow about ten yards from the tree line.

Nuli Singh and I made our own camp a short distance in the woods where the trees afforded a welcome windbreak against the chill, penetrating night wind that blew down from Nanga Parbat.

After we had eaten we got into our bedrolls, I with a meerschaum full of tobacco. This is one of the few luxuries I always permit myself on the trail—a pipeful of good Dutch tobacco, which, with careful smoking, will last more than half an hour. I smoked it down to clean white ash, my mind excited by thoughts of the Yeti, my nerves and body impatient with the urge to take to the trail. Had I been able to trust our bearers to stay put, there would have been no sleep for Nuli Singh and myself this night.

I TOSSED in my blankets trying to recall all I had ever heard about the mysterious Yeti. Discounting all the native embroidery and fanciful elaboration, minimizing all the local legends, those astounding tracks still remained to be explained. Was there really an Abominable Snowman, a weird monster that walked upright?

Something that Roy Chapman Andrews, the famous naturalist and explorer had said of the Amne Machin region of the Himalayas came to mind. Something about the "lost world" of fiction existing in fact, guarded by the towering peaks, the cavernous valleys and torrential rivers that present "impassable barriers for the communication of most forms of terrestrial life." Perhaps these barriers were not impassable to the monster Yeti.

I tapped the dottle out of my pipe and got up for my customary nightly check-up. All was peaceful and serene. Nuli Singh was already snoring in his bedroll. The Bhotias were huddled in blankets beside their fire under millions of deceptively low stars. And so I went to sleep with the pleasant smell of burning deodar cedar carried from the fire by the night wind.

IT SEEMED as though I had been sleeping but a few minutes when I was awakened by Nuli Singh shaking my shoulder. He was a Gurkha full of self-reproach and humiliation.

"The Bhotias have fled, *sahib*," he said. "Would that I had the sense to remain on guard!"

I looked out beyond the trees and saw that the bearers' campfire had gone out. I glanced at my watch automatically. It was still a half hour to dawn.

"This is equally my fault," I said, "I, too, should have been on guard. It is yet too early to follow a trail. Put on the tea."

We drank hot tea, impatiently waiting for the first light of day. I had already made my plans. The cowardly bearers, at this point, had become a liability. We were far better off without them in stalking the Yeti. Nuli

BAMBOO, pride of the Philadelphia zoo, was picked "the boy we would most like to have with us on combat patrol" by Korean GI's.

Singh and I had traveled light before, and he was at home in the Himalayas. We would cache the packs except for a few days' rations.

With the coming of false dawn we made for the Bhotias' campfire. As I emerged from the woods I got the greatest shock of my not uneventful life. The snow, near the ashes of the fire, had been bloodied for a considerable area. And there, plainly printed in the bloody snow was the track of the Yeti monster!

I bent over and picked up a small dark object. It was a torn fragment of Balaclava helmet.

"The Abominable Snowman!" I said to Nuli Singh. "He got our Bhotias during the night without a sound!"

"One, *sahib*," he answered. "The other, perhaps, escaped."

He pointed to the tracks. They had written their own story. The Yeti apparently had doubled on the trail, re-entering the woods from the other side. From the tracks emerging on this side of the woods it was apparent that it must have passed within 30 yards of us. Just why it had chosen to attack the Bhotias rather than us I shall never know. One thing was evident. It was not afraid of a fire.

From the point where it emerged between the trees to the campfire was a bit under 20 yards. It had attacked swiftly and unexpectedly, seizing one of the Bhotias—we could not determine whether it was Jumar or Utam—in its powerful arms. There was a set of man tracks, those of the escaping Bhotia, doubling back over the trail we had made the day before. And the track of the Yeti indicated that it had taken to the woods again with its victim. There were large *splashes*, not drops, of blood together with the tracks. There was no sign of a drag. The Yeti had carried the unfortunate Bhotia, either in its mouth or its arms, back to the woods.

Nuli Singh and I came to this conclusion at almost the same time. The Gurkha drew his kukri, the blade point laid against left forearm ready for instant action.

"Even now, *sahib*," he said softly, "the Metehkangmi may still be in these woods, gorging itself on the Bhotia!"

With rifle ready I led the way back between the trees, following the snowy tracks. Where the snow line ended, Nuli Singh found the trail. His eyes were keener than mine. He could see the splashes of blood beneath the rhododendrons very quickly.

We walked right through the woods. The Yeti had not stopped. Evidently it had been traveling at top speed. Near the other side of the woods we caught sight of something on a cedar at a height of about seven and a half feet. It was a piece of the fur jacket worn by one of the Bhotias. It was impaled on a jagged end of a dead and broken branch together with a ghastly piece of fresh flesh, part of a human arm muscle. The monster, in its haste, had bumped its victim against the tree and impatiently torn it free. I got a little sick to my stomach when I saw that and realized the Yeti's great strength.

On the other side of the woods we picked up the tracks again, as well as the blood splashes. For the next three quarters of a mile or so the latter appeared at less frequent intervals. Then we reached a point where the Yeti apparently halted. It had left several prints before continuing a track toward Buldar Peak, now almost due north. Nuli Singh pointed to the continuance of those tracks. There was no longer any evidence of blood.

We traveled for another three miles, following the snowy trail that veered slightly toward the Northeast. Then we came to another place where the Yeti had halted. From here the tracks led due East down a sharp slope, a pocket valley that formed the lower approach to the 22,408-foot Main Chongra Peak. And here the snow and the tracks ended.

For another half mile, over rocky terrain, we continued to search for prints or signs of the Yeti. And then we came to the edge of a deep, precipitous chasm. It dropped, I should judge, almost 2,000 feet, with an icy, roaring torrent, fed by the Rakhiot Glacier at the base. It seemed incredible that any earthly thing, not to mention a huge monster burdened by a human victim, could have made its way down the nearly sheer cliff-face of rock. But that, apparently, is what the Yeti did. We camped near the edge of the chasm that night and on the following morning I found a piece of fur from the Bhotia's jacket. The monster had descended there with its victim!

As A wild animal collector I have learned through bitter experience that foolhardiness seldom pays off. On the other hand, patience often does. I have bagged some of my rarest animal treasures by being patient enough to wait it out and let the game come to me. I tried to figure out the Yeti's movements and as I did, one startling thing stood out. The monster had sensed that it was being followed.

"When we first came upon the Yeti tracks the monster was heading for Buldar Peak," I explained. "The tracks continued in the direction of Buldar Peak until yesterday when they suddenly turned due East toward the Main Chongra. Never before have I known a homing animal to change its direction thus sharply on a long trail unless—"

"Unless it suddenly becomes aware that it is being followed," the Gurkha finished for me, "and would lead us away from its nest."

This was exactly the way I reasoned. The Yeti had descended into the chasm to throw us off the trail. Sooner or later it would reappear and make for the North—unless it could do so by swimming the icy river, climbing the opposite wall and working its way toward Buldar Peak on the other side of the chasm.

This seemed a gamble worth taking. Especially since I was stalking the most elusive, most spectacular of all monsters.

I sent Nuli Singh back to the cache for additional supplies, and I took up my patrol. When he returned we pitched our camp in a rocky cleft where we commanded a long, sweeping view of the cliff edge. Then we took up our wait.

That wait was the longest one in my life. For three weeks we watched for the Yeti to reappear. Then, with supplies running low, I was reluctantly forced to admit that I had lost the gamble. The Yeti monster undoubtedly had made its way back to its lair along the other side of the chasm.

OUR DISAPPOINTING trek back to the railhead at Raxual, the Indian border town that connects with a narrow gauge to Amlekganj in Nepal—Nuli Singh's home—took several days. On the way we passed through the little Indian village of Pavirani. One of our Bhotias, Jumar, had been there before us. He reported that he had barely escaped with his life from the clutches of a huge monster with long fangs and curling red hair that had carried off his friend Utam as well as Nuli Singh and a foreign white hunter.

Jumar was tragically right as far as Utam is concerned. But Nuli Singh and I, reports to the contrary, are still alive. And so, I believe, is at least one giant Himalayan Yeti, the least known, most fantastic monster on earth!

"INCREDIBLE MONSTER-MAN SIGHTINGS IN THE US"
JOHN KEEL
MALE, AUGUST 1970

Human, un-human
or something in
between? Where do
they come from,
where do they hide?
The authorities
don't know. But the
evidence is growing
that they do exist...

20 SCIENTISTS

From STRANGE CREATURES FROM TIME AND SPACE
by John A. Keel. Copyright © 1970 by Fawcett
Publications, Inc. Reprinted by permission of the author.

About the Author

JOHN A. KEEL has been on the
spoor of the weird ones for a quarter-
century. For that long he has been
tracking down the wild tales of aliens
from outer space, of the Big Foots
of California, of snakes that glow,
and of all the strange and terrifying and sometimes injurious creatures that ordinary citizens keep running into. He has become the top
man in the field of the inexplicable.

Keel began writing articles on UFOs
in 1945, two years before the great
UFOmania began. In 1952 he produced a Halloween broadcast from
Frankenstein Castle in Germany, and
in 1954 he saw his first flying saucer
—while exploring the Upper Nile on
an Egyptology kick. For years Keel
wandered about Asia in search of
the strange and occult. The last American to enter Tibet from the Indian
side, he spent months tracking the
Abominable Snowman. He has written books on UFOs, and articles on
all sorts of sightings.

INCREDIBLE MONSTER-MAN

A hunter is splashing alone through
a swamp. Suddenly his dog begins
to howl, flips his tail between his
legs, and runs off. The brush ahead
of the startled hunter stirs and a
great hoary shadow rises up, uttering an
unearthly screech. It towers above the man
by two or three feet. He is too surprised and
too paralyzed with fear to raise his rifle. The
thing shuffles off into the blackness of the
swamp to turn up months later elsewhere.

This drama has been acted so many times
over the years that the basic job of simply
cataloging such incidents is almost impossible.
The swamp creature is not necessarily a special breed of monster, though. In most cases
the descriptions are very similar to our mountaineering Abominable Snowman. We shall
call him the Abominable Swamp Slob, or
A.S.S., for short. While the ABSM thrives

28

TWO photos of "Bigfoot" taken in desolate mountain areas of West Coast show similarities . . .

PLASTER cast of "Bigfoot" track was made by Roger Patterson, who took motion pictures of enormous, hairy monster . . .

EXPERTS say humanoid creatures may be descendants of pre-historic times, as is Loch Ness monster, in model above . . .

SIGHTINGS IN THE U.S.
By JOHN A. KEEL

in forests and high places, the A.S.S. prefers low-level marshes and bayous. There's hardly a respectable swamp in the Deep South that does not boast at least one A.S.S. As usual, our local historical experts, the Indians, have many legends and stories about the swamp creatures. It would seem that all wet, dark, forbidding places are inhabited by unspeakable monsters of some sort. Frequently our Swamp Slobs blunder onto highways, dripping

with water and an ungodly stench, and try to flag down passing motorists. Perhaps one of these Slobs served as the original inspiration for the popular horror movie of some years ago, *The Creature from the Black Lagoon*.

At 7:30 P.M. on May 19, 1969, young George Kaiser was walking towards a tractor on the farm when his dog began to growl and bark. He (Continued on page 81)

29

A hunter is splashing alone through a swamp. Suddenly his dog begins to howl, flips his tail between his legs, and runs off. The brush ahead of the startled hunter stirs and a great hoary shadow rises up, uttering an unearthly screech. It towers above the man by two or three feet. He is too surprised and too paralyzed with fear to raise his rifle. The thing shuffles off into the blackness of the swamp to turn up months later elsewhere.

This drama has been acted so many times over the years that the basic job of simply cataloging such incidents is almost impossible. The swamp creature is not necessarily a special breed of monster, though. In most cases the descriptions are very similar to our mountaineering Abominable Snowman. We shall call him the Abominable Swamp Slob, or ASS, for short. While the ABSM thrives in forests and high places, the ASS prefers low-level marshes and bayous. There's hardly a respectable swamp in the Deep South that does not boast at least one ASS. As usual, our local historical experts, the Indians, have many legends and stories about the swamp creatures. It would seem that all wet, dark, forbidding places are inhabited by unspeakable monsters of some sort. Frequently our Swamp Slobs blunder onto highways, dripping with water and an ungodly stench, and try to flag down passing motorists. Perhaps one of these Slobs served as the original inspiration for the popular horror movie of some years ago, *The Creature From the Black Lagoon.*

At 7:30 P.M. on May 19, 1969, young George Kaiser was walking toward a tractor on the farm when his dog began to growl and bark. He looked up and saw a grotesque figure standing about twenty-five feet away. Whatever it was, it was the size of a man and covered with black fur.

"I watched it for about two minutes before it saw me," young Kaiser told investigator Bonnie Roman. "It stood in a fairly upright position although it was bent over about in the middle of its back, with arms about the same length as a normal human being.... I'd say it was about five feet seven or eight, in between there, and it had a very muscular structure. The head sat directly on the shoulders and the face was dark black, with hair that stuck out on the back of its head; had eyes set close together and a very short forehead. It was all covered with hair except for the back of the hands and the face. The hands looked like normal hands, not claws."

George was transfixed with shock and fright for a moment, then he made a move to get into the family automobile parked nearby. The creature made "a strange grunting sound," turned, jumped over a ditch, and ran down the road at high speed, quickly disappearing out of sight. Footprints were found in the dirt by the ditch. They showed three toes plus a big toe. Plaster casts were later made of these prints.

Back in 1931 an "escaped ape" was running around Long Island, only a few minutes from New York City. In June of that year half a dozen persons at Lewis & Valentine's nursery near Mineola, Long Island, excitedly reported the sudden appearance and disappearance of a fleet-footed "ape-like animal, hairy creature—about four feet tall." "Monster mania" struck Long Island. The police received so many alarmed calls that the Nassau County Police Department sent out ape-hunting details armed with shotguns. No circus was in town. A head count was taken of the gorillas in the nearest zoos. Nobody was missing. Still, the hairy little fellow kept pouncing out of bushes, scaring Long Islanders half to death. On June 29, Captain Earle Comstock organized a dozen heavily armed police patrols. They were joined by twenty hardy citizens armed with pitchforks and other weapons. The-four-foot-tall hairy thing must have seen the mob coming, and all the monster busters found were a lot of footprints: "The prints seemed to be solely those of the hind feet and were about the size and shape of a man's hand, though the thumb was set further back than would be the case with a man's hand."

The "ape's" final appearances were in the middle of July. A nurseryman named Stockman reported that his family had seen a gorilla thrashing about in the shrubbery near Huntington. Soon afterwards a farmer three miles away called in to report seeing the thing. Police found tracks at both places and tried to follow them, losing the trail in the nearby woods. That was supposedly the end of the Long Island "ape."

Or was it? This particular section of Long Island, with Huntington in the north, Mineola in the east, and Babylon in the south, constitutes a very interesting UFO "window." We have spent many days there in the past three years, talking to flying saucer witnesses and collecting some very odd information. There have been numerous monster sightings in a rather desolate hilly and wooded section south of Huntington since 1966. Neckers parked in an area known, appropriately enough, as Mount Misery claim to have been terrified by a giant seven-foot, human-shaped something. It turns up periodically in a place where many low-flying, glowing, saucer-shaped and cigar-shaped objects have been seen. The leading expert in Mount Misery is a young lady named Jaye P. Paro. Miss Paro is a reporter and radio broadcaster and has been studying the history of the area for years. She has made efficient and responsible investigations into many of the UFO and creature sightings, and in January 1969 she succeeded in photographing a very unusual being in the secluded woods on the top of the Mount. Fortunately she had a witness with her and he signed the following statement:

> At 8 A.M. on Sunday, January 12, 1969, I drove
> with Jaye P. Paro and Barbara LaMonica of
> Huntington, New York, to the area of Mount
> Misery for the purpose of taking photographs
> of the landscape. We pulled our car into a partial
> clearing on the left side of Mt. Misery Road,
> then decided to continue on foot. We decided to
> photograph an area that was located about five

hundred feet from our car.

Jaye was ready to take her first shot, when through the corner of my eye I caught a glimpse of a moving black object. Knowing we were completely alone in this desolate area, we were very scared. Immediately Jaye turned and snapped the first two pictures. The three of us were horrified to see the figure of something that resembled a human, disfigured face, long wild black hair, and dressed in a long black garment. It retreated immediately further into the bushes, made no sounds, and made no attempt to communicate with us. Frozen in her tracks Jaye dropped her camera. I picked it up and shot the two remaining pictures. Barbara started to run to the car. Jaye and I followed and we took off in a cloud of dust.

[signed] RICHARD DIMARTINO

What was it? A practical joker lying in wait on a bitter cold Sunday at 8 A.M.? Not very likely. A hermit? There are no rumors of a hermit living around Mount Misery. The photo depicts a dark blob with a very bushy head of hair extending a pale, long-fingered hand.

To demonstrate our theory that these events tend to recur in the same "window" areas year after year and even century after century, we will present a catalog of monster sightings summarizing many of the major and minor incidents of the past few years. We have organized this material by states, to give you some idea of the geographical dispersion of these reports. We have not tampered with these stories in any way. We present the facts as originally reported. We have, of course, greatly condensed each item. Some of these reports cover many pages. Some have included photographs, plaster casts, and lengthy tape recordings of the witnesses. Others are based upon lengthy newspaper stories written and published by competent local reporters. This catalog is by no means complete. We have not, for example, attempted to present even a fraction of the California "Big Foot" sightings, and we have weeded out the hundreds of sightings involving only the discovery of inexplicable giant footprints. We have also omitted, or tried to omit, the many unconfirmed or "hearsay" reports that flood our mail, but a few have been included and properly identified as such. As many statisticians will tell you, a sampling must be random if any valid conclusions are to be reached.

ALABAMA

1. A "Booger," as the locals called it, created quite a stir around Clanton, Alabama, in the fall of 1960. Several witnesses reported seeing a tall, hairy creature around Walnut Creek. A posse was formed and found footprints that resembled those of "a giant ape." Shortly after the posse quit the chase, the Reverend E.C. Hand saw the monster near Liberty Hill, grabbed his shotgun, and pursued it. But it got away.

"I can make my dogs catch a mule," Reverend Hand said, "But I could not get them to venture out toward the 'Booger'."

As time passed there were more reports. Some witnesses claimed the animal made a sound "like a woman screaming." Others said it sounded more like an elephant. It also prowled peach orchards, apparently sampling peaches.

Five years later, on August 30, 1965, the Union-Banner at Clanton carried this illuminating story: "Some six years ago several people out on Walnut Creek a mile or so from Clanton reported seeing some animal like a bear. It made some curious sounds at night kindly [sic] like a woman in distress. It ranged up and down the creek for a distance of some ten miles.

"Then some four years ago something made tracks in peach orchards some three miles south of Clanton, near large swamps. It was supposed to vanish into the swamps at night. A cement cast was made of the track, about the size of a person's foot but looking more like a hand. The cast is still somewhere in Clanton."

CALIFORNIA

2. "It ran upright like a man, swingin' long, hairy arms," said Ray Kerr of McKinleyville, California, as he described his sighting of "Big Foot" on Sunday, October 12, 1958. He was near Bluff Creek when he saw it. "It happened so fast, it's kinda hard to

give a really close description. But it was covered with hair. It had no clothes. It looked eight to ten feet tall to me."

Roy Wallace said he had seen a similar creature a short time earlier. It was hairy, walked stooped over, had long dangling arms, and was "four feet across the shoulders."

The mutilated bodies of four dogs were found in the area by Curtis Mitchell, an Indian, on the evening of Kerr's sighting. "They looked as if they had been ripped apart," he said. "One of them had apparently been slammed against a tree. The bodies were still warm when they were discovered off the Elk River road about five miles south of Eureka, California."

3. Charles Wetzel was driving home in Riverside, California, on Saturday night, November 8, 1958, and as he neared the point where North Main Street crosses the Santa Ana River, something leaped in front of his car.

"It had a round, scarecrowish head," he said, "like something out of Halloween.

"It wasn't human. It had a longer arm than anything I'd ever seen. When it saw me in the car it reached all the way back to the windshield and began clawing at me.

"It didn't have any ears. The face was all round. The eyes were shining like something fluorescent, and it had a protuberant mouth. It was scaly, like leaves."

Wetzel reached for the .22 pistol he carried in the car and "stomped on the gas."

"The thing fell back from the car and it gurgled. The noise it made didn't sound human. I think I hit it. I heard something hit the pan under the car."

There were long sweeping scratches on his windshield but nothing was found at the site. The next night a six-foot-tall black thing leaped out of the bushes near the Wetzel site and frightened another motorist. The Wetzel story was widely circulated by the wire services and has become a monster "classic."

4. Late in July 1966 two frightened teenaged girls reported they had been in a car near Lytle Creek outside of Fontana, California, when a "bush beast" suddenly stood up beside their vehicle. They described it as being 7-feet tall, with brown hair and covered with moss and slime. Their report kicked off a

monster epidemic and over 250 people, most of them armed to the teeth, poured into the area on a massive monster hunt. The San Bernardino County sheriff's office said that amateur "bush beast" hunters were swarming nightly over the barren foothills, filling the night with wild gunfire. The slime-covered ASS got away.

FLORIDA

5. In 1963 several persons on a ranch outside of Holopaw, Florida, said they had seen an ape-like creature running across a field. A "prominent cattleman and citrus grower" claimed he was in a group that been within a few feet of the creature and that "it was definitely an ape of some kind."

In 1966–67, the Holopaw "ape" was back. Eugene Crosby said it was 5-feet tall, hairy, very broad, and walked on two feet. It threw a tire tube at him. Other stories described how a six-foot-tall "ape" attacked two hunters on the Desert (Mormon) ranch. They are supposed to have shot at it and it went screaming into the darkness. Later an unoccupied tent house on the ranch was broken into, furnishings were broken and scattered, and blood stains were found.

6. A harsh, coughing sound made Ralph "Bud" Chambers of Elfers, Florida, look around as he was walking in some woods near the Anclote River in the summer of 1966: He saw a giant hairy thing standing in the trees. "The thing had a rancid, putrid odor like stale urine," Chambers said.

He hurried away and brought back a friend. They followed the creature's tracks into a swampy area. Chambers' dogs refused to follow the scent, but whined and could not be coaxed into going near the creature's trail.

Later Chambers had another sighting. He said the thing was over 7-feet tall, and "at least 4-feet wide" at the chest.

7. There were several hairy monster reports around Brooksville in 1966–67. In May 1967 Joan Whritenour was invited to a ranch near New Port Richey where strange three-toed tracks had been found. The county sheriff revealed that cattle were disappearing. No truck tracks or other evidence had been found to lead to the rustlers. "Just where does a rustler put a full-grown cow?" a sheriff's deputy asked Mrs. Whritenour. "Sure as hell not in his back pocket!"

KENTUCKY

8. Trimble County, Kentucky, was plagued with "monster mania" in June 1962. A farmer named Owen Pike said he saw the thing when it attacked and mauled his dogs, one a Collie, the other a German Shepherd. He described it as black, 6-feet tall, with hanging arms that reached to its knees. On June 8 Siles McKinney claimed the creature killed one of his calves. The calf's carcass was found fifteen feet outside of its enclosure, and the gate was still shut. Claw marks were found around the barn and traces of black hair were also discovered. Examination of the calf indicated it had been killed by a blow on the head. Other animals in the area disappeared or were found mutilated.

Sheriff Curtis Clem took the matter very seriously. Seven police dogs, a helicopter, and a posse scoured the area. Large footprints were found, like those of a giant dog. But various eyewitnesses attested that it was a large ape or bear. "A gorilla or a big something-or-other with reddish hair" was the general description.

MICHIGAN

9. Beginning around 1962 folks living in the vicinity of Sister Lakes, Michigan, started seeing something 9-feet tall that made a whimpering sound. Then, in May 1964 "monster mania" hit the region full force. A man named Gordon Brown told how he and his brother had seen the creature one night and followed its tracks. "We come to a tree," Brown said. "Well, I knew there weren't no tree there before. Well, we hightailed it right out of there."

Three teenaged girls met the creature in broad daylight while walking along a side road in Silver Creek Township. Joyce Smith fainted on the spot. Patsy and Gail Clayton stood motionless, paralyzed with fear, as the thing charged off into the underbrush.

"It didn't look like a man," Joyce said. Patsy described it as being about seven feet tall with "a black face."

John Utrup told the Cass County sheriff that he had seen the monster several times. One night as he was driving into his yard, he saw it standing behind a bush. "It had big, bright shining eyes," he said. Mrs. Utrup told of how one of her shepherd dogs chased the monster one night and came back with the pupil of one eye turned a pale blue color. Weeks later the eye returned to normal.

Many other witnesses came forward and were named in the extensive newspaper accounts. Hundreds of people flocked to Sister Lakes, and the usual futile monster hunt took place. Local drive-ins did a big business selling "monster-burgers," and station WSJM had a sponsored program of new monster reports and special "monster music."

In August 1965 the monster returned to Michigan, this time to the placid little community of Monroe, due east of Sister Lakes in Cass County.

Sixteen people reportedly encountered the monster in June and July 1965. Things really got serious when two attacks occurred in a single week. On Wednesday, August 11, David Thomas was driving a group of women home from a neighborhood baby shower when the thing jumped in front of their car.

Thinking that it was a neighborhood prankster, Thomas got out of the car to take a swing at it. When he discovered that it towered above his six-foot frame he prudently decided to return to the car.

It struck him in the back, he said, throwing him against the auto. He leaped back into it and drove off as the hairy arms thumped on the roof and fenders. Other people in the immediate area saw the creature that same night. Keith Mercure said he fired his shotgun at it. Some witnesses described it as "smelling moldy." Most agreed that it was at least seven feet tall, hairy, and had very long arms. It "grunted and growled like a mad dog."

MISSISSIPPI

10. Two truckers, William and James Cagle, were headed for Marietta, Georgia, on the Tuesday night, November 8, 1966. As they rounded a curve near Winona, Mississippi, a strange creature ran down a slope toward their vehicle.

"When my headlights picked him up, he was on our left side," James Cagle explained. "He was aggressive, angry, and ready to attack.... The face looked like a mixture of a gorilla and a human. The arms and legs were very large. The chest was at least 3-feet thick. His eyes glowed in the dark and did not seem to have pupils.

"It looked us over, then slowly raised an arm like the Indians do when they greet someone. I had seen all that I wanted. I floorboarded the accelerator."

MONTANA

11. Harold E. Nelson was driving across country when he pulled his camper off the highway to settle down for the night outside of Billings, Montana, on Wednesday, September 11, 1968. As he was gulping down a can of beans he heard a noise outside the camper, so he picked up a flashlight to take a look. When he opened the door he found a huge thing staring straight at him.

"It had an ape-like face but it was definitely not a gorilla," Nelson said later. "The head was slightly pointed, sloping down like the sketches of cavemen. The whole body was covered with reddish-brown hair. There were a few spots of white hair along the edge of the enormous shoulders. It stood erect, like a man, and must have weighed six hundred to eight hundred pounds. He was big—real big."

After a long moment of total immobility, Nelson scrambled back into his camper to find his gun. The creature peered in the door curiously and then turned and shuffled off into the darkness.

NEW JERSEY

12. Toward dusk on the evening of May 21, 1966, Raymond Todd and three friends were parked in an automobile in the Morristown National Historical Park, Morristown, New Jersey, when they saw a very tall ("at least 7-feet tall") entity ambling across the lawn. They described it as being faceless, covered with long black hair, and with scaly skin. What impressed them most was the breadth of the creature. It had huge shoulders, they said, and walked erect with a stiff, rocking movement. They were absolutely certain that it was not a bear or other known creature.

The quartet became hysterical and drove to the entrance of the park where they stopped cars and warned people that there was a "monster" on the loose. Todd stopped a car driven by a young lady (name withheld by request) and had her rush him to the Morristown Municipal Hall where he reported the encounter to the police. The police said that his fear and hysteria were genuine.

OREGON

13. In the fall of 1957 Gary Joanis and Jim Newall reportedly saw a giant human-like figure while hunting near

Wanoga Butter, Oregon. Mr. Joanis had just shot a deer, and
the tall being came out of the bushes suddenly, picked the dead
animal up with one arm, and walked off quickly with tremendous
strides. The creature was "not less than 9-feet tall" with very long
hair on its arms. It made a noise like "a very strange whistling
scream."

14. Two boys from Rosenburg, Oregon, told state police that
they had seen a fourteen-foot man-like creature in a nearby woods
on Wednesday, July 29, 1959. They said it was covered with hair,
walked upright, and had human characteristics. They saw it first
on the previous Friday but did not tell their parents because "we
didn't think anyone would believe us." They returned to the spot
again, armed with a rifle. The monster reappeared, and one of the
boys fired five shots at it from a range of about fifty yards.

"It ran off screaming like a cat, but louder," he said.

Police found human-like tracks fourteen inches long showing
five toes. The boys were certain it was not a bear.

PENNSYLVANIA

15. A six-foot-tall "person or thing" was seen by seven
persons on the shore of Edinboro Lake, Edinboro, Pennsylvania,
Wednesday night, August 17, 1966. "The witnesses fired at the
figure on two occasions with weapons they had taken along....
Apparently the creature was not hit," said the Erie, Pennsylvania
Times (August 19, 1966). A heavy UFO "flap" was taking place in
the area at the time. Another tall unidentified creature had been
seen on Presque Isle, July 31, some eighteen miles from Edinboro.
One report claimed that a man had come face to face with the
Edinboro monster near the lake and had been so badly frightened
that he was unable to speak for three days.

TENNESSEE

16. Brenda Ann Adkins reported meeting a hairy creature
on Monteagle Mountain, north of Chattanooga, Tennessee, in
the spring of 1968. She had stopped near the edge of a cliff to
take some pictures when she became aware of a nauseating odor
and heard a noise in the woods behind her. Turning, she saw the
thing lumbering toward her.

"I was absolutely frozen with fear," she said. "This thing was at least 7-feet tall and must have weighed several hundred pounds. I'll never forget his enormous chest and those huge arms and legs. His body was completely covered with blackish-red hair. The face was a mixture of an ape and a human. I still have nightmares about that afternoon. He seemed to be angry and was growling. I thought he would push me off the cliff or something. Then, he stopped about six feet from where I stood, cocked his head in a quizzical way, and just stared at me. He studied me for a few moments, then seemed to smile, made a little blubbering noise, and walked back into the brush."

WASHINGTON

17. At 4:00 A.M., on Wednesday, March 5, 1969, Don Cox drove around a bend on Highway 14 near Beacon Rock State Park in Skamania County, Washington, when a monstrous creature appeared on the road in front of his headlights. It was, he said, 8- to 10-feet tall, with a "face like an ape."

"It ran like a man and was covered with fuzzy fur," Cox stated. "I had just come out of a fog bank that had caused me to slow my car when I first saw what I thought to be a tree leaning toward the middle of the road.

"I slowed my car further and turned my headlights to high beam and it was then that I saw this fur-covered human form with the face of an ape. He ran across the road in front of the car, leaped up a forty degree slope and disappeared in the woods."

Deputy John Mason investigated and found smears that indicated that the creature had made an eight-foot jump up the embankment...a feat beyond the capabilities of any bear.

In April 1969 the Skamania County Board of Commissioners passed an ordinance making it illegal to kill a Sasquatch, providing a ten-thousand-dollar fine and up to five years imprisonment.

18. At 2:30 A.M., Sunday, July 27, 1969, Deputy Floyd Sund was driving along a deserted wooded road north of Hoquiam, Washington, when he had to slam on his brakes to avoid colliding with an animal standing directly in front of him. He got out of his car and pointed his spotlight at the animal. It was, he said, 8-feet tall, with a human-like face, but was covered with hair except for the feet and the hands. He estimated that it must have

weighed about three hundred pounds. Somewhat dismayed, he drew his pistol but the animal ran off into the woods.

Police searched the area for footprints the next morning but it was "too gravelly." Sheriff Pat Gallagher said he thought it could have been a bear. Deputy Sund grumbled, "It sure didn't look like one."

WEST VIRGINIA

19. In the summer of 1960, a group of young men were camping in the woods near Davis, West Virginia. One night one of them was cutting wood for the fire when he heard a noise and felt someone poking him in the ribs. He thought one of his friends was trying to scare him and turned around, annoyed, to find himself confronted with a "horrible monster." He described it: "It had two huge eyes that shone like big balls of fire and we had no light at all. It stood every bit of 8-feet tall and had shaggy long hair all over its body. It just stood and stared at us."

By the time the boys had recovered from their shock the creature had shuffled off into the darkness. They broke camp early the next morning. Gigantic footprints were found where the creature had been but the witnesses didn't feel like following them.

WISCONSIN

20. A large, powerfully built "man" covered with hair was seen by three men in the Deltox Marsh in Wisconsin on October 17, 1968. The same men, together with nine others, encountered it again on November 30. On the first occasion they tried to follow it but it eluded them in the thick underbrush. On November 30 the twelve men were combing the swamp looking for it. They found it but didn't shoot because "it was too man-like." Again it got away.

A number of interesting comparisons can be drawn from the foregoing. Viewed cumulatively, these random sightings reveal several hitherto hidden aspects. We can now categorize these events and speculate that there are two main groups. Group 1 consists of real animals possessing common characteristics of appearance and behavior. Group 2 are "monsters" in the true sense of the word and seem to be part of a paranormal phenomenon, like ghosts and flying saucers. That is, they are a problem for parapsychologists rather than biologists.

Witnesses to "monsters" very rarely report to the local newspapers or police. In our travels around the country we have uncovered many spectacular cases that had never received any publicity of any kind. Often, when the witness tells his family and friends about the incident he is so heavily ridiculed that he shuts up. In most cases, the man or woman who does report to the police or newspaper is not taken seriously. If you encountered a ten-foot-tall creature covered with moss and slime, with two huge, luminous red eyes, who would you tell? And do you think anyone would take you seriously?

These events are being taken more seriously now, by larger numbers of people. Our channels for communicating these experiences have improved greatly. The handful of well-equipped researchers involved now have more and better data to work from, and we are finally getting very close to a solution.

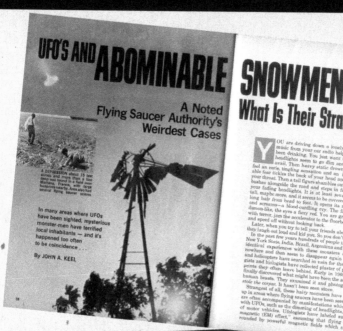

UFO'S AND ABOMINABLE SNOWMEN— What Is Their Strange Connection

A Noted Flying Saucer Authority's Weirdest Cases

By JOHN A. KEEL

A DEPRESSION about 15 feet across and more than a foot deep was found in a field near Molland, France, with large footprints nearby. Area also had several flying saucer scares.

In many areas where UFOs have been sighted, mysterious monster-men have terrified local inhabitants — and it's happened too often to be coincidence...

FOOTPRINTS were discovered in South Dakota after large hairy "monster" was seen by several campers in wooded area — and UFO was sighted...

Y OU are driving down a lonely country road late at night, lively music from your car radio helping to keep you alert. You haven't been drinking. You just want to get home to bed. Suddenly your headlights seem to go dim and you fiddle with the switch to no avail. Then heavy static drowns out the music on the radio. You feel an eerie, tingling sensation and an indefinable fear tickles the back of your head and dries your throat. Then a tall figure shambles out of the bushes alongside the road and steps in front of your fading headlights. It is at least seven feet tall, maybe more, and it seems to be covered with long hair from head to foot. It opens its mouth and screams—a blood-curdling cry. The face is demon-like, the eyes a fiery red. You are gripped with terror, jam the accelerator to the floorboards and speed off without looking back.

Later, when you try to tell your friends about it they laugh out loud and kid you. So you don't dare mention it again.

In the past few years hundreds of people in California, Michigan, Florida, New York State, India, Brazil, Argentina and dozens of other places have had identical experiences with these monsters and freaks who appear out of nowhere and then seem to disappear again into limbo. Posses using dogs and helicopters have searched in vain for these mysterious creatures. Zoologists and biologists have collected plaster of paris casts of the gigantic footprints they often leave behind. Early in 1969, two world famous scientists finally discovered what might have been the actual body of one of these half-human beasts. They examined it and photographed it. And then someone stole the corpse. It hasn't been seen since.

Strangest of all, these hairy monsters have a disturbing habit of turning up in areas where flying saucers have been seen, and their brief appearances are often accompanied by manifestations which have long been associated with UFOs, such as the dimming of headlights, radio static, and the stalling of motor vehicles. Ufologists have labeled such phenomena "the electromagnetic (EM) effect," assuming that flying saucers are sometimes surrounded by powerful magnetic fields which raise (Continued on page 74)

38

"UFOs and Abominable Snowmen—What Is Their Strange Connection?" pondered journalist John Keel in the October 1969 issue of *Male*. Keel, author of *The Mothman Prophecies* and one of the most respected and prolific authors in the fields of both cryptozoology and UFOlogy, passed away in 2009.

SIR ARTHUR C. CLARKE

"THE Reckless Ones" by Arthur C. Clarke in the October 1956 issue of *Adventure* features a cryptid as famous as its renowned author. The giant squid (*Architeuthis*) is an example of a former sea monster once thought to exist only in the exaggerated tales of rum-soaked sailors and ships' captains. It was not until 1925 when two tentacles of a colossal squid (*Mesonychoteuthis hamiltoni*) were recovered from the belly of a sperm whale that modern science was forced to reconsider the numerous reports from previous centuries of monstrous squid locked in death battles with chomping cetacean behemoths. To give a sense of perspective, it has only been since 2002 that Japanese scientists were able to photograph a mature giant squid alive in its natural habitat. It took until 2007 for a truly notable specimen of the colossal squid to be recovered by a commercial fishing crew from New Zealand.

Clarke is ruminating among the timeless greats of literature, as Aristotle and Pliny the Elder also wrote about the giant squid in their eras. The Kraken of Norse mythology is sometimes attributed by scientists to giant squid sightings, and these particular types of Kraken-like accounts are recorded in Greek and other seafaring cultures, too.

It is interesting to find Clarke writing about cryptids, but it should come as no surprise. After all, he wrote extensively about any and all range of curious natural and supernatural phenomena, albeit through a keenly skeptical viewpoint. His lucrative paranormal television shows were practically an in-house division of his literary output, including three different series bearing his name: *Arthur C. Clarke's Mysterious World* (1980), *Arthur C. Clarke's Mysterious Universe* (1985) and finally *Arthur C. Clarke's World of*

Strange Powers (1994). It might seem dubious that Clarke, who called himself "an almost total skeptic" in 1992, would want his well-respected scientific name and reputation associated with Bigfoot, the Loch Ness Monster, UFOs, ghosts, demons and crystal skulls. Yet he never disparaged that which was unknown to science as a priori fraudulent or suspect, whether the subject matter was quantum theory or cryptid hominids. Of his fascination with these topics he wrote, "I'm always paraphrasing J.B.S. Haldane: 'The universe is not only stranger than we imagine, it's stranger than we *can* imagine.'"

Clarke's connection to tales of the deep seas was intense and personal. He was an avid deep sea diver and underwater explorer throughout his life, discovering ruined undersea temple remains and shipwrecks. In many ways, Clarke's own exploits in uncovering lost treasures intact from sunken cargoes mirrors the "conquest of nature" tone prevalent in so many MAMs; hence the knowing, if wry, tone to his telling of "The Reckless Ones."

ADVENTURE

THE MAN'S MAGAZINE OF EXCITING FICTION AND FACT

SKID ROW
The Street Where
Anything Goes

**IS VIRGINITY
OUT OF DATE?**

A Shocking On-the-Spot-Story
**THE MURDER
OF KING ABDULLAH**

Oct., 25c

"THE RECKLESS ONES"
ARTHUR C. CLARKE
ADVENTURE, **OCTOBER 1956**
COVER BY MORT KÜNSTLER

THE RECKLESS ONES

Their hunting ways were secret, their quarry hidden to man.

But they were looking for big game, all right, the last, biggest

trophy of all — the Sea Thing some men called Death

by ARTHUR C. CLARKE

ALTHOUGH by general consent Harry Purvis stands unrivaled among the "White Hart" *clientele* as a purveyor of remarkable stories (some of which, we suspect, may be slightly exaggerated) it must not be thought that his position has never been challenged. There have even been occasions when he has gone into temporary eclipse. Since it is always entertaining to watch the discomfiture of an expert, I must confess that I take a certain glee in recalling how Professor Hinckelberg disposed of Harry on his own home ground.

Many visiting (*Continued on page* 58)

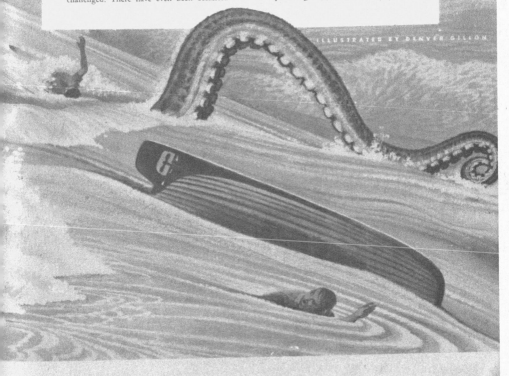

ILLUSTRATED BY DENVER GILLON

ART BY DENVER GILLON

Although by general consent Harry Purvis stands unrivaled among the "White Hart" *clientele* as a purveyor of remarkable stories (some of which, we suspect, may be slightly exaggerated) it must not be thought that his position has never been challenged. There have even been occasions when he has gone into temporary eclipse. Since it is always entertaining to watch the discomfiture of an expert, I must confess that I take a certain glee in recalling how Professor Hinckelberg disposed of Harry on his own home ground.

Many visiting Americans pass through the "White Hart" in the course of the year. Like the residents, they are usually scientists or literary men, and some distinguished names have been recorded in the visitors' book that Drew keeps behind the bar. Sometimes the newcomers arrive under their own power, diffidently introducing themselves as soon as they have the opportunity. (There was the time when a shy Nobel Prize winner sat unrecognized in a corner for an hour before he plucked up enough courage to say who he was.) Others arrive with letters of introduction, and not a few are escorted in by regular customers and then thrown to the wolves.

PROFESSOR Hinckelberg glided up one night in a vast Cadillac he'd borrowed from the fleet in Grosvenor Square. Heaven only knows how he had managed to insinuate it through the side streets that lead to the "White Hart," but amazingly enough, all the fenders seemed intact. He was a large lean man, with that Henry Ford-Wilbur Wright kind of face that usually goes with the slow, taciturn speech of the sun-tanned pioneer. It didn't in Professor Hinckelberg's case. He could talk like an LP record on a 78 turntable. In about ten seconds we'd discovered that he was a zoologist on leave of absence from a North Virginia college, that he was attached to the Office of Naval Research on some project to do with plankton, that he was tickled pink with London and even "liked English beer," that he'd heard about us through a letter in *Science*, but couldn't believe we were true, that Stevenson was okay, but if the Democrats wanted to get back, they'd better import Winston, that he'd like to know what the heck was wrong with all our telephone callboxes and could he retrieve the small fortune in coppers of which they had mulcted him, that there seemed to be a lot of empty glasses around and how about filling them up, boys?

On the whole the Professor's shock tactics were well received, but when he made a momentary pause for breath I thought to myself. *Harry'd better look out. This guy can talk rings round him.* I glanced at Purvis, who was only a few feet away from me, and saw that his lips were pursed into a slight frown. I sat back luxuriously and awaited results.

As it was a fairly busy evening, it was quite some time before Professor Hinckelberg had been introduced to everybody. Harry, usually so forward at meeting celebrities, seemed to be keeping out of the way. But eventually he was cornered by Arthur Vincent, who acts as informal club secretary and makes sure that everyone signs the visitors' book.

"I'm sure you and Harry will have a lot to talk about" said Arthur, in a burst of innocent enthusiasm. "You're both scientists, aren't you? And Harry's had some most extraordinary things happen to him. Tell the Professor about the time you found that U 235 in your letterbox...."

"I don't think," said Harry, a trifle too hastily, "that Professor—ah—Hinckelberg wants to listen to my little adventures. I'm sure he must have a lot to tell us."

I've puzzled my head about that reply a good deal since then. It wasn't in character. Usually, with an opening like this, Purvis was up and away. Perhaps he was sizing up the enemy, waiting for the Professor to make the first mistake, and then swooping in for the kill. If that was the explanation, he'd misjudged his man. He never had a chance, for Professor Hinckelberg made a jet-assisted take-off and was immediately in full flight.

"Odd you should mention that," he said. "I've just been dealing with a most remarkable case. It's one of these things that can't be written up as a proper scientific paper, and this seems a good time to get it off my chest. I can't often do that, because of this darned security—but so far no one's gotten round to classifying Dr. Grinnell's experiments, so I'll of talk about them while I can."

Grinnell, it seemed, was one of the many scientists trying to interpret the behavior of the nervous system in terms of electrical circuits. He had started, as Grey Walter, Shannon, and others had done, by making models that could reproduce the simpler actions of living creatures. His greatest success in this direction had been a mechanical cat that could chase mice and could land on its feet when dropped from a height. Very quickly, however, he had branched off in another direction owing to his discovery of what he called "neural induction." This was, to simplify it greatly, nothing less than a method of actually *controlling* the behavior of animals.

It HAD been known for years that all the processes that take place in the mind are accompanied by the production of minute electric currents, and for a long time it has been possible to record these complex fluctuations—though their exact interpretation is still unknown. Grinnell had not attempted the intricate task of analysis; what he had done was a good deal simpler, though its achievement was still complicated enough. He had attached his recording devices to various animals, and had thus been able to build up a small library, if one could call it that, of the electrical impulses associated with their behavior. One pattern of voltages might correspond to a movement to the right, another with traveling in a circle, another with complete stillness, and so on. That was an interesting enough achievement, but Grinnell had not stopped there. By "playing back" the impulses he had recorded, he could compel his subjects to repeat their previous actions—whether they wanted to or not.

That such a thing might be possible in theory almost any neurologist would admit, but few would have believed that it could be done in practice owing to the enormous complexity of the nervous system. And it was true that Grinnell's first experiments were carried out on very low forms of life, with relatively simple responses.

I SAW only one of his experiments," said Hinckelberg. "There was a slug crawling on a horizontal piece of glass, and half a dozen tiny wires led from it to a control panel that Grinnell was operating. There were two dials—that was all—and by suitable adjustments, he could make the slug move in any direction. To a layman, it would have seemed a trivial experiment, but I realized that it might have tremendous implications. I remember telling Grinnell that I hoped his device could never be applied to human beings. I'd been reading Orwell's *1984* and I could imagine what Big Brother would do with this gadget.

"Then, being a busy man, I forgot all about the matter for a year. By the end of that time, it seems, Grinnell had improved his apparatus considerably and had worked up to more complicated organisms, though for technical reasons he had restricted himself to invertebrates. He had now built up a substantial store of 'orders' which he could then play back to his subjects. You might think it surprising that such diverse creatures as worms, snails, insects, crustaceans and so on should be able to respond to the same electrical commands, but apparently that was the case.

"If it had not been for Dr. Jackson, Grinnell would probably have stayed working away in the lab for the rest of his life, moving steadily up the animal kingdom. Jackson was a very remarkable man—I'm sure you must have seen some of his films. In many circles he was regarded as a publicity-hunter rather than a real scientist, and academic circles were suspicious of him because he had far too many interests. He'd led expeditions into the Gobi Desert, up the Amazon, and had even made a raid on the Antarctic. From each of these trips he had returned with a best-selling book and a few miles of Kodachrome. And despite reports to the contrary, I believe he had obtained some valuable scientific results, even if they were slightly incidental.

"I don't know how Jackson got to hear of Grinnell's work, or how he talked the other man into cooperating. He could be very persuasive, and probably dangled vast appropriations before Grinnell's eyes—for he was the sort of man who could get the ear of the trustees. Whatever happened, from that moment Grinnell became mysteriously secretive. All we knew was that he was building a much larger version of his apparatus, incorporating all the latest refinements. When challenged, he would squirm nervously and say, 'We're going big-game hunting.'

"The preparations took another year, and I expect that Jackson—who was always a hustler—must have been mighty impatient by the end of that time. But at last everything was ready. Grinnell and all his mysterious boxes vanished in the general direction of Africa.

"*That* was Jackson's work. I suppose he didn't want any premature publicity, which was understandable enough when you consider the somewhat fantastic nature of the expedition. According to the hints with which he had—as we later discovered—carefully misled us all, he hoped to get some really remarkable pictures of animals in their wild state, using Grinnell's apparatus. I found this rather hard to swallow, unless Grinnell had somehow succeeded in linking his device to a radio transmitter. It didn't seem likely that he'd be able to attach his wires and electrodes to a charging elephant....

"They'd thought of that, of course, and the answer seems obvious now. Sea water is a good conductor. They weren't going to Africa at all, but were heading out into the Atlantic. But they hadn't lied to us. They were after big game, all right. The biggest game there is....

"We'd never have known what happened if their radio

operator hadn't been chatting to an amateur friend over in the States. From his commentary it's possible to guess the sequence of events. Jackson's ship—it was only a small yacht, bought up cheaply and converted for the expedition—was lying-to not far from the Equator off the west coast of Africa, and over the deepest part of the Atlantic. Grinnell was angling: his electrodes had been lowered into the abyss, while Jackson waited impatiently with his camera.

"They waited a week before they had a catch. By that time, tempers must have been rather frayed. Then, one afternoon on a perfectly calm day, Grinnell's meters started to jump. Something was caught in the sphere of influence of the electrodes.

"Slowly, they drew up the cable. Until now, the rest of the crew must have thought them mad, but everyone must have shared their excitement as the catch rose up through all those thousands of feet of darkness until it broke surface. Who can blame the radio operator if, despite Jackson's orders, he felt an urgent need to talk things over with a friend back on the safety of dry land?"

I won't attempt to describe what they saw, because a master has done it before me. Soon after the report came in, I turned up my copy of *Moby Dick* and re-read the passage; I can still quote it from memory and don't suppose I'll ever forget it. This is how it goes, more or less:

"'A vast pulpy mass, furlongs in length, of a glancing cream-color, lay floating on the water, innumerable long arms radiating from its centre, curling and twisting like a nest of anacondas, as if blindly to catch at any hapless object within reach.'

"Yes: Grinnell and Jackson had been after the largest and most mysterious of all living creatures—the giant squid. Largest? Almost certainly: *Bathyteuthis* may grow up to a hundred feet in length. He's not as heavy as the sperm whales who dine upon him, but he's a match for them in sheer size.

"So here they were, with this monstrous beast that no human being had ever before seen under such ideal conditions. It seems that Grinnell was calmly putting it through its paces while Jackson ecstatically shot off yards of film. There was no danger, though it was twice the size of their boat. To Grinnell, it was just another mollusc that he could control like a puppet by means of his knobs and dials. When he had finished, he would let it return to its normal depths and it could swim away again, though it would probably have a bit of a hangover.

"What one wouldn't give to get hold of that film! Altogether apart from its scientific interest, it would be worth a fortune in Hollywood. You must admit that Jackson knew what he was doing: he'd seen the limitations of Grinnell's apparatus and put it to its most effective use. What happened next was not his fault."

Professor Hinckelberg sighed and took a deep draught of beer, as if to gather strength for the finale of his tale.

"No, if anyone is to blame it's Grinnell. Or, I should say, it *was* Grinnell, poor chap. Perhaps he was so excited that he overlooked a precaution he would undoubtedly have taken in the lab. How otherwise can you account for the fact that he didn't have a spare fuse when the one in the power supply blew out?

"And you can't really blame *Bathyteuthis*, either. Wouldn't *you* have been a little annoyed to be pushed about like this? And when the orders suddenly ceased and you were your own master again, you'd take steps to see it remained that way. I sometimes wonder, though, if Jackson stayed filming to the very end...."

"HUNT FOR THE HALF-MAN, HALF-APE..."

"HUNT for the Half-Man, Half-Ape of North America" from *Men*, November 1969 combines the narrative journal-keeping frequent to the horror stories of H.P. Lovecraft with the killer hominid meme to engaging effect. None of the hunters' names are legit, and the sunglasses airbrushed atop one "Pete Cernan" are as risible as they are entertaining.

The story interweaves cryptozoologic fact and fantasy, a hallmark of the genre. Note the narrator reads a news clipping referencing Belgian zoologist Bernard Heuvelmans' statement

Pre-Historic Man May Still Be Alive

BRUSSELS — Somewhere in northeast Asia or on the opposite side of the Bering Sea in Alaska or British Columbia a kind of pre-historic man resembling the Neanderthal, may still be living.

This possibility is . . . In . . . lates bulletin of . . .

dead only a few years, of such a man.

It . . . on De . . . stone, . . . ex . . . n . . .

to have been shot.

Heuvelmans quotes an American geologist, Jack Arthur U rich, as testifying that the my terious being must have bee frozen into the ice artificial only a few years ago.

He says Hansen told him . . . it's "exhibit" . . . one in 190 . . . was su . . . been found . . .

Enlarged detail of an ape man from Gil Cohen's Men *cover art.*

about the Minnesota Ice Man (a supposed cryptid in a block of ice that exhibitor Frank Hansen once toured to flocking crowds in the 1960s). A pioneer in the field with a legitimate academic background, Heuvelmans set a high standard for future cryptozoological researchers. Name-dropping Heuvelmans offered a form of shorthand scientific validation designed to short-circuit the doubters (at least long enough to be entertained by the story).

But unless you are a historian, it's not the research that sustains "Hunt for the Half-Man, Half-Ape of North America" for a modern reader. Rather, it is the sense of danger and trepidation that builds as you flip each page. Author Tom Christopher crafts a scary "cabin under siege" storyline that retains an elemental fright factor. The vivid descriptions of the monster, the blood-stained drawings left behind by a vanished witness, as well as the bleakly ambiguous ending, all combine to give the story a white-faced pallor. It blends classic motifs in Bigfoot literature (a protagonist attacked while in cabin confinement) with adventure story mechanics and plot structure, such as the classic told-within-a-flashback narrative construction. Again, the skeptical editors back away from the cryptid killer they've meticulously set before the reader as a real possibility—allowing doubting readers of the period to dismiss it as all so much hokum before going under their barber's snipping blades.

The Book Everyone's Talking About

HONOLULU MADAM

The outspoken autobiography of an Hawaiian girl who became a sex legend

NOV.

MEN

50¢
3/

A HUNTER'S INCREDIBLE TRUE STORY
Pursuit of North America's
APE MAN

1969'S
NEWEST CRAZE
VACATIONS FOR MATE-SWAPPERS ONLY
— a top investigator's inside report

SNEAKY NEW TRAP
FOR USED-AUTO BUYERS **HOW THEY BUILD "HALF-BREED" CARS**

$5.95
Book Bonus **'BREAKOUT'**

"SHOCKING AND UNFORGETTABLE...RAW AND HONEST...
MUST READING BY AN EX-CON." — The Journal

STIR-MAD CONS
ON A BRUTAL
48-HOUR
TERROR SPREE

Pre-Historic Man May Still Be Alive

HONOLULU
MADAM

A GO-GO DANCER, A SALESGIRL AND A COLLEGE COED TELL...
"HERE'S WHAT WE MEAN BY BETTER SEX"

AMAZING SURVIVAL ORDEAL OF THREE
WHO FOUND A BRAZILIAN TREASURE
THE GREAT JUNGLE PAYROLL HUNT

"HUNT FOR THE HALF-MAN,
HALF-APE OF NORTH AMERICA"
TOM CHRISTOPHER
MEN, NOVEMBER 1969
COVER BY GIL COHEN

SHOCKER

HUNT

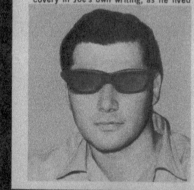

Joe Hunrath (above) went into Canada's wilderness alone to find the ape man. Worried about his friend, Pete Cernan (below) searched and found instead a startling discovery in Joe's own writing, as he lived it.

THE whole thing began a couple of years ago when Joe Hunrath and I were up in Cassiar, British Columbia, hunting caribou. There were five of us up there that year, all guys from back home in Idaho. But Joe Hunrath and I were the only ones in the hunting party that had made the trip to this section of British Columbia regularly every year for the past six years.

We were staying in the same cabin, in the wilderness up above Telegraph Creek, that Joe and I had used for the past six springs. There was great hunting up around Cassiar; Caribou, moose, grizzly bear, wolf, Stone sheep and mountain goats. We'd never come back empty-handed from any of our past trips. And this time, just two days after we'd got there, a couple of us had bagged a mountain goat apiece, and Joe—the best shot among us—had got himself a bull moose.

"Nice shooting, Joe," I said and meant it when we'd dragged the carcass back to the cabin that night and began skinning it. He'd brought the moose down with five shots from his .308 Winchester, drilling the shots into the animal's chest, one almost on top of the other, leaving the head undamaged.

"Hell," Joe said, "he was practically on top of me when I opened fire. I would've had trouble missing him."

Joe was a very quiet guy. He'd been pretty much a loner all his life and he wasn't easy to get close to, even though we'd been friends for quite a while now. But I could see he was pleased when the whole gang of us celebrated his kill with a beer party in the cabin that night.

It was the next day that this odd thing happened that was to change Joe's life—although at the time I didn't realize how important it was to become. We were in the woods about a mile and a quarter from the cabin, near the same place where Joe had shot his moose the day before, when we flushed out a big buck, with massive antlers, from the trees.

The startled buck plunged from the clearing and into the brush and all of us spread quickly, moving in different directions into the woods to encircle him. A few minutes later I heard Joe yell, "He's headed back into the clearing. Get him!"

I ran back and reached the clearing just about the same time as a couple of the other guys got there. The buck was standing, head upraised, well down from us. And before any of us could get a shot off, the buck bolted

(Continued on page 32)

OF THE YEAR...

FOR THE

HALF MAN- HALF APE

Of North America

By PETE CERNAN as told to
TOM CHRISTOPHER

This is a scientific artist's reproduction of the ape man, just as
Joe Hunrath's diary described him.

31

ART BY GIL COHEN

The whole thing began a couple of years ago when Joe Hunrath
and I were up in Cassiar, British Columbia, hunting caribou.
There were five of us up there that year, all guys from back home
in Idaho. But Joe Hunrath and I were the only ones in the hunting
party that had made the trip to this section of British Columbia
regularly every year for the past six years.

We were staying in the same cabin, in the wilderness up
above Telegraph Creek, that Joe and I had used for the past six
springs. There was great hunting up around Cassiar: Caribou,
moose, grizzly bear, wolf, Stone sheep and mountain goats. We'd
never come back empty-handed from any of our past trips. And
this time, just two days after we'd got there, a couple of us had
bagged a mountain goat apiece, and Joe—the best shot among
us—had got himself a bull moose.

"Nice shooting, Joe," I said and meant it when we'd dragged
the carcass back to the cabin that night and began skinning it.
He'd brought the moose down with five shots from his .308
Winchester, drilling the shots into the animal's chest, one almost
on top of the other, leaving the head undamaged.

"Hell," Joe said, "he was practically on top of me when I
opened fire. I would've had trouble missing him."

Joe was a very quiet guy. He'd been pretty much a loner all
his life and he wasn't easy to get close to, even though we'd been

friends for quite a while now. But I could see he was pleased when the whole gang of us celebrated his kill with a beer party in the cabin that night.

It was the next day that this odd thing happened that was to change Joe's life—although at the time I didn't realize how important it was to become. We were in the woods about a mile and a quarter from the cabin, near the same place where Joe had shot his moose the day before, when we flushed out a big buck, with massive antlers, from the trees.

The startled buck plunged from the clearing and into the brush and all of us spread quickly, moving in different directions into the woods to encircle him. A few minutes later I heard Joe yell, "He's headed back into the clearing. Get him!"

I ran back and reached the clearing just about the same time as a couple of the other guys got there. The buck was standing, head upraised, well down from us. And before any of us could get a shot off, the buck bolted and bounded back into the trees right about where Joe should have been. We could hear the buck thrashing around in the underbrush and I expected the crack of Joe's Winchester to come at any moment.

Instead, I heard only the sound of the buck receding into the brush in the distance, and a few minutes later Joe came walking slowly out of the trees, rifle under his arm.

"Hey, what happened," I shouted to Joe. "How come you missed him?"

Joe looked up as if he had forgotten we were there. He had a strange, strained look on his face and he started to say something and then just shook his head and came on toward us, walking slowly.

I knew Joe well enough to know that he couldn't have been afflicted with "buck fever," that paralyzing inability to shoot when suddenly confronted with game, which sometimes comes over green hunters.

"So what the hell happened?" I asked again. All the other guys were standing there with me looking at Joe. He pushed the bill of his hunting cap back with the barrel of his rifle, shook his head, and said, "I saw the damnedest thing back there." He paused and then in a rush added, "A big hairy thing—kind of man-animal. It was the ugliest, weirdest-looking thing, or creature, I've ever seen. And fast! It sprang out of the brush about a yard or two in front of the buck and before I even had time to take a good look, it was gone." He looked at each of us in turn. "You know what I'm talking about?"

Nobody said anything for a minute. I could tell the rest of the guys were kind of embarrassed. I figured they thought Joe had made up a cock-and-bull story to explain why he hadn't shot the buck.

Joe's face flushed dark purple then. He must have guessed what was going through the guys' minds.

"Godammit," he yelled, "don't you believe me? I'm telling you I saw this big hairy thing, about 6-feet tall. It looked like a man, except its body was completely covered with a thick coat of hair."

There was no mistaking the sincerity in Joe's voice, but still I couldn't blame the guys for not taking him seriously. One of the guys said, "No more beer for you tonight, Joe," and that broke the tension. Everyone then began joking with Joe about the hairy creature and at first I saw him stiffen with anger but a few minutes later he shrugged and I relaxed.

There were some jokes about Joe's "abominable hairy man" from time to time during the rest of our stay in the cabin, and even for a while after we'd gone back home to Idaho a week or so later. But I saw Joe pretty regularly, and some of the other guys frequently, during the next year. Gradually the guys stopped joking about what Joe said he had seen, and I forgot all about it.

Joe and I both drove trucks for the same trucking outfit, although not working on the same truck. Our jobs often took us to various points around the state, but almost never beyond the borders of Idaho. I didn't see a lot of Joe at work. But all through that summer and winter we played poker, or went to ball games or bowling or double-dated pretty regularly.

AND then, early that spring, toward the end of March, I heard from one of the guys in the dispatcher's office that Joe had taken off for a three-week vacation. He hadn't said a thing to me about it the last time I'd seen him, and I figured, knowing Joe, he'd just decided he wanted to get away by himself for a while. When a month went by and Joe still hadn't gotten back, I decided to call his house and see if his family had heard from him. I got his sister on the phone and she said, No, nobody had heard a word from Joe. She didn't sound too concerned. She said, "You know how Joe's always been. He kind of comes and goes. He's not one to be tied down to an exact schedule—especially when it comes to hunting."

It was just a couple of nights later that I ran into Ernie Anders, one of the guys who'd been on the trip with Joe and me the previous spring. I hadn't seen Ernie for a couple of months and we had a couple of beers together. While we were drinking and shooting the bull, Ernie happened to mention Joe and asked about him. I just told him Joe was okay. And then Ernie took a newspaper clipping out and passed it on to me, asking if Joe had said anything about it.

The clipping was about six weeks old, and I hadn't seen it when it appeared in the newspaper. The clipping read:

> PRE-HISTORIC MAN MAY STILL BE ALIVE:
> BRUSSELS—*Somewhere in northeast Asia or on the opposite side of the Bering Sea—in Alaska or British Columbia—a kind of pre-historic man resembling the Neanderthal, may still be living. This possibility is advanced in the latest bulletin of the Belgian Institute of Natural Science. Its author, Belgian zoologist Bernard Heuvelmans, believes that in a small American town he might have seen the body, dead only a few years, of such a man. It happened, he says, on December 17, 1968, in Rollingstone, Minn., when a fairground exhibitor named Frank D. Hansen, showed him the body of "a six-foot human male of virtually normal proportions but covered with a thick coat of hair." The body was preserved in ice, and from wounds in his skull and left arm he appeared to have been shot. Heuvelmans quotes an American geologist, Jack Arthur Ullrich, as testifying that the mysterious being must have been frozen into the ice artificially only a few years ago.....*

By now I was plenty worried about Joe, figuring that he'd seen the clipping and had gone back up to British Columbia for proof that the pre-historic man-animal was there. That's the kind of fool thing he was capable of. So the next day I went in and asked for an immediate emergency leave of absence, or my vacation time, from the job. They didn't like it much at the place, but they gave me two weeks as vacation.

Soon I was on my way to Cassiar, British Columbia. It's hard to say what I expected to find at the old cabin. I hoped maybe Joe'd be there, cooking up a potful of game, and I'd look foolish. As it turned out, Joe wasn't there. But even before I went inside, I saw signs that somebody had been there recently; there were horse tracks around the cabin that had been made since the winter snowfall.

Inside I noticed Joe's .308 Winchester lying on a table. I didn't like that. It wasn't like Joe to go anywhere outside the cabin without his rifle. I picked up the rifle and looked it over. It had been cleaned and oiled since the last time it had been fired, but there was a light film of dust on it.

It had been a long, hard day and I should have been ready to turn in but I was restless and uneasy. I built up a fire in the stone fireplace and began rummaging through the cabin looking for some clue to explain what had happened to Joe. Then I came across a notebook marked "Diary," in the drawer of the table. I noticed a piece of paper sticking out from between its pages. I opened the notebook-diary to the page and saw that what had been sticking out was the newspaper clipping—the same one Ernie had shown me about the possibility that a pre-historic man might still be alive in British Columbia.

I quickly leafed through the diary and saw that there were several entries in it in Joe's handwriting. The first entry was on March 28. I took the diary over by the fireplace and sat in the chair and read what he had written for that date:

"I'm writing round about midnight. I spent the whole day out in the woods. I ain't seen anything yet. But I could hear movement out there—movement different from the animal kind—and I sensed something out there. Both my horses have been jumpy ever since we got here. I heard them whinnying all night long last night. And today when I got back to the cabin I could see where the horses had been pulling at their ropes, and how they kicked the ground up all around the lean-to. Right now, the horses are making a lot of racket like they're scared."

There was nothing written under March 29. But on Sunday, March 30, there was this:

"I saw 'the thing' today! It was the first time since I came back. It or he or whatever the hell you wanna call it was in a clearing down by the pond five miles south of here.

"Man, it was something to look at, too. Too bad I didn't have any goddamn camera to take pictures of it. The camera got busted up. The camera and my telephoto when my pack horse bolted seeing a snake.

"The man-animal or animal-man was resting near the pond. There were some bones scattered around him on the ground. So I figured he'd just finished eating. And since he didn't know that I was watching him, I had a good chance to get a good look this time. He was near 6-feet tall, and built heavy. Heavy body, head, arms, and legs. His arms were longer than those of a man, and he stood upright on his legs. He looked more like a man than an ape, except for the hair all over him, and the face. The face was more ape than man—a flat, caved-in looking thing. He also had a big, squashed-in nose, small eyes, and thick rubbery lips. The teeth were animal-like, too, and jutted out. He was scary-looking. At the same time he was also kind of great-looking because I had the feeling I was seeing a creature from long ago. I had my rifle with me but I wouldn't want to shoot a creature as rare as this.

"After a while he suddenly seemed to sense that I was there. He raised his head, and shot out of the clearing so fast that it was like I was watching one minute, blinked my eye, and he was gone. He ran upright, and moved so swiftly there was hardly a sound. Now my problem is: How am I going to get proof of what I've seen...?

Joe tried to make some rough sketches of the man-animal. He was no artist, but by reading his description and looking at his sketches, I could see a little bit of what the thing looked like.

THERE was nothing written in the diary under the next two days. But on April 2, Joe had this to say:

"For the last two days I stayed out in the woods all the time. I made a very important discovery, too. There's more than one of the animal-man creatures out there—there's a small group

of them! I've tried to draw what they look like on the two pages
before this one in the diary. Some of the creatures are smaller than
the others. I wonder if they're females. The larger ones I figure
are males. I tracked the group for most of one day—yesterday—
but finally lost them. They must have some place, a cave or
something, where they hole up in. I wish I could find it. I'm going
looking again tomorrow."

I flipped to April 3, and read:

"This was a bad day. I was out in the woods early and found a
couple of the hairy creatures moving through the trees just ahead
of me. I started after them, but they disappeared. Then something
strange happened. They began popping up all around me every
once in a while. After a while it dawned on me for the first time
that they had spotted me. That they had spotted me and were
watching what I was doing. That I wasn't tracking them—they
were tracking me. I could hear them grunting back and forth to
each other.

They were all over the place, popping up first on one side
of me, then the other, and in front and back of me. I was afraid
they were going to jump me. I panicked. I fired on them for the
first time. I kept firing. I used up almost all my ammunition. But
they're swift and elusive. I don't even think I winged a one of
them. I'm convinced that they meant to kill me. I think the rifle
was the only way I held them off. I made it back here to the cabin,
but I heard them behind me all the way, tracking me. When I got
back, both of the horses were gone! The ropes had been bitten
through. Tonight, I admit it, I'm scared to death. I wish I hadn't
been so damn foolish and come up here alone."

I flipped the pages rapidly now, reading on, April 4:

"Stayed in cabin all day. I'm sure the hairy sons of bitches
were moving around outside about sundown. I shot at them. But
I ain't certain whether I hit 'em or not. Am running low on grub.
God I'm scared. Gotta do something soon. But what?"

April 5:

"I decided to walk out of the cabin today. But when I went
a few yards, the goddamn monsters came at me. Shot right out
of the brush.... Had to use up all my ammo getting back inside
the cabin.... Just finished the last of the grub. Have to think of
something soon."

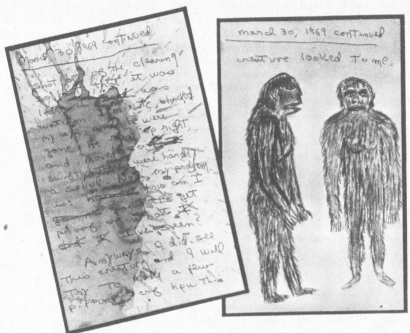

These coffee-stained pages from Hunrath's diary, shown for the first time, may be the first clues that the ape man indeed exists.

April 6:

"Stayed inside the whole lousy day. Food's all gone. So's my ammo. I ain't seen a sign of the hairy creatures once today. But I'm too scared to go out. Got a bad case of the shakes. Real bad. I ain't shook like this ever before in my whole life. Can't stop.

"If they're still out there, I'm finished. Jesus, please help me. Please, dear God...."

April 7:

"It's two days now that I ain't seen a sign of the hairy creatures... Am going to have a look around outside. If I don't see them, am going to hike back to town today."

That was the last entry in the diary. I guessed that Joe stuck the diary back in the drawer and meant to take it along with his other gear when he started back to town. But now, it appeared, he had just vanished. I put the diary in with the rest of my stuff and went to bed.

I DIDN'T sleep much that night, and early next morning I saddled up my horse, packed on my gear, and rode back to town. I decided not to tell anybody in town about the diary, but I told them Joe had disappeared from the cabin and I wanted to organize a search party to go back and look for him. About seven men in town volunteered to go along and we rode back that same afternoon to look for Joe.

For the next three days we searched the woods in every direction around the cabin but we didn't turn up any sign of Joe. Nor of the hairy, "pre-historic" men or whatever it was Joe had seen. Funny thing, though, after we'd finally given up the search and were riding back to town, one of the men, one of the guides who often hunted up in that area, said, "Did you notice a peculiar thing while we were looking for Joe? There were no animals around anywhere. Where do you reckon they had all gone to?"

I never did tell the rest of the men in the search party about the diary Joe left behind. But after I got back to Sandpoint, I began thinking about it, and decided to contact some magazines and see if they'd be interested in printing the story. Now you've just read it.

I figured I could do at least that much for my friend, Joe. I know he'd have wanted the world to know what had happened.

EDITOR'S NOTE: *The editors of* Men *magazine would like to state for the record that we neither believe nor disbelieve that a creature such as the one described in the article you've just read actually exists. To use a favorite scientific term, it's possible; not probable. However, we printed the article which the author brought to us because we do think it's interesting and fascinating.*

Men's adventure magazines are justly famed for their dynamic and explosive cover art, but "quiet" covers—like this Yeti encounter by artist Mark Schneider—generate tension in the calm before the storm. ("The Abominable Snowman Seen Again," *Sir!* September 1953)

"THE 'THING' AT DUTCHMAN'S RIG"

ECHOING the influence of Arthur Conan Doyle's Professor Challenger stories, "The 'Thing' at Dutchman's Rig" by Joseph Mavitty, which appeared in the aptly named *Showdown* from November 1958, tells of a relic dinosaur species running amok in the jungles of New Guinea. While few serious cryptozoologists have posited that the probable Allosaurus or T. Rex portrayed in this story is actually still remnant, there are claims in the crypto field of other dinosaur species being alive to menace mankind. For example, the fabled Mokele Mbembe, a Congo-based legend which purports to describe a very much alive sauropod species, is well-known by enthusiasts. Similarly, "MacDonald's Nightmare Safari" (included later in this collection on pg. 193) from the August 1959 edition of *Man's Conquest* contains scenes of a giant, man-eating lizard that also follows along this line. Both stories are classic to the genre, in that they slowly, methodically build verisimilitude by offering a specificity of details about their respective geographic regions. This formula was designed to set a believable stage for the action, as well as offer a needed educational background for exotic locales many readers had scarcely heard of prior, let alone had any relevant knowledge about. In many ways, many of these narratives adroitly combined the dry details of a typical *National Geographic* report mixed with the exciting adventure aspects of Doyle's *The Lost World*.

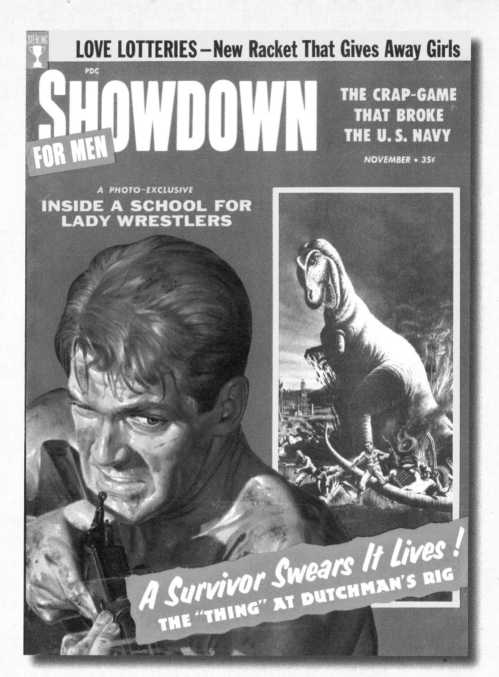

"THE 'THING' AT DUTCHMAN'S RIG"
JOSEPH MAVITTY
SHOWDOWN, **NOVEMBER 1958**
COVER BY GEORGE GROSS

by JOSEPH MAVITTY

GIGANTIC thunderclouds towered blackly over the Bismarck Range of New Guinea's mountainous interior, signaling the beginning of the rains. We were chugging along the upper reaches of the Sepik River, heading for that great unmapped region beyond the headwaters, somewhere in an area on the Dutch-British frontier marked *Undeveloped* on official charts. It is a land of unknown tropic valleys and poisonous green jungles where cannibal headhunters await the foolhardy adventurer, the intrepid explorer, and the scientist. The time was November 1955, at the start of the monsoon season.

I was worried about those huge black thunderheads over the mountains. A cloudburst up there would certainly mean a flash flood below, and our expedition of small river-boats rode so low in the swift water—due to heavy loads of men and oil drilling equipment—that we were sure to be swamped.

It was a question of time. We were possibly five hours from our destination, and I had no way of knowing how long the first flood would take to race downriver from the towering mountains, where those thunderheads were already spilling their millions of tons of water.

After the first hour of rain, the river swelled and rose, and the current ran so fast I was forced to lead my boats along the tangled banks of mangrove roots in order to make some headway upriver. It was a risky maneuver but a river's current is always slower at its banks.

After three hours the river was swollen almost to flood stage, and we were nosing very slowly ahead in a 12-knot current. I ordered my crews to make fast our towing lines from stern to bow, so that all three boats were linked together like mountain climbers—in case a sudden avalanche of water should catch one of my rivercraft unready.

The clouds kept pouring tons of water upon the distant mountainsides and after the fifth hour I heard a low roar from dead ahead, and I knew the flood wall would soon appear around a bend upriver. But just then we reached our destination—a small tributary of the upper Sepik—and we entered the mouth of the stream, pulling in from the Sepik River and out of the path of the oncoming flood.

As the third boat was about to enter our haven, the flood wall raced around a bend in the Sepik, catching the small craft on her stern port quarter. Only the fact that I had strung my three boats together saved her from being torn away by the flood crest.

We traveled another hour upstream and finally beached by a green field of towering kunai grass at the base of a tall red cliff. We were a few valleys north of Wilhelmina, a Dutch settlement. According to my contract with the East Indies Investment Company, I was supposed to drill for oil in the center of this kunai grassland.

Cholly, my chief rigger, saw the first sign of trouble when we beached our boats. During World War II, he'd spent two years in the New Guinea jungles, living with a tribe of headhunting cannibals, after he was shot down following a bombing raid on Jap-held Rabaul. He knew the back country of this island better than any other white man. After the war he joined up with me, and we went barnstorming around the world as oilmen, prospecting in the Middle East, drilling in Brazil, bossing gangs in the Arctic—and now sinking a hole in New Guinea, where a Dutch investment company wanted me to bring in the black gold that has long been known to lie in a vast reservoir below those prairies of nine-foot-tall kunai grass and the vast reaches of towering rain forest.

Cholly was a wiry little guy with curly black hair and sharp eyes, one of Brooklyn's finest sons, a tough street fighter, a daredevil rigger with more than one fall to his score, and crazy about the oil game.

He came running along the sandy riverbank now, and I saw trouble in his eyes. He didn't say anything until he reached me, and then he spoke quietly so as not to alarm the others, my gang of Dutch drillers and the Papuan porters.

"Joe, we better get out of here," he whispered. "Get the boats in the water quick, and let's blow!"

I was surprised, because my curly-headed little friend didn't scare easily. "What's up, Cholly?"

"Better come with me," he said. "You wouldn't believe it if you didn't see it with your own eyes."

Groot, one of my Dutch drillers, was bossing some natives unloading gear, and I spoke to him quietly as Cholly and I walked past his boat: "Stop work for now, Groot. I'll let you know when to start."

Then I followed Cholly to the downriver end of the beach, and there he ducked behind a low red *guava* bush. I had to get down on my hands and knees to follow him, being about twice Cholly's build.

"How the hell did you ever get around behind this bush in the first place?" I complained brushing leaves out of my face.

He looked grim and said, "Here's what I brought you to see." (*Please turn to page 66*)

From out of New Guinea's primitive jungles comes the most incredible creature of our time. Dozens of horrified men were witness to its fantastic strength, but only one man survived it. Here, for the first time, is the story of the monster that came back from a million years ago—to kill!

ARTIST UNCREDITED

Gigantic thunderclouds towered blackly over the Bismarck Range
of New Guinea's mountainous interior, signaling the beginning
of the rains. We were chugging along the upper reaches of the
Sepik River, heading for that great unmapped region beyond the
headwaters, somewhere in an area on the Dutch-British frontier
marked *Undeveloped* on official charts. It is a land of unknown
tropic valleys and poisonous green jungles where cannibal
headhunters await the foolhardy adventurer, the intrepid explorer,
and the scientist. The time was November 1955, at the start of
the monsoon season.

I was worried about those huge black thunderheads over the
mountains. A cloudburst up there would certainly mean a flash
flood below, and our expedition of small river-boats rode so low
in the swift water—due to heavy loads of men and oil drilling
equipment—that we were sure to be swamped.

It was a question of time. We were possibly five hours from
our destination, and I had no way of knowing how long the first
flood would take to race downriver from the towering mountains,
where those thunderheads were already spilling their millions of
tons of water.

After the first hour of rain, the river swelled and rose, and
the current ran so fast I was forced to lead my boats along the

tangled banks of mangrove roots in order to make some headway
upriver. It was a risky maneuver but a river's current is always
slower at its banks.

After three hours the river was swollen almost to flood stage,
and we were nosing very slowly ahead in a 12-knot current. I
ordered my crews to make fast our towing lines from stern to
bow, so that all three boats were linked together like mountain
climbers—in case a sudden avalanche of water should catch one
of my rivercraft unready.

The clouds kept pouring tons of water upon the distant
mountainsides and after the fifth hour I heard a low roar from
dead ahead, and I knew the flood wall would soon appear around
a bend upriver. But just then we reached our destination—a small
tributary of the upper Sepik—and we entered the mouth of the
stream, pulling in from the Sepik River and out of the path of the
oncoming flood.

As the third boat was about to enter our haven, the flood wall
raced around a bend in the Sepik, catching the small craft on her
stern port quarter. Only the fact that I had strung my three boats
together saved her from being torn away by the flood crest.

We traveled another hour upstream and finally beached by a
green field of towering kunai grass at the base of a tall red cliff.
We were a few valleys north of Wilhelmina, a Dutch settlement.
According to my contract with the East Indies Investment
Company, I was supposed to drill for oil in the center of this kunai
grassland.

Cholly, my chief rigger, saw the first sign of trouble when
we beached our boats. During World War II, he'd spent two years
in the New Guinea jungles, living with a tribe of headhunting
cannibals, after he was shot down following a bombing raid on
Jap-held Rabaul. He knew the back country of this island better
than any other white man. After the war he joined up with
me, and we went barnstorming around the world as oilmen,
prospecting in the Middle East, drilling in Brazil, bossing gangs
in the Arctic—and now sinking a hole in New Guinea, where a
Dutch investment company wanted me to bring in the black gold
that has long been known to lie in a vast reservoir below those
prairies of nine-foot-tall kunai grass and the vast reaches of
towering rain forest.

Cholly was a wiry little guy with curly black hair and sharp eyes, one of Brooklyn's finest sons, a tough street fighter, a daredevil rigger with more than one fall to his score, and crazy about the oil game.

He came running along the sandy riverbank now, and I saw trouble in his eyes. He didn't say anything until he reached me, and then he spoke quietly so as not to alarm the others, my gang of Dutch drillers and the Papuan porters.

"Joe, we better get out of here," he whispered. "Get the boats in the water quick, and let's blow!"

I was surprised, because my curly-headed little friend didn't scare easily. "What's up, Cholly?"

"Better come with me," he said. "You wouldn't believe it if you didn't see it with your own eyes."

Groot, one of my Dutch drillers, was bossing some natives unloading gear, and I spoke to him quietly as Cholly and I walked past his boat: "Stop work for now, Groot. I'll let you know when to start."

Then I followed Cholly to the downriver end of the beach, and there he ducked behind a low red guava bush. I had to get down on my hands and knees to follow him, being about twice Cholly's build.

"How the hell did you ever get around behind this bush in the first place?" I complained brushing leaves out of my face.

He looked grim and said, "Here's what I brought you to see."

I looked at it. But I didn't believe it.

The "it" was a pawprint or footprint—about a yard and a half long. It looked like the print of an enormous bird, but several hundred times bigger than the biggest condor of the Andes or the eagle of the Rocky Mountains. The footprint had three toes and a heel, and the talons of the toes had dug deep holes in the soft earth.

There was a second footprint about four yards away and another an equal distance beyond that. These three prints led into the nine-foot-tall kunai grass and disappeared there, but Cholly and I could see a swath 12-feet wide running into the high grass and away toward the jungle at the far side of this prairie. Something immensely long and heavy had dragged a five-inch deep trench in the earth as whatever creature it was walked along.

"What do you make of it, Joe?"

I hardly heard Cholly's question.

"Joe," he repeated urgently, "what's it all about?"

"Damned if I know," I said, glancing over my shoulder to see if we had been followed, for I knew that if my native porters saw those prints and that trench, I would lose my entire labor force.

But then the rainstorm from the mountains reached us as it spread over the land. It would stay with us now, every day until the end of the rainy season.

And as the rains came down, I watched the giant clawprints and the long trench between them wash away in the downpour.

I made my decision. "Cholly," I said, "this is just between you and me." I had to shout into his ear to be heard above the roar of the monsoon cloudburst. "Say a word about this to the others, and the porters will run out on us. Maybe the Dutchmen too. It means a lot of money, Cholly...."

"Yeah," he agreed, "ten thousand bucks for you, no matter what, and another ten grand if we bring in oil." Cholly squinted against the driving rain. "But it's only money, Joe...."

"It's only a hell of a lot of money, fella," I countered.

"The Dutchmen and the porters just get wages," Cholly answered, which surprised me, because I had never heard him talk like that before.

"You get a bonus, Cholly," I reminded him.

"Keep it," he said, and now I could see he was angry about something. "I don't want it," he added, starting to turn away.

"Hold on, fella," I growled, beginning to get a little angry myself. "You contracted to do a job. So did the Dutchmen. And so did those porters...."

"They can't even read!"

"So what! This is their island and their jungle, and everything in it. If there's some kind of big animal back there in the rain forest, it's their animal. These Paps take their chances like everyone else, the same as the Dutchmen, and the same as you and me—unless you're running out on the job."

I never saw the little guy look so hard as he did at that moment when he said, "If the money means more to you than these men's lives, O.K. I'm with you, because like you said, I contracted to do a job, and I'll do it. But I don't have to like it, and

I don't think I have to like you for it, either."

He turned his back on me then and scooted through the grass, and when I followed he broke into a run down the beach and cursed the men into work as he ran.

Cholly never smiled but once after that moment, when he said, "I should have stayed in Brooklyn."

But by then it was far too late for Cholly.

We worked every day, Sundays included, in the rain most of the time, and in short order we had the rig up and ready. For power I used my three riverboats' wood-burning steam engines to drive a series of electric generators, and thus in the middle of the New Guinea jungles we had a modern oil rig run by electricity. Fuel wood was plentiful and of course thoroughly wet because of the steady rains, but the boats' furnaces burned so hot the wet wood only raised its burning point still higher, and our steam-driven generators hummed around the clock with a steady whine that you could hear on the far side of the kunai prairie. It took us a week to get rolling.

With the operation going full blast and my drills biting deep into the rocky shell that covers New Guinea's vast subterranean lakes of oil, I thought little about the giant clawprints that Cholly and I had seen. Meanwhile every day my Papuan porters gathered firewood for the furnaces, going out into the deep rain forest, where there were ordinarily very few serious dangers. The New Guinea jungles were then known to be among the safest in the world—except of course for the presence of cannibals and headhunters. There were no tigers, no rhinos, and hardly any poisonous reptiles, merely a few parrots and tree kangaroos.

On the other hand, this particular area was at that time still unexplored, and nobody *really* knew what was in it. As for me, I *knew* what I had seen: something that seemed impossible to me then, but truth is in fact stranger than fiction. Those giant clawprints could have been made by only one animal, and as a mining geologist I knew which animal was the only one that could have made clawprints a yard and a half long, with a four-yard stride, and a tail heavy enough to drag a trench in the earth. Such a beast would stand upwards of 20-feet tall and about 45-feet from tip to tail. But I told myself such a creature simply could not exist, not even in New Guinea, regardless of the evidence I had seen.

And then one night we heard it.

The sound split the night like the scream of a gigantic wounded horse. It came about midnight, echoing across the kunai prairie like the splitting, shattering sound of lightning cracking the night sky.

It brought the Dutchmen and the Papuans running out of their tents yelling at each other in sudden fright. At first we all thought the well had come in with a terrible explosion, but when we saw the rig drilling steadily and everything normal, we gathered around the working lights and just stood there, waiting and wondering.

All but Cholly and me. *We knew.*

The gargantuan voice that shrieked out of the jungles and across the grassland could only belong to the beast that had made those huge clawprints back at the river's edge. If I had any doubts before, I had none now. I even knew the scientific name of the animal, but I dared not speak it. Had I said its name, not a man in my crew would have believed me.

My Papuans were already crowding around their *luluai,* a kind of chief and witch doctor combined, who was busily painting his face and chanting ritual formulas to counter the black magic that they all believed to be out there in the night beyond the yellow pools of our working lights. The Dutch drillers, however, were merely arguing with each other as to the cause of the fearful noise.

The Paps were dancing and chanting their magic rituals, and the Dutchmen went on arguing, while Cholly and I stood watching them.

"You gonna tell them now," Cholly asked, "before it's too late?"

"No," I said. "Tell Groot and the Dutchmen to mix in with the Paps and try to get them back to the tents. Then douse the standing lights...."

"Putting out the lights won't be enough, Joe," he said. "The thing can still hear the rig working."

"I'm not stopping the rig for any damn animal, and I don't care how big it is!" I growled.

"A lot of men's lives..." Cholly began. His voice was hard and cold, and he wasn't even looking at me as he spoke.

"You've got your orders!" I said curtly. "Get to work!" Hell, I thought, better men than any of these Paps and Dutchmen had run nitro trucks up and down mountains because that was their job. And as any fool knows, a nitro truck is a hell of a lot more dangerous than all the dumb animals in the world, no matter how big the animal.

But I knew how Cholly would answer that, so I kept it to myself. He'd look up at me out of those snapping black eyes and say, "Well, Joe, a nitro trucker at least knows what he's up against, and he takes his chances. But these poor saps are in the dark...."

I'll admit it now, I felt pretty lousy about the whole thing. But I had a job to do, and I needed every man I had to finish this job.

Figure it this way: The world's oil reserves are dwindling. Those oil deposits we now have are in many cases not only getting smaller very fast but are also in more or less hostile territory. Oil turns the wheels of industry, and if industry stops there are millions of workers idle, unemployed, and going hungry. Like other mining geologists, I knew there was a big lake of oil lying below the island of New Guinea, and the Dutch had hired me to go in and tap that lake.

It wasn't just the $10,000 I could make on this job, or even the 10 grand bonus for bringing in a well.... There was a hell of a lot more at stake, and I meant to go all the way.

I wanted to say all these things to my old buddy, but I already knew his answer: "Is it worth the life of a man?" He didn't think so, and I knew that much. But I thought it was, and there wasn't much point in discussing it. My way, or his way.... That's all there was to it. And I was boss.

Next day we had one hell of a time getting the Paps to go out into the jungles beyond the kunai prairie. But my three wood-burning steam engines ate up a lot of firewood, and I couldn't run the electric generators without steam power, so I ordered some of the Dutch drillers to run the Paps back to work with force if necessary. Though the Dutchmen were scared enough themselves, they weren't superstitious, and they could control their fears. But the Paps were fit to be tied—goggle-eyed and gibbering with terror. We worked them anyhow. Every white man carried some kind of sidearm, a revolver or an automatic, and all you had to do to get a Pap moving in the direction of the jungles was to touch your sidearm and give him a hard look. He moved all right.

This big Dutchman Groot was boss of the drillers, under Cholly of course, and Groot was too stupid to be afraid of anything, so he straw-bossed his men and the Paps under them like there was nothing out there in those jungles to be afraid of. But the day after the "Thing" woke us up with its screaming in the night, we all got another surprise—and what happened to Groot surprised me most of all, because he fell apart like a rag doll.

It seems one of the gangs of Paps got separated from the others in the jungle, and Groot was running this particular gang at the time. Well, they walked straight into our monster....

They were chopping and bundling firewood, and they had all but forgotten last night's terror, when suddenly the tall trees were shoved apart and the monster crashed through, seeing the men at once and instantly attacking. They fled howling into the underbrush, but not before three of them had been mangled in one scooping motion of the animal's great mouth.

"Und ve heard dis big ting crunch dem in its jaws!" Groot told me later, shuddering and sweating with fear as he told the horrible story. "I shoot de pistol until is empty, and I hit every damn time de animal in its face, but de bullets not hurt him, not even make blood come. I hear de bullets go *ping! ping! ping!* ven dey strike him—like bullets bouncing off rocks, eh? Vot you call ricochet, yes?"

The natives had to be held under armed guard while I talked to the other Dutchmen. Cholly stood by, and Groot interpreted for me. He was a big blond man about six feet two and close to 300 pounds, which gave him a slight edge over me if it came to a showdown. Cholly and I *used* to call him the Pig because of his small round blue eyes and his long snout-like nose, not to mention his vicious temper. Also, when he was angry, his strangely high-pitched voice squealed like a stuck pig's dying shriek.

He was angry now. So were all the Dutchmen. But not in the same way.

Groot the Pig had seen the "Thing." The other Dutchmen hadn't, and they couldn't believe him when he claimed it stood more than three times the height of a man and was maybe 50 feet long. He said it had a mouth big enough to take a cow in one bite, and they couldn't believe that either.

He said we ought to abandon the rig and head for the boats at once, but the other Dutchmen argued that half a dozen men with rifles could track down the creature and kill it.

As for me, I wondered. I didn't think our rifles had enough penetrating power for the "Thing's" armored hide.

But I was willing to try it, and I sided with the other Dutchmen against Groot the Pig. There was one hell of a row, with the Pig squealing in Dutch and English and threatening to blow up the whole damn rig with a bottle of nitro if we didn't agree to hit the boats and head downriver at once. It was a very tricky situation, because the Pig was the only squarehead who knew any English, while Cholly and I didn't know one word of Dutch. But I speak a little French and a lot of Spanish, so I tried first the one and then the other, and my Spanish found a friend—a boy who remembered some Spanish he learned in school.

"*Deténgalo pronto!*" I told the lad: "Arrest him quickly!"

That was a mistake, because when the young fellow pulled his gun, Groot saw what was happening and got himself ready real fast. Dumb as he was, the Pig knew something was up when I started jabbering French and then Spanish at his men. Groot fired first, killing my Spanish-speaking friend instantly, which of course made him guilty of murder.

I didn't hesitate after that. I put a shot through his gun arm and then rushed him. It was only a flesh wound, and while it knocked the gun out of his grip, it didn't cripple him, so I had a fight on my hands. I belted him a good one in the guts, knocking out his wind, and when he jack-knifed I hit him in the face with my knee, following with a locked-hands rap against the back of his neck. It was over in seconds. Then the other Dutchmen carried him to his tent and left him there under armed guard.

Afterwards we organized a quick safari to see if we could dispose of the "Thing" with our rifles. We had some old Springfields, the 30-caliber Model 1906 that I have always found the best all-around utility rifle. It fires a steel-jacketed slug that can penetrate three standing men or a heavy oak plank. Its range is three miles, with high accuracy up to 1,000 yards. It will even shoot one mile straight up if you have any reason to. We used it for sniping in the Raiders during World War II, since the Garand wasn't very accurate at long ranges, though it had superior firepower.

Five Dutch drillers, Cholly, and I headed across the broad kunai prairie for the jungle on the far side, where Groot and his gang of Papuans had seen the "Thing." Visibility was close to zero because kunai grass grows about 9-feet high, but by the time we were close enough to the jungle to be able to see its tall trees, we also saw our quarry.

The "Thing" crashed out of the jungle and onto the open grassland, looking for prey. The high grass protected us from its view, and we were able to sight in long and carefully, and slowly squeeze off our shots.

"Aim for the eyes," I whispered to Cholly. I tried to get this idea across to the Dutchmen, but without a common language I'm not sure they savvied. They were all good workers, though, and I guess they figured about the way I did.

The range was around 600 yards. We had to shoot offhand, or standing, as prone or kneeling or sitting positions were impossible in the tall grass. Shooting offhand at 600 is no way to win shooting matches, even with no wind or drift problem, and as a result we didn't strike the creature's eyes, but many bullets did glance off the armored hide of his face, while others chipped away at the massive chest. It was a damn big target even at that long range, standing upwards of 20-feet tall, as Groot had reported, and it looked about 50-feet long, though you couldn't be sure because much of its long tail lay hidden in the grass. And as Groot had also said, its mouth was big enough to take a cow in one bite.

We emptied our rifles into the creature's face and body, and all we accomplished was to make it angry. Not hurt in any way, just roaring mad. God how it screamed. I think the sound would have deafened us, but we ran pell mell for camp when our ammunition was gone, and put a few more hundred yards between us and it.

Back at the drilling site, we could see the "Thing" standing tall and slimy gray against the green front of the jungle, swinging its enormous head back and forth, looking angrily for its attackers—the invisible gnats that had stung its heavy hide.

I think the Papuans were ready to riot, and I don't think my Dutch drillers would have tried to stop them, but then the "Thing" turned its back on the prairie and went back into the jungle, shoving aside tall trees the way we walked through kunai grass.

Immediately everyone started jabbering excitedly—merely from release of tension. The Dutchmen laughed and horsed around, shoving each other and shouting whatever Dutchmen shout when serious danger suddenly passes. Cholly took off his sun helmet and wiped his forehead and muttered something about a close call.

I just watched. I had been afraid the whole gang would turn yellow then, run for the riverboats, and leave one of the most important test wells of my life just standing there on the kunai prairie.

I figured on coppering my bets now. I would move everything but our actual drilling equipment down to the boats, and henceforth we would sleep aboard them, and live and cook on them, though it would mean about a mile's hike to work for each shift on the rig. And I was starting to get this idea across to the Dutchmen, with the help of what few German words I remembered from a course I took in mining school, and a lot of sign language....

But suddenly the well blew in. One of the easiest, quickest wells I ever scored. And how she blew! The fountain of black gold geysered up some 200 feet, and the levees we had shored up to hold the oil for just such an eventuality soon held a wide brimming lake of the crude black stuff. And not too crude, either. This would be high-test stuff, you could smell it. We capped the hole.

And we celebrated that night, the Dutchmen, the Papuans, everybody—even Cholly, who still hadn't smiled since that day he found those first claw prints, the day he and I argued whether I had the right to risk my men's lives without their knowledge and consent. Cholly celebrated now with the rest of us, but he wasn't happy, he didn't smile, he just got drunk and then went to his tent.

But he had a word to say to me before he staggered off into the darkness. "Joe," he said, "you got 20 thousand bucks coming now, right?"

"Right," I answered.

"And one dead Dutchman and three dead Paps, right?"

I didn't answer, and he didn't wait for an answer. He just reeled away toward his tent, and I went and got drunk myself.

Everyone got drunk. This was a mistake.

The monsoon rains coming down every day had mucked up the earth all over that kunai prairie, so that a herd of elephants could have walked right into camp without our hearing so much as a single footfall. Which is just what happened.

Sometime after midnight, with the rain coming down like a waterfall, that ungodly shriek we had heard before began again. But this time it was a hundred times louder, and it brought everyone out of his drunken stupor and onto his feet. We rushed out of our tents, all the Dutchmen and the Paps, and we found the monster among us, standing high above our tents, its head swinging around, its huge fiery eyes darting about, looking for live meat.

We were as helpless as sitting ducks. The Papuans ran for the river, but the great beast scooped them up by twos in its long jaws. The night was horrible with screaming as those jaws chomped down on their victims.

My Dutch drillers stood their ground as long as they could, firing rifles and pistols into the animal's armored hide—with no apparent effect. Then the Dutchmen broke and ran for the river, but the "Thing" rushed them and snapped them up in its great mouth the way a dog hurriedly wolfs down a panful of meat scraps.

Groot was free to fight now, and he and Cholly and I kept firing our weapons, aiming at the creature's eyes, but it did no good: if our bullets actually struck their mark, 30-caliber was too small to do much harm, if any at all. And suddenly we had no more ammunition.

"Run for the nitro!" I yelled.

We headed for the nitro tent, the last three men alive, so far as I knew, and I doubted that anyone had yet escaped the "Thing's" great scooping jaws.

It saw us then and lowered its head to attack. Cholly and I ducked into the tent just as the beast got Groot. We heard his screams and the crunch of his bones as the giant jaws clamped down on him.

Then we were outside the tent again, each of us with bottles of nitro in his hands. The creature had ambled a short distance away toward the lake of oil by the rig. It was bending down as if to drink at a fresh water lake, and I laughed like a madman.

"Cholly!" I yelled. *"Come on! Throw the nitro into the oil. Let's blast that damn thing off the face of the earth!"*

Cholly didn't even look at me when he said, "I should have stayed in Brooklyn."

He just ran toward the oil pond with a bottle of nitro in each hand—and me right beside him with my own hands full of death.

The "Thing" was wading into the lake of oil when we got within throwing range. We threw together, then dropped flat on the muddy earth. Even so, the explosion picked us up and flung us across the ground, rolling us like tumbleweed in front of a high wind.

When I stopped rolling, I scrambled to my feet and saw the "Thing" still standing in the middle of the pond, which was aflame now, and so was our enemy—flaming like a great dragon and screaming insanely as it wallowed about in the lake of fire.

I looked around for Cholly. He lay still and pale where the nitro explosion had thrown him up against the base of a tree. He was dead.

I could go on to tell you how I lost all three of my boats on the trip downriver when a flash flood caught up with me, and how I finished my trip down the Sepik River in one of the boats' dinghies—alone. But none of that seems to matter much now.

I did what I set out to do, I brought in New Guinea's first well, and now the world has a few more years' supply of precious fuel for the wheels of industry. But at what cost! I wonder if it was really worth it.

As for the terrible creature that killed off my men, I was sure from the beginning that nothing could have made those gigantic clawprints we first saw along the riverbank—except King Tyrannosaur. The scientific name is *Tyrannosaurus rex*, and the last of the species is supposed to have died some millions of years ago during the Pleistocene geologic period. Fossilized bones have been found in Montana and South Dakota, but none had ever been reported from New Guinea.

How to explain the presence of a creature supposedly extinct all this time? Frankly, I can only guess. Perhaps radioactive fallout from the Pacific or Siberian H-bomb tests activated an accidentally preserved egg of the King Tyrannosaur —since we are nowadays blaming practically every misfortune on the fallout.

But none of that seems very important to me now when I remember poor little Cholly.

As he said, "I should have stayed in Brooklyn!"

"A MAN FROM ANOTHER AGE"

THE basic structure of these stories is often remarkably similar, as "A Man From Another Age" by Mike Flint, which appeared in the November 1958 issue of *Man's Illustrated*, demonstrates.

The editors claim that Mike Flint is an actual explorer of the Himalayas, when in reality the name is a probable pseudonym, and the story is outright fiction. But as a composite figure drawn from real-world figures such as Sir Edmund Hillary, Eric Shipton, and others, "Mike Flint" acts as an able avatar, well-versed and, more importantly, well-equipped to bring down his intended specimen with nary a concern for bringing one in alive.

The character of "Doc" cites sections of the book *The Story of Everest, 1921–1952* by W.H. Murray as factual proof of the existence of the Yeti. Again, this is prime MAM technique in action, using known facts with an editorial bend that suggests everything presented is beyond question, even when the material included is added for dramatic effect. The best example of this is when the heroes encounter the willing Gandaki River native women, who are very eager to bed down for fun and shelter with our delighted protagonists. This sudden left turn into consensual sex in the last place the average reader would expect such activities to happen is precisely why MAMs were so popular with their audiences. There were as many willing wanton wenches in every remote region the protagonists explored as there were varieties of menacing monsters. And while doubtlessly actual explorers have co-mingled scientific research with intimate native interactions throughout history, it was rarely as likely to happen as in a men's adventure story.

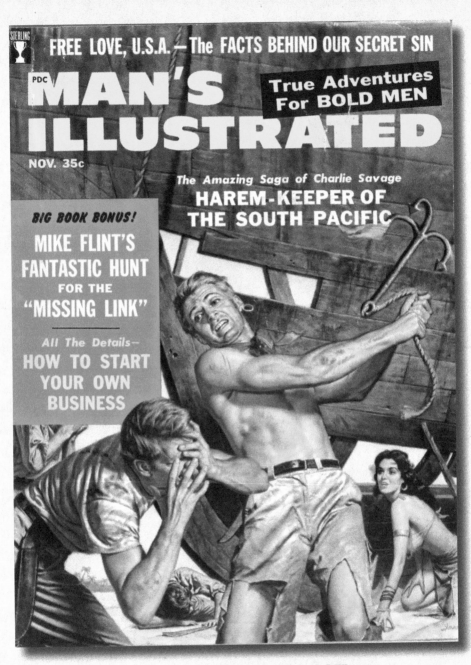

FREE LOVE, U.S.A. — The FACTS BEHIND OUR SECRET SIN

PDC

MAN'S ILLUSTRATED

True Adventures For BOLD MEN

NOV. 35c

The Amazing Saga of Charlie Savage
HAREM-KEEPER OF THE SOUTH PACIFIC

BIG BOOK BONUS!
MIKE FLINT'S FANTASTIC HUNT
FOR THE
"MISSING LINK"

All The Details—
HOW TO START YOUR OWN BUSINESS

"A MAN FROM ANOTHER AGE"
MIKE FLINT
MAN'S ILLUSTRATED, AUGUST 1959
COVER BY STANLEY BORACK

The "Abominable Snowman" is the mystery man-beast of the high Himalayas.   Here is the true

A MAN FROM ANOTHER AGE

by MIKE FLINT

EDITOR'S NOTE: Almost every spring at the height of the mountain-climbing season in the Himalayas, news stories date-lined Katmandu, Nepal, or Calcutta, India, report new sightings or tracks of a Yeti, otherwise known as Abominable Snowman. Newspapers and magazines continue to refer to the Abominable Snowman as though there was just one and not a breed.

But breed it is and horror it can be, but only Nepalese natives who have reason to fear its nocturnal attacks regard it with superstition. Other authorities besides big game hunter Michael Flint have seen an Abominable Snowman, and its tracks have been photographed. Tensing Norkay, the Sherpa who conquered Mt. Everest with Sir Edmond Hillary, has seen the skulls of two Yeti in two Nepalese monasteries. Dr. G. N. Dutt, Indian geologist, has not only seen the same skulls but at dusk one day saw the hairy, pin-headed beast itself. He also interviewed a native who fought with one and subsequently died from the infected wounds caused by its scratches. Eric Shipton and W. H. Murray, famed English mountain climbers, photographed a Yeti's tracks in snows not 24 hours old. The Swiss Mountain Climbing Expedition to Everest in 1952 reported sighting the tracks of "un abominable homme des neiges."

Why, then, hasn't this beast been photographed, or captured? There are many good reasons. One is that it is a nocturnal creature that roams the mountain slopes between 13,000 and 20,000 feet and is uncannily elusive. At such frozen heights men have a tough enough time plodding along in the rarified air without thinking of running after the swift-footed creature. Nor would they risk firing guns, for fear of starting avalanches which might engulf them.

To those who have seen an Abominable Snowman or its tracks, there is no mystery about its existence. But what tortures their imaginations and impels them to follow its tracks is the suspicion that it may be half beast, half man. It was this compulsion which sent Mike Flint off on his expedition.

MINUTES BEFORE I heard the sound, my two hounds suddenly sprang to their feet, their hackles stiffening as they stood tense at the tent flap, growling in their throats. Nothing had stirred them all evening, neither the chatter of the coolies bedding down by the fire outside nor the distant wild screams of the snow leopard.

Then I heard whatever it was that must have alerted them. It began with a gull-like mewing, then rose fiercely, excitedly, in a series of canine yelps, and broke off abruptly with a

(Continued on page 48)

story of one adventurer's hunt to capture the weirdest creature of our time.

BOOK BONUS

ARTIST UNCREDITED

EDITOR'S NOTE: *Almost every spring at the height of the mountain-climbing season in the Himalayas, news stories date-lined Katmandu, Nepal, or Calcutta, India, report new sightings or tracks of a Yeti, otherwise known as the Abominable Snowman. Newspapers and magazines continue to refer to the Abominable Snowman as though there was just one and not a breed.*

But breed it is and horror it can be, but only Nepalese natives who have reason to fear its nocturnal attacks regard it with superstition. Other authorities besides big game hunter Michael Flint have seen an Abominable Snowman, and its tracks have been photographed. Tensing Norkay, the Sherpa who conquered Mt. Everest with Sir Edmond Hillary, has seen the skulls of two Yeti in two Nepalese monasteries. Dr. G.N. Dutt, Indian geologist, has not only seen the same skulls but at dusk one day saw the hairy, pin-headed beast itself. He also interviewed a native who fought with one and subsequently died from the infected wounds caused by its scratches. Eric Shipton and W. H. Murray, famed English mountain climbers, photographed a Yeti's tracks in snows not 24-hours old. The Swiss Mountain Climbing Expedition to Everest in 1952 reported sighting the tracks of "un abominable homme des neiges."

Why, then, hasn't this beast been photographed, or captured? There are many good reasons. One is that it is a nocturnal creature that roams the mountain slopes between 13,000 and 20,000 feet and is uncannily elusive. At such frozen heights men have a tough enough time plodding along in the rarified air without thinking of running after the swift-footed creature. Nor would they risk firing guns, for fear of starting avalanches, which might engulf them.

To those who have seen an Abominable Snowman or its tracks, there is no mystery about its existence. But what tortures their imaginations and impels them to follow its tracks is the suspicion that it may be half beast, half man. It was this compulsion that sent Mike Flint off on his expedition.

Minutes before I heard the sound, my two hounds suddenly sprang to their feet, their hackles stiffening as they stood tense at the tent flap, growling in their throats. Nothing had stirred them all evening, neither the chatter of the coolies bedding down by the fire outside nor the distant wild screams of the snow leopard.

Then I heard whatever it was that must have alerted them. It began with a gull-like mewing, then rose fiercely, excitedly, in a series of canine yelps, and broke off abruptly with a snarl. It seemed to come from somewhere up the slopes of the Imja Khola Gorge.

Both dogs were quivering, and then Omar whimpered, turned, and slunk off into a corner of the tent, ashamed to look at me. Bongo held his ground as I turned down the primus lamp and went to the flap and looked out into the night. The campfire was smoldering and in its light I could see that the blankets where the coolies had been sleeping were empty. I'd had my suspicions as to what that horrible banshee howl was, and now that the men had fled, I was sure.

"Ang Phar," I called, grabbing my flashlight and going out, with Bongo at my heels.

A moment later there was a rustling among the bushes and Ang Phar walked silently toward me. "Sar?" He was my chief Sherpa guide and if he'd never known the meaning of the word fear, he did now.

"Where are the men?"

"They run away," he said. "Come back in morning. Afraid. The—" he gestured toward the slope where the sound had come from and hesitated, as though fearing to say the name of the beast that struck superstitious terror into the minds of Nepalese natives. *"The Yeh-teh,"* he whispered.

My hunch was right. It was the cry of the *Yeh-teh*, or Yeti, the Abominable Snowman, that had frightened the coolies off. And then the sound came again, closer, louder, and this time the yelping ended in what seemed like a wild, gleeful laugh. Ang Phar began to tremble, his face white.

I ran back to the tent and got my snare, my rope with the ends weighted like an Argentine bola, to trip up and immobilize the beast if I got close enough to it. "Build up the fire!" I told Ang Phar. "He won't come near you then!"

I ran across the clearing and started up the slope, with Bongo silently trotting alongside of me now, waiting for the command to go.

"All right, Bongo," I yelled, *"Go get him!"* He raced ahead as I clawed my way up the bushy, moonlit slope. A few minutes later I reached the plateau where I could see the bright moonlight gleaming on the snout of the Khumbu Glacier which stretches out toward Mount Everest. I stopped and listened, and then I, heard Bongo's bark off to the left among the rocky ledges near the Pass. I ran toward it, stumbling, as I readied my rope. The dog's barking got louder, and it sounded wild with fear as it suddenly blended with the crazy cry of the Yeh-teh. Bongo's bark suddenly became a long series of yelps and whines—and then it stopped.

I kept going, flashing my light ahead of me now, clambering over the ledges and searching the pockets among them with the beam.

At last I found Bongo, but the Yeh-teh was gone. The big mastiff lay across a ledge with his back broken, as though he'd been hurled there by a terrible force. His stomach was ripped open and his guts were spilled out in a pool of blood. Now I began to feel something of the fear that had turned Ang Phar jittery and caused the coolies to run. Stubbornly I flashed the light around among the ledges, hoping in my heart I wouldn't see anything.

I didn't. I turned around and first walked, then ran, toward the slope that led down to the camp. I hadn't seen the Yeh-teh, but I knew now what manner of beast it was. Whether it was a monkey, as some said, or part bear, as others claimed, or half-human, as the natives feared, didn't matter. I'd just found out that it was a blood-thirsty murderer.

It was in the bar of Spence's Hotel in Calcutta, India that

my adventure got its start. Spence's is the spot where travelers back from *shikars* (or *safaris*, as they say in Africa), gather to blow about the tiger they shot, and British, French, Swiss, or German mountaineers stop en route to or from expeditions to Annapurna, Nanga Parbat, Dhaulagiri, or Mount Everest for a drink and a discussion of their dreams. Actually my involvement in the escapade was due to curiosity, conversation, and committing myself when cornered.

There were six of us sitting around one of the big tables. Bill Gregory, an alcoholic English mountaineer who never seemed to make it beyond the base camp of any expedition; Dr. Govind Chetsingh, better known as Chet or Doc, an Indian M.D. whose hobbies were zoology, anthropology, talking, and drinking; myself, an American who never could stay put anywhere long but had been hanging around India the last four years acting as interpreter, guide, hunting companion, and shill for tourist agencies catering to wealthy travelers looking for excitement; and three strangers in fancy hunting clothes, the only one of whose names I caught was Randell, a Canadian.

Billy was off on one of his stories about an adventure he'd had in the high Himalayas, and he was a pistol with a yarn. Everyone sat enthralled as he came to the end of it: "I was numb with cold and didn't think I'd ever make it across the *col*—I'd just lost my way, it was as stupid as that. Then suddenly I looked up and saw this figure—was it a man? I couldn't tell. But I knew by some instinct that if I went toward him I wouldn't go plunging off down the scree or over a cliff. He was about 200 yards away and as I got nearer I saw that it wasn't a man—not really—but a hairy fellow who looked like a primitive man. He had an acorn shaped head and hair all over him and the sun glinted on what seemed to be fangs. I'd been keeping my eye on him to make sure of my way—but suddenly I looked down to get my footing, and saw these monstrous tracks in the snow, like enormous bare human footprints. It shook me, I can assure you. I stopped, and looked up, but the creature had disappeared. I'd never gotten any closer than 100 yards of him, but I knew then that at last I'd seen the Abominable Snowman."

There was a moment's silence at the table, and I looked around the room and sized up the female talent as I waited for the reaction to Billy's story. As I say, he was a pistol at spinning a yarn and I never knew whether to believe him or not. Neither, apparently, did the others.

Then the Canadian called Randell laughed, as though testing to make sure Billy wasn't pulling his leg. "You really believe in this Yeti—isn't that it?—this Abominable Snowman?"

Billy raised an eyebrow and looked hurt. He picked up his swizzle stick and began stirring the drink the waiter had put in front of him. Before answering, he lifted the drink, looked at it carefully, and sipped approvingly with the aplomb of a connoisseur—and then slugged it down fast like a skid-row bum. "Of course!" he said, stroking his thin moustache with an unsteady finger. "Others have seen the beast—the creature—or whatever it is. And famous climbers like Eric Shipton have even photographed the footprint."

Randell still smiled suspiciously, but when his two companions snorted and got up to go he stayed put. "See you later," the spare, bald, and middle-aged Canadian said to his friends. Then he turned back to Billy. "Did any of the others on your expedition see the Yeti?"

"I don't think you believe me, Randell," Billy said with the exaggerated dignity of one who's had too much to drink. He snapped his fingers for the waiter to bring him the same again.

"Of course I do—" muttered the Canadian in the voice of a man humoring a drunk.

"No you don't," insisted Billy. "No one else saw the Snowman that trip—but they did see his tracks. We didn't get pictures because it was so bloody cold that the camera shutter froze stuck and so," he made an empty gesture, "I have no proof. *But it is true.*"

Billy, a handsome devil who reminded me of Ronald Colman in his prime, was hurt and as angry as it was possible for him to get. Somehow I knew he wasn't lying.

"He probably did see him, Randell," said Doc Chetsingh quietly. "Plenty of reliable Sherpas—the Nepalese natives—have seen the Yeti. And I've talked with many mountaineers who have come across its tracks."

"Then it's not just a myth?" Randell asked.

Doc shook his head. The squat, chubby Indian wore thick glasses that gave his liquid brown eyes an almost hypnotic quality. "It's a myth only so far as the superstitious natives have exaggerated its powers and frightened travelers have distorted its size. But there's no doubt that it exists. It roams the region between the timber line and the snow line of the Himalayas— roughly, that's between 13,000 and 18,000 feet. They're a hardy breed."

"They're a breed? You mean there's more than *one* Abominable Snowman?" Randell asked. "Then why aren't they seen more often?"

I'd had quite a few gin-and-tonics so I decided to get a word in and show off what little I knew. "They're nocturnal characters for one thing," I told him. "For another, there aren't many expeditions into the Himalayas—and when white men with cameras do pass through you can't expect the Yeti to come jumping out to be photographed. Especially since the climbing expeditions travel with scores of coolie bearers and Sherpa guides—"

"That's a formidable group for a creature that travels either by himself or with just his mate," Doc broke in. "No matter how savage he may be, he'd be frightened off by that many men." Doc went on to run down the known history of the Yeti, referring to episodes in which Sherpas had fought with them, natives had mysteriously disappeared from spots where their footprints met those of the Yeti's, and the accounts Tibetan monks gave of the *shupka*, their name for the creature. He referred to Eric Shipton's story, which was confirmed by W.H. Murray in his book, *The Story of Everest*. Murray was a mountaineer who sighted the Yeti tracks three days after Shipton. Doc also brought in the evidence of Dr. G.N. Dutt, an Indian geologist who interviewed natives who had seen and even fought with the monster.

"It's fascinating," Randell said.

"The whole thing has intrigued me for years," Doc sighed, "and I've always wanted to do something about it. Track it down—see what kind of creature it really is. Some people try to pass it off as a species of langur monkey—others say it comes from the bear family. Others who've seen it swear it's more than ape. I'd like to find out. Funny thing is, in three days I have to go up to Namche Bazaar which is right in the heart of the Yeti country. There's been an outbreak of smallpox up there and I'm awaiting some serum before going up to relieve the doctor that's there." He shrugged his shoulders. "It would cost money to outfit a proper expedition to hunt the creature and try to bring one back alive. And you'd need good, experienced men—like Billy here, with mountain climbing experience—and you, Yank, because you're a good stalker and hunter."

"Just call on me any time you dig up the money, Doc," I laughed. "I'm sick of leading wealthy squares around on *shikars* just so's they can shoot a trophy to take home." I looked at Billy. "It should appeal to you too, Gregory."

"It'd be wizard," he said. He gave Randell a malicious grin, and added, "Then if we brought one back, *some* people wouldn't doubt my stories."

Randell laughed. "I'm sorry," he said, "but you can't blame me. After all, up until now I've just heard the exaggerated stories—the myths, I guess." He turned to Doc and asked seriously, "You mean you'd actually hunt this monster if you could outfit an expedition?"

Doc laughed wryly. "Like a shot. But—"

"And you two would go with him?" Randell continued.

"Sure," I said, and Billy nodded. "But the combined income of the three of us would hardly pay for our personal camping gear—"

"Then let me finance the expedition," Randell said, suddenly taking command of the conversation as he got on a subject he apparently was intimate with—money. "Now I'm curious too. I couldn't survive the climb or the altitude but I'd like to have my name associated with the project." He pushed his chair back and got up. "Is it a deal?" he asked crisply.

We looked at each other, slightly dumbstruck, and just nodded. Anything would have sounded good, the way I was feeling.

"Good," said Randell. "Tonight you figure out just how much money you're going to need—and don't skimp, mind you—and I'll go round to Barclay's Bank and cash a draft as soon as you give me the estimate tomorrow morning."

He shook hands with each of us in turn and as he came to Doc he said, "I noticed when you talked about the Yeti you didn't call it a beast or an animal—you kept referring to it as a *creature*. Does that mean that you figure it might even possibly be some kind of human monster?"

Doc looked startled, almost as though the man had eavesdropped on some secret thought. Then the Indian gave him a slow mysterious smile. "Now that's a very intriguing thought," he said cryptically, "and I'll let you know how right it is as soon as we get our hands on one of the—er—*creatures*."

Randell had the money for us next morning within an hour after we'd presented him with our estimate of what it would cost to outfit and supply the expedition. Randell's only kick was that we'd failed to include salaries for ourselves, and insisted on throwing in a couple of thousand rupees per man as an advance. It never occurred to any of us—not at the time, at least—that we'd have been smart to invest it in life or accident insurance.

We had no trouble getting our visas confirmed at the Nepalese consulate since we were accompanying Doc on his errand of mercy, though we'd never have had a prayer of getting into Nepal if we'd been a party of hunters or unscheduled mountain climbers. It takes practically a government edict to get permission to go mountain climbing, while any shooting that has to be done is left to government patrols, which only kill tigers, panthers, bears, wolves, and snow leopards when they turn marauder and attack cattle and people. Bringing guns into the country is taboo, and since we were quite possibly going to need them in self-defense against the Yeti or whatever else we might encounter, our only hope was to smuggle them in.

Accordingly, when Doc and Randell took off for Katmandu, the capital of Nepal, Billy and I got a plane for Delhi, India. There we bought a Land Rover, a glorified British jeep, and loaded it down with supplies and equipment. We dismantled our guns and hid the parts amongst our tools, Alpine gear, tent poles and stakes, and then took off across the United Provinces for the Nepalese border.

"All I hope," said Billy as we bumped through the elephant grass and choking dust en route north, "is that these ruddy border guards won't know the difference between a gunstock and an Alpenstock. Granted we want to capture a Yeti alive, but I'm damned if I want to try to do it unarmed. If the guards take our guns away, we've had it."

"We'll just have to practice some more with the bolas," I said. "Right now the only thing I can be sure of snaring is myself." The bola, the "lasso" used by the Argentine gaucho, or cowboy, was the most practical solution to the problem of catching the Yeti.

The short length of rope has weights at its ends, and is swung around over the head until it gains terrific momentum, and then let fly at the animal you hope to bring down. The rope strikes your quarry's legs, tripping it up, while the weights whip around to securely entangle them.

As it turned out, we were needlessly worried about the border guards, for although they actually handled some of the gun parts while examining our luggage, they weren't aware of it and passed us through the customs station at Negalpan.

Then we started the slow climb into the Himalayan foothills, stopping overnight at the Dak bungalows, the government rest houses that are used by travelers in the wilds.

We made slow forward progress as the foothills steepened, but we were climbing to eight, nine, 10,000 feet, and the nights were getting colder. By day, however, a hot sun beat down on us and the rapidly changing temperatures and the rare air proved exhausting. As we lurched along the rocky trail beside the Gandaki River late one afternoon, we spotted a Dak bungalow in the distance and decided to put up for the night. We weren't far from Riri, but we weren't sure whether the town had been hit by the smallpox epidemic. Even though we'd been inoculated in Calcutta against just about everything, we didn't want to take any chances.

As the Land Rover chugged up to the bungalow I suddenly heard screams in the distance. I quickly shut off the motor and listened. We heard the shrill sounds again, mingled with laughter and a babble of talk.

"Women!" said Billy, fingering his moustache and popping his eyes comically.

We jumped out of the Land Rover and headed for the river where we found a couple of tethered donkey carts that contained salt and rice. We pushed through some wild bushes to the river bank and there, not a dozen yards away, were four naked Nepalese girls thrashing around in the water and throwing lotus leaves at each other. None of them was more then 18, but these girls, it was enchantingly obvious, matured early.

Suddenly one of them turned toward shore to grab for a handful of lotus leaves, which float like lily pads in the river, and spotted us. She gave a startled cry and squeaked something to her friends. They all looked up, standing unembarrassedly waist-deep in the water, and just stared. We stared right back.

I smiled, and one of them giggled and said something to her friends. Slowly they waded out of the river and approached us, all jabbering at once, and laughing when we failed to understand their language. I tried a little Hindu, which didn't register. My throat was a little tight and I noticed beads of sweat on Billy's forehead as the four girls stood in front of us completely nude, their only covering their sleek black hair, which clung wetly to their dusky shoulders.

They were amazingly friendly and completely unashamed of their nudity, and when they started toward a clearing in the bushes they motioned for us to follow. There they had laid out their clothes, bright-colored saris, which they took their time putting on. As they combed out each other's hair and tucked lotus blossoms above their ears, one of the girls spotted our Land Rover through a gap in the bushes.

Instantly she went into a flurry of talk and began gesturing excitedly. From the sign language I realized she was asking us if we were sleeping that night in the rest house. Outside of a few common expressions and some technical words needed when we bought supplies, I knew no Nepalese. I just nodded, and the girls started laughing, jabbered some more, and then ran to their donkey carts.

I looked at Billy, mystified. "What'd I do? Looks like they're leaving."

"Oh, not a bit of it," he chuckled. "They just ran to feed the animals and get some rice to make supper. They said they'll be spending the night in the rest house too—"

I just looked at the guy, remembering suddenly that he'd been on four expeditions in Nepal and spent months in the company of native coolies and Sherpas. "Why, you dog, you," I said, "I must have looked like a fool making with the sign language. Why didn't you talk to them?"

Billy laughed and shook his head slowly. "I wasn't trying to make a fool of you, Mike, believe me. It's better that they think we're complete strangers. If they learned that I'd been here before they'd be afraid I knew one of their relatives—one of the guides maybe, or a porter—and the chances are they'd be right.

We're near the region where we hired our natives, you know. So it's best to play dumb and then they'll behave naturally." He gave me the moustache-twirl bit, and the wolfish wink. "*Real* naturally."

We went to the Land Rover and dug out some rations, the primus stove, and a couple of pressure lamps, which we took into the rest house. As soon as we dumped the stuff on a table, Billy ducked out and brought back the transistor radio which he quickly tuned in and got some music. He turned it up loud and a moment later the girls came running in to marvel at the gadget.

With the two lamps burning brightly and the table covered with blankets we got from the car, we had quite a gala feast, and when it was over the girls ran to the river and washed up the dishes as Billy and I lay back on a couple of the beds and smoked. When they came back they made signs for us to turn the light down low and turn up the radio.

They took turns dancing, and when they weren't dancing they sat close beside us on the beds and watched the girl who was performing. They couldn't have been more graceful as each one went through her dance, which was a cross between a Tibetan Temple Dance and a strip tease. It was all interpretative and entirely individual, each girl throwing in little variations that progressed from gentle fluid movements to wild, abandoned, whirling and leaping. The girls' hair, which they'd worn knotted at the nape of the neck, came loose and swirled around their heads as they spun right out of their saris and came to rest naked in a

cross-legged Buddha posture on the floor. Throughout the entire performance the music played seductively and the fragrance of the lotus blossoms was heavy in the air.

I stroked the soft skin of the girl who sat beside me, and she looked at me with large, liquid eyes. "This is what Nirvana, the Buddhist heaven, must be like," I muttered to Billy.

"You're so right," he said.

Suddenly the girl beside me got up and went across the room and pulled back the covers on one of the beds. She dropped her sari on the floor and got into bed as the other girls followed across the room. She propped her head up on the pillow and looked across at me and smiled. She closed her eyes tight, and shivered expressively. I didn't need an interpreter to get the idea that she was cold in there by herself. She patted the blanket suggestively, smiled, and said, "—Ah cha?"

That was one Nepalese expression I knew.

"Ah cha!" I said; okay.

I stood up and turned out the first lamp, and as soon as Billy made his way across the room I turned out the other. I had no trouble finding my way to where I was going in the darkness, and a moment after I'd gotten settled I heard a giggle from one of the other girls.

"Ah cha?" she called from her bed.

I couldn't answer that one. I didn't know the native word for maybe.

Three days later we rolled into Katmandu and found Randell holed up in the Nepal Hotel, impatiently waiting for us. It was an ancient relic of a place, drafty and full of worn and faded luxury.

"Quite a place," I grinned at Randell, looking around the cavernous lobby where our drinks were served.

"I have a distinguished bed," grumbled Randell. "I'm certain that Kipling slept there—" He gulped his drink, and continued, "—very recently."

He briefed us on what he'd arranged so far, and Doc's plans for getting the show on the road. Doc had hired porters and Sherpas from Panga, which was unaffected by the smallpox epidemic. It was only a day's march from Namche Bazaar. Randell showed us the spot on the map, an elevation a few miles from Namche Bazar in the Dudh Kosi Valley, where we were to rendezvous with the men in two days.

"Doc's at Namche Bazaar now," Randell said. "He doesn't want you to risk the disease, despite all those inoculations you got in Calcutta, so you're to bypass the town and set up your camp. He'll contact you soon after you arrive."

Randell had bought another jeep, which was garaged in back of the hotel, loaded with supplies. He couldn't take the altitude much longer and he was going back to Calcutta where we were to keep him posted on all developments. The next morning we took off with Billy driving the Land Rover and I the jeep, and headed for Namche Bazaar. It was an awesomely beautiful trip through the valley, on all sides of which rose snow-capped peaks not one of which was under 20,000 feet. In the distance, to the northeast, a veil of snow clung to the leeward side of Mt. Everest and puffy white clouds hung around its base.

We skirted Namche Bazaar to make our presence known, and then proceeded to the elevation east of town where we set up our camp. After raising our tent and sorting out the supplies, we waited for Doc to appear.

He arrived some hours later sitting in a basket-chair strapped to the back of a native porter, and trotting alongside them was a wispy-bearded old man who wasn't even breathing hard after his climb. Doc jumped down and before he said a word he headed straight for the primus stove on which we had tea brewing. He poured himself a cup, laced it liberally with gin from a bottle sticking out of Billy's rucksack, and gulped it down. Then he grinned with satisfaction and looked at us owlishly from behind his thick glasses.

"I've been living on Benzedrine for the last five days," he said, "and this is a nice change. It's been hell down in the village. The doctor I came to relieve is sick, and I've had a devil of a time trying to keep the sick natives in the emergency hospital I've set up. Some of them sneak out and go into the hills to take care of their yak herds." He picked up a couple of tin mugs and filled them with tea, powdered milk, and molasses and handed them to the porter and the old man.

"The old one here is Sarkay," Doc said. "He can't speak English. But the porter will be able to interpret for him. Right, Tamang?"

"Yiss, sar," grinned the broad-shouldered native.

"Sarkay was up on the slope rounding up a couple of strays
the other evening—it was three days ago," Doc said. "He was
following their trail and suddenly he got an uncanny feeling that
he was being watched. He looked around, thinking he'd see one of
the other villagers, but all he saw in the twilight was a movement
in some bushes, which he blamed on the wind. He continued
looking for his wandering yaks and took a trail that put him
downwind of the spot where he'd seen the rustling bushes. Then
he smelled an appalling stench that sent a shiver of fear through
him. He knew instinctively that he was being watched—probably
followed—and that the unseen thing was a Yeh-teh."

"Just by the smell?" I asked.

Doc fixed himself another cup of tea and went on. "Yes.
In Nepalese, Yeh-teh means literally 'wild man of the snows,'
but the Tibetans call it *Metch Kangmi* or *Shupka*. *Kangmi* means
'snowman,' but *metch* means filthy, dirty, unwashed to a disgusting
degree, and stinking. Hence, abominable. They can be smelled 100
yards away if the wind is right—or wrong, I should say. Sarkay
knew damn well there was a Yeti nearby and he started to run just
as the sun sank behind the mountains, and plunged the slope into
darkness. He was in a terrible spot because he was near the edge
of the ravine, and if he kept going he might lose his footing and
go over. He was scared to death of the Yeti but he was a lot more
scared of certain death if he fell—so he turned back and started
yelling for help at the top of his lungs. He walked cautiously
back along the trail—yelling from time to time to give himself
courage."

And then, Doc went on, just as Sarkay reached the pile of
stones that marked the safe path down the slope to the grazing
grounds, the Yeti leaped out at him. Sarkay didn't see a thing
but he felt the creature's hot breath on him and he nearly passed
out from the awful stench. Suddenly the Yeti grabbed at him and
Sarkay screamed in terror—and just as abruptly as the creature
had materialized, he disappeared. Then Sarkay staggered down to
the valley, nearly out of his mind with fear."

I thought about the story a moment, and then looked at
Bill. He shook his head slowly and grinned. "Sounds like a case
of hysteria to me. He didn't see anything, and he *says* that the

creature grabbed him. As for the smell, a powerful superstitious fear such as Sarkay's could have exaggerated any sensory experience."

Doc nodded. "That's what I thought too." He turned to Tamang. "Tell Sarkay to open his robe."

Tamang rattled off something in Nepalese and the old man obediently opened his robe and revealed his chest and stomach. I had to turn away after one look. Three deep scratch marks and the faint trace of a fourth extended down from his collarbone to his navel, and every one of them was oozing a yellow-black pus. Then I got a full whiff of the foul stench of the man's wounds. Quickly Sarkay covered up again and clasped the robe tight around his neck in an attempt to contain the noxious odor.

"That was the result of a mere *grab*," Doc said. "I've put all sorts of medicines on those lesions and they just won't heal. It's almost as though the creature is so filthy that it's poisonous. And I haven't got the antidote yet."

"That's good to know just in case we should snare one," Billy said. "We'll keep clear until we can lasso and bind his ruddy paws."

"*Or hands,*" Doc said slowly. "*Did you notice the wounds on Sarkay's body? They're exactly like the scratch-marks that a human hand would make!*"

Doc had to get back to the town to tend to his patients, but he said he'd be back in the morning when the Sherpas and coolies from Panga showed up. He had arranged for the delivery of a couple of huge hounds from Darjeeling, in northern Bengal, and they were due to arrive the next day. The dogs were trained to take English commands and, having been used on commercial *shikars*, were obedient to strangers—once properly introduced by the trainer. They'd been used to hunt wild boar and bear in Bengal, Sikkim, and Bhutan and were supposedly able to tree or tear apart anything twice their size.

Just as Doc was boarding the chair on Tamang's back he remembered that he'd brought something along for us. From under the chair he unstrapped half a dozen books he'd picked up in Katmandu, all dealing with sightings of, and experiences with, the Abominable Snowman.

"A lot of this stuff is sheer nonsense," he said, "since some wild tales told by terrified natives are included. But I recommend

Ralph Izzard's book, *'The Abominable Snowman,'* and Shipton's
and Tilman's books. There are some magazine articles tucked
in among them too, written by scientists who've speculated on
just what manner of creature it is from the evidence that's been
gathered so far." He mounted the chair and Tamang stood up
as Sarkay walked over beside him. "I'll bring these two back
tomorrow," Doc said, "so Sarkay can show you exactly where
the Yeti attacked him—and maybe you can start tracking from
there. By the way, I'd advise you to keep a roaring fire going by
the entrance to your tent. The natives say that fire's the one thing
sure to keep the Yeti away." He tapped Tamang's shoulder, said
good night, and the trio moved down the hill.

That night, as we kept the fire blazing outside our tent, we
skimmed through some of the books, and Billy kept nipping at
the bottle of gin. I read that the Yeh-teh is commonly believed to
be a hulking, thick-set creature, covered with coarse brown fur,
and has arms that hang to its knees. It stands anywhere from five-
foot-four to five-foot-eight, according to most reports, though a
company of hard-bitten Sikh soldiers who sighted one all swore
that it was 12-feet tall. It walks and runs on two feet, even uphill,
and never scampers on all fours like a bear or an ape, which has
been consistently proved by its tracks. Leading zoologists believe
it is somewhere in the category between ape and man. Until they
had more evidence, no scientist dared come out and write that it
was the "missing link."

Despite early beliefs that the Snowman's "feet were on
backwards," with the toes pointing aft, all recent sightings as
well as the pressure-indentations in its tracks contradict this. Its
diet consists chiefly of voles, or mouse hares, marmots, and rock
rats, which it kills by hurling against rocks and then disembowels,
tossing away the guts and eating the rest. It avoids populated
areas but has been known to kill cattle and attack humans. The
only real physical evidence of the Yetis' existence, in addition to
the rumors of sightings and the photographs of its tracks, are a
couple of scalps in a Buddhist temple at Pangboche village. These
have been seen and examined by many scientists who've visited
the temple, and they cannot identify the helmet-shaped, pointed-
peak, coarse-furred scalps as belonging to any animal known
to science. These scalps are thicker than yak-hide and covered

with reddish, bristly hair several inches long. The scalps would fit perfectly the acorn-shaped head of the big-fanged, wrestler-necked monster many witnesses have described.

Tensing Norkay, the Sherpa, who with Sir Edmond Hillary reached the summit of Mount Everest, includes stories of the Yeti in his autobiography. His father encountered one on the Barun Glacier, a female with long hanging breasts, and it ran away whistling shrilly when it saw him. So strong was his superstition of the evil spell the Yeti cast that he was sick, and for a while near death, for almost a year. He saw another one years later, and in each case he noted that the creature ran like a human being and not an ape.

I was so absorbed in my reading I nearly jumped a foot when I heard a loud metallic crack. I looked up to see Billy examining his Webley .38 pistol. He was swaying a little and I looked down at the gin bottle and saw it was empty. He spun the chamber and then examined it closely when it stopped.

"What the hell are you doing?" I asked.

He looked up and gave me a lopsided grin. "Just seein' what kind of luck I'd have these days," he said. "Used to play Russian roulette with this bloody sidearm once—and they tell me I was *lucky* I didn't blow my brains out." He put the gun down on the bed beside him, and looked at me with all the exaggerated earnestness of a drunk who was about to tell you something confidential.

"You know, Yank—I mean Mike—we've got to catch that bloody beast," he said, trying to focus his eyes. We've got to—*I've* got to. All my life a bloody failure. Charming boy. Charming man. Ev-a-body's pal. Kicked out of school. Booted out of Cambridge. Reinstated, and then booted out again—"

"All right, Billy," I said, embarrassed. "Why'n't you get some shut-eye?"

"No, no Mike. Got to tell you this. Get it off my chest." He hiccupped, picked up the gin bottle, saw there was a drop left, and drank it. "Along comes World War II. Chance to make a name for myself—or end all my troubles. It didn't much matter which. Parents fed up with me anyway. What happens? I join the Rifle Brigade and when the Jerries break through, I run out on my buddies like a scared rabbit. But no one ever caught me because that was just before the retreat to Dunkirk. I come home a hero like all the rest, but then I get sent to Africa. Out there on patrols I was scared. Damned scared. That's when I used to play Russian roulette—hoping I'd lose so I wouldn't have to be scared any more. When the Germans attacked I ran from the fighting again. This time my men—and my fellow officers—they saw me. I was court-martialed. 'Lack of moral fiber,' they call it. In other words, no guts. A coward. Cashiered and reduced to the ranks. Made me a hospital orderly. Believe me, I—"

"You shouldn't tell me this, Billy. How—"

"*Billy!* By God, doesn't that just fit the situation? Billy! Who the hell ever heard of a grown man of 36 being called Billy?" He spat contemptuously. "No one but me—because I never bloody well grew up and couldn't get anyone's respect. So as I was saying, I finished out the war as a hospital orderly and when I got back to England I found that everybody knew about what happened and my parents and my girl wanted no part of me. My father offered me an allowance with the condition I get the hell out of England. So I came to India. I was going to prove to everyone I was a man. The bottle helped me feel that I could make it."

He broke off, reached down to rummage in his kit bag, and came out with another bottle of gin. I knew better than to say anything. He bit out the cork and took a long swig.

"I was real brave when I was drunk—but I meant it even when I was sober. I was going to do something heroic. So I joined up with a mountain climbing expedition, and then another, and another. Everest. Nanda Devi. Nanga Parbat. Kang Peak. What happened? Every time the same thing. Ol' Billy can't make it beyond the base camp. Hasn't the guts to climb the faces, walls—the tough part. Always that way."

He slapped the cork on the bottle and dropped it on his bed. "But now I'm going to do something." He lay back on his pillow. "That Yeh-teh is the challenge. If I catch that beast it'll blot out everything in the past. And I'm going to get that ruddy monster if it kills me!"

He didn't say anything after that. He passed out cold.

The next morning Doc and his two companions, as well as the dogs, the Sherpas, and the coolie porters arrived on schedule.

Ang Phar, famous in the Himalayas for his strength and bravery, was the *sirdar*, or leader, of the contingent, which consisted of three Sherpa guides and 12 porters.

Our first job, while Sarkay was still in shape to do it, was to reconnoiter the area where the old man had had his encounter with the Yet-teh. It was a long haul up the steep slopes that leveled out here and there to permit grazing. At last we came to the pile of stones near where Sarkay had been attacked. Through Tamang, the interpreter, we got a vivid picture of the old man's experience and how the Yeh-teh attacked him. We had a clear view of all paths leading up and down the slopes. Billy drew a rough sketch of routes to explore up the glacier as well as down along the timber line, far east into the Dudh Kosi Valley. High up at 19,000 feet was the Nangpa La Pass, where Yeh-tehs had been seen from a great distance. Doc told us that some of the clearest Snowman tracks ever seen had been discovered in the snows there by the natives. Our pursuit of the beast might even take us up there, adding the hazard of the climb to the menace of the monster.

As we went back down to our camp I thought of all the effort and danger involved in the hunt, and what it meant to each one of us connected with the expedition. To Randell, our backer, capturing the Yeh-teh meant prestige and automatic admission to Explorers' Clubs everywhere. It would give his wealth a little glamour. To Doc, it meant scientific renown, and the making of him as a zoologist and a person of consequence in India. And to Billy it meant redemption—the atonement and justification for a life that had been a scandalous succession of cowardly failures.

And what did it mean to me? What was my motive?

Suddenly I stopped as I realized what it was, and started to laugh.

The Sherpas kept going, politely ignoring me, but Doc and Billy stopped, looking at me in concern. "What's so funny, Mike?" Doc asked, instinctively looking close for a sign of fever.

"Nothing," I grinned. "Just something that struck me funny."

Bill tapped his finger to his temple and smiled. "Poor chap's around the bend. Daft, these Americans!"

We moved on. Billy was so right. Daft, touched in the head. Just a typical American with that inborn yen for adventure. A screwball whose only reward would be kicks, and perhaps the satisfying of a curiosity.

It was enough. More than enough.

That night the Sherpas celebrated their association with a new expedition, as was the Himalayan custom, by throwing a brawl in which gallons of *chang* and *rakhsi*, the native beer and wine, were consumed. And the next morning, despite heads that pounded, we started training for the grind ahead.

I worked with Neppu, the dog-trainer, and learned all the commands and got the confidence of Omar and Bongo, the hounds, while Billy spent his time practicing with the bola. Then we switched exercises, and I worked with the "lasso" until I could bring down Ang Phar, acting as a running quarry, 9 times out of 10 from 20 yards away. At night when Doc was able to get away from his medical duties for a while, we planned our overall strategy and networked the map with routes we'd explore. The smallpox epidemic was going to keep Doc from making the climb up the slope with us, which I figured was just as well. The short, chubby doctor was no tiger for exercise and he'd only have slowed us up on the climb.

During these shakedown days there'd been no reported sightings of the Yeh-teh; nothing had been seen of any of "them" since Sarkay's experience. It was decided that Billy and I would split up the men and supplies and proceed via separate roundabout routes to a rendezvous at the 15,000 foot level, where we'd meet four days hence. That way we'd cover twice the area and investigate double the number of suspected Yeh-teh lairs as we climbed.

I took Ang Phar and six of the coolies, while Billy's detachment consisted of the other two Sherpa guides and the remaining half-dozen porters. When it came to the dogs, I asked him which one he wanted.

"Take 'em both," he said, not meeting my eye. "I—I don't seem to—to be able to work with them."

It was true that he had gotten only half-hearted cooperation from the hounds during the training period, and it was because his commands lacked decision and crisp authority. Remembering his drunken confession, I could almost read his thoughts: *It's no use*, I could hear him telling himself, *even the dogs don't respect me*. It was a damn shame that Billy, one of the nicest guys I'd ever met, had to torture himself with his feelings of guilt and self-doubt.

After we'd loaded each porter with a rucksack containing about a *maund*, the Nepalese weight unit of 80 pounds, we took off. Billy's group started climbing immediately while I proceeded on down the valley of the Dudh Khosi, or "River of Milk," which flows from the melting glaciers of Everest. After traveling a few miles we started a gradual climb, and by evening we were on a wide plateau overlooking the village of Damdang.

We set up my tent but the coolies didn't bother with theirs; they wouldn't sleep in a shelter until we reached the snow line. I spent the early part of the evening planning the next day's route with Ang Phar, and before going to bed I put my bola in a handy spot and my gun under my pillow. It was just as I was starting to take off my clothes that the two hounds leaped to their feet and started growling; it was the night that Bongo was killed by the Yeh-Teh.

When I got back to camp after that wild chase, I told Ang Phar what had happened and the next morning we went up the slope to look for the dog's body. It was gone. When I looked at Ang Phar's face, I saw that he was really shook up, more so than the night before. People of the western world may think of the Oriental face as emotionless and inscrutable, but anyone could have seen the shadow of terror crossing Ang Phar's face.

"*Chutrey?*" he said aloud, more to himself than to me. "*Metrey?* Which Yeh-teh is it?"

I remembered what I'd read in Tensing's autobiography about the Sherpa beliefs. They believe that there are two types of Yeh-teh: the *chutrey*, which lives on small animals, and the *metrey*, which is a maneater. Ang Phar seemed to be thinking that anything that would kill and make off with a huge beast like Bongo was obviously no *chutrey*.

I clapped him on the back and said cheerfully, "Forget it, Ang Phar. Let's not worry until we see the thing."

Ang Phar shrugged and bent to look at the faint trace of a blood-stained footprint on the ledge. "It is not easy to forget, sar," he said looking up. "Not when I have bad dreams of *metrey*, the maneater, ever since I am baby."

Frightened or not, Ang Phar was above all a dutiful Sherpa

guide and set out to do the job he was being paid for. He
tracked the faint footprints of the Yeh-teh, just smudges really,
and followed them as they became nothing more than subtle
impressions on the gravel or earth. He finally lost the trail on the
rock ledges just above the timber line.

"I feel he is somewhere near," Ang Phar said. "Perhaps hiding
in the crags above us. They sometimes make what we call 'nests'
of bushboughs in the rocky places. Perhaps the dog Omar can
trail him."

I explained that I'd left the dog behind because of his terror
last night, and hadn't wanted to make things worse by letting him
see Bongo's remains.

"It is just as well. He would have seen the blood of his friend
today. But the dog will be all right for trailing." We turned and
started down the slope and suddenly I understood why Ang Phar
had said, *"I feel he is somewhere near."* My skin crawled at the back
of my neck as I sensed that from some hidden place the creature's
eyes were on me.

Suddenly I was hurled to the ground as a terrific force hit me
in the middle of my back, and a moment later I found Ang Phar
on top of me, grabbing me hard to keep me from sliding down the
slope. We both got up quickly and Ang Phar pointed to a rock the
size of a basketball that bounced on down the slope.

"The Yeh-teh threw that," Ang Phar said. "I had a sudden '
fear—and turned around—and saw hairy arms raised just over
that cliff." He pointed upward. "And then the rock came and I had
no time to yell. I just knocked you down."

I shook his hand and he grinned at me. "That's why the dog
will be all right for trailing. Fear make eyes, nose, and ears very
sharp."

And thank God for your sixth sense, too, I thought, as we headed
for the camp.

The porters had returned to the camp when we got there,
sheepishly avoiding my eyes because of their shame at having
deserted me the night before. I didn't say anything, but Ang Phar
gave them hell, and in a little while they were scurrying around
getting things ready to move to a spot up the valley where we'd
meet them later.

I put a leash on Omar. Then I tried a few practice throws

with the bola before hitching it to my belt and starting out after
the Yeh-teh with Ang Phar. We went back up the slope and circled
for miles looking for an approach to the cliff from which the
Yeh-teh had hurled the stone. En route we crossed its footprints
and Omar, trembling slightly, had apparently caught a scent and
sniffed along ahead of us trying to pick it up again as we climbed
around the rocky ledges.

Suddenly as we reached what seemed to be the northern
approach to the cliff on which the Yeh-teh had holed up, Omar
started straining at the leash and whimpering. I let him pull me
and presently we rounded a rock abutment and the dog began
yelping wildly. He was like a Geiger counter gone berserk. All
over the cliff lay the foul-smelling waste of the Yeh-teh, but what
had really sent Omar wild was the partly gnawed skull of Bongo,
lying amidst the bones and fur of the Yeh-teh's past meals. Omar
sniffed once at Bongo's skull, then started to growl. There was a
setback in the cliff a little further on, and here we found the Yeh-
teh's nest.

It was like a bed of boughs that campers make, with the
exception that it smelled to high heaven. Omar nearly pulled my
arm out of its socket as he charged around looking for the beast.
Deep in the setback we found more bones, and then Ang Phar
gave a startled grunt and bent over and picked up a shredded
bit of bright red cloth. He threw it aside and began rummaging
among the bones and in a moment picked up what looked like a
human thighbone, and after a few busy moments, the scattered
bones of a human hand. He stood transfixed for just a moment,
and then slowly turned and looked at me.

"*Metrey,*" he said. "It's the maneater. There is no doubt."

With a sense of desperation I gave Omar his head, and he
pulled me, with Ang Phar following closely, around a rocky ledge
that stuck out from a sheer wall of stone rising high above us.
The ledge narrowed, and then ended abruptly. There was nowhere
to go but up or down—a sheer drop below, and above, a straight
wall of rock. We backed cautiously to a wider section of the ledge
and I turned to Ang Phar.

"Where could it have gone?" I said.

He pointed up the wall that no mountain climber without
an alpine axe, pitons, and rappels could hope to get up or down.

There was no hand-hold or foot-hold apparent anywhere.

"That is one reason we fear them," said Ang Phar. "They can climb anywhere—they are like ghosts." He shuddered as he looked over at the crushed bones. "They are monsters."

It was late in the afternoon when we met the coolies at the designated spot and found them in a state of fearful excitement. They kept looking up the mountain, and then down toward the little village of Shaksum, which lay in the valley far below. It didn't take Ang Phar long to find out what it was all about: a Yeh-teh had raided an outlying dwelling a few nights before and made off with a little girl. The child had wandered off while her father was tending his yaks, and when he went searching for her he found her tracks intercepted by the broad, bare footprints of an animal that could be nothing but a Yeh-teh.

"Those must have been her bones we found," I said, and Ang Phar nodded sadly.

That night the men refused to camp near my tent, telling Ang Phar that I was risking the Yeh-teh's wrath and that the creature would single me out for its vengeance. The men went down to a lower plateau and built a huge fire. After building a fire for me, Ang Phar made the excuse that he would stay below with the men so they wouldn't run off. And then, unaccountably, Omar broke away just after darkness and raced down the mountain, and I never saw him again.

It's not hard to be superstitious when you're left alone on a mountainside with a vivid memory of the ghastly sight you'd seen that afternoon. Ang Phar had left a good supply of wood, which I fed to the fire to keep a bright blaze going, and I found myself turning the pressure lamp in the tent higher than usual. Sounds magnified and I found myself brooding as I strained to identify them.

The fire waned at last and I decided to hit the sack. I didn't get out of my clothes, however. I just lay down on top of my sleeping bag. It was cold, but some inner fear kept me from being too aware of it.

And then, as I lay in the darkness, I heard again that frightful, fiendish howling of the Yeh-teh in the distance. I sat up as it was repeated a few minutes later, and it seemed closer. Then suddenly, not far away, I heard a shrill scream. I leaped up, grabbed my

flashlight and bola, and went outside. The moon was full behind
a sky of scattered clouds, and in the bright light I saw a shadowy
figure running along the plateau. My mouth turned dry and I felt
a sudden surge of fear as I started after it. I guess I must have
yelled as I let fly with the bola and saw that it was a successful
cast. The figure went down and there was a muffled scream and a
moan. Cautiously I moved forward, remembering Sarkay's raking
wounds and the poisonous pus that oozed out of them. I flashed
my light ahead of me, and then my beam shone on my prey.

But it wasn't the Yeh-teh.

It was a lovely young girl, her eyes wide with horror and her
hand up to hold off her unseen attacker. She did a double-take
when she must have realized that the Yeh-teh wouldn't be holding
a flashlight. She had cut her forehead when she fell, and it was
bleeding slightly. Her sari was up around her thighs and she had a
small cut above her knee.

"Ah chah," I said, coming closer. "It's O.K." She trembled as I
bent over and untangled the rope that had wound itself around
her knees and thighs. Then she sat up and modestly pulled her
sari down.

"Thank you," she said.

"You speak English?"

"Yiss, sar. My father was Sherpa guide. An' I work for while
in Katmandu for English."

"What are you doing up here?" I asked, helping her up, and

leading her back to my tent.

She didn't answer, and for a moment I had a sudden wild notion about human sacrifices to appease the monster. But I dismissed it. I put my arm around her and felt her whole body trembling.

We went inside the tent and I lit the lamp and dug around in my luggage for the first aid kit. She sat down on my cot, and in a few minutes I had the wet gauze ready to cleanse her wounds. As I turned I saw that her eyes were glazed; she was suffering shock, and her whole body was shaking violently.

"I am so frightened," she said.

Then I noticed that beside her on the bed was a *kukris*, a long native knife. I didn't say anything then, but gave her a sedation pill and cleaned up her cuts. I fixed her a drink of tea-and-whiskey, which she sipped, and in a little while her jitters stopped and the glaze left her eyes. She was a beautiful girl. Her mouth was full-lipped and her figure, to which the sari clung tightly, was perfection itself. Though she was young, she was all woman.

"And now will you tell me what you were doing up here?" I asked, nodding at the knife.

"Oh," she said, with an embarrassed look that quickly turned to anger. "It was silly, perhaps—but you heard of the little girl that the Yeh-teh took?"

"Yes," I said.

"That was my niece, Tami," she said. "Everyone was sad, but I—Nimma—I was angry as well as sad and I decided that I would kill the Yeh-teh. I do not believe in ghosts or evil spirits like many Sherpas. I believe it is animal I can kill."

"Or kill you, Nimma."

She asked me if I was the man who was hunting the Yeh-teh and as soon as I said I was, she wanted to know if she could go along. She actually looked surprised when I said it was impossible; she was so determined to get revenge on the Yeh-teh that such a request didn't seem absurd.

"However," I said, "you're not going down the mountain alone tonight."

"No," she said, smiling slyly. "I shall have to stay here with you."

I could read every thought behind that sly look: she was

going to do everything in her power to persuade me to change my mind. And then, to my surprise, she said with complete frankness, "I am a woman, sar, don't forget." Her laugh tinkled pleasantly. "I will not let you alone until you let me go with you."

So far the Yeh-teh hadn't been able to frighten me into hitting the bottle, but this dainty dish drove me to pouring myself a man-sized mug of whiskey and downing it in a couple of quick gulps. When the drink hit bottom, she was lovelier than ever, if that were possible.

"It won't do any good," I said without conviction. "You can't come along."

Her eyes twinkled and she moved over on the cot. "Come sit down," she said. "You must be tired."

The moment I sat down she got up, took my mug, poured me some more whiskey, and gently pushed me down onto my pillow. Then, hushing my one protesting remark, she undid my boots and helped me out of my hunting jacket, and made me sit up a moment as she slipped my sweater off over my head.

"What next?" I wondered taking another long drink. This was one determined girl.

I looked up as she unfastened the pin that held her sari at the shoulder and I got a momentary flash of her naked beauty just before she turned out the lamp.

The next thing I knew she was breathing in my ear, "Now I shall try to make you change your mind."

Nimma didn't succeed in persuading me to take her along, but in the morning she reluctantly went back down the mountain when I promised that we would go to Katmandu together as soon as I had accomplished my mission.

Ang Phar came up shortly after she'd left and reported that half of the men had run off in the night, and that we'd have to leave some supplies behind. This left me with Ang Phar and three men. After caching a large portion of our supplies, we struck out for the spot up the mountain where we were to rendezvous with Billy.

We skirted the cliff where we'd seen our Yeh-teh, hoping to pick up a trail. Though Ang Phar and I were experienced trackers, we had no luck at all. I was pretty sure that the Yeh-teh had left the area. It was a back-breaking climb and it grew steadily colder as we went up the mountain. Flurries of snow began to hamper us as we reached 14,000 feet. After three days hiking we got to the saddle of the ridge where we were to meet Billy, and as we crossed into a wild terrain of scree and jagged rocks, we saw the camp pitched on a plateau above the prearranged spot.

When we reached the camp, Pasang, the chief guide, said that Billy had come across the trail of the Yeh-teh the day before and had followed it up into the snow.

"I wanted to go with him," Pasang said, "even though the men were afraid. But he wanted to go alone. He would not let me join him."

I believed him. "What did he take with him? Has he food?"
"Very little," said Pasang. "Not more than one day's rations, and this will mark the end of the second day. He had that rope with the balls on the end—and a *kukris*. That's all."

"No gun?"

"No. He said to fire a gun up here at this time of year might start an avalanche."

I looked at Ang Phar. "We'll have to go after him right away."

"No, sar," he said. "We cannot. We have a full day's climb already and it will be dark before we get started. We must wait until morning."

I had to agree that it would have been crazy, because I could hardly stay awake in this rarified atmosphere after our exhausting climb. And so after a good night's sleep, Ang Phar and I took off at dawn over the route described by Pasang, who had watched Billy in the distance during his first day's climb. Soon after starting out we came across his trail, finding indentations in the scree that were a pace apart, and clearly indicating that he was headed for the glacier. At one point we came across the spoor of the Yeh-teh, and knew then that the trail Billy was following was a fresh one.

"It could well be the same Yeh-teh that we were after," Ang Phar said.

"Yeah—and Billy doesn't know that the damn thing's a maneater."

All through that day we climbed, and toward evening we came upon an empty can of C-rations. We were only a few hours march from the glacier, and the icy cliffs that rose up from it glistened in the sunset.

In the morning Ang Phar and I made short work of gathering up our tent and starting the climb after Billy. Soon we were in snow, and I was startled suddenly to see that Billy's welted footprints strode alongside the long wide tracks of a Yeh-teh.

We hastened our pace as we came to the glacier and started
the slithering climb up. We roped ourselves together and Ang
Phar's ice-ax, which he normally wouldn't have used for this
gradual, but slippery, ascent, was a great help in speeding up
our climb.

Suddenly in the distance came a terrible screeching. It was
the cry of a maddened Yeh-teh, and the shrill laugh at the end
sent shivers down my spine. A few more minutes of climbing
and we reached a high point in the glacier. We heard the Yeh-
teh yelping again, and suddenly Ang Phar grabbed my arm and
pointed.

On a cliff of ice not more than 200 yards away we saw two
figures, just dark puppets that seemed to dance backwards and
forwards toward each other.

"They're fighting," Ang Phar said hoarsely. *"Come."*

I shrugged off the rope that held me to Ang Phar and started
to run. As we came closer, I could make out the reddish color of
the beast, which stood erect like a boxer and clawed at the dark-
suited figure, which was Billy. I saw the sudden glint of Billy's
knife as they came together, locked in a terrible struggle, and then
I saw the animal fall. We were still too far away to get a good
view of the beast, and Billy was only a dark figure. I saw him
bend over the beast, then turn and walk away.

I shouted, and Billy waved. He started our way, sliding down
the icy cliff to the flat of the glacier, and picking himself up at
the bottom staggered toward us. He fell and picked himself up,
and lurched on again. Ang Phar and I kept running and finally we
reached him as he picked himself up for the third time. I tried to
help him but he pushed me away.

He was a horrifying sight. His jacket and sweater were ripped
through and his bare chest was a mass of blood and hanging
flesh. His pants were in tatters from crotch to boot-tops and blood
dripped down on the snow. I looked at his face and saw that his
left cheek was laid open from his temple to his chin. I caught the
glint of naked bone. But he was grinning happily.

"Mike, old boy! It's good to see you! Mike! I did it!" he cried
hoarsely. Blood dribbled out of the corner of his mouth. *"For once
I did what I set out to do, Mike! I got me my Yeh-teh! I won, Mike, I
won!"* He waved his hand back toward the cliff. *"He's lying there
dead—the first Yeh-teh that any man—"* He coughed, and the blood

gushed out in a torrent. *"I knew that someday, Mike, someday I would do it—"*

Before we could catch him he slumped to his knees and pitched forward on his face.

I didn't have to feel his pulse to know that he was dead. Billy had died in his moment of self-vindication, killed by the thing he had conquered.

When we climbed the cliff to find the Yeh-teh it was gone. There was no doubt that it was dead, for the creature had dragged itself from the bloody battleground to the edge of a deep crevasse. Streaks of blood were on the chasm walls marking its passage down. It lay somewhere in the bottomless crevasse, forever lost, defiant in the end to elude man; determined to thwart his efforts to bring back to civilization evidence to prove that the Yeh-teh was not a myth.

And so I turned away from the crevasse with the question pounding over and over in my mind: I knew it was not a myth, but what was it? I had seen it, like so many others, from a distance, but I had no evidence to produce and I could not put a name to it.

The one man who could have answered my questions was dead. We wrapped Billy in our tent and carried him down the mountain.

The whole valley turned out for his funeral, and Billy Gregory was buried among the heroic Sherpa guides who had died as they fought to conquer Everest, Nanda Devi, Annapurna, and the other great challenges. On his headstone, in English and Nepalese, they put his name, and underneath the simple legend: *He conquered the Yeh-teh.*

As I told Randell later, when he, Doc, Nimma and I sat in the hotel at Katmandu and discussed the expedition, it didn't matter what they inscribed on his headstone—for I knew that his greatest triumph had come when he conquered himself.

Eisner Hall of Fame comics artist Matt Baker provided the illustration for "I Hunted Prehistoric Men," a tale drawing on lore related to *Almas*, a purported relic species of early man. (*Courage*, January 1958)

THUNDERBIRDS

"MONSTER Bird That Carries Off Human Beings!" by Jack Pearl (an Anglicized *nom de plume* for writer Jacques Bain Pearl) from *Saga*'s May 1963 issue covers the Thunderbird, a giant predatory species common to some Native American indigenous tribes, particularly in the Pacific Northwest and Southwest cultures. Tribal myths vary in details, but the essential qualities are common: The solitary Thunderbird is so named because of its ability to cause thunderous claps with its mighty wingspan, blast lightning bolts from its eyes, and swoop down on unsuspecting tribal members, carrying them away to certain doom. For most non-Natives, the beast described most likely conjures images of Pterodactylus, a fossilized species familiar to filmgoers in such inaccurate but influential movies as *Rodan*, the original *King Kong*, and numerous other films. In this manner, "Monster Bird That Carries Off Human Beings!" plays upon these already planted images in readers' minds, then takes imaginative flight, extending the potential dangers of said terror birds to the next thrilling (but highly improbable) level.

Typical of MAM cryptid coverage, scientists of unclear accreditation are produced to help convince skeptical readers that reports of Thunderbirds, while fanciful, may have factual components. A certain Dr. R.J. Young from California (no university is credited), described as an ornithologist by profession, claims that it's very possible the Thunderbird sightings can be attributed to huge condors with wingspans ranging as wide as "twenty-five feet."

The claims that Thunderbirds carried away humans is perhaps a retelling by the author of an *Arizona Champion* article from March 10, 1892, bearing the headline "Exciting Rescue of a

Child That Had Been Carried Off." The more preposterous claims in the article about the downing of jet aircraft by the flying monster seem based mostly on the author's vivid imagination, though cited sources add a level of authenticity to the proceedings that is again classic to MAMs.

The actual event reported is based on the crash of United Airlines Flight 297, a Vickers Viscount 745D, on November 23, 1962. Likewise, the specified Civil Aeronautics Board chief of safety investigation officer, George Van Epps, did finally conclude that a flock of swans was to blame, having been sucked into the jet's rear stabilizers, causing them to disintegrate in mid-air. But the author of "Monster Bird That Carries Off Human Beings!" goes one step beyond, attributing misleading quotes to Van Epps in which he all but cryptically concludes only a massive bird on the order of an unknown species could have caused such damage.

While cryptozoological readers will be understandably disappointed by such confabulation, it is a true Fortean bit of synchronistic timing that the cited date, November 23, is precisely one year to the date President Kennedy was later assassinated in Dallas. This use by Pearl would seem in poor taste, until one considers the fact that this issue of *Saga* was published in May of 1963, and that it also eerily features Kennedy on the cover, complete with a flashing explosion near his forehead as it depicts a doomed aircraft flight.

Cryptozoologist/author Ken Gerhard, who has written about Thunderbirds in his book *Big Bird! Modern Sightings of Flying Monsters*, explained when I queried him: "As far as airline disasters, I am familiar with the allegations regarding the flight you mention, but I'm skeptical about such claims. I am not personally aware of any evidence linking Thunderbirds with airline disasters."

But as his own work in the field suggests, the phenomena of Thunderbirds is far from extinct as a subject for serious cryptozoologic inquiry. In his work, Gerhard cites reports of the *Kongamato* (which translates as "breaker of boats," owing to its habit of destroying watercraft), originating in Western Zambia, Angola and Congo as evidence of a Thunderbird-related phenomena, as well as the *Ropen* ("demon-flyer") from New Guinea, to illustrate the global continuity of the Thunderbird trope, be it fact or fancy.

DOCTOR TELLS Why Great Ladies Pose Without Clothes

SAGA

THE MAGAZINE FOR MEN · MAY 35¢

WAR
HERO
WHO HAUNTS
JACK
KENNEDY

NEW CUBAN INVASION!
How and When

"MONSTER BIRD THAT CARRIES OFF
HUMAN BEINGS!"
JACK PEARL
SAGA, MAY 1963
COVER BY ROBERT ENGEL

MONSTER BIRD *THAT CARRIES OFF HUMAN BEINGS!*

BY JACK PEARL / ILLUSTRATED BY JOHN McDERMOTT

A phantom killer roams our skies. Is it a freak of nature—or the Indians' legendary Thunderbird?

The supernatural and the superhuman have exerted a powerful attraction on people through the ages. The ancient Greeks feared their one-eyed Cyclops and half-man, half-bull Minotaur. Europe, in the Middle Ages, was awed by tales of vampires and werewolves—both of which still get occasional testimonials today. In Asia, the legendary monster is the phantom "Abominable Snowman," the reputed man-beast, shaggy-haired and ten feet high, who roams the snowy wastes of the Himalayas. A few years ago, the respected and serious sportsman, Sir Edmund Hillary, who conquered the world's highest mountain, Mt. Everest, led a costly expedition into the Himalayas to try to capture a **yeti,** as the Snowman is locally known. ■ Here in the United States, one of the most popular 20th Century myths or mysteries—according to your preference—is the "flying saucer." But recently there have been reports of still another terrifying apparition—a bird of prey so monstrously large and

ART BY JOHN MCDERMOTT

The supernatural and the superhuman have exerted a powerful attraction on people through the ages. The ancient Greeks feared their one-eyed Cyclops and half-man, half-bull Minotaur. Europe, in the Middle Ages, was awed by tales of vampires and werewolves—both of which still get occasional testimonials today. In Asia, the legendary monster is the phantom "Abominable Snowman," the reputed man-beast, shaggy-haired and 10-feet high, who roams the snowy wastes of the Himalayas. A few years ago, the respected and serious sportsman, Sir Edmund Hillary, who conquered the world's highest mountain, Mt. Everest, led a costly expedition into the Himalayas to try to capture a yeti, as the Snowman is locally known.

Here in the United States, one of the most popular 20th century myths or mysteries—according to your preference—is the "flying saucer." But recently there have been reports of still another terrifying apparition—a bird of prey so monstrously large and strong that it can carry off a human being or dive into an airplane hard enough to cause a catastrophic crash. This flying beast—often called the "Thunderbird"—is more than a legend. It has been seen by eyewitnesses, although no one is sure of its species. Few people have gotten close to it and lived....

In 1933, a doctor from a mining camp near Ivanpah, California, reported he had been summoned to an isolated farmhouse to attend a man, a woman, and a three-year-old child, all seriously lacerated about the head and torso. The man and his wife, badly shaken but in complete control of their senses, told a story that made the short hairs bristle on the doctor's neck.

The husband had been working in a field when he heard his wife scream. Running back to the house, he rounded the front porch and saw a horrifying sight. About 40 yards from the house, where his child had been playing, a terrible struggle was taking place between his wife and the biggest bird he had ever seen. The child was lying between his wife's legs screaming and covered with blood, while she swung a stove poker in an attempt to fend off a vicious attack by the creature. The bird—it looked like a giant vulture or eagle—was ripping at his wife with its claws and huge beak. One swipe of a wing, which the man estimated to be at least 12-feet long, sent her sprawling. The husband picked up an axe that lay on the porch and joined the battle. He got in one good blow—"right in the shoulder joint, and I must have struck an artery because the blood spurted like a fountain." Enraged by the wound, the bird attacked with renewed fury, grabbed the axe with its beak and seized the man with its sharp talons by the shoulder and buttocks. According to the man's story, the great bird then lifted him 10- or 12-feet off the ground as he battled to grab the monster's neck with his hands. He was unsuccessful, but abruptly the bird dropped him and flew off. He assumed that the wound he had inflicted on the bird had weakened it—an assumption that was later borne out when the skeptical doctor visited the scene of the encounter. In the doctor's opinion, there was more blood on the ground than could have been shed by any three human beings— even if they had bled to death. That a violent and vicious battle had taken place, he had no doubt. He also attested to the fact that the wounds on the three victims—who all survived—could only have been inflicted by enormous talons.

An Indian who had accompanied the doctor to the farmhouse said that for generations big birds had been swooping down from the high mountain peaks and carrying away Indian children and livestock.

"What kind of birds?" the doctor asked. "Eagles?"

The Indian shook his head. "Thunderbirds," he said.

Only two years ago, there was another sighting, on the US east coast.

In May, 1961, a New York businessman was piloting his private Piper Cub up the Hudson River Valley when an object, which he first thought was another plane, dove at him out of the sun, "like a fighter plane making a pass." Blinded by the glare, he was unable to make a positive identification at that instant. Outraged, he turned his plane to get a glimpse of the other ship, which had climbed up behind him at about "five o'clock," in Air Force jargon. To his amazement, the sky was empty except for a huge bird, now about a third of a mile off, drifting lazily "with scarcely any movement of its wings." It is difficult to estimate size in the sky, without any known object available for comparison, but he recognized that it was "a damned big bird, bigger than an eagle. For a moment I doubted my sanity because it actually looked more like a pterodactyl out of the prehistoric ages...."

Frightened, he turned the plane again and headed away at full throttle. The bird flew after him for 10 minutes, keeping up with the plane easily, though making no effort to close the distance between them. At last, its curiosity apparently satisfied, it swooped off in another direction, to the man's relief.

When he later related the incident to his family and friends, they advised him either to be fitted with glasses or to give up flying!

Similar experiences have been reported by scores of private pilots, as well as veteran commercial pilots, in which mammoth birds have been sighted. One pilot had this to say, alluding to the extreme difficulty of estimating size and distance while high above the earth: "You see another airliner in the distance and it may look no bigger than a pigeon. The same thing is true of birds. There's no reliable way of judging the size of another object in the air unless it's almost on top of you. In 1947, I almost collided with a bird over Arizona. My co-pilot and I couldn't believe our eyes. It came down from the left and passed beneath us, just missing us by a hair. There was no doubt about my judgment that time. The thing had a wingspan of at least 30 feet... Afterward I got to thinking. God knows how many monsters, just as big, there are flying in the air over the isolated mountain regions... You just don't realize it unless they get close to you...and I never want to get that close to another one again!"

The experience of this pilot suggests an obvious question: If the bird and the plane had not missed by that hair's breadth, what would the consequences have been? More to the point, can a bird actually cause an air disaster?

Collisions between birds and aircraft are more frequent than is commonly believed. In 1957, a goose crashed through the cockpit windshield of a DC-3 and injured the co-pilot. The plane landed without incident. In 1960, a flock of starlings was sucked into the engine intakes of an American Airlines Electra taking off from Boston's Logan Airport, causing a tragic crash. The files of the Civil Aeronautics Board (CAB) abound with reports of similar freakish accidents.

Shortly after noon on November 23, 1962, a United Airlines Viscount was making a routine approach to Washington, DC, International Airport. It was a bright, sunny day with unlimited visibility and minimum air turbulence. Radio communication between the plane and the Washington control tower was normal. There was not the slightest hint of trouble, much less total disaster. Then, abruptly, the Viscount disappeared from the tower's radar screen.

On a farm in Ellicott City, Maryland, a boy looked up from his chores to witness a sight he had never expected to see: a huge airplane diving vertically toward the woods to the southwest of the farm. As he watched, paralyzed with horror, the plane crashed and exploded in the trees with an impact that caused the ground to tremble beneath his feet.

On November 25, in an official statement to the press, George Van Epps, chief of safety investigation for the CAB, announced: "We have evidence of a bird strike on the (plane's) horizontal stabilizers and associated elevators, both left and right... The fact is we found both left and right stabilizers back in the flight path, which indicates in-flight separation...."

Both halves of the 35-foot, all-metal stabilizer were found almost a half-mile behind the crash. And on both were matted the blood, feathers, and flesh of an unidentified bird.

But what kind of bird was it that could disable a huge aircraft like the Viscount turboprop—built to endure the stress and strain of high speed, the giant force of wind and storm—disable it so badly that it would spin out of control to disaster? It is a question that air experts and ornithologists alike have been asking themselves—and each other—and, so far, none of the answers have satisfied anyone.

Leon Tanguay, safety director of the CAB, declared about the bird theory: "I have never known of such a thing to happen. I'm not sure that this happened!" But neither he nor anyone else can explain the feathers, blood and flesh on that stabilizer torn off by terrific impact.

The Chief Medical Examiner of Maryland, who examined the gory remains of the creature plastered to the stabilizer, said cautiously: "I've got a foot-square piece of the carcass. It's white with down below the feathers—it couldn't be anything else but a swan!" He didn't convince the investigators from CAB and FAA. One of them said, off the record: "There's talk that it was a swan or a goose. But only one bird! It doesn't add up."

So unconvinced were the investigators that Army helicopters were assigned to hedge-hop the fatal route the plane had followed from Baltimore to Washington "in an effort to find more carcasses or remains that might indicate this to be a flock instead of a single bird," explained Mr. Van Epps. "They found nothing," he added uneasily.

Among pilots, civil and military, the swan or goose theory produced outright contempt. A former World War II fighter pilot, now flying for a commercial airline, said, "That swan would have to be straight out of a science-fiction movie.

Take a look at the stabilizers on a big plane sometime. They're built to take strain. They have to be. Without the stabilizer, the pilot has no control. During the war I saw big Flying Fortresses come back with their stabilizers shot to hell by machine guns and cannon shells. Nobody can tell me that a swan could tear one loose from the ship!"

Another pilot—now an aeronautical engineer—asks a more intriguing question: "What I'd like to know is how this 'bird' managed to get through the arc of the props and hit the tail? You look at the design of the Viscount. It would almost be impossible unless...? Unless we assume that it actually swooped in from the side, behind the wings, was able to buck the slipstream, then deliberately dove into the tail section. It's ridiculous! What kind

In 1962, an airliner mysteriously crashed near Washington, DC.
Investigation produced evidence it had been hit by an enormous bird.

of a bird could do that!"

What kind of bird, indeed? A bird that could rip a section of
solid metal off the tail assembly, a slab of metal 35-feet long and
238 square yards in area, rip it off like a slice of balsawood off a
child's toy plane?

The answer seems obvious. A bird big enough to carry off a
sheep or a calf or a man. A Thunderbird.

But does such a creature really exist? The evidence would
seem to indicate that it does. Allowing for a normal amount of
magnification induced by fear, hysteria, and vivid imagination in
the frequently recorded encounters between bird and man, there
has to be some substance to the stories. Farmers, businessmen,
airline pilots, doctors—respectable, sane citizens from all walks
of life—cannot all be written off as eccentrics or liars.

Nesting on craggy pinnacles in desolate mountain sections of
North America are birds of a size that few humans have ever seen
or imagined.

Is it possible that these birds are oversized eagles whose
glands have gone wacky, the way human glands sometimes run
wild and produce giants 10-feet tall? The American Museum of

Natural History scoffs at this idea, claiming that the largest eagle
ever reported in the United States had a wingspan of 10 feet.
It qualifies this statement, however, nothing that "incompetent"
witnesses have sworn that they have seen eagles with wingspans
of up to 20 feet.

What about a condor?

There is some evidence to support this theory. Ornithologist
R.J. Young of California believes that the giant condor, a species
of vulture, or the California vulture itself may be the true
Thunderbird. At one time the condor could be found in great
numbers all along the west coast of North America. At present
these huge birds are fast becoming extinct, victims of the same
destiny that exterminated the great monsters of prehistoric
times. The condor has failed to adapt to the radically changing
environment of the past century. By conservative estimates, the
"average" condor has a wingspan of 12 feet; its body is up to
5-feet long, fleshy and muscular; the head and neck are bare above
a white collar of soft down; the beak is thick, strong, and cruelly
curved. One specimen in a Chilean zoo had a wingspan of 15 feet
and regularly consumed 18 pounds of raw meat as a daily diet!

Consider the plight of a wild creature that requires 18
pounds of meat a day to survive, battling to exist in our
modern civilization where wild game, its natural prey, is rapidly
disappearing. For centuries condors would swoop down from their
craggy nests 15,000 feet above sea level to kill their food on the
plains and in the valleys. But now, with cities and towns spreading
out across the countryside, reducing wildlife, the condor is slowly
starving to death. But there are the rare ones, the strongest,
the biggest, who still inhabit the High Sierras and other lofty
pinnacles in the clouds.

"Although many of my colleagues will not agree," Dr. Young
states, "I would say it is not only possible but likely that certain of
the species, which have endured, are great hardy creatures with
wing spreads up to 25 feet." Although the condor is normally not
aggressive, preferring to eat dead flesh or kill off dying animals,
any species is capable of some change. As Dr. Young points out:
"The timidest of creatures are converted to fighting tigers when
hunger and the instinct for survival motivate them."

Therefore, it is not too preposterous to assume that a giant

condor or California vulture, maddened by hunger, might
occasionally invade the lowland domain of man and carry off a
fat lamb, a sheep, or even a child: This is no more unlikely than
an eagle swooping down at midday on the busy, noisy streets of
Chicago and laying hold of a fox terrier—which did happen in
November 1962.

A condor, conceivably, might become curious about another
flying thing near it in the sky. The highest and fastest flyer of
all the birds, it could easily overtake a small plane cruising at
moderate speed. But obviously, it could not keep pace with a
modern airliner, nor could it get close to one except by accident.
However, we know that somehow this did occur on November
23, 1962, when tragedy overtook the Viscount turbo approaching
Washington. Some bird—a big bird—collided with the tail of that
plane and demolished a 35-foot sheet of vital stabilizer. Could it
have been a condor?

Even Dr. Young, who is willing to accept the idea of a 25-
to 30-foot condor or vulture rejects that idea. According to the
reference books there are no condors in the eastern part of North
America. "To the best of our knowledge they have become extinct
in the United States," says Dr. Young, "except for isolated sections
of the Southwest."

Thoughtful people agree that contemporary explanations
for these strange attacks and maimings certainly are needed,
but question the existence of huge birds, larger than anything
we imagine as native to our continent. Is there any precedent or
evidence from the past for such assumptions?

In simple societies without written language, the storyteller
occupies a predominant place in the tribal hierarchy. It is he who
teaches the young about the heroic deeds of their ancestors,
communicates the traditions of the tribe and stimulates them to
deeds that will carry on this heritage. And in the tales that survive
among the native people of the North American continent,
monster birds appear again and again. In fact, centuries before
white men came to the continent, a cult of the Thunderbird
bound native tribes together in a strange, almost religious
alliance. From the Bering Strait to the Isthmus of Panama,
dozens of different tribal legends tell of monster birds that dwelt
in high mountain fastnesses, preying on living creatures, including

men. About 1400 AD, when North America was in the grip of
"The Little Big Freeze," and life—plant, animal and human—
was being ravaged by ice and snow, the Thunderbird (the name
appears to have originated during this period) deserted its lofty
habitat and came down into the valleys seeking food. Here began
the legends of the bird that carried away children and even grown
men when it could not find animal food.

"Preposterous," modern, sophisticated ornithologists assert.

Still, in Southern California, while excavating in asphalt
pits for fossils, geologists uncovered skeletons of Indians and
bison alongside the bones of birds which, when reconstructed,
resembled huge vultures with an estimated wingspan of over
25 feet. The folklore of this region tells of a Thunderbird that
attacked a beached whale and literally ripped it apart, carrying
great hunks of blubber off into the mountains.

Allowing for a certain amount of deistic exaggeration (for the
Thunderbird was regarded as a god), the number and consistency
of such stories, spread among many scattered tribes over the
length and breadth of the entire continent, suggests that a "super
bird" such as the Thunderbird did exist.

That such a monster came to be called the Thunderbird
and was regarded as a deity is quite natural. The ancients of
the Americas, like their counterparts in Greece, Rome, and
Scandinavia, understandably created a god for every unexplained
phenomenon of nature, so after a few centuries they had sea gods,
rain gods, fire gods, and, of course, thunder gods. In the simple
reasoning of the Indians and the Eskimos, thunder and lightning
came from the sky and the giant bird came from the sky, too.
It seemed natural that the rush of his powerful wings churned
up thunder; the blinking of his golden eyes flashed forks of
lightning.

Primitive art throughout the North American continent
found a common motif in the Thunderbird. His visage is easily
recognizable atop totem poles, on leather shields and tepees, and
in the crude drawings on cave walls. Most of the representations
of the Thunderbird are strikingly similar. The American
Indian's depiction of it is as good a criterion as any. It is
surprisingly modern in its geometric design, and bears a marked
resemblance to the American eagle, except that the Indians made

a clear distinction between the "big" eagle and the "monster" Thunderbird.

The 18th and 19th centuries provide countless stories of huge birds attacking farm animals and human beings. Most of them came from campfire sessions among hunters and mountain men who spent a lifetime in the Rocky Mountains or the Appalachians. The famous scout Jim Bridger described how a "giant bird, too big for either an eagle or a vulture," attacked a tethered mule and lifted it off the ground. Bridger and a companion held onto the animal's legs, and eventually the bird loosened its grip and flew away.

Daniel Boone claimed to have seen a Thunderbird carry away a five-year-old Indian boy. A dozen arrows and a volley of shots were supposedly pumped into the creature without effect. But campfire tales, primed by freely circulating jugs of "white lightning" and the natural tendency of strong men to outdo each other even in storytelling, cannot be taken too seriously.

But other reports cannot be ignored. In the year 1886, the Tombstone, Arizona *Epitaph*, which helped make Wyatt Earp famous, published a photograph of a huge bird nailed to a wall. The newspaper said it had been shot by two prospectors and hauled into town by wagon. Lined up in front of the bird were six grown men with their arms outstretched, fingertip to fingertip. The creature measured about 36 feet from wingtip to wingtip.

In 1889, a group of revelers at the Oriental Saloon in Tombstone got to talking about that picture and made fun of the two prospectors who claimed to have killed the bird. By chance, one of the old silver hunters was standing down at the far end of the bar. "If you're so damned smart," he challenged them, "why don't you go out where we got the bird. There's plenty more of 'em nesting in the tops of them mountains. You'll see for yourselves."

The party of happy drunks took off at once for the scene where, allegedly, the Thunderbird had been shot. By the time they reached the spot, it was almost dawn and the whisky was beginning to wear off. The fun seemed to have gone out of the adventure. With aching heads, they built a fire and rolled up in their blankets to sleep it off.

Just as they were dozing off, one of the men got up and

went into the bushes to relieve himself. Minutes later, a terrified scream sent the others bolting out of their bed rolls, wide awake.

"God help me! It's got me!" the unseen man in the woods screamed. "Aghhhhh!"

Grabbing rifles and pistols, the men ran in the direction of the screaming man, believing that a bear or some other wild animal had attacked him. In the first gray light they could make out his footprints in the damp earth, leading to a clearing in the woods. Suddenly the men stopped dead. The footprints ended abruptly in the middle of the clearing. They looked at each other in bewilderment.

"What the hell," one man said nervously. "He disappeared into thin air."

Instinctively, they all looked upwards, and, almost as if this gesture was a signal, the terrible screaming, which had ceased for a few moments, now started again—only this time it came from directly over their heads, high in the air.

"*Let me go, lemme go, lemme gooo....*" Gradually, it faded into the distance.

Shaken, wild-eyed, but sober, all four men who were present later signed sworn statements testifying to the truth of this incident.

One of the most eerie Thunderbird incidents occurred in 1944, in a California internment camp where Nisei, Americans of Japanese origin, were held during World War II. Over a period of months, more than a half-dozen internees disappeared from this camp, and it was thought they had escaped. In the course of the thorough interrogation that followed, to figure out how the Nisei had escaped and who had helped them, the only thing investigators could get out of the other internees was that a "giant bird" had carried off the missing men. The angry soldiers assumed that they were being "taken" by the Japanese Americans, who had been fraternizing with local Indians working around the camp. These Indians habitually told wild stories about a monster bird that lurked in the lofty mountain peaks. This opinion was reinforced when two of the Indians rushed into camp one morning, shouting excitedly that they had seen a Thunderbird kill and carry off a man the night before.

This particular camp had enjoyed a minimum of security

until then, because the inmates were "good risks." But from this point on it bristled with machine guns and watch towers, double guard details and powerful searchlights ringing the fence at night. The prisoners stopped disappearing and the matter ended there —temporarily.

Usually when Japanese American internees escaped from the camps, they would be picked up again in days or weeks, while trying to sneak in or out of the homes of friends or mingling self-consciously in Chinese sections, hoping they would be accepted by their brother Orientals. It rarely worked.

Strangely, none of the internees who escaped from this camp ever turned up again—during the war or after. They had, literally and figuratively, disappeared into thin air! So claimed their fellow inmates—and the Indians.

These stories are typical of many reported through the first half of the 20th century in mountain states, both west and east. Pennsylvania is, significantly, one of the most popular sources of Thunderbird sightings. Just recently one of these reports was received by *Saga* from a Pennsylvania resident who wrote: "...In April, 1922, I was standing at my gate alone after the sun had gone behind the mountain when a bird, which I first thought was a blue heron, flew overhead with a slow, flapping motion of its wings. As it was lighter in color than a heron, I watched it fly past a pine tree with branches that spanned 50 feet. Its wingspread was two-thirds the width of that pine. For 35 years I never mentioned the incident for fear someone would think I was crazy. Then, on March 27, 1957, a young man rushed into my house shouting excitedly. 'There's a bird flying around out there and it's a monster!'

"The bird had disappeared by the time I got out of the house, so I went back inside and made a phone call to the local American Legion Post. I asked the steward there if he had heard anything about a big bird flying toward the Susquehanna River. He said he hadn't, but went outside to ask the crowd in the street. A chorus of people answered him, saying that they had seen it fly across the river at Westport, Pennsylvania. The consensus was that it had a wingspread of at least 25 feet.... One week later another Thunderbird flew over my house and was later sighted flying up Halls Run...."

Let's return for a moment to the Indian legends of the Thunderbird. Folklore tells us that when the native tribes of North America migrated east as the Little Big Freeze slanted down across the continent from the northwest, they encountered a multitude of Thunderbirds while crossing the mountains. The predator birds, always ravenous, killed many braves, squaws, and Indian children. In retaliation, hunting parties sought out their nests and ruthlessly destroyed both the eggs and the young of the Thunderbird. The Indians noted particularly that the Thunderbird was not a nesting bird, by conventional nesting standards—including those of the eagle. Frequently the Thunderbird's eggs and young lay on crude beds of sticks on the bare mountain tops, with no protection from the elements. This may be the vital clue to the identity of the mysterious Thunderbird, for it is a fact that the condor is the only existing bird in the world whose nesting habits follow this pattern.

So, in their westward movement, the Indians exterminated as many of these big birds as they could discover. Certainly no one would suggest that they could have destroyed all of them. The surviving Thunderbirds—or condors—gradually died off as a result of the natural attrition described earlier. But can even an expert be absolutely certain that every last one of them died? It seems quite possible that on some remote, inaccessible peak of the Appalachian Mountains a hardy strain of the breed has endured. A dozen, ten, perhaps fewer, but certainly strong, wily birds who could survive where the rest of their species was dying out.

Some people, although they live in the areas where people have been attacked, refute their own neighbors' evidence—but are unable to offer any explanation for the terrible wounds inflicted. Others scoff at the reports, snorting: "Ah, that's just another Loch Ness Monster or Abominable Snowman that nobody's ever seen! It'll end up like the Cardiff Giant—and just as phony."

Neither hasty acceptance nor stubborn hooting at the facts makes sense. Only after thorough investigation of every new sighting and monster bird incident, and scientific analysis of the facts, will we come close to an acceptable answer. For sophisticated people of the mid-20th century, contemplating visits to other planets within a decade, must have the answer when forms of life from the savage past seem unwilling to die out even in the alien conditions of our glass-and-neon civilization.

Detail of artist John Asaro's woman-hungry Sasquatch from "America's Terrifying Woodland Monster-Men," *Saga*, July 1969

"MACDONALD'S NIGHTMARE SAFARI"
JIM MACDONALD
MAN'S CONQUEST, AUGUST 1959
COVER BY GEORGE GROSS

norm eastman

MACDONALD'S NIGHTMARE SAFARI

by JIM MACDONALD

Geologist Jim MacDonald studied diaries and reports for years before starting out on the most incredible diamond hunt in modern history.

■ CARRYING Oliveira's wife over my shoulder and dragging him along under my arm was too much. When I stumbled and fell for the last time the Morcegos head-hunters were no more than a spear's throw behind us, whistling their shrill bat-like cries.

Relieved of the Oliveiras' combined weight, I could stand and look around for a place to make a showdown. That's when I saw a faint glimmering through the dense jungle ahead of us.

"*Come on!*" I growled, jerking the Oliveiras to their feet. "*There's a clearing up ahead!*"

They were too exhausted to stand alone, so I slung Maria over my shoulder again and grabbed her husband under his arms and headed for the clearing. It was only 50 yards away, but the Morcegos weren't much further behind us and coming on fast. Maria's 120 pounds felt like a ton on my shoulder. And half-carrying, half-dragging even a small man like Oli-

MORE

Jim MacDonald knew just where to find the fabulous diamond field hidden in Brazil's Mato Grosso. Now all that stood between him and a billion dollars were the greedy Oliveiras, a tribe of Morcegos cannibals — and a mysterious man-eating lizard.

MAN'S CONQUEST

ART BY NORM EASTMAN

Carrying Oliveira's wife over my shoulder and dragging him along under my arm was too much. When I stumbled and fell for the last time, the Morcegos head-hunters were no more than a spear's throw behind us, whistling their shrill bat-like cries.

Relieved of the Oliveiras' combined weight, I could stand and look around for a place to make a showdown. That's when I saw a faint glimmering through the dense jungle ahead of us.

"Come on!" I growled, jerking the Oliveiras to their feet. *"There's a clearing up ahead!"*

They were too exhausted to stand alone, so I slung Maria over my shoulder again and grabbed her husband under his arms and headed for the clearing. It was only 50 yards away, but the Morcegos weren't much further behind us and coming on fast. Maria's 120 pounds felt like a ton on my shoulder. And half-carrying, half-dragging even a small man like Oliveira is work for mules. I wanted to drop them, or at least him, but I stretched screaming muscles until I staggered into the clearing.

I quickly dropped them both and for a breathless instant stood amazed at what I saw.

The open space was a natural clearing some 50 paces wide and roughly circular. The thick jungle wall crowded up to the edge of the clearing, and within this strange circle a full tropical moon flooded everything with silver radiance, illuminating a field of giant crystals that stood around us like a forest of huge quartz boulders thrust up through the earth's thick carpet of moss.

They dazzled in the moonlight, some gleaming blue like sapphires, others flaming red like rubies, many of brilliant emerald green, yellow, or the iridescent crystal of blue-white diamonds, an immense jewel box of gargantuan gems, some of them higher than a man!

A spear glanced off a tall blue-white crystal next to me. I cursed the Oliveiras. *"Take cover, you damn fools!"* They suddenly found the strength to crawl behind one of the big rocks, and I flopped down behind a big blue-white stone and unlimbered my Winchester shotgun. I threw the Enfield rifle across to Oliveira and tossed his wife the pistol. Then I peppered the dark jungle wall with birdshot.

The Morcegos' piercing, bat-like cries were immediately punctuated by screams of pains. But the savages didn't run! They let loose a shower of flint-tipped spears that struck sparks from the huge crystal boulders. On my left I heard the Enfield roar and the pistol chatter angrily.

Suddenly spears and darts were coming from all directions, for the Morcegos had surrounded the clearing now and were bombarding us from every side.

I dodged among the rocks and blasted away with the shotgun until I had no more ammunition. I threw down the gun and looked around for the Oliveiras. I could hear them shooting, but for the moment I lost track of them in the moonlit maze of crystals.

Then I saw their gunflashes and started running toward them. The Morcegos broke out of the jungle just as I dropped down behind the Oliveiras' rock.

Raul Oliveira stopped shooting. The rifle fell from his fingers. His hands shook uncontrollably, and he began gibbering and laughing wildly.

I grabbed the Enfield and blazed away at two hideously painted Morcegos as they came around the edge of the rock. I blasted both of the hairy savages, but more came on. I emptied the rifle into them, but there were still more Morcegos.

Tugging an ammo clip out of my belt, I turned to get Maria's pistol. But just then she cried out and fell back against the rock with a spear rammed through her left shoulder.

She dropped the pistol and it skittered away over some smaller crystals. I scrambled frantically to pick it up, but before I could reach it a dozen hairy Morcegos closed in screaming....

I first met these Morcegos Indians during World War II, when I was with a special detachment of U. S. Army Engineers laying out a chain of airstrips across the Brazilian jungles, early in 1942.

Because of German interests in the international diamond trust, we weren't getting enough industrial stones from South Africa to supply the needs of our factories for drills and cutting edges. Though Brazilian diamonds are not hard enough to make good drills, being mostly fancy gem stones, they were better than nothing in those days.

From our airstrips, loads of diamonds were flown in light planes out of the Mato Grosso, which until long after the war was a very dangerous place full of head-hungry Indians like the Morcegos.

Some of the tribes were friendly, however, and traded with us as we worked our way through the jungles, hacking out these landing strips. They told us fantastic stories about lost cities, strange races of people in the heart of the rain forest, mysterious monsters that were worshipped as gods—the very things Colonel Fawcett reported about his own explorations in this area only 18 years earlier.

But I wasn't interested in bizarre animals, lost cities, and strange races of men. It was diamonds that most impressed me about the Mato Grosso. The small stones panned out by the placer workers along the riverbanks had to come from a source. There had long been a mystery about the location of the mother lode. When we came along in 1942 no one had yet discovered the volcanic "pipes," which are the mother lode of every diamond field in the same way that a big gold deposit is at the source of every panning of gold dust and nuggets. I knew this much, with only a bachelor of science degree in mining geology.

When the war was over, I went back to the Colorado School of Mines and finished my studies, and for several years afterward worked as an oil prospector in Venezuela and Brazil.

During that time I developed a theory about the possible

location of the mother lode of Brazil's diamond workings.

Armed with this theory and about $1,000, I landed at Rio de Janeiro's International Airport on January 7, 1958, with the intention of going to a region in the Mato Grosso known as the Mato Bruto, which was totally unexplored at that time. In fact the Brazilian government wasn't issuing travel permits to any unauthorized expeditions going into the Mato Grosso at this time, and especially not into the Mato Bruto.

This I knew in advance when I applied for a permit to travel in the interior. I presented myself as an ordinary tourist with a camera.

It was then I first met Raul Oliveira. He was chief of the Bureau of Indian Affairs, as we call our own agency in Washington.

"You say the purpose of your trip into the Mato Grosso is pleasure, *Senhor* MacDonald?" he inquired politely. He was a sad-

eyed little Brazilian with curly hair and a small, neat moustache.
The pin stripes on his blue serge suit made you dizzy if you
looked at them too long and the pomade on his hair smelled like
a perfume factory on a hot day. And Rio does get awfully hot in
January, the middle of summer south of the Equator.

I said, "Yes, I have long wanted to take a walking tour of the
Mato Grosso around Cuiabá. I understand the area is peaceful
now and has become one of your new National Parks." I figured
that sounded innocent enough, even to a suspicious bureaucrat.

"It *was* peaceful, *Senhor* MacDonald," he said. "But recently
bands of Morcegos Indians from the interior have been seen
near settlements. The Morcegos have not yet been tamed.
Consequently very few permits are being issued for travel in the
region."

"What's the usual permit fee, *Senhor* Oliveira?" I asked. In
these matters it's always best to be completely frank in Latin
American countries.

"Well, *Senhor* MacDonald," he said, studying the top of his
desk very carefully as he considered how much to ask. Arriving at
a figure, he went on, "*Before* the Morcegos trouble, the permit fee
was only fifty American dollars...."

"And now?"

"It's slightly higher—double, to be exact."

"By all means, let's be exact," I said, reaching for my wallet. I
peeled off five 20s and laid them on his desk.

Without raising his eyes, he scooped the hundred into a
drawer, slammed it shut, and locked it, pocketing the key. Then he
opened another drawer and took out some official forms.

"Now we must fill these out," he said.

I protested. "But I just gave you a hundred dollars for my
permit! What's this about forms now?"

"You are merely applying for a permit, *Senhor* MacDonald," he
said softly and patiently as if to a small child.

"And then?" I demanded. "When do I get my travel permit?"

"As soon as your application is processed, which will take but
a few days," he assured me, adding, "I will call you at your hotel—
the Grand Hotel Amazonas, is it not?"

I've paid bribes before to public officials, but this looked more
like a holdup.

"Don't call me, I'll call you!" I said, and left. Another minute and I'd have busted him right in the jaw.

I spent the next three weeks phoning Oliveira about my travel permit, and when I wasn't on the phone I was sitting on a bench outside his office, waiting for the arrogant little wise guy to come out and tell me, "No, *Senhor* MacDonald, not yet! Sorry...."

During those three weeks I spent my nights trying to forget the days, which is a lead-pipe cinch in Rio. The *carioca* girls are the world's greatest, running an even first place with the girls on Havana's Prado. They're big where you want them big, and small where you want them small, and they never think of anything but *amor*. That's how I spent my nights.

Meanwhile, my hotel room was searched. Nothing was stolen, but when I returned one night with a gorgeous blonde I picked up in one of Rio's wilder gin mills, I looked in the dresser drawer for a bottle of bourbon and I saw immediately that someone had been through my things. I happen to be very orderly in my personal habits, like always putting the cap back on the tube of toothpaste and arranging my two hairbrushes just so in the drawer.

I didn't waste any time thinking about this problem at the moment because of this crazy blonde, but the next day as I sat in Oliveira's waiting room, I thought it over.

Two weeks had already passed, and I still hadn't received my permit to travel into the interior. It struck me that such a delay meant only one thing—*I was being investigated.*

As part of my long preparation for this expedition, during the years since the war, I had studied not only the Portuguese language but everything else I could about Brazil—and to some extent Latin America in general. My years as an oil prospector in South America had taught me one thing if nothing else about these semi-dictatorships: the thoroughness of their secret police.

I knew it was more than likely that I was on record in Brazilian government files as having been with the US Engineers in the Mato Grosso in early 1942. This fact alone, considering our mission in Brazil during World War II, would be enough to alert their counterintelligence organization. The government is jealously interested in everything connected with diamonds, desperately fearing the international diamond syndicate, which

has long tried to get into Brazil's rich diamond fields. I was a
natural suspect, if you looked at it from their point of view.

I got my travel permit after three weeks. It came when I was
spending my usual morning in Oliveira's waiting room. I was
going to offer him another bribe, when he came out of his office
and took me inside, personally leading me by the elbow. He sat me
down in front of his desk and broke out the cigars.

"Here is your permit, *Senhor* MacDonald," he said, handing
me the $100-paper, signed, sealed, and rubber-stamped a dozen
times. I didn't bother saying thanks. And I didn't take a cigar. I
only wanted to get out of there. I rose to leave.

Oliveira remained seated. "I suppose you know," he said, "that
it's against the law to carry firearms into the Mato Grosso. Our
policy is to protect the Indians, not shoot them."

"I'm aware of that," I said, thinking of the pistol, the rifle,
and the shotgun in my hotel room, and all the ammunition I
intended to carry with me.

Traveling in the more settled parts of the Mato Grosso
without guns is usually safe enough now. In fact a great area
is becoming a vacation ground for Brazilians. But I was going
beyond that and into the Mato Bruto, the unexplored heart of the
Mato Grosso, where guns were definitely needed. I didn't intend
to face a gang of head-hunting cannibals with nothing in my
hands but a compass and a map.

At the same time, I remembered that my hotel room had been
searched, and I wondered how much Oliveira knew.

I guessed how much when he said, "By the way, *Senhor*
MacDonald, my wife and I are taking my annual vacation at this
time, and we too have planned a walking tour of the new Mato
Grosso National Park."

"That's very interesting," I said, edging toward the office
door. "I hope you both have a very nice time." His announcement
surprised me. I wasn't sure what to make of it.

"Perhaps we'll meet in the interior, then," Oliveira was saying
as I backed into the hall.

"I certainly hope so!" I said, just to give him something to
worry about. I had plenty to worry about myself. I was beginning
to get the idea Oliveira had found out what I was up to, and
instead of alerting his government, he was going to tag along on

the richest diamond hunt in history.

He and his wife boarded the train the next morning, and of course they had tickets for a berth in the same car with me.

As soon as Oliveira saw me, he mugged astonishment and came rushing to my end of the car with outstretched hand. I stood up and gave him the phoniest handshake of my life.

"*Senhor* MacDonald," he gushed, "what a delightful surprise!"

"Yes, it certainly is," I agreed, staring past him at his wife, who was looking straight into my eyes. She had a look that spoke volumes, if the volumes were written by Boccaccio and illustrated with certain postcards you can buy from any newsboy in Rio.

"Come meet my wife," Oliveira said.

He led the way up the aisle and made the introductions. Maria Oliveira held out her hand. I took it the way you take a small living animal. She had delicate hands and feet, but the rest of this woman was built big for her size. She was the same height as her husband, about five feet four, but blessed with enough equipment for a much taller woman. She was very conscious of her physical possessions, the kind of sexy female who always seems to be on the verge of breaking into a belly dance. She was beautiful, too, in a strange way, with fiery golden hair, ebony eyes and tawny skin. Heavily sensual red lips parted in a frank and healthy smile, and her white teeth looked like they wanted to take a bite out of me. There was a delicate tension about her nostrils that bespoke the restless wife. The palm of her hand was moist in mine.

I had no doubts about her. I only wondered *when*....

The three of us spent the day together, sitting in the club car and talking. And waiting for each other to slip up and tip his hand. Maria and I did most of the talking, I noticed, with Raul Oliveira listening and saying little. Maria asked me about my work, and I talked about mining geology—mentioning nothing, of course, about diamonds. She tried to make conversation about the Mato Grosso, and I pretended to as much ignorance as I thought I could get by with.

Meanwhile Maria was giving me the business, crossing and uncrossing her legs, each time hiking her skirts up a little so I could see that beyond her black silk stockings and black garters, she was also wearing black panties.

At one point during the first afternoon, Maria said, "Perhaps we shall meet in the Mato Grosso."

After supper, while we were having brandies, she said, "It might be fun to make the trip *together*, don't you think *Senhor* MacDonald?"

I hesitated, looking for a way to say no, but her husband broke in then, saying, "We'll have all day tomorrow to talk about the trip. We don't reach Corumbá till evening... Shall we go to bed?"

Later I lay in my berth with the lights out, watching the landscape roll past the window under a rising full moon. The Trans-Brasil railroad from Rio to Corumbá at the Bolivian border is one of the wildest jungle trips in South America, cutting straight through the primeval rain forest, with Indian villages alongside the roadway and hordes of monkeys cavorting next to the tracks. After Corumbá, the trip upriver into the Mato Grosso. I wondered how to get rid of the Oliveiras.

I wasn't surprised when Oliveira's wife crawled into my berth. I had the idea all along that he was the kind of man who would use his wife this way. With her delighted cooperation of course. And mine. She slipped between the curtains and started taking off her robe. The lights of a station were flashing by, and I could see why her husband had that sad, worn-out look. She was *too* much! Even among the very mature figures of Brazilian women, Maria's was outstanding. After shrugging off her robe, she flung herself upon me and covered my mouth with hers. She moaned and her hands went wild.

I wasn't thinking about Oliveira just then, but afterward, as we lay watching the moonlit landscape roll by like a technicolor travelogue, I asked her, "What about your husband?"

She smiled. "Do you care?"

"No," I admitted. "I'm just curious. Did you dope his hot chocolate or cut his throat? In other words, where is he now, and what's he up to?"

"I don't know," she said. "I told him I was going to the ladies' room. When I go back I'll tell him I got into a long talk with another woman I met in there."

"How long is this talk going to be?"

"It's over right now," she said, pulling on her robe. "I must go back. Perhaps there will be another chance—at the hotel in Corumbá, on the riverboat, or maybe even in the Mato Grosso...?"

She left then, and I did some heavy thinking. It figured the Oliveiras were trying to box me in. At first Raul hadn't shown any unusual interest in my trip, not knowing its true purpose. But after three weeks of undercover investigation, the travel permit came through and Oliveira was suddenly so overjoyed he announced his *own* trip into the Mato Grosso! Too coincidental to be accidental! He *had* to know something.

The government's investigation must have turned up the fact that diamond geology was my specialty—and also no doubt the information that I had this theory about the *location* of the mother lode, which feeds the Brazilian diamond fields. That's as far as they could go without asking me personally, because no one knew *where* I mentally put the big *X* on the map and said, "There it is, the greatest lode of diamonds ever known!"

At most, they knew my general theory, but not its most important fact—the exact location. Apparently Oliveira knew this much, since it was enough to make him try to tag along, by hook or crook, even if it meant using his wife to work on me.

I couldn't escape from the Oliveiras. At Corumbá, which was as far as we went, I checked into the local hotel for the night, and of course the Oliveiras took a room on the same floor.

Maria did the Pullman berth scene again, and this time she came out flat with it: *Would* I take her and her husband along with me on my Mato Grosso walking tour?

"I can't," I alibied, "and don't ask me why."

So naturally she asked, "Why?"

"I can't tell you," I stalled.

"Does Raul know?"

"Nobody knows," I said, not really surprised that she didn't trust her husband. I'm sure the feeling was mutual.

"Tell *me!*" she pleaded, toying with the hair on my chest. "I can keep a secret!"

"All right," I said, not laughing at that last remark, "I'll tell you... I'm not a mining geologist at all!"

"What?"

"I'm a zoologist, and I'm on the track of one of the century's biggest discoveries!" I wasn't making this yarn up on the spur of the moment. I'd given the problem some thought, and the only lie I was about to tell her was the detail about me being a zoologist.

"What's a zoologist?" she asked, just about as baffled as I wanted her to be.

"I'm a scientist," I explained, "and I specialize with creatures in the animal kingdom. And right now I'm after one of the rarest animals alive!" I looked her square in the eyes. Would she go for it? "Have you ever heard of the Guardian?"

"The Guardian? No, I don't think so. What does it guard?"

"That's the mystery," I said. "There are reports that many tribes deep in the Mato Grosso are worshipping a strange white beast, which they call the Guardian because it's supposed to guard a great treasure." This much was true and was well known in Brazil—not that such a creature actually existed, but that the forest Indians said it did.

"You don't actually believe this?" Maria, it seemed, was one who didn't believe *everything* she heard.

"Believe in it? I'm sure of it!" I said firmly. "What's more, I have a theory about it, which some of my colleagues in the states think is pretty fantastic." I was playing it close to the truth. If she knew the difference, I hoped she'd show it. She did.

"Yes?" she said as she slipped into her robe, "and what is your theory?" She didn't even try to hide the skepticism in her voice.

I had no more doubts. The Oliveiras *knew!*

But I went on. "I think the so-called Guardian is really a huge albino lizard," I explained, playing it out to the end. "This occurs very rarely in the animal world—especially among jungle lizards. We don't know how it has survived, because its strange white coloring makes stalking and hunting for food almost impossible. Also, its size, about twenty feet long, is something of a phenomenon. But I imagine in certain parts of the deep rain forest, conditions are favorable for this form of life...." I was still at it when Maria quietly left the room, forgetting to slam the door.

I thought that story *might* shake the Oliveiras, but if Maria told Raul about my white lizard, he apparently didn't believe I was after the albino any more than she did.

The next day as I was sitting in the bow of the riverboat and watching the green jungle walls slide past, Oliveira came up to me and laid it on the line.

He said, "I happen to be very familiar with the Mato Grosso

area around Cuiabá. Perhaps if we traveled together I could be of some use to you. In addition, I have a permit to carry guns."

I said, "Thanks, *senhor,* that's very kind of you, but I may stay around Cuiabá for a few days before taking off for the interior. Of course if you and your wife haven't left by the time I start my trip...." I didn't think stalling would help me any, but I had to try.

"That's very good of you!" he cut in, grasping my hand and sealing the agreement, as he perhaps thought. Or perhaps not. Raul Oliveira was as tricky as a cat.

Late that afternoon we passed through the famous Brazilian diamond workings, which I hadn't seen since the war. For miles along the riverbanks I saw thousands of men panning for diamonds with reed-mesh screens, as they have been doing for generations.

Oliveira approached me again as I watched the panners from the boat's rail.

"Somewhere upriver," he remarked, "lies the source of all the diamonds found around here."

I said nothing.

He went on, "But the source has never been discovered. Someday a lucky explorer will become the richest man in the world!"

Still I said nothing. He talked about theories, and he showed that he knew the subject. General João Prêto, the Brazilian explorer, Oliveira said, believed the mother lode lay deep in the earth beneath the Mato Grosso. Oliveira had everything right about Prêto's theory except the location of the lode.

I didn't reply to this conversational gambit. It was clearly a trick. I knew Prêto personally. He believed the original diamond lode lay high in the Andes Mountains, thrust up during those cataclysmic upheavals in prehistoric times that raised new continents and sank old ones. Prêto's theory was really the opposite of what Oliveira had said, but if I showed I knew this, I'd tip my hand. So I said nothing, though I was sure it was already too late.

My own theory was an extension of General Prêto's, the difference being that I believed the mother lode had been shifted to one side of its original location, not raised by the Andes nor plowed under by turnings of the earth's crust. I believed the lode had been shifted from the outer Mato Grosso to the even more primeval Mato Bruto.

But Oliveira got none of this out of me, and that night Maria tried again. We were lying in my cabin, smoking when Maria said, "You were joking about the big animal, no?"

"No," I said. "I was serious. I believe the Guardian does exist. It could be a giant white lizard as I think."

"But what if you do find this thing?"

"I'll photograph it," I said, still playing it straight. "With this evidence, I'll be able to get up a proper scientific expedition." With such questionable evidence, I'd probably be laughed out of the scientific world. But it was better than telling her where I expected to locate the greatest mother lode in the world.

Maria bit her lip and looked doubtful. When she left to go to her own cabin, I think she was slightly convinced. But the next morning as we left the riverboat at Cuiabá, her husband came up to me and asked, "Do you know yet when you want to start the trip?"

"No, I haven't decided."

He wore a very serious look. "One of the boat's officers informs me that a decree will be announced tomorrow forbidding anyone to enter the Mato Grosso National Park until further notice!"

That did it. I had no doubt Oliveira could get the local Park officials to close the area for a few days. In other words, this was the squeeze. Oliveira was forcing me to start my trip *today*—right now, so I couldn't slip away from him.

He guessed right. I *had* intended ducking out on the Oliveiras during the night. I could have been halfway to the Mato Bruto before they had breakfast.

This was the showdown, and Oliveira stood there with his eyes fixed on mine, waiting for my decision. If I kept trying to shake him, he could close the trails that led into the area. On the other hand, if I agreed to take him along, no one else would get in my way, and I'd have a legal permit for my guns.

Of course Oliveira would be able to follow me to the biggest natural cache of diamonds in the world.

We were on trail before noon.

At first I took well-traveled footpaths, setting a fast pace and hoping to lose the Oliveiras while we were still in the National Park area of the nearer Mato Grosso. Beyond that point, I wouldn't even leave a US Marine alone—especially with Morcegos head-hunters in the vicinity.

By nightfall we'd been on trail six hours, and I was tired. The Oliveiras were completely done in, and they sagged to the ground when we stopped for the night. They couldn't even take their own packs off. I had to help them, but this gave me the chance to go through their things, which I did very quickly over their noisy protests. But I found nothing unusual and no guns.

However, I, carried an arsenal of three weapons, a Winchester 12-gauge shotgun for birds and people who got too close, one of the famous old Enfield "Jungle" rifles, and a Spanish MM-31 of the Luger type, firing a 30-round clip. All this was a load to pack, but I had planned to carry the stuff myself anyway, and I didn't want the Oliveiras handling guns. Not with my back exposed.

I built a cook-fire of damp wood, starting it with dead bamboos and old coconut husks, and while the fire was building up a good bed of coals, I slung the hammocks. By then the Oliveiras were able to move again.

Maria offered to cook the meal. I let her try. It turned out there were two things that woman excelled in, and cooking was one of them.

I knew I'd miss her both ways. But I had to get rid of the Oliveiras before we reached the end of the Mato Grosso forest and struck into the unknown tract of the Mato Bruto—which would be the following afternoon if I kept up a good pace.

After supper I damped the fire and we all climbed into our hammocks. I half-expected Maria to come climbing into my net when I heard Raul snoring, but I guess she was too worn out by the long trek.

I had a hard time staying awake, but when I felt sure they were both asleep I swung out of my hammock and silently gathered my gear together. I had my pack cinched and was slinging it onto my back when one of the straps caught on the canteen and made enough noise to wake the dead.

A spotlight snapped on and caught me in its guilty circle. Raul said, "What's going on?"

Maria woke up then and grumbled something sleepily.

I had the bright idea I might go ahead anyway and make my escape. What could the Oliveiras do about it? By the time they got into their boots, I'd be far away and hiding in the bush.

But as I went on slinging my pack I heard something else— the tiny sharp metallic click of a safety catch!

So I dropped my pack and got out the hammock again. While I was tying it to a pair of trees Raul kept the flashlight on me.

When I started to climb in, he said, "Toss me your boots!" I took them off and threw them to him. "Your extra pair also!" I threw them to him. "Now drop your gun belt!"

I did. Then I swung into the hammock. I watched him get out of his net, gather up my boots and the guns, and walk on down the trail with them. He came back a few moments later without them.

"You're crazy!" I yelled across at him.

"Maybe," he replied, climbing back into his hammock, "but if you're barefoot and unarmed you won't go far, no? Good night!"

Maria spoke up now. "Raul! What about the Morcegos?"

He said, "They haven't been seen in three days. The forest is perfectly safe. Go to sleep!"

But she went on, "Raul! What about the monster lizard that *Senhor* Mac-Donald...?"

"There are no monsters, idiot!" he snapped. "Now shut up, and go to sleep!"

A moment later I felt a warm breath at my right ear, and Maria's hushed voice whispered, *"Kill him! Do it now!"* I said nothing. She went on, *"He's going to kill you! He said so! After you find the diamonds...!"*

I turned and took Maria's head in my hands and brought her ear close to my mouth. I whispered, *"You kill him, he's your husband!"*

She jerked away from me, cursing furiously.

Oliveira woke up again, but by the time he got his flashlight on, Maria was back in her hammock. He played the light over our nets for a few seconds, then switched it off, and that ended the night's activities.

After this I didn't try to shake the Oliveiras. I just took it for granted they'd be along when I found what I was looking for.

There wasn't anything I could do about it unless I wanted to kill Raul. And I didn't. Though I knew he had something like that in mind for me. Especially after his wife was nice enough to tell me about it. But I still had to *find* the diamond lode. He wouldn't try killing me before that.

In the morning Raul went into the bushes and brought back my boots and guns, and after a light breakfast we hit the trail.

From this point until we reached the Mato Bruto it was still possible to turn a gun on Raul and force him and his wife to go back. Except for one thing: You don't point a gun at a man unless you're willing to shoot him. He might call your bluff with his own gun, and I distinctly heard a safety catch snapped off when I tried to desert the Oliveiras the night before.

I've never had to kill except in self-defense, and I hope I never will. A fortune in diamonds isn't enough to make me do it. The war was no exception. We had to defend ourselves against untamed Indians (I think they were Morcegos), who attacked us once. Their name means Bat People. They rushed our detail when we were clearing some jungle for an airstrip along the edge of the Mato Bruto. It happened at night, which is the way with most primitives, and before we could drive them off they got one of our sentries. We found his bones the next day. Picked clean, *but uncooked.* The Bat People had eaten him raw. After that we shot at Morcegos whenever we saw them.

You couldn't mistake them for other Indians. They're very short, bow-legged and long-armed, hairy all over, and naked. Very dark, almost black, they paint their faces white, and they file down their teeth to needle points in the manner of most cannibals. They build no fires, plant no corn, build no houses, but live in holes they dig in the muddy jungle floor, breed like rabbits, and devour their own kind. Raw. Which in itself is not uncommon among aboriginals. But the Morcegos eat their victims *alive.*

Maybe we were a little fast on the trigger during the war, but after seeing what happened to that sentry....

I had not seen these horrors in 16 years when we walked straight into one of the Morcegos' mound villages on our second day out of the Mato Grosso and well into the Mato Bruto rain forest. It was noon and the sun directly overhead filtered eerily through the tall canopy of dripping treetops 100 feet above, while here below among giant roots and great tree ferns the air was steamy and our clothes clung wetly to our bodies. We were tired and hungry and in need of rest when we threaded our way through a bamboo grove and suddenly came out into the open.

Before us lay a cluster of earth mounds, perhaps 20 of them, each with its entrance hole, and among them a few of the Morcegos' young were playing like hairy pups. One of them saw us and shrieked his strange high-pitched cry, which is why the head-hunters are called the Bat People. Several adults were nearby, grubbing in the ground for worms.

They looked up and saw us and started shrieking, and suddenly Morcegos were pouring out of their ground holes like large hairy bats, brandishing spears and short darts.

As long as there was a chance they wouldn't attack, I was willing to skirt their village peacefully. But if they got tough I knew what to do. They got tough, all right, with a shower of spears and darts.

"Run for it!" Oliveira shouted. *"Come on!"*

Maria grabbed my arm. "My god, what'll we do?" she cried.

"We'll run," I said, *"but straight ahead!"* I handed her the MM-31 and Raul the Enfield. I kept the shotgun.

"They'll kill us!" Maria was screaming.

"Not before we kill a lot of them!" I yelled at her. "Now, when we start running, start shooting! And don't stop for anything! When your guns are empty, keep on running! I'll tell you when to stop. *Now let's go!"*

I led the way, charging straight through the mound village, blasting away with the shotgun as fast as I could shoot. Behind me I heard the rifle and the MM-31. The suddenness of our assault scared the Morcegos, and most of them scurried into the jungle to throw spears from the protection of the trees. The Bat People are known for their sneak night attacks, they never stand and fight.

I raced ahead until we were through the village and well into the jungle again, where we had to stop and cut our way through a dense brake of bamboo. Here I quickly reloaded the MM-31 and the Enfield and handed them back to the Oliveiras. I stuffed a stick of shells into the birdgun and started through the bamboo brake—one hell of a trap to be caught in if the Morcegos had come after us just then. But they waited till dark.

Apparently they followed us the rest of that day and watched for us to make camp at nightfall, for the dim green light of the rain forest had scarcely faded away when their first eerie shrieks came piercing through the dark like bats' cries.

"Drop everything but the guns and follow me!" I shouted at the Oliveiras.

"What are you going to do?" Raul demanded. There wasn't enough light filtering through the treetops to see his face, but you could hear the fear in his voice.

"We've got to keep moving!" I said. "Here we're sitting ducks!"

"I'm not going!" he whispered huskily. "Maria! Where are you? Come here!"

Maria was hanging onto my shoulders and saying over and over, "You've got to get us out of this!"

I shook her loose. "If you panic, you're dead!"

Then I moved out and they followed close behind. I shoved straight into the massed jungle growth. It was too dark to look for a trail. We made a lot noise, and of course the Morcegos knew where we were all the time.

But it was just as dark for them. I felt the breath of darts flicking past and heard the thud of spears striking tree trunks close by. Whenever I thought I saw a ghostly shadow flit among the trees, I cut loose with the shotgun, scattering birdshot all over the area. I scored a few times. This kept the Morcegos at a little distance, and we plunged ahead through the tough webbing of liana vines, tripping over roots, slogging through knee-deep mud, and time after time sinking up to our bellies in foul water, with unseen things slithering around our legs.

The jungle was alive with night animals hooting or snarling, jabbering in the treetops, padding stealthily along the mud floor, and pairs of golden eyes were everywhere in the darkness.

I walked straight into a Morcego before I saw him or he saw me. I shoved the muzzle of the 12-gauge against his gut and blasted a hole through him. The impact slammed him back into the brush, but it didn't kill him instantly, and his dying screams echoed through the hot night air.

I heard Raul somewhere behind me cry out, *"Help me! I can't make it! Help me!"*

I started back to see what I could do and bumped into Maria.

She gave a startled cry and said, "Oh, it's you!" Then, "Listen! Don't go back there! Leave him!"

Raul heard her and yelled crazily, "Don't leave me! You bitch, I'll kill you if we get out of this! Help me! Help me!"

Maria was holding my arm. "Get out of my way!" I said, shoving her aside. I kicked around in the darkness trying to find Raul. I found him collapsed in the mud.

"I can't go on!" he moaned.

"You hurt?"

"No, but my legs have given out. I haven't any strength left!"

I pulled him up, but his legs were trembling so violently he couldn't stand alone. I slung the rifle over my shoulder and grabbed him under one arm to help him walk. Then I started out again, but now it was slow going, lugging Oliveira along and trying to use the shotgun at the same time.

Maria held up a little longer, but when she caved in, it was all the way. She couldn't even walk with help. I holstered the MM-31 and threw her over my shoulder, which left me a free arm to help Raul.

I don't know how far we traveled this way, but after another hour I was ready to drop the Oliveiras and let the Morcegos have them.

Then I saw that strange light glimmering faintly far ahead through the jungle, and with the strength of desperation I hauled the Oliveiras to the clearing before I let them drop to the ground.

I was dumbfounded by what I saw in the clearing. I had *stumbled* across the very thing I was searching for, the long-sought mother lode of Brazil's diamond workings—the volcanic "pipes" that feed the world's richest diamond fields!

As I stood staring at the forest of giant multicolored crystals, the Morcegos came charging out of the jungle into the moonlit clearing and saw us. They shrieked and threw a wave of spears and darts, striking the crystal boulders. None of us was hit, but it scared the Oliveiras into taking cover.

I jumped behind a giant crystal and tossed the Enfield and pistol over to Raul and Maria. Then I pointed my shotgun at the jungle wall and began blasting away, cutting down Morcegos by twos and threes in the wide-spreading pattern of birdshot. This kept them away for a few moments, but then came a shower of spears from every side. The savages had surrounded the clearing!

With no place to hide, I began to move quickly from boulder to boulder, blazing away at Morcegos wherever I saw one, until I ran out of shells. Throwing away the useless gun, I looked around for the Oliveiras. I heard two guns shooting, and when I located their flashes, I ran over to them, dropping down behind their rock just as the Morcegos charged out of the jungle in a screaming horde.

Raul broke down completely. He shook so hard he couldn't hang onto the rifle, so I grabbed it from him and started picking off Morcegos as fast as I could snap the trigger. I emptied the magazine and threw the rifle down.

I had one more 30-round clip for the MM-31, but as I reached to take the gun from Maria, a spear suddenly struck her in the left shoulder, and a gang of hideously painted hairy Morcegos came running through the rocks with their spears poised for the kill....

Then a loud and chilling scream followed by a long hiss burst over the jungle and the moonlit field of crystals. For a long moment afterward, there was absolute silence around us.

A blast of hot and fetid air swept over us like the stench of a thousand unburied corpses.

The sound came again, this time within yards from where we were hiding, and the scream echoed through the night.

Suddenly the foliage on the edge of the jungle parted and a huge white head jutted out of the undergrowth. We saw the golden eyes and the red tongue flitting in and out of its wide, ugly mouth.

The Guardian!

It hissed again, and the Morcegos turned tail and ran for cover, but before the first of them got there, the monster charged out of the jungle, its claws scraping loudly on the crystals and its mouth gaping.... It was the gigantic albino lizard—20-feet long, with a jagged jaw five-feet wide. That immense jaw scooped up the Bat People as they ran. Then I suddenly knew why the natives worshipped this monster as a god. Because its white coloring prevented it from hunting animals, *it had turned maneater*. I had to turn away from the gruesome sight as the creature chomped down on two Morcegos.

Oliveira was lying on his back, shaking like a man with malaria. His mouth hung slack and saliva drooled down his chin. He was pure fear.

Maria was trying to pull the spear out of her shoulder. I yanked it loose. She nearly fainted, but she hung on, cursing like a drill sergeant.

Suddenly and without a word Oliveira scrambled to his feet and ran for the jungle. He might have made it, too, but for his wife.

She didn't shoot her husband. She fired a shot at the Guardian instead, hitting it on the thick scaly armor just below the eye, which stung it and brought the huge head around to look for its puny attacker.

It saw Oliveira running, and in one swoop it snapped him up in those great jaws. I can still hear his bones crunching and his terrible dying screams.

I grabbed the pistol from Maria and headed for the jungle myself while the monster was still busy with Oliveira. I didn't give a damn what happened to Maria now, but she was right behind me. When we reached the cover of trees, I stopped.

I shoved the last clip into the MM-31 and stuck it in my holster. I probably wouldn't need it again, for the Morcegos had fled in the other direction, back toward their mound village, and I intended to head due south until I came to a branch of the Paraguay River.

Maria was standing close to me. The Guardian was kicking up a storm back in the field of crystals, roaring and slamming around, looking for more fresh meat.

"Maria," I said, "you're a lousy shot!" She tried to explain. "I aimed for the eye!"

"Whose?" I asked.

"If I had more bullets," she went on, ignoring my comment, "I would have hit it!"

"That's real noble of you. You didn't have to shoot at all, you know! The Guardian was too busy with those Indians to even see your husband. Raul might have got to the jungle all right if you hadn't helped him!"

"Well, what do you care? Now you don't have to share your discovery with him!"

"Or with you either, baby!"

She smirked. "Don't forget, I know where it is now!"

"I'm not forgetting," I said. "But I'm wondering if maybe I should just leave you here...."

Her eyes bulged. "You wouldn't!"

"Are you sure?" I countered. At the moment even I wasn't sure, but it seemed like the best idea I'd had since we started.

I turned my back on her then and started to walk away. But I heard a certain familiar metallic click, like a gun's safety catch, so I stopped. *What gun?*

I slapped my holster to see if the MM-31 was still there. It was.

An explosion behind me and a stab in my back spun me around. I saw Maria dimly in the forest gloom, standing there with a small gun in her hand. It was the gun I thought Raul had that night when he caught me in the beam of his flashlight just as I was trying to sneak out on them. He had the flash, all right, but his wife must have had the gun. I couldn't tell at the time because of the darkness. And now she'd shot me with it!

The wound wasn't deep. It was only an 18-caliber pellet
from a lady's gun. They hurt but seldom kill unless they strike
a vital place like the head or spine. Maria's little lead bullet was
embedded in my thick back muscles, not serious but painful.

She thought she'd killed me. She dropped the pea-shooter and
flung herself upon me, sobbing hysterically.

Her left shoulder was wet and sticky against my chest, still
bleeding from the spear wound. And the hole in my back hurt like
hell. I wasn't bleeding much, however, because the bullet acted as
a plug. But something had to be done about Maria. So I made her
give me her panties to use as a bandage, and this stopped the flow
of blood. Then I took her brassiere and made a sling for her arm,
to keep the shoulder wound as quiet as possible.

Two days later we staggered into a village of tame Indians
on a branch of the upper Paraguay. They ferried us down to
Corumbá in a balsa canoe. One of them dug Maria's bullet out of
my back and stuffed the hole with a well-chewed leaf. It healed
very quickly.

At Corumbá we split up. I left Maria at the river jetty. It was
early evening, hot and thick with bugs, and a small crowd had
gathered to see the two dirty, ragged, beat-up whites who had
floated down from the Mato Grosso.

"We could be partners," Maria said. It was the last moment,
and she had one foot on the dockside ladder, the other still in the
boat. "After all, you and I have meant something to each other!"

"I saw what you did to your last partner, Maria."

"I didn't shoot him!" She turned back to me now, leaving
the dock ladder. "I shot the Guardian! I was only trying to help!
Besides, you know Raul was going to kill you when we got close
to civilization again! I was trying to help *you!*"

I gave that one about two seconds' deep thought. Then I
picked her up and put her on the ladder and quickly shoved the
canoe away from the jetty. I told the rowers to make for Puerto
Suárez on the Bolivian side of the river. On the Brazilian side,
Maria had only to blow the whistle and slap me in the cooler.
That is, if she felt she needed help from the authorities.

When I looked back from mid-river she was blazing with
anger and yelling for a cop to chase me. She was a wild sight to

see, standing on the river jetty with that golden hair flying and her arm in a sling, a blood-soaked bandage around her shoulder....

At Puerto Suarez I took a plane to La Paz, and then on to New York, where I've spent the last 10 months raising money and men for another expedition into the Mato Bruto.

I'll be ready to go again at the end of Brazil's present rainy season. This time I'm going properly equipped, and from the Bolivian side—down the Guaporé River and then overland to the Mato Bruto, where I expect no difficulty in locating that field of volcanic "pipes" again. I'm taking along a knee mortar in case of another attack by Morcegos, and a high-powered elephant rifle for the Guardian if it shows up.

I have no doubt about finding the mother lode again, but I often wonder about Maria. She can't get there much before me, because everyone has to wait for the rains to stop. But I have no doubt that she'll be there.

And to tell the truth, when I think of that woman, though she's as treacherous as a wolf, her luscious body and the memory of her wild lovemaking still make my head spin and my hands itch to get hold of her.

No, I won't be sorry to see Maria....

"I ENCOUNTERED THE ABOMINABLE SNOWMAN"

Following in the snowy footsteps of some of our earlier tales, "I Encountered the Abominable Snowman" from the September 1960 issue of *Rage* by "Sonam Taki" ("as told to Richard Platt") outlines the familiar quest by a Westerner into the Himalayas in search of the Yeti. The key difference in this tale is the portrayal of the "Yeh Teh" as adept not only at snatching yaks, but likewise young Sherpa women and children—before easily climbing to safety to devour its prey.

The sister of a guide is abducted by a Yeti, and the mission transforms from one of innocent exploration into a desperate gambit to rescue the snatched girl before she is consumed. This level of bloodthirsty behavior, while unusual, is not altogether rare in actual Yeti legends—which accounts for Sherpa guides typically being the first to drop their load and scramble back down the mountainside for safety whenever they encounter any evidence of an Abominable Snowman.

Whether or not any part of this story is fact-based, there frequently lurks an underlying reliance on actual case lore in men's adventure magazine yarns that is yet again successfully exploited here to provide chills and thrills.

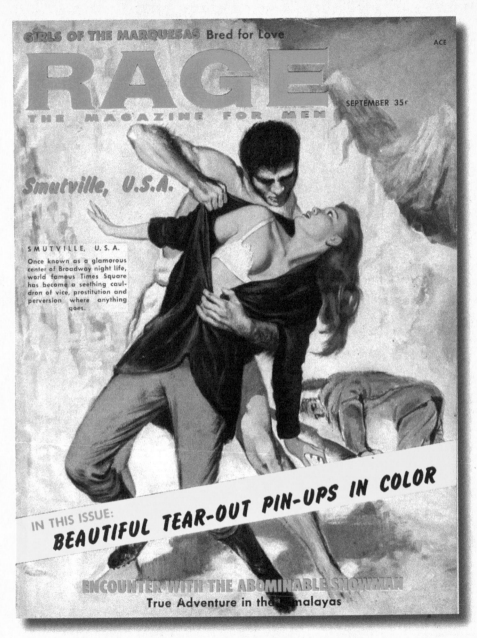

"I ENCOUNTERED THE
ABOMINABLE SNOWMAN"
RICHARD PLATT
RAGE, SEPTEMBER 1960
COVER BY JOHN DUILLO

8

I ENCOUNTERED THE ABOMINABLE SNOWMAN

I fired once, and then again . . . there was no sign of the bullets striking the monster.

ARTIST UNCREDITED

EDITOR'S NOTE: *Sonam Taki is a Sherpa guide, one of the natives of Nepal who live in the Himalaya Mountains, and spend their lives traversing the slopes of Everest, Annapurna, and the other great peaks that make up the "top of the world." Sonam is a veteran of numerous climbing expeditions, but his most incredible exploit occurred in April 1959, on the slope of Kanchenjunga just above his own village. This is his own account of that exploit, as he told it to Richard Platt in Darjeeling, India, a few months afterward. A well-educated Sherpa, who speaks English, knows how to use modern guns and exploration equipment, and is not carried away by local superstitions, Sonam is a reliable observer and a clear-headed one. This is his story, just as he lived it.*

I was at the little settlement of my tribe on the slope of Mount Kanchenjunga, which is the third highest mountain in the world. It was just before the storm season, early in the month of April. We were right below the Zemu Gap, a pass 19,000-feet high that cuts through from the Tibetan side of the Himalayas on the northeast, to the Nepalese side, on the southwest slopes.

There have been signs of the Yeh Teh (Abominable Snowmen) for many years around the Gap. We knew they were there. We had seen their tracks, and two of the oldest men had seen one of them at a distance years before. He was very big, over

7-feet tall, and broad, and covered with heavy, reddish brown hair, and had a tall, pointed head. The hair covered his whole body, but not his face. And when the men from our tribe followed him, they could not keep up with him. He climbed straight up a steep wall, and disappeared into the Gap.

Another time one of our yaks strayed away, and I followed his tracks in the snow. Suddenly they were mingled with tracks like those of a barefooted man, only bigger than the feet of any man, and there was snow kicked up and marks of a fierce struggle and much blood, and the yak's tracks ended there, but the giant man footprints went off again, and behind them there was the bloody track of the yak's body being dragged along. Finally the tracks disappeared against the foot of a rock face too steep for any man to climb without a rope and a pick. But a small streak of blood high up on the rock told the story. The Yeh Teh had gone up the rock carrying the yak with him.

I looked at that and trembled. What could any man do if he caught up with such a monster? The strongest man would never be a match for the Abominable Snowman. And yet I dreamed of someday seeing this strange creature. I was to see that dream come true in a way that would always haunt me.

On that day in April of last year, it happened.

My friend, Bhuta Rau, came running down the trail, waving to me and shouting something I could not understand as I stood in front of my stone but scanning the sky for a coming blizzard. I watched him for a moment and then I realized that he was very frightened and was shouting the same thing over and over. I started toward him, and then I heard it.

"Rana. Rana's gone. It's got Rana. It's got Rana!"

"What's got Rana?" I cried as I approached him. Rana was his young sister—a small, soft-voiced girl with great dark eyes as rich as velvet, skin like flower petals, and the face and form of a beautiful woman-to-be. She was only 16 years old, but already was gazed at with unconcealed longing by men from the nearby villages. Since their parents were dead, Bhuta, who was 24, looked after her closer than most fathers do their daughters.

"Yeh Teh, Yeh Teh! Yeh Teh has Rana—There—There!" He waved his arm furiously in the direction from which he had come, and up, up the slope, toward the Zemu Gap. There was an agony of fear in his face, and his voice was shrill with terror.

He turned back. "Please, bring help! Follow me! I am going back after her," he shouted over his shoulder.

I tried to hold him a minute, and find out more about it, but he shook off my grip, and started running. He only looked back once more, and there was utter desperation in his face.

"I saw the tracks. Yeh Teh carried her off. I must catch them. Come quickly," he called as he ran.

I felt a chill of fear as I thought of Rana in the grasp of the creature who had carried off a yak and climbed the rock faces a man couldn't find a grip on. I turned and shouted to the other men, and when they came running, I told them what had happened. We hurried after Bhuta. He was far ahead of us, running among the rocks, but we could still see him. As we rushed after him, I thought "he has no chance of catching the monster, but if he did, what could he do?" And, I wondered, what could any of us do? Poor, pretty young Rana. She was certainly lost. And if any of us should overtake the snowman, we would be lost, too.

The full force of the horror struck me, and I felt the full taste of fear, for myself, for all of us, for Bhuta and Rana. But at the same time I was aware of a terrible fascination—was I really going to see the monstrous snowman at last, face the dread Yeh Teh, which I had heard about and talked about myself for so long?

Out of the village, Bhuta reached the open slope and began to climb. He went out of sight momentarily, but we continued to move toward the spot where he had been. We still had his tracks before us and we were watching them as we hurried along. The wind was stronger and little flurries of snow were beginning to whip into our faces, but we could still see his tracks. There was not enough to cover them. We climbed up around a cut in the rocks where we had last seen Bhuta, and I heard a shout from my left.

One of the men was standing pointing at the ground, a look of horror on his face. We looked down. It was not Bhuta's tracks he pointed at. It was the spot where the monster of the rocks had struck. We saw a couple of footprints that were clearly Rana's, and beside them, coming down from above were those of the Yeh Teh. It was clear what had happened, fearfully clear.

Rana's tracks came from below. The Yeh Teh's came down

from above. Then Rana's simply stopped. And the monster's headed back up among the rocks. They were the same huge prints I had seen before. And there was almost twice the distance between them that there was between any of ours. He must be huge, I thought again. The other men, too, were gazing at the tracks in a kind of shocked fascination. I gripped the .30-30 rifle I was carrying a little harder. After all, three of us had guns, powerful, modern rifles. We might be able to help still. There was no blood. Only the monster's tracks, followed by Bhuta's. Maybe Rana was still alive.

Without saying a word we looked at one another and plunged ahead. The going got harder. The trail we were following now went straight up the mountainside. A little further on we came onto a ledge that jutted out from the face and we looked up. I caught sight of Bhuta, and shouted, pointing. The others looked up. He was very far ahead of us, far above us. He was practically running up the mountain. The wind was rising and more snow was coming down.

"Come," I shouted, "we must catch up before a blizzard starts. We must not lose Bhuta."

"He is climbing like a fiend," one of the men said.

We started after him, climbing faster than before, as fast as we could. I tried to keep him in sight, but it was impossible. He would appear and disappear as he went among the rocks, or as I went behind a boulder. Ahead of the others, I shielded my eyes and looked up again. Suddenly Bhuta reappeared, or seemed to, much higher up, edging out onto a sheer, open stretch.

"It can't be him...that high," I thought—and then I realized, as I got a better look. There was a figure up there, but it was not Bhuta's. It was too big for him, too big for any man. And there was a huge bundle on the shoulders. I was looking at the Yeh Teh—the creature called in English the Abominable Snowman. There it was! And the bundle across its shoulders must be Rana.

I screamed something then. I don't know what. I only know I was shouting and rushing up the slope, waving the others on behind me. They saw then, and there were gasps of astonishment and fear for the girl, but everybody climbed faster, even while they chattered about the incredible size of the Yeh Teh. And as we climbed, all eyes strained upward toward the figures there.

The monster was moving fast, but did not seem to be
hurrying, and did not seem to be aware of any pursuers. He cut
across the face of the slope for a while and I wondered about
Bhuta. He must have gained too, I thought. And just at that
moment I saw him.

He had attained the open stretch behind the monster and
was climbing with the frantic speed of a madman. He was much
closer than I had expected he could be, and with the Yeh Teh's
delay Bhuta might soon be up to the level with him. Most of the
distance between them now was lateral. Bhuta had not cut across
the slope when the monster did; he had continued going up.

Now the monster was approaching a jumble of rocks and
cuts in the surface. If he went into them, he might slow down. If
he cut back to more open ground, he would turn back closer to
Bhuta. And if he did, what could Bhuta do?

"Hurry, hurry." I screamed at the others. "We must hurry.
Bhuta may catch up with him soon, and he will need help. He can't
stop the Yeh Teh by himself. We have to catch up."

We redoubled our efforts, but we were still a good distance
below them. The Yeh Teh had entered the cut in the face, and
paused. He seemed to be picking around among the rocks, idly
hunting for something, still unaware of us, or Bhuta. Bhuta was
as high on the slope now as his quarry, and he was moving across,
toward the rocks, going a little above them.

The Yeh Teh disappeared among the rocks, and then,
incredibly, reappeared without his burden. He had put Rana down.
My heart sank. She must be dead, I thought. Bhuta stopped, too,
crouching forward and looking. I knew that he was thinking the
same thing I was. He was only about 30 yards from the rocks now,
and the Yeh Teh was bound to see him soon.

We were about 150 yards below. I could see the big, reddish
figure of the Yeh Teh clearly, but the face was turned away from
me. He was a big, lumbering thing, but he moved among the rocks
with ease. He turned half toward us, and I had a glimpse of a
light-skinned face, without the hair that grew everywhere else on
the seemingly naked figure.

Bhuta had gone higher, and reached the edge of the cut,
keeping some rocks between him and the monster. Now he was

no more than 20 yards from the Yeh Teh. I wanted to call to him, but I knew that was foolish. He looked down and saw us, and motioned toward the lumbering, hairy figure. Then he ducked down behind some rocks, and I realized he was moving to the Yeh Teh. It was useless for him alone, I knew. He had no gun. I wanted to yell at him, but I only urged my companions on fiercely.

We were less than a hundred yards away when it happened. The giant, red, shaggy shoulders were only partially visible among the rocks, and we could not see Bhuta at all. But a small figure appeared near the Yeh Teh, crawling among the rocks.

My heart pounded. We all stopped and gazed in amazement. It was Rana, crawling away from the monster. She was alive, and apparently not badly hurt, if hurt at all. She darted up and ducked behind a rock, away from the red shoulders. She still did not know anybody was near, it was clear, for she was not trying to move toward us. We were scrambling, struggling up as hard as we could in the flying snow and the biting wind. The snow was still coming only in flurries and was not heavy. We could still see.

Rana started to run. She cut out on the open slope. The monster saw her, and turned in pursuit. In her frantic flight she stumbled and fell in the snow, and the great figure, moving with surprising speed was almost upon her when Bhuta stood up behind him, and charged the huge thing. We heard a faint cry in the wind as Bhuta yelled to attract the Yeh Teh's attention. Rana saw her brother then for the first time, and screamed. The monster paused for a moment between them, then reached for Rana, and got a hand on her. She squirmed away, however, and left him holding a piece of her yak-hide skirt. And at that moment, brave Bhuta leaped full on the back of the monster with his small knife in his hand. That was the only weapon our comrade carried.

We were within 50 yards of them by then, but lower down on the slope. I saw Rana run not away but toward the monster. She wanted to help her brother. I paused and fired my gun in the air, risking a snowfall, to distract the Yeh Teh's attention, but nothing happened. The furious fighting Bhuta was clinging to the back of the Yeh Teh, trying, it seemed, to climb up on the huge form, and for a moment they were one mass of struggling limbs.

Then the Yeh Teh reached back with one huge arm, and before our horrified eyes plucked Bhuta from his back by the neck.

The monster pulled Bhuta over his head, holding him out in one
hand in the air. Rana's scream could be heard over the wind. The
Yeh Teh then peered down over the rocks directly at us and flung
our friend through the air down the slope toward us, flung him as
we might fling a leather coat.

Bhuta's body struck in front of us and tumbled down the
slope almost to our feet. The monster stared down at me from
no more than 25 yards above. He looked as big as the side of the
mountain. His face was horrible, but it was not an animal's face.
It was that of some monstrous kind of man I'd never seen before.
The nose was slightly flat, and the forehead sloped way back.
The eyes were small, and deep set in the huge hairy head, and the
mouth was wide and ape-like with long, crooked teeth. He shook
his head angrily at us.

I got the broad breast full in the sights of my rifle. I fired
once and then again, quickly. I could not have missed, but there
was no sign of the bullet striking the monstrous face or form.
The guns of my friends also exploded. We must have hit him but
he did not show it in any way. Then he turned and grabbed up
the screaming Rana who tried to run down the mountain toward
Bhuta's inert form.

The monster flung her over his shoulder as though she were
no heavier than a rabbit, and turned and swung up the mountain
away from us. Through the wind Rana's horrified scream pierced
my ears and my heart. None of us shall ever forget it, I know. Her
face was contorted with terror as she looked down at us for one
terrible moment. It was the face of a young girl who had lived
through a nightmare. Then it was lost behind the rocks as the Yeh
Teh ran up the slope.

We rushed after him, but he pulled away from us easily. Bhuta
was dead when we got to his body. I hardly paused over my friend,
because I wanted to try to reach his sister, but the Yeh Teh moved
with incredible speed among and behind the rocks. I had one more
glimpse of Rana's face frozen into a mask of pure terror, but she
did not cry out anymore.

We kept the monster and the girl in sight for some time, but
when we reached the top of the pass at Zemu Gap, we never saw
him again. We followed the tracks up into the gap, but there the
snow was coming down thicker and the path was swallowed up.

We carried Bhuta back to the village, and gave him honorable rites, for he had died bravely, but nobody will ever know what happened to his lovely young sister. She has not been seen or heard of since. She was not dead when I last saw her, but perhaps it would have been better for her if she had been.

I'll never forget her face, nor the terrible face of the Yeh Teh, the thing of the rocks. I saw him too clearly. But I still don't know what devilish kind of creature he actually is. I do know though, that he exists. I had awful proof of that.

I <u>Know</u> Monsters Live on Everest!

Are the "abominable snowmen" of the Himalayas fact or fable? Here — for the first time — is an American climber's own story of his encounter with the man-beasts of 20,000 feet

The darkness hid it, but it was there. The icy air was heavy with its musky stench, the sounds were those of a large beast.

Though no creature is visible save a shadow across the snow, the climber's eyes speak volumes. Will the ice axe be enough? A tense, uncredited illustration from *Argosy*, February 1954. The issue's cover is by artist Frank McCarthy.

TRUE

THE MAN'S MAGAZINE

December 25¢

PAUL GALLICO · COREY FORD
STANLEY FRANK · LUCIAN CARY
TREGASKIS · MAURICE ZOLOTOW

A Fawcett Publication

CHRISTMAS GIFT ISSUE

"What-Is-Its of the Sea"
Ivan Sanderson
TRUE, Dec. 1948
cover by Tom Lovell

DECEMBER 1948

True

THE MAN'S MAGAZINE

W. H. Fawcett, Jr. . . . President
Roger Fawcett . General Manager
Ralph Daigh . Editorial Director
Al Allard . . . . Art Director
William E. Rae . . Supervising Editor

H. Van Valkenburg . Art Editor
Clyde Carley . Associate Editor
John DuBarry . . . . Aviation
T. J. Naughton . Associate Editor
Len Bowman . . . . Managing Editor

Pete Barrett . . . . . Outdoors
John P. English . Associate Editor
Walter Schmidt . Associate Editor
I. S. Berlin . . . . . . Research

Bill Williams . . . . Editor

CONTENTS

What-is-its of the sea

People who say there's no such thing as a sea
serpent don't necessarily know what they're
talking about. Take the case of Captain
Jason Seabury, for instance, who caught one
monster by harpooning it in the eye

BY IVAN T. SANDERSON

*Scottish-born Ivan T. Sanderson's repu-
tation as a naturalist is based upon his
participation in many scientific expeditions to the East Indies, the Aru Islands,
and the West Indies, and his leadership
of a zoological expedition to West Africa,
sponsored by the Royal Society and the
British Museum. Author of numerous
scientific papers, he is perhaps better known for his two books,* Animal
Treasure *and* Caribbean Treasure.
—The Editors of TRUE

art by JOHN PIKE

Once upon a time—and only a short while ago, at that— sea monsters were thought to be dolorous figments of happy Elizabethan imaginations. Up till a year ago they were just perennial fillers found in the newspapers when all the current wars were slowing down. Now the darned things have been cropping up every month. In the face of all these reports, we need to evaluate the arguments against accepting their validity.

Take the record during the past year. In December, 1947, the master of the SS Santa Clara, seconded by two officers, reported striking a 40-foot what-is-it with an eel-like head and a long neck three feet in diameter, off the North Carolina coast. In January, the press of British Columbia broke out in a rash of stories about sea monsters and even produced a corpse which, however, turned out to be that of a large shark. In February, Florida put in its two-bits' worth with photos of vast, three-toed tracks meandering out of the sea and all over a sandy beach. In March, British Columbia was back with its camel-headed, long-necked, off-shore visitor. In April, something was reported off the California coast. In the meantime, Australia, England, and India suffered a number of visitations from the deep.

Perhaps you will remember the cryptic wireless message received by the US Hydrographic Office last December 30, which was widely published:

> "Lat 34.34 N Long 74.07 W. 1700 GCT struck marine monster either killing or badly wounding it period estimate length 45 feet with eel-like head and body approximately three feet in diameter period last seen thrashing in large area of bloody water and foam sighted by Wm. Humphrey chief officer and John Axelson third officer."

This was dispatched by the captain of the SS Santa Clara, en route to Barranquilla, Colombia. When the ship returned to New York, the press descended. The result was the usual crop of fatuous write-ups in which, inevitably, liquor was mentioned as often as the sea monster. Certain pertinent facts were reported, however: notably that the matter was entered in the log and in red ink, as required for disasters and unusual events. As one New York daily pointed out, "There is a fine of $500 prescribed for false entries in a ship's log."

It appears that precisely at noon, 118 miles due east of Cape Lookout, third mate John Axelson suddenly spotted the head and body of a large animal sticking out of the sea. He yelled and the captain, navigating officer, and chief mate joined him at the rail. The ship was doing eighteen knots and the animal was by this time about 60 feet astern. They report that it "sort of humped over and started thrashing around." Mr. Axelson made some sketches of what he saw and all witnesses describe the animal as having a flat head about 5-feet long, shaped like that of an eel, a neck 18-inches thick and 6-feet long, and a body twice as thick, of which some thirty feet showed above the surface. The animal was dark brown in color, slick, and shiny. It was left rolling and thrashing about in bloody foam.

Here is the age-old enigma of the seas, and the travesty that follows. An enormous unknown beast is seen in broad daylight by a number of professional mariners trained to observe everything upon the sea. They are hard-working, well-educated, responsible men with good jobs. They do not drink on duty, not only because of regulations but because such people just don't. The animal is hit and believed mortally wounded. The ship is not stopped, no boat is lowered, no attempt is made to investigate, photograph, or collect the beast. It is simply entered in the log and a wireless report made. The ship docks, the press arrives, jokes are made about liquor.

The press appeals to the professors and experts, who promptly state that people not trained as zoologists never know how to describe what they see. It is suggested or stated flatly that the animal was probably a line of playful dolphins, a large fish, a whale, a log, a piece of giant seaweed, a deflated navy blimp, or something equally mundane. In this case they picked an oarfish, saying it could be 50-feet long. The actual statement made to one reporter is a near classic: "Often two people seeing the same thing will describe it differently afterward. The seamen said the body was round, but a flat surface may look round from a distance. An oarfish is what we call a compressed fish—narrow from side to side but wide from top to bottom. It's possible what they saw was a large porpoise, but more likely it was an oarfish."

It approaches plain insult to ask the public to believe that professional mariners cannot tell the difference between a long, laterally compressed fish without neck, and an animal with a large head, slender neck and a body twice as thick. It is positively inane to suggest that any seaman could mistake such an animal for a porpoise. As a matter of fact, many more sailors hold a definite belief in the real existence of the enigma than the average zoologist might suppose. They wisely say nothing as a general rule, for fear of ridicule. Occasionally they become aggravated, or when they retire, are apt to "relate their experiences." A good example is found in Sir Arthur H. Rostron's book, *Home From the Sea.*

Rostron writes of the time he was chief officer of the Cunard Liner Campania. The ship was off Galley Head entering Queenstown, Ireland, one evening in 1906, when Rostron noticed something sticking out of the sea. He ordered the vessel swung away a point to avoid the "snag," which they passed at about 50 feet. Then he saw to his amazement that it was the head and neck of some enormous animal, which rose about nine feet out of the water. The neck was about a foot thick and the head, as he described it, kept looking "from side to side for all the world as a bird will on a lawn between pecks."

Rostron made sketches of the beast on a white dodger-board and later showed them to his captain, who was more than skeptical. After the Campania docked at Liverpool, however, reports appeared in the papers of a man found adrift in a small boat at the opposite side of the Bristol Channel. He reported that his boat had been attacked by a monster exactly answering the description of that seen by Rostron and other Campania officers.

Reports of this kind can be multiplied almost indefinitely. They have been made by people of every seafaring nationality, and by more coastal landlubbers over the world. Professional seamen of every kind— from luxury-liner captains, naval officers, whalers, and fishermen to uneducated primitives in dugout canoes — have reported the same thing time and again. Women with telescopes, parsons in yachts, ordinary citizens in rowboats, Chinese smugglers in junks, thousands of Sunday strollers in New England, and even two zoologists off Brazil have watched these animals sometimes for hours, sometimes for days.

Can all these reports be cases of mistaken identity? All hoaxes, jokes, or plain lies? If liquor is the cause, why do exactly the same kind of animals invariably accompany the alleged delirium tremens, appearing only on or by the sea throughout the world? Why don't we get any pink elephants or at least a few technicolored whales? Is it wishful thinking or some atavistic product of folklore? Can it all be mass hallucination, as some scientists always contend? And what, incidentally, is mass hallucination?

All these explanations are, however, only negative and, be it noted, are put forward by people who were not present when the alleged incidents occurred. In all the hundreds of cases reported, there is not a single instance that I know of in which an eyewitness disagreed with other eyewitnesses.

Skeptics often put forward other arguments against the existence of these creatures. One that they cannot exist, is really quite fatuous and can be dealt with very simply. It should have been demolished long ago by the discovery that the kraken, in which Norwegian fishermen had believed for centuries, really existed. This turned out to be a giant squid, now known to science as Architeuthis, which sometimes attains a weight of over two tons and is not only a very real but a fairly common animal. The fact that almost anything can exist in the sea was demonstrated when a fish 5-feet long, and belonging to a group of which all members were thought totally extinct since the Dinosaur Age, was brought up alive in a commercial trawl off South Africa in 1938.

There are three more arguments, which at first sight appear to be devastating. First, that no specimen has ever been captured; second, that none has ever been washed ashore; and third, that no piece of one is in any museum. I would advise the utmost caution in accepting any such notions as final. Let us examine the record.

Almost the first fact that springs to mind is that, if the what-is-its really do exist, there is one group of professional seamen who, above all others, should know about them. I refer to whalers, who for centuries have roamed the oceans expressly searching for large marine beasts. Yet in all the published literature on the subject, and there is considerable, I have yet to find one case recorded by a whaler.

Dr. Townsend of the old New York Aquarium is said to have made an exhaustive search of the logbooks of old whalers, but failed to find a single report. It seems that he either did not probe far enough, or looked in the wrong logs. It appears, in fact, that the logbooks of whalers have not been properly examined at all, because in 1932 the editor of the *New Bedford Standard-Times* caused a search to be made in the Old Dartmouth Historical Museum and literally dozens of reports and many illustrations came to light. Among these was a quite matter-of-fact account of the actual capture of an enigma.

In the year 1852, Captain Jason Seabury of the whaleship Monongahela, was off his ship in a whaleboat when one of these long-necked, small-headed creatures surfaced and rushed the boat. "I instinctively held out my harpoon," he writes, "and its sharp point entered the eye. I was knocked overboard and felt a deep churning of the water around me. I rose to the surface and caught a glimpse of the writhing body, and was again struck and carried down. I partly lost consciousness underwater but recovered it. When I rose again in the bloody foam, the 'snake' had disappeared and I shouted, 'Pick up the line.'"

Captain Seabury's harpoon had taken fast and the monster was mortally wounded. The Monongahela seems to have come up with them, and three other boats were lowered. The account goes on to say: "We lanced the body repeatedly without eliciting any signs of life. While we were at work he gradually rose to the surface and around him floated what I took to be pieces of his lungs, which we cut out with our lances. To make sure, we continued to lance, eagerly seeking for his life. He drew himself up from the water and we pulled away to safety and then witnessed the dying struggles of the monster. The revolutions of the body were rapid as lightning, seeming like the revolving of a thousand enormous black wheels."

Captain Seabury was a young man and of good education, as his description indicates. His closing observations: "It was a male, the length 103 feet, 7 inches. We cut the snake up but found great difficulty and had to flense him," (i.e., strip off the blubber). The most interesting facts in this account are Captain Seabury's obvious belief that the animal had lungs, and his ready statement that it was a male, both of which would indicate that it was not some enormous fish. They are definite statements that, combined with the precise measurement and the remark about the difficulty encountered in cutting up the beast, lend an air of great authenticity to the account.

This report can be attributed by skeptics to any of the regular causes—liquor, lies, a joke, a hoax, or perhaps even to wishful thinking. It can hardly be called a case of mistaken identity, be attributed to folklore, or explained by mass hallucination.

We can scarcely conceive of a company of hard-bitten whalers flensing a whale under the mass hallucination that it was a sea serpent. We can only take the report at its face value, but it might be wise in future to refrain from stating dogmatically that no unknown sea monster has ever been caught.

Further, we might be well advised to adopt the same cautious attitude regarding the contention that no example has ever been beached. Indeed there is considerable evidence that quite a number of such monstrous jetsam have been washed ashore. When investigated properly, the vast majority of such reports turn out either to be pure rumor or hearsay, or to concern some animal already known to science but not to local residents. The most popular seem to be basking sharks or the rarer whales, in an advanced state of decomposition. When the flesh has been abraded from the vertebral column of a basking shark, all but trained zoologists may well be excused for thinking it to be the remains of some vast sea serpent. Such was the object washed ashore at Port Alberni, British Columbia, early this year. First reported as being 72-feet long, it later shrank to 45-feet. It was just a long string of obviously fishy vertebrae with a blob of rag-like flesh at the front end.

However, quite a number of the beached corpses defy identification. Perhaps the nastiest example was a vast mass of boneless flesh no less than 21-feet long, 7-feet wide, and nearly 5-feet high—washed up on a Florida beach in 1896. It was first thought to be the body of a gigantic octopus, and then the "tank" from the head of an enormous sperm whale. However, it was examined by no less an authority than Professor A.E. Verrill, who stated, with commendable simplicity for such a real expert, that he had no idea what it was. Ever afterward, he believed implicitly in the existence of unknown marine monsters.

This is by no means the only carcass the waves have thrown up that could not be identified, even by experts. There are records of dozens of such horrible things. In 1921 something odd, probably only a decomposed whale, was washed ashore at Cape May, New Jersey; in 1928 a nondescript corpse of large dimensions and covered with what was described as "white hair like that of a polar bear," was beached in South Africa; in 1928 also, a black-and-white striped mess turned up on the beach at Fonseca in El Salvador; in 1930 a 45-foot what-have-you was found on Glacier Island, Alaska.

This is merely a few years' sample, taken at random. Other periods are just as bad. Some are worse. In 1885 an astonishing carcass was reported washed ashore on another Florida beach. This was inspected by a reliable-sounding gentleman named the Reverend Gordon of Milwaukee, and other witnesses. It lacked a head but had a long serpentine neck, a spindle-shaped body with two flippers, and a long, tapering tail. It was nearly 50 feet in length. Unfortunately, a hurricane blew up that night and despite all efforts to save the prize it was carried back to sea.

Even when the true nature of such beached corpses is determined, the real identity of the beast is seldom reported. The matter is quietly dropped. But there are incidents of quite another kind that are even more silently buried. I refer to the corpses that cannot be identified or over which recognized experts do not agree. There was a beauty late in 1934, which you may look up for yourself in the files of, for instance, *The New York Times* for November 23rd of that year, and in subsequent issues. This account brings us to our third postulate; namely, that no part of a so-called sea monster is as yet in our possession.

The news item described a 30-foot corpse with four flippers and an elongated backbone, found on a beach at Henry Island, British Columbia. The coast there is a great place for sea monsters and the locals are very conscious of their presence, even having a name for them—Cadborosaurus, or "Caddie" for short. This corpse was taken to Dr. Neil Carter, the expert of the Division of Domestic Fisheries, who with consummate perspicacity said that "in life it must have been slender and sinewy." It was covered with hair mixed with quills and was a mammal. However, Dr. Clemens of the Government Biological Station at Nanaimo said it was a basking shark, which is a fish. Finally, it is reported that the officials of the Provincial Museum in Vancouver pronounced it to be the remains of the last surviving Steller's sea cow, a large relative of the manatee, and a mammal thought to have become extinct in the middle of the last century.

Are we seriously asked to believe that a group of trained zoologists is unable to distinguish a fish from a mammal? The idea is absurd to almost any high school student. The whole matter was hurriedly dropped; no final conclusion seems to have been published and, what is more, no explanation of this omission appears to have been forthcoming. The remains must presumably be lying in some museum and one wonders if they will continue to do so. This is an unpleasant thought, rendered no less disturbing by the case of the kraken.

Despite the fact that this great sea monster was, as we have said, known to mariners for centuries, it had been confidently dismissed by the shore skeptics as a mass hallucination or something, until an actual specimen, admittedly injured and half dead, was brought from Newfoundland to New York at the end of the last century by the same Professor Verrill. It was then disclosed that for years bits of kraken had not only been used as bait by the cod-fishers of the Grand Banks, but also had been reposing in bottles of alcohol in several large museums. You begin to wonder what other priceless treasures may be hidden away in the recesses of these institutions. There was one that had some skulls of Neanderthal man, unlabeled, in an old hat box, for a decade. Perhaps there is a skull of a young sea monster in some museum labeled "Old adult male seal; locality unknown."

Here we have thousands of people, the great majority presumably sane, of all nationalities and walks of life, for centuries reporting substantially the same kind of animals. They defy ridicule, they sign statements and they make little sketches. At the same time we are confronted with the spectacle of the best brains in our communities, specializing in the study of nature and animals, and presumably steeped in the tradition of science—which is the investigation of the unknown—flatly denying that any of these people have seen what they say they have. Worse still, we find some of them even denying the possibility of such creatures' existence, while their colleagues continue fishing even worse monstrosities out of the seas.

Disappearance of an alleged sea monster into a museum is burial of an orthodox kind. There is interment of a somewhat more iniquitous nature, which I call cremation by ridicule. An example:

In British Columbia in March 1947, it appears that two ordinary citizens went out fishing. One had what was, in this case, the great misfortune to be of Greek ancestry, and to be leader of a "Polar Bear Club" whose members took a dip in the icy sea each New Year's Eve.

The other drove a cab for a living, had the first name of Oscar, and obviously did not want to be quoted. Some large strange beast appeared near their boat, and the darned fools said so on landing. The press got to work and a reporter produced the following little funeral oration:

"It looked like a horse—you know, the kind of horse that resembles an indignant cow or else a wolf, or even maybe a mad dog with accusing eyes and a pompadour. Confusing, h'm? Just the same, that's the best available description of British Columbia's newest and weirdest sea monster. The witnesses: Peter Pantages, Vancouver restaurateur and 365- days-a-year English Bay swimmer, and an inscrutable taxi-driver known only as Oscar. Mr. Pantages, his eyes still bulging, and with a stunned hoarseness in his rich Athenian accent, told the story today, world rights reserved, reproduction in whole or in part strictly on the up-and-up. 'It happened Wednesday evening about 6 o'clock,' said Peter the Peerless."

The incident is then given as described by Mr. Pantages, with considerable emphasis on his difficulty with our language. Another version from a rival paper accused both witnesses of insobriety, lying, and otherwise heaped uncalled-for contumelies upon them. This sort of facetiousness is not journalism. It deliberately hampers the furtherance of knowledge but it is unfortunately only too common, especially in those fields that lie on the borderland of zoological knowledge.

What then of positive evidence for the existence of large, as-yet-unknown animals in the various seas and oceans? Here we encounter an enormous mass of facts that would be most baffling to any honest skeptic if he were prepared to analyze them without bias. Several serious thinkers and renegade zoologists have pondered this question, and there is substantial agreement in their conclusions.

First of all, and with few exceptions, the reports agree very closely on the form of the animals seen, despite the fact they cover two centuries and originate from all the oceans. The animals described almost invariably have small, earless heads; a mouthful of teeth; whiskers; long, serpentine necks; barrel- or spindle-shaped bodies; four flippers—two forward and two aft—long, tapering tails; and they are sleek like a wet sea lion. Many reports speak of manes or frills extending down the neck and often along the spine. Sometimes these are continuous, sometimes notched, or divided into a series of finlike projections. In the matter of size, there is considerable variation but then all animals are small when born— there is great variation in the size of adult whales. There may also be secondary sexual differences, so that the males might bear manes and the females be devoid of them. There might even be more than one species.

In the matter of behavior, there is even closer agreement. The animals reported seem to be more prevalent off rocky, indented coastlines like Norway, West Scotland, and New Zealand. They are almost always reported in calm weather. When observed near a coast they seem to be just puttering about, while on the open ocean they are always going somewhere, often at great speed. Report after report bears this out.

Norwegian fishermen who have always believed that these enigmas compose a real family of marine animals, contend that they are harmless but frightfully inquisitive. Innumerable reports second this, describing the beasts as rising out of the depths to inspect or to follow ships, bathers, or the shoreline, just as do seals. At the same time, they appear to be terrified of thrashing screws (screw propellers).

But in the manner of locomotion there is the closest agreement. When under way the animals are described as having a vertical undulatory movement so that when near the surface a series of humps protrude from the water. Moreover, when the paddles have been seen they are always said to flail together in pairs. Further, when going all out, the head is reported to be held stiffly forward on the long neck and at a slight upward angle, like a sea lion.

There is no real reason why a lot of large mammals such as described could not exist, popping their small heads or only their nostrils above water to breathe at long intervals, like whales, never disclosing themselves by "blowing" or "breaching," or in any other manner except when the sea is glassy and still. They could breed on the high seas, as do whales, live on fish in deep water by the edge of the continental shelf and, like the kraken, come into shallow waters only when old, injured, or blown there by storms.

The many descriptions, when analyzed together, seem to indicate the existence of one or more species of large mammals related to the seals, with bodies shaped like the ancient fossil marine reptiles known as plesiosaurs. That they are mammals and not reptiles seems to be indicated by the sleekness as opposed to scaliness of their hides, and by the frequent reports of whiskers. Blue whales, which are cylindrical and tubby, grow to more than 100 feet in length. A slender creature with thin neck, long tail, and overall length of 175 feet, would be much less bulky and in no way mechanically impossible for an aquatic animal.

We have seen that the oceans may still harbor all kinds of fantastic creatures—fish 5-feet long that ought to have been fossilized 60 million years ago, thousands of three-ton squids measuring 50 feet, and who knows what completely unknown animals.

It is clear, then, that none of the arguments put forward by the skeptics holds much water. They are all negative, often rather silly and sometimes, on analysis, just not true. In fact there seems to be a regular conspiracy to prevent any suggestion that there might be unknown large creatures in the sea that do not as yet have long Latin names.

The reason is that we have not so far got a stuffed one in a museum, and until this lack is remedied, scientists are perfectly entitled to be skeptical. In the meantime, we can make their lives more bearable by refraining from facetiousness and by doing all in our power to rectify the omission. If the current volume of reports is any indication, our chances of filling this niche in the museum would appear to be rather bright.

ABOMINABLE SNOWMAN SIGHTED
ARGOSY EXPEDITION TRACKS TEN-FOOT BEAST

ARGOSY

AUGUST 75c

THE MYSTERY OF EASTER ISLAND BY JOHN DOS PASSOS

BACK FROM THE DEAD! HERE'S HOW THE RUSSIANS DO IT

$1,500,000,000 TREASURE YOURS IF YOU CAN BEAT THE U.S. MILITARY TO IT

The August 1971 issue of *Argosy* cryptozoologist Loren Coleman calls "almost legendary," detailing Harold Stephens' research on the "Malaysian Bigfoot," Orang Dalam. Coleman's 2006 conversation with Stephens about the expedition can be read on the Cryptomundo.com website.

A.M. LIGHTNER

As IF in perfect cumulative distillation of the preceding Yeti stories, "The Stone Monster" by A.M. Lightner takes all that has come before in men's adventure magazine crypto fiction and renders it down into one potent monster tale.

Lightner was actually a pseudonym for female author Alice L. Hopf, a naturalist who also wrote books and magazine articles about a variety of subjects, ranging from children's books to serious scientific examinations of various zoological species such as Monarch butterflies, Komodo Dragons, and even arachnids. She also authored many science fiction books primarily aimed at young adults, including such titles as *The Galactic Troubadours*, *The Space Plague*, and S*tar Dog*, as well as a trilogy, *The Rock of Three Planets* series. Further adding credo to her expertise in the examination of cryptid species by way of actual scientific background, she was a passionate entomologist, right down to being a chairwoman of the 1956 Annual Meeting of the Lepidopterist Society held in New York City.

While such a background is not completely unusual among MAM authors, who included such science-driven men as Ivan T. Sanderson and the like, Hopf's gender most certainly *is* atypical; hence the genderless pseudonym of "A.M. Lightner." But for modern readers, Hopf signals the introduction of a trend line that has only exploded in more recent times in actual cryptozoology: The rise of female researchers in a field once dominated exclusively by men.

"Lightner" deftly uses terminology germane to the field, such as labeling her Yeti as a hominid. And without divulging a key plot point, "The Stone Monster" also references historical eyewitness accounts in which captured or cornered humans were able to trick the menacing cryptid with foodstuff.

As this diversity of accurate, nonfiction facts combined with exploitative, unrealistic (but thrilling!) fictionalized stories by talented authors hopefully reveals, the Yeti was a cryptid goldmine for the men's adventure magazines. This unpredictability of tone and content made each new issue of such magazines a pleasure to encounter, as they exhibited a healthy sense of anarchy and imagination. This was not to be undervalued in a time when conformity was emphasized in most forms of culture. Widely read in large pass-along numbers in communal male-bonding centers such as barber shops and the like, men's adventure magazines radiated a sense of verboten subversiveness that made them irresistible.

THE NEW GOLDEN

ARGOSY

NOVEMBER, 50¢

FOR MEN

CALLING ALL ADVENTURE LOVERS:
WORLD'S NEWEST GOLD RUSH WANTS YOU!

EXPOSED:
CRIME'S ANGRY YOUNG MEN

WW II's WILDEST FLIGHT:
"FLAP YOUR ARMS REAL HARD, GENERAL!"

THOSE ZANY
GYPSY GUN TRADERS

SPECIAL SECTION:
ANYBODY CAN TAKE GOOD PICTURES!

EXTRA BONUS:
$3⁹⁵ BOOK
ED LACY'S
LATEST THRILLER

ROBIN HOOD, '63:
BIG BOOM IN BOWS AND ARROWS

"THE STONE MONSTER"
A.M. LIGHTNER
ARGOSY, NOVEMBER 1963
COVER PHOTO BY GEORGE X. SAND

WHAT WAS THIS INHUMAN THING HE HAD SHOT—THIS THING THAT HAD COME UP FROM THE DEPTHS OF HELL TO STALK THEM—AND COULD BURY THEM UNDER TONS OF ROCK AND SNOW TO AVENGE ITS WOUND?

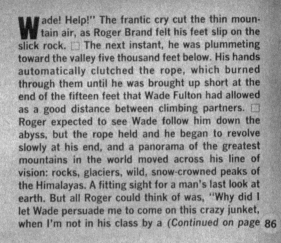

Wade! Help!" The frantic cry cut the thin mountain air, as Roger Brand felt his feet slip on the slick rock. □ The next instant, he was plummeting toward the valley five thousand feet below. His hands automatically clutched the rope, which burned through them until he was brought up short at the end of the fifteen feet that Wade Fulton had allowed as a good distance between climbing partners. □ Roger expected to see Wade follow him down the abyss, but the rope held and he began to revolve slowly at his end, and a panorama of the greatest mountains in the world moved across his line of vision: rocks, glaciers, wild, snow-crowned peaks of the Himalayas. A fitting sight for a man's last look at earth. But all Roger could think of was, "Why did I let Wade persuade me to come on this crazy junket, when I'm not in his class by a (Continued on page 86

the STONE MONSTER

BY A. M. LIGHTNER
ILLUSTRATED BY JACK DUMAS

ART BY JACK DUMAS

"Wade! Help!" The frantic cry cut the thin mountain air, as Roger Brand felt his feet slip on the slick rock. The next instant, he was plummeting toward the valley 5000-feet below. His hands automatically clutched the rope, which burned through them until he was brought up short at the end of the 15 feet that Wade Fulton had allowed as a good distance between climbing partners. Roger expected to see Wade follow him down the abyss, but the rope held and he began to revolve slowly at his end, and a panorama of the greatest mountains in the world moved across his line of vision: rocks, glaciers, wild, snow-crowned peaks of the Himalayas. A fitting sight for a man's last look at earth. But all Roger could think of was, "Why did I let Wade persuade me to come on this crazy junket, when I'm not in his class by a mile? Now we'll both be dead—and not even a tough mountain!"

The young man was amazed at how much his mind could review in perhaps ten seconds, for just then Wade's tanned, seamy face appeared over the cliff's edge and his voice floated down.

"You all right, Roger? Remember what I told you. Your feet against the rock and climb. Don't leave all the work to me!"

Then he realized he was already inching up the cliff. Wade was doing his job on the rope! Resolutely, he forced himself to release his grip and reach up to begin the laborious climb. At the same time, his feet sought the cliff face and he found himself using the techniques his friend had been pounding into him for the past week.

It turned out to be easier than he had anticipated, and soon he had pulled his six feet of bone and muscle to safety on the ledge. Wade was resting with one hand on his ice axe, which was driven into a rock crevice to take the strain on the rope.

"Welcome back to the living!" he said. "I guess you think that was a near thing."

"As near as I want to come." Roger was glad to hear that his voice was steady. "And without you...."

"That's what I've been telling you," Wade lectured. "As long as there are two—partners who understand each other.... You'd have done as well by me, I'm sure."

"Don't kid yourself," Roger laughed. "We'd both be down at the bottom!"

Wade stood up and stuck the axe back in his pack. "Rest a minute until you get your breath back."

Another way of saying, get your nerve back, Roger thought, as he got to his feet, relieved to find his terror had almost drained away.

"I'm afraid all the hazards are at your end of the rope."

"In that case, I'll chance them. It's not much farther to where I told the Sherpas to make camp."

The rest of the climb was easy and in another 15 minutes they came out on a level spot where their Sherpas Ang and Pemba, were already busy.

Later as they lay in their tent, listening to the shouts and laughter of the Sherpas around their fire of yak dung, Roger asked his friend, "Do you really think we'll find any animals? What could live in this wasteland of rock and ice?"

"You'd be surprised," Wade told him. "There's a whole chain of life: lizards and insects and, of course, the Tibetan rat. That would be something interesting for the museum. No tail, rather like a guinea pig. They say it's the food of the yeti."

The younger man pricked up his ears. "That's the Abominable Snowman, isn't it? Think we'll see one of those?"

"Frankly, no. Science has about decided there's no such animal. Tracks could be those of beasts, distorted by melting snow."

"Oh, but people have seen it!" Roger hated to have the most interesting possibility ruled out as a myth.

"Not many. And people get excited...mistake a bear for something else. Perhaps a wild mountain hermit."

When Roger sighed in disappointment, Wade explained, "I'm only quoting the arguments I've been given. Nothing would please me more than to run into a yeti. Hell, I'd be famous if I could bring one back, dead or alive!"

"You wouldn't shoot it? A rare animal, like that!"

"Probably impossible to get one alive unless you could lure it into a trap. The adults are supposed to be huge, and strong as gorillas."

"But if it's so rare, and you shot it...." Roger loved animals and preferred his specimens alive.

"Same thing with the panda. No one believed it existed until one of the Roosevelts shot a specimen. Now they're protected, of course. And so is the yeti, in most places. But I'm going to put my gun sights on animals I know exist—ibex and foxes. And you'll do well to do the same with your camera."

"Don't worry about that. Lead me to an animal and I'll photograph it."

"Leading," said Wade, "is the job of the Sherpas. Ang and Pemba are expert trackers. Tomorrow should see some action."

Roger reflected that today had brought plenty of action as far as he was concerned. But the talk had pushed his fear into the back of his mind. As the temperature dropped, he curled up in his warm sleeping bag and soon was dreaming of seven-foot snowmen with fangs a yard long. The next thing he realized, Wade was shaking him awake, thrusting a cup of hot tea at him.

"Drink that. The Sherpas are making breakfast. But I want to take a look round that bluff before the sun gets up. You can see a Himalayan sunrise, too."

Roger gulped his tea and began looking for his camera.

"Don't bother with that," Wade told him. "Won't be enough light."

But the young man had a stubborn streak. Rather than waste time looking in his rucksack, Roger swung the bag over his shoulder and followed Wade up the trail. He could dig out the camera later.

The track ran along the edge of the ridge, and in the predawn, the miles upon miles of jagged peaks were veiled in early mist, with only a hint here and there of their overpowering majesty. Wade was a few yards ahead, and Roger hurried to catch up, but his pack slowed his progress.

The man passed from sight where the trail rounded the bluff. Almost immediately, Roger heard a high, peculiar whistle and then Wade's shout. He put on a burst of speed and almost fell over his friend around the corner.

"It's him! Holy saints, it's it!" hissed Wade, his hands shaking with excitement as he cocked his rifle.

"What?" Roger looked wildly around.

They were on a grassy ledge where the trail widened, and scrambling down the slope was a medium-sized animal, hard to identify in the tricky light.

"It's a yeti or I'm a baboon!" cried Wade, raising the rifle.

At that moment, the creature stopped and turned to look at them. Perhaps it thought it had run far enough for safety. It straightened up—four to five feet, Roger guessed—and turned a face to them, so human in caricature that he cried out to his friend.

"Don't shoot! It may be a man!"

"With that hair and face?"

"How about your hermit? Or a bear?"

"That's no hermit. And if it's a bear, I want it."

"But you mustn't shoot it! It's too much like us. Let me get a picture first." And Roger scrabbled in his bag for the camera.

"Nobody believes a picture these days. Too easily faked. This is my chance to be famous."

"Just wait one moment!" Roger pleaded. "Perhaps we can catch it alive."

But the strange animal wasn't waiting. On two legs, it walked quickly away down the slope. Soon it would be hidden among the rocks. Wade raised his gun.

"Sure, Roger, I'd rather have it alive. But we haven't a chance, and a dead specimen's better than none."

The younger man put out a restraining hand. Without knowing why, he felt it a crime to shoot the manlike creature.

"Please! Don't kill it! There must be another way. Don't!"

The shot rang out and the animal staggered a few steps, then rolled down the slope. Wade gave an exultant shout.

"Got it, by God! A real yeti! The abominable snow—"

His words were cut short by an ominous rumble that seemed to echo the shot. As though nature were protesting the murder of her child, the ground beneath their feet began to move and slide.

"Look out!" yelled Wade. "Avalanche!"

He turned to run back to the shelter of the bluff, but before he reached it, he was overtaken by a mass of racing ice and snow. A huge section of the glacier above them had been jarred loose and now was tearing down the mountain, bearing rocks and bushes along with it, obliterating everything in its path.

Roger, too horrified to move, saw Wade struck down by a flying boulder and carried away toward the valley below, and then he himself was falling, faster and faster into darkness and oblivion, while a mountain of snow and debris seemed to smother the life out of him.

The sun was a bright ray, a searing knife that blinded his eyes. Roger turned his head to escape, as he tried to remember where he was and how he got there. He should be dead, according to all the rules. Wade must be dead. But avalanches are unpredictable. They do weird things. Like leaving him on a pile of rocks when he should be 20 feet under. At that, perhaps Wade, too....

Cautiously, he picked himself up. He was at the bottom of a hole...a couloir...a crevasse. He sought unsuccessfully for the right mountaineering term. Whatever it was, the avalanche had plugged up the exits. He was in a trap. How long had he been here and what chance of rescue? The sun was directly overhead, so it must be noon and he had lain unconscious all morning. He limped around his prison, vainly searching for some way to climb out. The walls seemed vertical rock and above hung the debris of the avalanche. He saw no landmark that could point to their night's camp, where friendly Sherpas might be organizing his rescue.

On the off chance that Wade might still be alive or that the Sherpas could hear him, he began to call: "Wade! Wade! Ang! Pemba! Here I am! Help! Help."

His cries seemed to travel from peak to peak, but only the echoes came back to him. By a perverse fate, he, the incompetent novice, had been spared, while Wade, the expert, had died. He remembered Wade's frantic yell as the hurtling rocks bore down upon him, and one part of him mourned the friend who had taught him the science of the mountains. At the same time, his brain told him that he might be as dead as Wade in a few days. It was only a matter of time. Without help, he'd never get out of this hole.

But the mountains were coldly silent to his cries. Or were they? Suddenly, quite near, he heard a squeak, a whistle and a rattle of brush. And there in the farthest corner of his prison, behind a pile of rock and broken bushes, was the animal that had started it all. Roger stared in disbelief and the creature stared back with anxious, frightened eyes.

Its reddish brown hair was covered with dirt and sand and the shoulder was streaked with blood where Wade's bullet had hit. Its neck was nonexistent, giving the shoulders a hunched appearance, and the head had an odd, pointed shape, sloping backward from the forehead. Its half-seen feet hinted at the manlike structure indicated by the famous footprints. Was this how the ancient Neanderthal had appeared? Or some other early cousin of Man, now extinct save in this one, inhospitable niche?

It was holding its hurt arm with the other hand and furtively trying to lick the wound, but the spot remained beyond its reach. Roger judged the animal had been knocked out much as he had been, and that his shouting had aroused it. Well, the yeti was a famous climber of mountains. Perhaps it could find a way out, and where it went Roger would follow. He began to walk slowly toward it. It whistled in alarm and peered fearfully from side to side, but there was no escape from Roger in this small arena, and suddenly it bared its teeth with a hissing sound.

The man stopped. Without doubt, he could overpower the creature if he tried, but it was wounded and frightened and as shaken up as himself. If there was any possibility of its climbing out of this trap, it would never do so in its present condition. Roger wished he could do something about its shoulder. He himself had suffered numerous cuts and abrasions that could benefit from first aid.

He began to search for the pack he had been carrying when

the avalanche hit. To his great joy, he spotted a corner protruding from a pile of rubble and soon had dug it out. The camera, of course, was a total wreck. But emergency rations were there, his ice axe, and most important, the first-aid kit. He spread it out: band-aids, antiseptics. He selected a roll of gauze, some scissors, and the sulpha powder, and approached the animal again.

Once more, he was met by snarls and hisses. He could see that his ministrations weren't going to be welcomed, so he sat down and attended to himself. Squatting by the open kit, he applied sulpha and Band-Aids to his worst cuts. As he finished, he looked up and found the yeti watching him. Roger began to talk to it quietly.

"That's how it's done, pardner. Nothing to it. Can't possibly hurt."

But at the sound of his voice the animal shrank back against its pile of rubble and peered at him with frightened eyes.

"Okay. So you don't want to take advantage of the miracles of modern medicine."

His monologue to the yeti was really an attempt to buoy his own morale, and as he repacked the first-aid kit, he reflected that the best medium for making friends with an animal is food.

He emptied his rucksack and looked over his meager rations: a small packet of biscuits; one can of jam and three of sardines; dates, and chocolate. He ought to ration himself, he realized. But for how many days? Was it better to eat as little as possible, while his strength drained away? Or to eat well now and use the energy in an all-out effort to escape? Roger knew that only an idiot would consider giving any of the food to an animal. But if by winning its trust he could get the animal to help him out? Only an idiot would think of such an idea—but Roger was thinking.

He looked at the yeti, which had approached him again. He looked up at the rock and ice surrounding him and knew he would never get out without help. With sudden determination, he picked up his knife and began to open one of the tins of sardines.

He could hear the yeti inching closer as he worked, and when the tin was open he speared a fish with his knife and held it out to the animal. But its trust was not to be won so easily, and it scuttled away to a safe distance.

"Good to eat," the man urged, and demonstrated by picking

up a second sardine and devouring it with smacking lips.

The yeti was torn by indecision. It inched forward and oozed back.

"All right," said Roger. Have it your way." And he threw the sardine so that it landed at the yeti's feet.

It picked it up with the fussiness of a finicky child, smelled of it, peered closely at it, then popped it into its mouth. A remarkable caricature of a smile spread over the yeti's face.

"I told you so," said Roger. "But you've got to come and get it."

Again the yeti hesitated. It sidled up almost within reach and then backed away, all the while whistling in a worried way. Roger dropped the fish on the ground two feet away. The animal rushed in and grabbed it. The third sardine was finally taken from Roger's fingers. By the time they had emptied the can, the yeti was squatting beside Roger, watching avidly as the food was divided.

He considered his remaining supplies. Reluctantly, he put the cans back in his pack, but he kept out a bar of chocolate. What would the yeti make of candy? He broke off a small square and offered it. There was no doubt about it. It made a tremendous hit. The animal smacked its lips and then watched in dismay as Roger ate two squares in succession. The man then made his first attempt to touch the creature.

By moving slowly and gently, whistling the while in an imitation of the yeti's expressive calls, and rewarding its trust with chocolate, he soon had the yeti nestling up to him. It even let him examine its shoulder, and Roger cut away the matted hair and sprinkled sulfa on the wound.

By now the sun had left their narrow sky and the gully was deep in twilight. Already, the cold Himalayan night was making itself felt. Roger realized that he would have to make a fire if he was to survive until morning. With much effort, he managed to dig out a few bits of shrubs and bushes that had been carried down or buried by the avalanche, but the pile was pitifully small. It could only burn for a few hours. He heaped them all by the corner that was the yeti's hiding place. A few larger rocks gave some protection from the wind, and Roger rearranged them into the semblance of a cave. Then, as night closed down, he lit the fire.

At the first crack of the blaze, the yeti scampered away, whistling its objections. But soon it returned, for the man was occupying its personal retreat, and also the man had come to represent food. Roger let the animal creep into the farthest corner among the rocks, while he tended the fire at the front. He had filled his pan with ice from the glacial debris and soon had melted it to water over the fire. Then he counted out their supper rations. The second can of sardines was opened. The strange creature crept close to Roger to get its share, and the warmth of their two bodies filled the little den. He decided that they might as well eat some of the jam and biscuits. And they finished off with a few dates. Roger emptied out his rucksack and spread it on the ground, and when the last branches had gone into the fire and it had burned down to embers, man and hominid curled up together in dual attempt to fight off the cold.

Roger slept. Well before dawn he was awake, rubbing his limbs to restore circulation. As he moved, the yeti snuggled closer, making whimpering noises in sleep. Perhaps this was a young animal dreaming it was back in the family den, warmed and protected by its mother.

Roger slipped out of the shelter and stretched himself in the half-light. The sky above gave promise of the rising sun. He collected more ice and stirred the ashes, adding the few sticks he had say for that purpose. Just enough to melt water for breakfast. The yeti came close and watched. It was right there to demand its share when Roger opened the last can of sardines. They also divided the remaining biscuits and jam. The dates and chocolate were saved for later.

In the growing light, Roger walked around the gully, examining the walls for the best possible exit. At last he noted a crevice high up above a wall of ice and debris. If he could reach that, there might be sufficient hand- and toe-holds to climb out. But how to get to the first hold? Whistling and calling, he lured the yeti to the spot, but no amount of pointing could bring the animal's attention to the matter in hand. All it wanted was chocolate.

"No more food until we get out here," he told it. "From now on, pardner, you've got to work for a handout."

But the yeti had a one-track mind, and finally in desperation, Roger took his axe and began to cut in the ice and avalanche debris, hoping to carve out steps as Wade had taught him. Soon he was absorbed in constructing hand- and toe-holds.

He had advanced a few feet and was busily at work, while he clung precariously to the cliff, when the yeti began to whistle. Then without warning it scrambled past him, using his first steps, then leaped to Roger's shoulders and thence the bottom of the crevice. With a shower of little stones and excited squeaks, it disappeared among the rocks and bushes in the fissure, leaving Roger to wipe the dirt from his eyes and stare in amazement.

"Well, I'll be damned!" he exclaimed. "That's the payoff!" The beast gets out and I'm left right here. Showed me the way, all right—for a yeti!"

But before he had time to deplore stupidity, there was more scrabbling in the bushes and the yeti's brown face peered out at him. It began to whistle in an insistent manner that could best be interpreted as "Come on up."

Roger climbed up his few steps, then swung his axe toward a possible belay.

He was stretched to his limit up the wall when the yeti reached down a long, hairy arm. Miraculously their hands met. But the animal did not clasp, as a man would. Instead, it seized hold of Roger's wrist and gave a mighty jerk. Roger literally flew up the cliff and landed beside the beast in a shower of stones that almost knocked the breath out of him.

For a moment, he was afraid to move: first, lest they both slide back into the hole, and then lest he find a bone broken. But the yeti was impervious to such fears. Already, it was scrambling further up the cleft, whistling for Roger to follow. Carefully, he picked himself up, collected his axe, and pulling himself up by roots, branches, anything that came to hand, he managed to climb after his rescuer and out onto a safe ledge.

There he sat down to collect himself and take stock of the situation. He had escaped from the trap, all right, and the animal had helped him. But where did he go from here? At this altitude, he did not have the boundless energy of the yeti, now disappearing over the rocks. He had only a little food left, so he must not waste time. If he could find his way down to the

valley, chances were that he could locate a settlement. But even
that was doubtful, as this country was thinly settled, some even
unexplored. Still, down he must go, being careful not to start
another avalanche in the process.

At first he followed the yeti, but when he found a way that
seemed to go down more quickly, he took that in preference.
As he scrambled downward, he heard the animal whistling in
protest.

"That's all right, pard!" he called. "You go your way and I'll
go mine. This is where we part."

The creature sat on a rock and continued to whistle. Roger
ignored it and went on down until he was stopped by a cliff.
There was no way around and no way down. Reluctantly, he
climbed back the way he had come and soon found himself sitting
on the rock by the yeti.

"Oh, hell, you win!" Roger told him. "This is your territory
and you should know. But I want down, pard." He pointed, hoping
the idea might get across.

"Whee!" said the yeti, and held out its hand.

It was offering Roger something that looked like moss. When
the man did not react, the animal stuffed a handful into its mouth
and began to chew. Roger stared.

Food! It was giving him food. He remembered reading that these
creatures, inhabitants of the forest, come up on the rocky slopes
to look for a salty moss or lichen. Cautiously he accepted a pinch.
It had an odd taste. He chewed it up, but did not dare eat more.
He put the rest in his pocket.

"I'll wait till I'm really hungry," he said, and then stopped
because the animal was begging again, holding out its hands and
whistling insistently.

What do you know, he thought, it wants to trade its food for
chocolate!

"Well, I haven't any to spare, and you've got your own grub,"
he told it.

Then he thought better of it. The little fellow had gotten
him out of that hole when he could just as well have run off. He
deserved a reward. Carefully, Roger broke off one small square
and handed it to the yeti, who ate it quickly.

"Come on," said Roger. "Time to get going. Can't spend another night here."

The yeti was quite willing to go. It started off at its pell-mell pace, running bent over on two legs, and Roger was put to it to keep up. This time, he followed where the animal led. Soon they entered a beautiful montane forest. Ancient pines brooded above dense rhododendrons and ferns and moss carpeted the ground. Now they were on a trail. Roger could not be sure if it was an animal's or a man's, but hoped for the latter. At one point, they turned off the path, the man following reluctantly until he heard the splash of running water. They squatted across from each other at a pool, both drinking thirstily. The yeti raised its face from the water and stared as Roger drank the water from his hands.

"I'm sorry I'm so civilized," he told it. "No doubt, your way is much more efficient." And he laughed when the animal tried to copy him, but failed to keep its fingers together.

While they rested, the yeti continued to beg. It seemed to know that Roger was hoarding the chocolate. And although he divided up the last dates, it was the candy the creature craved.

"Got to keep something in reserve," he told it, and started off down the trail. The yeti soon scuttled ahead of him and set a fast pace.

Toward evening, they emerged from the forest onto a little knoll. Far down a meadowed slope Roger could see a cluster of stone houses. He stared in disbelief. Somehow—by chance or by intent—the yeti had brought him back to the village whence he and Wade had set out a few days before. Smoke was rising from a chimney and the man imagined he could smell Sherpa stew. With a shout of joy, he began to run down the slope, but a soft whistle brought him to a stop. The hominid stood where he was, holding out his hands in a pleading gesture.

"Okay, pard," said Roger, searching his pockets for the last of the chocolate. "So you want to be paid off. You've earned it and I won't need it."

He left the yeti licking its fingers, and started once more down the slope. When he looked back a few minutes later, the knoll was empty. He thought sadly of Wade, who would have brought in the beast at any price. But the idea of this climbing partner confined in a zoo or stuffed in a museum did not appeal to him.

He began to run again as he neared the huts, and some men came out with shouts of "Sahib Roger!" They surrounded him, shaking his hands and pounding him on the back and all talking at once in Urdu with a sprinkling of English.

"What'll I ever tell them?" he thought. "Nobody will believe me—the Sherpas, the newsmen, the world. I've no proof, no pictures, not even a scrap of hair."

And then as he looked at Ang and Pemba and saw their joy at his return, he knew they would believe. They were part of that older culture of the East—unlike the scientific western mind, which does not want to believe what it cannot understand. As he followed them back to the good food and warm shelter, he told them:

"If you meet a yeti that's crazy about chocolate, be good to him!"

"THE APE-MAN MONSTER OF TENNESSEE"

"FACE-to-Face With the Ape-Man Monster of Tennessee" from
Man's World, October 1973, is a perfect example of cryptid
storytelling. It plays as a straight recounting ("As told to Ted
Gross") of an actual incident, even if the editors proclaim doubt
as to the creature's existence in the introduction.

The plot centers on a young couple who venture into the
Appalachian wilderness only to encounter a relic hominid intent
on interrupting their blissful idyll. Notice how the basic details
are almost identical to Teddy Roosevelt's 1892 chronicle (bad
odor, aggressive nature, night siege, giant footprints, etc.). The
modern romantic couple are not trappers, but they are still
interlopers, and they are accosted in a similar fashion by a hostile
cryptid. Without revealing plot twists, scribe Ted Gross plays
the conclusion for a scientific denouement that is unexpected,
but not unusual for the genre. Each new cryptid entry in men's
adventure magazines added details and heightened theories about
the hominids they portrayed. In a deliberate Darwinian pun, they
evolved with the growing base of readers by diversifying with
variable story adaptations.

The tale also reveals how blurred the lines often were
between veracity and lack thereof when the tag-line "based on a
true story" appeared. Typically such a statement indicated readers
could expect anything *but* the truth. So to add authenticity, the
fictionalized entries were often laced with actual cryptid details,
if slightly or entirely altered by the creative authors. "Face-to-
Face With the Ape Man Monster of Tennessee," for example,
offers an opening litany of supposedly actual encounters with an

Appalachian Bigfoot, but none of the witness names offered appear in my research. ("Earl Shackleton" may actually be a wily reference to Sir Ernest Shackleton, the famous British explorer of the Antarctic.) Whatever the origins, names in these stories were as likely fabricated as nobly changed to protect the identity of witnesses. Deadlines always loomed, and rates paid by most publishers were minimal—factors that did not favor follow-up research or depth of detail. But in part, the liberty to take the drier, less sensationalized crypto articles and add a zest of fantastic literary aspiration (and outright monster horror) is what made the fictional men's adventure stories such fun excursions.

$7.95 BOOK BONUS Airline stewardesses forced into a life of crime OCT.

THE HOUSE OF CAPTIVE CALL GIRLS

Harry 'Big Moose' Franklin's one-man rescue mission has to be 1973's most incredible adventure saga." —NEW BOOKS

60¢
15p

02413

man's world

TRUE
FACE-TO-FACE WITH THE APE-MAN MONSTER OF TENNESSEE:
Campers' Eyewitness Report On Their Terrifying Showdown

The Female Sex Cycle: What You Must Know
FACTS ON HORMONES AND EMOTIONS TO ADD EXCITEMENT TO YOUR LOVEMAKING

WHEN WOMEN PROWL:
Five Reveal The Special Kind of Men And Passion They Seek

THE DIRTY TRICKS OF THE GASOLINE BUSINESS
Tips That Will Save You Hundreds of $$$ At The Pumps

TRUE
A vengeance-crazed killer goes after the man who'd sent him to prison
MADMAN OF THE EVERGLADES

TRUE
"WE FOUND MUSSOLINI'S SECRET $60 MILLION TREASURE CAVE"
Three Yanks unravel a WWII mystery that's baffled experts for 29 years

THE STRANGE EROTIC RITES OF THE POLYNESIANS
—A sexologist's in-depth study

"FACE TO FACE WITH THE APE-MAN MONSTER OF TENNESSEE"
TED GROSS
MAN'S WORLD, **OCTOBER 1973**

FACE-TO-FACE WITH THE APE-MAN MONSTER OF TENNESSEE:
Campers' Eyewitness Report On Their Terrifying Showdown

Art by Gil Cohen

32

TRUE

EDITOR'S NOTE: The editors of this magazine do not necessarily believe that a prehistoric creature resembling a half man, half ape (as described by those who claim to have seen him) exists in modern times. Nevertheless, we sent a writer to interview those eyewitnesses and to tape-record their impressions. What follows is based on those interviews. . . .

O N November 14, 1958, Samuel T. Harmon who lived with his wife Jessie on a small farm near the Southern reaches of the Appalachian Mountains reported sighting a strange-looking creature on his property. It was night at the time and there was a violent thunderstorm. "I went out to check on the livestock," Harmon was quoted as saying, "and I (Continued on page 74)

As Told To TED GROSS

33

ART BY GIL COHEN

EDITOR'S NOTE: *The editors of this magazine do not necessarily believe that a prehistoric creature resembling a half-man, half-ape (as described by those who claim to have seen him) exists in modern times. Nevertheless, we sent a writer to interview those eyewitnesses and to tape-record their impressions. What follows is based on those interviews....*

On November 14, 1958, Samuel T. Harmon who lived with his wife Jessie on a small farm near the Southern reaches of the Appalachian Mountains reported sighting a strange-looking creature on his property. It was night at the time and there was a violent thunderstorm. "I went out to check on the livestock," Harmon was quoted as saying, "and I saw this man coming out of the barn door. Leastwise, I thought it was a man. But then there was a flash of lightning and I saw him clearly for a moment. It made my hair stand up on end. He was big and his body was all hairy. He wasn't wearing clothes and he had a face like a gorilla I saw once at a zoo. Before I could do anything he high-tailed it into the woods with a pig under one arm, a couple of chickens under the other...."

Two years later, August 18, 1960, there was a raging brush fire in the general vicinity of the Harmon farm. Earl Shackleton, one of the community's volunteers fighting the fire, claims he caught sight of "the scariest-looking thing I ever laid eyes on. It ran through the smoke and into the trees near the mountains. I first thought it was some kind of animal, but it ran like a man...."

In the spring of 1965, a married couple from New Jersey, Ernest and Mary Jo Rindluff, were fishing in a stream in the same region near the Appalachian Mountains when they spotted something moving through the brush on the opposite side of the stream. "Mary Jo saw it first," Ernest Rindluff recalls, "and she whispered to me. Then both of us saw this ugly face staring at us. We couldn't see the rest of the body. But that was an ape's face if I ever saw one. Mary Jo screamed, and it ran away. Afterwards, I went across the stream and saw that all the bushes there had been trampled, as if a powerful man had pushed through them...."

On October 13, 1968, three years later, Boyd Tyler and Davy Kinsman, both experienced woodsmen, were camped in one of the cabins along the Appalachian Trail used by hikers. "About morning," Kinsman said later, "Boyd and I both woke up when we heard something prowling around outside. We went to the door to look. It was kind of gray and misty outdoors, but we saw this huge man or animal or whatever. It took off when we opened the door but we saw enough to scare the hell out of us. Damnedest-looking thing I ever saw. Big hairy body with, like, an animal's head on it...."

Jay Y. Redfield, who regularly hunts in the vicinity of the Appalachians where the strange-looking creature was reported being seen, decided, in 1970, to track down whatever it was with his pack of dogs. "I spent 14 days in the mountains and brush," Jay Redfield claims. "There was something out there all right. The dogs sensed it. But whatever it was, was too smart for the hounds to catch." Two nights after Redfield returned to his farm—on April 9, 1970—all six of his dogs were killed in the pen behind the house. The dog's skulls had been crushed and their bodies clawed. Redfield found a single, giant footprint in the soft mud near the dog pen. The footprint looked like that of some enormous animal, except that there were five toes clearly outlined in the mud—exactly like the left foot of a human....

None of the preceding incidents were known to Jim and Elaine Blair, who lived near New York City, when they went camping in the Tennessee Appalachians in June 1973. They planned to spend a week in the wilderness area, and arrived well-provisioned with tent, food, and clothing, which they carried in knapsacks. The Blairs had been married for four years and both were experienced campers.

Originally, the Blairs had hoped to spend their first night in one of the campers' cabins. But it began raining heavily that first day, and after hiking for several hours through a solid downpour, they began looking for a spot to pitch their tent and make camp for the night. An hour later, Jim finally spotted what he thought was a likely place to stop.

The site was a scooped-out section in the base of a mountain, with enough rock over-hang to shelter a fire. As soon as they had put their tent up, Jim Blair went searching for dry firewood while his wife began opening their supplies to prepare a meal. Jim knew that darkness would come early because of the rain, so he worked swiftly to gather enough wood to last the whole night. When he returned, he was surprised to find his wife peering out of the tent, anxiously waiting for him.

"What's wrong, Elaine?" he asked, piling the firewood under the rock shelter.

"I don't know what it is, Jim," she said, coming up to him. "But while you were gone, I suddenly became very frightened."

"Frightened?" Blair asked. "Of what? We're a million miles away from anybody and anything."

"Yes, but that's just it," his wife answered, "This place is so lonely it's spooky. And the whole time you were gone I had the feeling I was being watched. The feeling was so strong that finally I decided to go into the tent."

"It's probably nothing," Blair said lightly, "except that you're chilled and tired. Soon as I get the fire going and fix a couple of drinks, you'll be fine."

BLAIR tried to reassure his wife, but he himself was disturbed by her actions. It wasn't like her to behave in that manner. She had spent plenty of time in places far more desolate and lonely than this one and had never been bothered. Nor was she a particularly nervous person; usually her nerves were steady and calm. On the other hand, Blair knew that his wife had an almost sixth sense about danger—and it was this knowledge, as much as anything else, that bothered him now.

Soon, he had a roaring fire going back against the mountain, and its flames seemed to push the shadows back as night fell. Elaine Blair had cheered up considerably by the time they had their drinks and ate a meal of steak and baked potatoes. Afterwards, they sat for a long time drinking fresh-brewed coffee and listening to the beat of rain against the tent and the trees.

Blair built up the fire before they turned in for the night and knew, despite his fatigue, that he would awaken periodically to keep the fire going until daylight. The rain was still falling as Blair crawled into his sleeping bag. His wife was already dozing.

Several times during the next few hours, Blair awoke, went outside with the flashlight and threw fresh wood on the fire.

On the last trip he made, he glanced at his watch and noticed that it was close to 4 A.M. The steady rain was still falling. He decided he could sleep for the rest of the night and burrowed down in his sleeping bag again.

Less than an hour later he came awake suddenly when he heard his wife calling his name. He was instantly alert and out of his sleeping bag. He saw her standing inside the opening of the tent with the flashlight in her hand. It was still dark outside and he could hear the rain falling.

"What is it?" Blair asked, hurrying over to his wife.

"There's something out there," Elaine Blair whispered urgently. "I heard it when I woke up—something making a kind of grunting sound. Then, when I got to the front of the tent, I caught a glimpse of something moving. That's why I called you."

Blair wished he had a gun. He thought it might be some wild animal, a bear perhaps, which had been attracted to the camp. He'd have to scare it away, but he didn't want to approach whatever it was unarmed.

"Stay inside," Blair said to his wife, pushing past her. "Give me time to get to the fire and get a piece of burning wood. Then shine the flashlight and see if you can pick up whatever it is out there."

Elaine Blair nodded wordlessly.

Blair had just reached the fire and bent to snatch up a burning branch from the fire when his wife screamed: "Jim! My God, Jim! Look!"

Holding the flaming length of wood in his hand, Blair twirled
and ran toward his wife who was standing outside the tent. She
was holding up the flashlight and its powerful beam shone on
the face and part of the body of a grotesque-looking creature.
It was standing upright and was somewhere around 6-feet tall.
Its shoulders and chest were covered with thick hair and were
muscular. But the face was something else: ape-like, with a
pushed-in look. The eyes were small and squinting, the lips thick
and rubbery.

For a moment the creature seemed hypnotized by the beam
of light shining into its eyes. But, in the next moment, it moved
swiftly toward Elaine Blair, grimacing and exposing jagged,
animal-like fangs. Elaine Blair screamed and Blair hurled the
burning tree branch. The blazing torch arched through the
dark air straight at the ferocious creature. A couple of sparks
pinwheeled out from the burning wood and showered down on the
figure. It bellowed with pain and disappeared into the darkness of
the trees. The burning torch tossed by Blair sizzled briefly on the
soggy ground where it had landed and was quickly extinguished
by the rain.

"Jim, did you see what I saw?" Elaine Blair asked in a shaky
voice.

"I saw it," Blair answered, his own voice shaking, "but I'd
swear it was impossible."

"But what was it?" his wife asked.

"Damned if I know," Blair said, "because nothing exists,
animal or human, that looks like what I saw."

"That's it exactly," Elaine Blair said. "It looked part animal,
part-human; a half-man, half-ape. But there are no such things."

"No," Blair said, "of course not." But he remembered that
from time to time reports had appeared in the newspapers of
evidence that a species of prehistoric man might still exist in
remote areas of the world. He remembered there had been one
report as recently as 1968 that indicated a kind of Neanderthal
man might be still living in Alaska or British Columbia. Was this
just such a specimen?

Blair had no more time to dwell on such notions. In the faint,
gray, half-light of early dawn he had just noticed something he'd
overlooked before in his excitement: All the lower ground beyond

the base of the mountain and the tent was covered with several inches of water, and the water was rising rapidly.

It occurred to him that the rains had probably flooded the nearby streams and rivers, which were plentiful in the area. He decided it was time to break camp and head for higher ground. (The Blairs had brought no radio with them so they could not know that on that early morning of June 22, 1973, the most ravaging storm in Eastern US history was pounding not only the area they were in but the whole northeast mainland. Before the storm, named Agnes, ended, at least 109 people died, the homes of half a million more were destroyed or damaged, and 131 counties—including the one the Blairs were visiting—and 25 cities, were to be declared disaster areas.)

BY DAYLIGHT water was streaming down from the mountainside to add to the flooding. Jim and Elaine Blair packed up their tent and supplies to leave. They were sloshing around in water up over their ankles.

Jim Blair's first inclination had been to try to go back the way they had come. But soon after they set out in that direction, they were wading through water up to their waists and still rising. What was even more terrifying was that the flood waters had a strong current running through them. Weighted down by the packs on their backs, the Blairs were in very real danger of losing their footing and being swept away in the ever-growing flood waters.

"We've got to go back," Blair shouted to his wife, pointing to the side of the mountain they'd just left. As they made their way, it briefly seemed to Jim Blair that perhaps the strange animal, or man, or whatever it was they'd seen, might have been driven to their camp by the storm and the waters.

It took them several hours before they saw the mouth of a cave dwelling well up the mountainside. Blair approached it cautiously. He stood in front of the cave and shone the beam of the flashlight inside until he was satisfied it was empty. The cave was a natural shelter. From where they were, they could see the flood waters still rising below.

It was damp inside the cave and there was a strong, musty, animal scent in the air. The top and sides of the cave were solid rock and wet with moisture. There was a dirt floor and there were a few animal bones scattered around. Blair knew the cave had been used as a den for some animal—perhaps a bear or maybe even the strange creature they'd seen earlier. But there was no evidence that it had been occupied recently, and he decided it would likely be safe for them to stay there until the flood waters began to recede.

They shucked their equipment and rested for a while.

"Jim," Elaine Blair said finally, "what do you really think we saw this morning?" she shivered.

Blair considered for a moment before he answered. He knew they might still have a long wait in the woods before they could make their way back to civilization and he didn't want to alarm his wife if he could avoid it.

"Honey, I don't honestly know. Maybe it was just some mountain man from around these parts who thought it would be a funny idea to dress up in a costume and try to throw a scare into us city folks."

"You say that," his wife said, "but I don't think you really believe it."

"Believing that," Blair said, "makes more sense than believing there's really a half-man, half-ape like the one we saw. Anyhow, whatever the hell it was, it appeared as scared of us as we were of it. I doubt that it'll bother us again. Meanwhile, the rain'll probably end soon and we'll be able to get out of here."

But the rain didn't end and the wind began to blow, flattening the tops of the trees and whipping up the surface of the water that continued to rise. Blair had begun to suspect by that time that this was more than a passing summer storm, although, of course, he still couldn't know the real extent of it.

They had plenty of canned food and since they couldn't build a fire, they opened cans of corned beef, beans, and fruit and ate them. Several times that day, Jim Blair had an uneasy feeling that he and his wife were being watched. He frequently went outside the cave into the pouring rain to look for prowling animals or for the unknown creature they'd seen earlier. But he was not able to spot anything. That night, Jim and Elaine spread their bedrolls on the damp ground in the cave and got into them. Blair stayed awake all night watching the cave entrance in case anything entered.

Elaine dozed fitfully.

Just after dawn the next morning, when the rain had tapered off to a light drizzle, the Blairs packed up their bedrolls and food supplies and left the cave. They had decided to discard their tent to lighten the load since they would still have to wade through the water flooding the ground below.

When they got down the mountain, near where they'd camped two nights before, they saw that the flood had receded slightly but that the water was still deep and treacherous. Blair roped his wife to himself, and together they waded out into the water, which reached, in places, up to their armpits.

Before they were out of sight of the cave, Blair once again had the uneasy feeling that they were being watched. He turned and looked back quickly at the cave and thought he caught a blur of movement on the ledge overhanging the cave entrance. But it all happened so swiftly that he couldn't be sure that it wasn't just a shadow. They came around a bend in the side of the mountain shortly after that and carefully made their way through the muddy water.

Tree branches, roots, silt, and leaves brushed past them as they fought their way through the flood waters. A couple of times, snakes floated by but presented no real danger. About two hours after they had left the cave and entered the water, they had a bad moment when Elaine lost her footing and was pulled under by the eddying water. She screamed and Blair was almost pulled off his feet before he regained his balance. He grabbed the rope that bound her to him and pulled her up on her feet and into his arms.

He was holding her in his arms when he glanced up and suddenly saw it. "Look! Elaine, look!" he shouted, turning her around in the water. She saw it, too: a small wooden cabin perched on a high trail about five yards above them—the kind of cabin they'd been looking for ever since they entered the woods.

Blair half-carried his wife through the water and up a muddy slope to the cabin. He kicked the unlocked door open, lifted his wife into his arms and carried her inside. The interior of the cabin was simple and bare. There was a rough, wooden table with a couple of hurricane lamps on it, wooden benches on either side of the table, double-decker bunks against one wall, and a fireplace with cords of wood piled next to it.

"It's just sheer heaven!" Elaine Blair laughed, twirling around the room.

With the rain still tapering outside, they unpacked their supplies. Blair built a blazing fire in the fireplace and Elaine cooked a hot meal. After they had eaten, Blair pushed back from the table and said, "Honey, I think I should go see if there's a way we can get out of these woods. Why don't you stay here where it's dry until I get back."

Elaine Blair shook her head firmly. "No," she said. "If you go, I go with you. I'm not staying in these woods by myself." He knew that she was remembering the creature they'd seen.

THEY waited until the fire had died out, and left all their supplies behind. They'd decided they would return to the cabin whether they found a way to get out of the flood, or not. As it turned out, they spent over two hours trying to find high ground across the rolling waters below with no success, and finally had to return to the cabin.

As they approached the cabin again, Jim Blair came to a sudden stop. The cabin door, which they'd shut when they left, was now standing wide open. Blair went forward, keeping his wife behind him. He went to the side of the cabin first and looked through the window. He was relieved when he saw the place was empty. But, a few minutes later, when the Blairs entered the cabin, they immediately saw that there had been a visitor.

Jim felt a tingling chill along his spine as he examined the cabin. The benches were overturned, firewood was scattered across the floor and, most terrifying of all, the table and floor was strewn with cans, which had been ripped open by brute force and bent and crushed. All of the cans had been emptied and there was fresh blood on most of them and bits and pieces of fur.

"It's been here, Jim!" Elaine Blair shrieked hysterically. "It's been right here in this cabin." She would have rushed out if Blair hadn't restrained her.

Blair, too, wanted to get out of the cabin; for one thing the place had an almost unearthly stench that gagged and choked him. But first, he wanted to collect some evidence of the creature that had been there. There was a small quantity of blood in one of the cans where it—which was the only way Blair could now think of the creature—had cut itself. Blair emptied one of the canteens, poured the blood in it, and screwed the top on tight.

"Let's go," he said quickly and the two of them left, leaving behind everything that was in the cabin.

At that moment, the Blairs didn't know it but their curious adventures were almost at an end. Less than an hour later they were rescued by a helicopter, which had come to search the area for stranded hikers.

A few days after the Blairs returned home, Jim had the blood he'd found in the cabin analyzed at a laboratory. The report: "NOT HUMAN, NOT ANIMAL—*BLOOD TYPE UNKNOWN.*"

Later, Jim Blair said sadly of the incident: "I sure as hell don't know what I saw for sure. But the thing that bugs me is I keep thinking how we send men out into space to try to contact some advanced form of life there. Suppose this poor creature was a link to millions of years in the past?"

EDITORS' POSTSCRIPT

The *Cryptozoology Anthology* editorial team is spread out across the US, and we use WeTransfer to share files. After transferring the final image needed for this book (artist John Duillo's 1970 Bigfoot portrait for *Man's Action,* featured on pg. *3*), we were greeted by this download screen on the WeTransfer site:

We considered it a good omen.

ACKNOWLEDGMENTS

THE EDITORS would like to acknowledge Loren Coleman for his invaluable help, and his keen understanding of the influence of men's adventure magazines on cryptozoology. We gratefully acknowledge Lyle Blackburn, Nick Redfern, and Ken Gerhard, all of whom provided personal insight and professional acumen. These respected authors/researchers have published numerous well-written books on cryptozoological phenomena; interested readers are directed to those works for further information on the subject.

Thanks to Sharon Lee Lomurno, Editor of the *Bigfoot Field Reporter*, for her early support for this book; and to Brian Impey and the other cryptozoology buffs in the Monsters, Mysteries & Mayhem Facebook group for their infectious enthusiasm and inspiration.

Thank you Ann Behar and the Estate of Arthur C. Clarke, Cheryl Keaton and the Estate of John A. Keel, Malcolm and Christine at Mystery & Imagination Bookshop, Guillermo del Toro, Mark Alfrey, J. Elliott Swanson, Kata Pinter, Laszlito Kovacs, Jason Cuadrado, Andy Biscontini, Bill Shute at Kendra Steiner Editions, Greg Sullivan, Mark Leonard, Paul Silva, Scott Somerndike, Morgan Roberts, and all our pals in the Men's Adventure Magazines group on Facebook.

ROBERT DEIS

As always, special thanks to my wife Barbara Jo, for putting up with my time- and space-consuming interest in vintage men's pulp adventure magazines that she doesn't quite understand, but graciously tolerates and supports.

DAVID COLEMAN

My sincere gratitude to my wife and lovely family, whose unwavering support is still the greatest unsolved, but enormously cherished, mystery of them all.

WYATT DOYLE

With thanks to Sandee Curry and my family.

FOUND! LOST PULP TREASURES

MENSPULPMAGS.com

MEN'S ADVENTURE MAGAZINE
HISTORY

FROM **ROBERT DEIS**,
FEARLESS EDITOR OF

WEASELS RIPPED MY FLESH!

HE-MEN, BAG MEN & NYMPHOS

CRYPTO ZOOLO GY ANTHOLOGY

COVER GALLERIES
and PULP ARTWORK

PIN-UPs &
Glamour Girls

art by John Pike from True, *December 1948*

cryptozoologymuseum.com

MAN UP!

For 28 bare-knuckle short stories and reminiscences by some of the toughest writers ever to punch a typewriter . . .

For a shirt-ripping, gut-punching anthology collecting two-fisted writing torn from the pages of long-lost vintage men's adventure magazines of the 1950s, '60s and '70s . . .

For outrageous, 100% *true* tales of sex, crime, combat, jungle queens, beatnik girls, LSD experiments, animal attacks, and nymphos. Always nymphos . . .

WEASELS RIPPED MY FLESH!

TWO-FISTED STORIES FROM MEN'S ADVENTURE MAGAZINES OF THE 1950s, '60s & '70s

featuring

LAWRENCE BLOCK

JANE DOLINGER

ROBERT F. DORR

HARLAN ELLISON

BRUCE JAY FRIEDMAN

WALTER KAYLIN

KEN KRIPPENE

MARIO PUZO

ROBERT SILVERBERG

WALTER WAGER

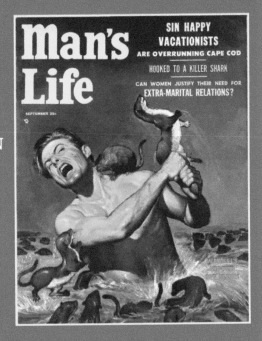

man's Life

SIN HAPPY VACATIONISTS
ARE OVERRUNNING CAPE COD

HOOKED TO A KILLER SHARK

CAN WOMEN JUSTIFY THEIR NEED FOR
EXTRA-MARITAL RELATIONS?

SEPTEMBER 25¢

edited by
Robert Deis

with Josh Alan Friedman & Wyatt Doyle

Gunfighters. Lovers. Kings. Surf Pack
Assassins.

The World of
MEN'S ADVENTURE MAGAZINES'

Scores of great authors wrote for men's adventure pulps—**Elmore Leonard, Jim Thompson, Richard Matheson, Lawrence Block,** and **Harlan Ellison,** to name a few. But the wordsmith writers for *Man's World* and *True Action* envied most was **Walter Kaylin.**

Leaving an indelible mark on three decades of sweat-soaked pulp fiction, Walter Kaylin tackled testosterone-fueled subjects from Westerns to war, secret agents to sex sirens, Nazis to *noir*. His frequently over-the-top plots and characters scaled new heights of ingenuity and invention, while setting the standard for the kind of unapologetic savagery and excess that made men's adventure magazines notorious—then and now.

Walter Kaylin's He-Men, Bag Men & Nymphos hits like a clenched fist; get yours or get out of the way!

edited by Robert Deis and Wyatt Doyle

Ladies' Men.   He-Men.   Bag Men.   Nymphos.

WALTER KAYLIN

WILDEST WRITER

"Walter Kaylin, come back!"

— Mario Puzo,
author of *The Godfather*

THE
MEN'S ADVENTURE
LIBRARY

original magazine
illustrations by
(from left): George
Eisenberg, Don
Neiser, Al Rossi, Earl
Norem, Joe Little,
Earl Norem, Samson
Pollen, Gil Cohen

FROM THE MEN WHO BROUGHT YOU
WEASELS RIPPED MY FLESH!

HE-MEN,
BAG MEN
& NYMPHOS
COLOR EDITION
classic men's adventure magazine stories by
WALTER KAYLIN

edited by Robert Deis and Wyatt Doyle

new texture   MENSPULPMAGS.com   WALTERKAYLIN.com

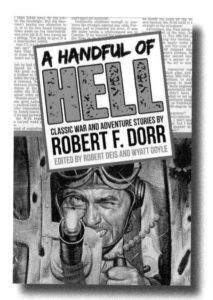

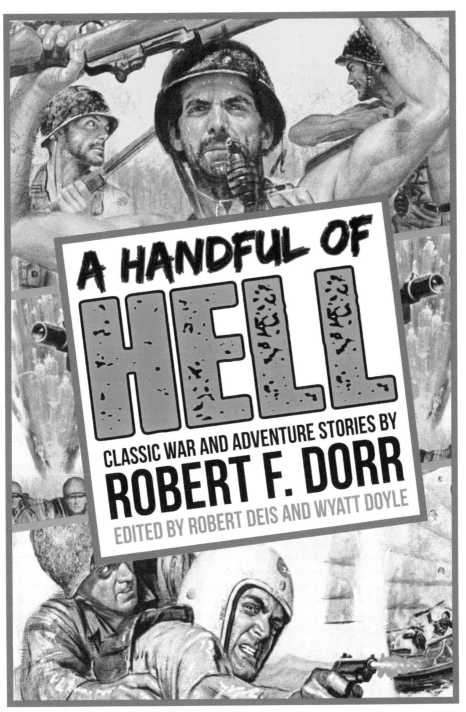

A HANDFUL OF HELL

CLASSIC WAR AND ADVENTURE STORIES BY
ROBERT F. DORR
EDITED BY ROBERT DEIS AND WYATT DOYLE

A NEW KIND OF MEN'S ADVENTURE COLLECTION

OUTLAW biker gangs have been a cultural obsession for over half a century, inspiring countless books, news reports, television shows, exploitation movies . . . and men's adventure magazines.

This oversized, full-color album from The Men's Adventure Library collects the very best of the mags' *three decades* of biker artwork— only the wildest covers and hardest-punching interior spreads, by masters of two-fisted pulp illustration, most unseen for years. From "The Combat Angels" to "Sex Life of a Motorcycle Mama," *Barbarians on Bikes* is a one-of-a-kind visual history . . . Read it like you stole it.

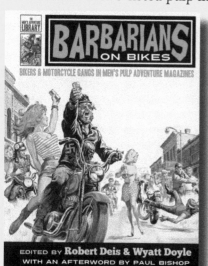

KNUCKLE-DUSTING COVERS & ROWDY ILLUSTRATIONS! STOMPED ON EVERY PAGE

PAPERBACK, EBOOK, AND DELUXE EDITION HARDCOVER WITH ALTERNATE COVER ART AND EXCLUSIVE CONTENT

THE MEN'S ADVENTURE LIBRARY

BARBARIANS ON BIKES

A NEW TEXTURE PUBLICATION

A high-octane visual archive from vintage men's pulp adventure magazines

BIKERS & MOTORCYCLE GANGS

EDITED BY
Robert Deis & Wyatt Doyle

AFTERWORD BY
Paul Bishop

Pollen's women

THE ART OF SAMSON POLLEN EDITED BY **ROBERT DEIS & WYATT DOYLE**

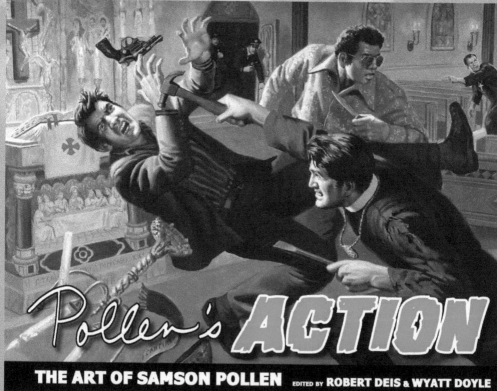

Pollen's ACTION

THE ART OF SAMSON POLLEN EDITED BY **ROBERT DEIS & WYATT DOYLE**

"They might say something like, 'Well, the hero has an automatic weapon in one hand and he's carrying a woman in another hand, and she's holding a dog and they're climbing up a cliff.' So I'd have to come up with a solution. What I would do is visualize it. I'd try to look at the scene as I'd see it in my imagination. That's the part I liked the most: Trying to make sense out of something and create a story of it in my mind, then translate that into a painting."

— Pollen

THE ART OF SAMSON POLLEN

EDITED BY **ROBERT DEIS & WYATT DOYLE**

MensPulpMags.com   # new texture

DELUXE HARDCOVERS AVAILABLE NOW

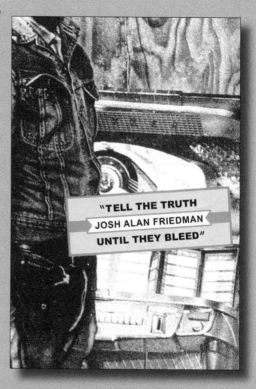

1965. Flashpoint of the Civil Rights Movement.

In every major American city, interracial tensions threaten to boil over into violence.

And in Glen Cove, Long Island, Josh Friedman finds himself on the front lines of the battle for racial equality.

Josh is nine.

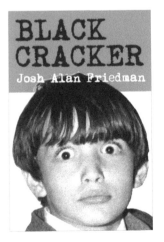

Race. Segregation. Doo-doo jokes.

BLACK CRACKER

an autobiographical novel
by Josh Alan Friedman

WYATT DOYLE

STOP REQUESTED

WYATT DOYLE

ILLUSTRATIONS BY
STANLEY J. ZAPPA

WYATT DOYLE
DOLLAR HALLOWEEN

I need reg/
tuxedo and a
top Hat!

words and pictures by wyatt doyle

"[**Doyle**] has the elliptical, post-modern zen understatement of a Richard Brautigan, with a poet's gift for the carefully-chosen detail and a playwright's gift for dialogue.

"I admire his eye for the unexpected juxtapositions of detail among the seemingly mundane, juxtapositions of detail that provide a window of insight into life, into society, into truth. This quality is as strong in his fiction as it is in his photography."

—**Bill Shute**,
Kendra Steiner Editions

STOP REQUESTED *stories*
illustrated by Stanley J. Zappa
softcover and deluxe hardcover

DOLLAR HALLOWEEN *photographs*
hardcover

I NEED REAL TUXEDO AND A TOP HAT!
photographs/stories
88-pg softcover
104-pg deluxe hardcover

BUTY-WAVE IS NOW CLOSED FOREVER
photographs
88-pg softcover
104-pg deluxe hardcover

JORGE AMAYA DOESN'T LIVE HERE ANYMORE *photographs*
88-pg softcover
104-pg deluxe hardcover

new texture

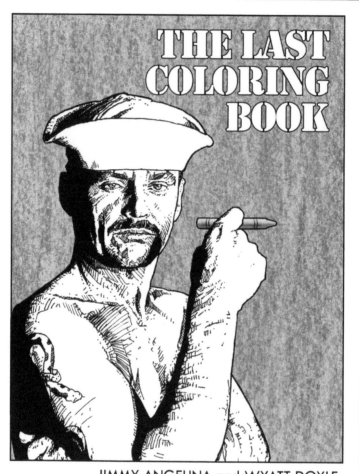

JIMMY ANGELINA and **WYATT DOYLE**

Ceci n'est pas un coloring book

lastcoloringbook.com

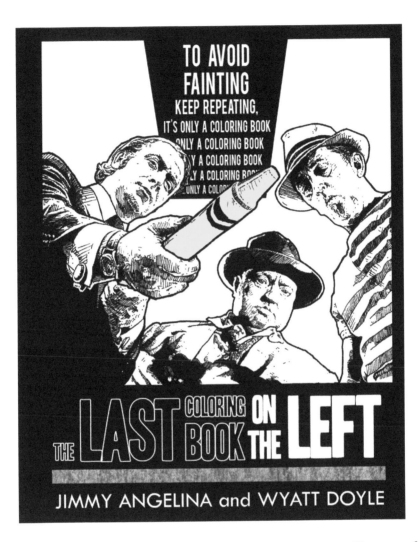

Ceci n'est pas un coloring book [1] non plus

new texture

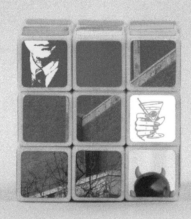

"Someone, I don't know who, has been stealing things from my desk..."

Richard Adelman
TEACHER TALES

SCHOOL'S OUT
...completely.

PAPERBACK, EBOOK, AND
DELUXE HARDCOVER

new texture

The Revolution will be on the Moon.

n u l u n a

Andrew Biscontini

SOFTCOVER, EBOOK, AND DELUXE HARDCOVER

new texture

new texture

Lightning Source UK Ltd.
Milton Keynes UK
UKHW021854041220
374641UK00008B/278